"TORPEDOES AT TWO-SEVEN-ZERO!"

As Brent swung his glasses frantically, a torpedo struck the oiler in a half-empty gasoline tank. Thousands of gallons of high test gasoline and fumes ignited in a catacylsmic explosion that rocketed the entire superstructure and a pair of twisting derricks straight up hundreds of feet on the tip of a tongue of brilliant yellow flame. Men leaped into the sea to be engulfed by flames, flopping like wounded seals.

Brent focused, catching four white bubbling trails off the starboard beam. "Four more! Range one thousand, bearing zero-nine-zero relative! Heading straight for us!"

"Right full rudder!" Fujita ordered.

"It's too late!" Mark Allen screamed. "We have no time!"

"We have no choice!" Fujita shouted back.

Steaming at least twenty knots, the giant carrier *Yonaga* heeled and turned slowly, so very slowly, toward the approaching doom.

ACTION & ESPIONAGE
from Zebra Books

THE LEADER AND THE DAMNED (1718, $3.95)
by Colin Forbes

Adolf Hitler didn't commit suicide in his Berlin Bunker in 1945—the burned body that was found was his double! From England to Berlin, from the Kremlin to Palestine, Ian Linday is under the threat of death because he holds the earth-shaking knowledge that Hitler is a fake.

STATE OF EMERGENCY (1767, $3.95)
by Basil Jackson

It was a strange signal that caused T.V. sets to explode and radios to vaporize killing hundreds of Americans. One scientist races against time to uncover the truth—which is about to bring the U.S. and the Soviets to the brink of Armageddon.

THE ELIXIR (1809, $3.95)
by James N. Frey

Hitler's most secret weapon—a blood-red liquid that would have created an immortal Nazi super race to rule the world forever—has reappeared as the centerpiece of the world's most expensive auction. Only death can seal the bargain for THE ELIXIR.

TERMINAL (1968, $3.95)
by Colin Forbes

One by one, wealthy American patients are dying in brutal suffocating agony. It is all part of a sinister conspiracy that could alter the political shape of the globe forever. But, for those fighting to prevent international chaos, too much knowledge spells certain death!

THE LAST PATRIOT (1403, $3.50)
by James N. Frey

The press calls him the most notorious killer who ever lived. The White House cringes in fear of him. The public wants his blood. But Chandler Smith believes in America and has vowed to set it free—no matter who he has to kill.

Available wherever paperbacks are sold, or order direct from the Publisher. Send cover price plus 50¢ per copy for mailing and handling to Zebra Books, Dept. 2093, 475 Park Avenue South, New York, N.Y. 10016. Residents of New York, New Jersey and Pennsylvania must include sales tax. DO NOT SEND CASH.

RETURN OF THE SEVENTH CARRIER

BY PETER ALBANO
AUTHOR OF THE SEVENTH CARRIER

ZEBRA BOOKS
KENSINGTON PUBLISHING CORP.

ZEBRA BOOKS

are published by

Kensington Publishing Corp.
475 Park Avenue South
New York, NY 10016

First printing: June 1987

Printed in the United States of America

To the loyal members of the crew: Mary Annis, Carla, Lisa, Vincent, and Laura, who weathered every storm and survived the final battle.

ACKNOWLEDGEMENTS

I am indebted to airline pilots William D. Wilkerson and Dennis D. Silver who not only explained how to fly antique aircraft, but advised on performance characteristics as well. For solving technical problems with computers, ciphers, and radar, my grateful thanks to Dr. Roland W. Koch. I would also like to thank Master Mariner Donald Brandmeyer for helping with the innumerable problems that can confront a carrier at war.

Finally, my gratitude to Jane Smith who transformed my scribbles into a legible manuscript.

PREFACE

Hidden by a sliding glacier in a secret anchorage in a cove on Siberia's Chukchi Peninsula in 1941, the Imperial Japanese Navy's largest carrier Yonaga was trapped in ice for 42 years. Manned by samurai and commanded by Admiral Hiroshi Fujita, the crew subsisted on fish and seaweed while maintaining the ship, aircraft and weapons in top fighting trim. Many crewmen died, but in 1983 the carrier broke loose and steamed south through the Bering Sea, her crew determined to carry out their orders to attack Pearl Harbor. Surprising Pearl Harbor's defenders, Yonaga's airgroups destroyed carrier Tarawa and sank battleship New Jersey off Ford Island.

While a shocked world counted the dead, a Chinese system of laser equipped satellites malfunctioned. All over the world the skies were filled with killer beams and every jet and rocket was instantly destroyed. Only reciprocating engines were able to function. As a global scramble for World War II ships and planes ensued, Admiral Fujita and the crew of the Yonaga realized their carrier was the most formidable fighting force in the world. . . .

Chapter One

Pressing his left rudder pedal and moving the control column slightly to the left, the combat air patrol leader, Commander Yoshi Matsuhara, dipped the port wing of his Mitsubishi A6M2, sending the lithe white Zero into a counterclockwise turn. Free of his parachute straps—samurai considered parachutes and radios cumbersome junk—he turned his head in jerky movements, honoring the timeless ritual of the fighter pilot; first to the left, then straight ahead, and then to the right, and finally high above the black cowl where the sun pulsed fiercely in a clear sky. It was here that the greatest danger lurked. "Watch out for the killer in the sun," his old instructor had told him at Tsuchiura when he had first been accepted in pursuit school in 1938.

The commander was not concerned about his tail. Trailing and maintaining formation twenty meters off his elevators, like they were attached by invisible umbilicals, were his wingmen since China: Lt. Tetsu Takamura on his port side and naval air pilot first class, Hitoshi Kojima to starboard. They were the best; Takamura with five kills of Arab aircraft and Kojima with three. Added to his eight, his "three" had accounted for more than a staffel in the recent fighting, enhancing their karmas and assuring themselves a place for their spirits in the Yasakuni Shrine.

The glorious day matched his mood. There were mountainous cumulus clouds on the southern horizon, true, but the sky overhead was brilliant blue vault, and he could feel the heat of the sun's rays piercing the perspex of the canopy and caressing his face with warm, friendly fingers. Below, the Atlantic was a cobalt plain marred only here and there by occasional whitecaps, which marked the mounting swell. To port, riding his dipping wing tip, he could see the great carrier *Yonaga* slashing the blue carpet, bow like the sharp point of a *wakazashi* ripping a *shoji*, cleaving the infinite rollers and leaving a widening white scar to the horizon. And the five American destroyers shepherded the great warship like courtiers fawning over a shogun; Capt. John Fite leading and appearing to pull the carrier with the string of his own swirling wake while two other graceful *Fletchers* charged to *Yonaga*'s port and the remaining pair to starboard.

From 2,000 meters, size was lost. In fact, *Yonaga*'s 300 meter flight deck was a postage stamp, flying on the wind. Even after all these years and hundreds of landings, thoughts of putting the Zero down on that heaving deck brought a hollow feeling to his stomach.

But the safety of the carrier was in his hands. He tore his eyes from his home of forty-three years, adjusted his tinted goggles and glanced at the sun. Nothing. Nothing at all.

He moved his eyes to his gauges which told him fuel was low and forty minutes of his patrol still remained. The tachometer read 2,000 rpms. A quick adjustment brought the finely pitched propeller down to 1,750. With a touch like a fine feather, he grasped the throttle, moving his eyes to the pressure gauge where the needle quivered at 80 centimeters of mercury—all the manifold pressure the 950 horsepower Sakae could take. After backfiring twice and vibrating its objections, the engine settled down to its usual steady roar. But Yoshi knew he could ask no more of it.

When he heard the Sakae backfire, Brent Ross was standing high on the flag bridge of carrier *Yonaga*, crowded with four lookouts, a talker, and two junior officers. Twisting his head back, the young six foot two inch, two hundred ten pound ensign brought his glasses up in a line just above the ships clutter of radar antennas. He caught a glint. Then rolling his thumb over the focusing knob, he brought three Zeros into focus. Soaring like gleaming seagulls taking the breeze on rigid wings, the graceful Mitsubishis brought a sigh. Matsuhara and his wingmen. Added security in a world gone mad—a world stunned by the orbiting Chinese laser system that grounded all jets and rockets. A world where terrorists and madmen led by Moammar Kadafi gathered old warplanes and ships, bullied their neighbors, and seized hostages by the shipload.

True, *Yonaga* had defeated the Libyan strongman; his coalition of Egypt, Jordan, Lebanon, the PLO, and Syria in their campaign against Israel. But Kadafi

13

had carriers, destroyers, and possibly some big-gunned ships with which to press his *jihad* against the Japanese—a people he hated as much as he did the Israelis and Americans.

Lowering his glasses and bending his knees slightly, Brent braced himself as the great carrier challenged the mounting southeast swell like a battering ram, her prow smashing through the relentless breakers, sending white-dappled water and sheets of spray flying in lacy curtains.

It was a strange day, but here in the central Atlantic just 180 miles east of the Cape Verde Islands, there were many strange days. Overhead, the sun glared in a clear sky, painting the spray playfully with the colors of the rainbow, while to the south great buildups of cumulus clouds threatened in infinite shades of gray, flickering with lightning and cascading rain in such torrents that the horizon was obscured and the ship's radar screens showed almost solid blips. From this brew the rollers marched in endless rows like attacking infantry.

Sighing, the tall blond ensign turned, running his eyes over the ship's flight deck. And what a deck: Longer than three football fields, the massive steel rectangle was punctured by two elevators; one fore and one aft. The young American gripped the windscreen as the ship defeated another comber, the impact sending vibrations through every frame and plate, blue water and spray flying. Feeling the exhilaration that came with this endless war, Brent smiled and leaned into the wind, filling his lungs and reveling in life as only a man at sea can when clean air fills his lungs and cold spray stings his cheeks like thrown

14

gravel.

By craning his neck, Brent could see the ship's foretop and the barrels of a dozen anti-aircraft guns in exposed mounts. Farther aft, he found a ship's single funnel—tilted outboard in Japanese style—supporting searchlight platforms and hung with life rafts. Gun galleries surrounded the flight deck, over 200 25 millimeter and five inch dual-purpose guns pointed skyward like thickets of young saplings.

On the flight deck, a half-dozen ready Zeros squatted like angry grounded hawks, tied down in rows of three from amidships aft. Once every hour the Sakaes popped and gasped to life as crew chiefs warmed oil and cylinder heads. And half the ship's guns were ready, too, steel-helmeted pointers and trainers staring at the sky from their steel bicycle seats while loaders lounged against gun tubs and ready boxes.

Brent felt a presence behind him before he heard the voice—a voice that rustled like dry leaves, yet commanded with the cutting edge of a sword. "Be alert—Kadafi has the long memory of a lunatic," the voice rasped.

Turning, the ensign's eyes found a spectral, almost macabre figure standing close behind. Not more than five feet tall with a leathery face riven and seamed by a hundred years, Adm. Hiroshi Fujita stood erect despite the ship's motions. He was helmeted and dressed in number two green battle fatigues, matching the dress of every man on the bridge. Binoculars hung at his waist. Looking down, Brent was struck by the eyes—eyes that defied time, alert and glowing with intelligence.

15

Close behind the admiral, the ancient executive officer, Capt. Masso Kawamoto, rocked with the ship on spindly legs. Bent and skeletal, the captain wore every one of his ninety years on his scabrous face and in his dim eyes.

Two seamen lookouts turned from their huge binoculars, which were so enormous they were mounted on steel stanchions bolted to the deck. Speaking angrily, Fujita turned to the seamen. "Back to your watch! The Cape Verde Islands are there." He waved a tiny hand. "Easy range. Do not break your vigilance for anyone—not even Amaterasu."

The men whirled back to their glasses so quickly that one sailor's helmet spun from his head and clattered on the steel deck like a dropped pot. In one motion, the terrorized rating scooped up the helmet and returned to his glasses.

Grunting and raising his glasses, the old admiral leaned on the windscreen between Brent Ross and the talker who stood rigidly, huge helmet covering his earphones, mouthpiece close to his lips, and eyes locked on Fujita.

Captain Kawamoto staggered to the windscreen where he supported his bent frame with gnarled hands, leaning like a twisted, windblown pine.

Without turning or lowering his glasses, the old admiral spoke. "You have the youngest and best eyes on the ship, Ensign Ross."

"Thank you, sir."

Lowering his glasses, Fujita inclined his head toward the big American. "Tell me, Mr. Ross. If you were commanding this vessel, where would you expect your enemy to lurk?"

"Submarines, admiral?"

The old sailor shook his head. "For this discussion, we will leave submarines to Captain Fite."

The ensign nodded understanding. "The African coast. Dakar is at extreme range, admiral, but it is Arab. Bombers might make it, but without fighter cover." He gestured overhead. "Our CAP would cut them to pieces."

"The Cape Verde Islands, ensign?"

"They're Portuguese, admiral."

"Do you think that matters in today's world, ensign?"

Brent scratched his chin. "Not really," he agreed, sensing a deep concern masked by the game. Brent had enjoyed the euphoria that followed the carrier's smashing victories over the Arabs. But euphoria could be followed by complacency, and complacency might lead to carelessness and disaster.

The admiral's had swept the semicircle of the eastern horizon. "Then where, ensign? From which quadrant would they come?"

"Not out of that clear sky, sir. Our radar would pick them up at two hundred and fifty miles — ah, I mean four hundred kilometers."

The old man nodded agreement. "The storm?"

"Treacherous . . . dangerous. There are drafts there." He inclined his head at the horizon. "That can tear the wings off a Heinkel," he added.

"But, indeed, cover," the admiral said. "An unexpected place. And radar is receiving returns from those squalls." He pointed to the gray masses, slanting in solid curtains under the towering clouds. Then, turning to one of the lookouts, he said, "Seaman

17

Koshiro, maintain a watch on the storm. Report anything—even a seagull."

"Aye, aye, sir."

The admiral turned to the talker. "Radar, keep a close watch on the storm. We may have a raid from that quarter—close on the water."

"To escape turbulence and our radar search, admiral?"

"Of course, ensign."

Almost as if the admiral's words had been a prophecy, the talker shouted, "Radar reports many blips bearing one-four-zero moving in the storm, admiral. May not be squalls."

Hurrying to the forward end of the platform where a voice tube led to the armored command center in the pilot house and followed by the talker who plugged into a new receptacle, Fujita glanced at the battle ensign whipping at the gaff. He shouted into the voice tube, "Left full rudder, steady up on one-two-zero, speed twenty-four." He commanded the talker with the speed and precision of a machine gun: "Sound the general alarm. Ready pilots, man your planes. To the signal bridge, make the hoist course one-two-zero, speed twenty-four, two block pennant one. To the radio room, inform CAP and escorts of possible raid bearing one-four-zero. CAP intercept. Set Condition Zed. Adm. Mark Allen to the bridge."

Honking like frightened geese, Klaxons blared to life throughout the ship. Immediately, a half-dozen Sakaes roared to life. There were the shouts of officers, the shrill twitter of boatswains' pipes, the thump of boots on decks and ladders, the clang of steel on brass as breeches received five-inch shells, and the excited shouts of gun-layers as weapons were cranked skyward. Adding to the cacophony was the hollow sound of hundreds of steel doors slamming shut deep in the bowels of the ship as watertight compartments were "dogged down." Then, far below in the heart of the ship, an electrician's mate threw a switch, and the high-pitched whine of hundreds of blowers dropped octaves and faded as *Yonaga*'s ventilation system was shut down. The great carrier was holding her breath.

When the alarm was sounded, Commander Matsuhara had just led his "three" in a swing far to the east of the carrier. After the command, "Edo leader, this is Iceman. Radar reports many aircraft bearing one-four-zero. Closing at a high speed out of the storm. Intercept," had crackled in his earphones, he had shouted his acknowledgment into his microphone. Then, disdaining the radio, he had stabbed a finger upward and waggled his wings. Instantly, Takamura and Kojima reflected the command. With hurried, yet precise movements, the commander jammed the throttle to the panel, kicked right rudder and pulled the column back while thumbing the ring of the gun button from Safe to Fire. Under full military power, the Sakae roared like thunder before a typhoon, rocketing the fighter upward until Yoshi hung on his propeller, and the horizon dropping out of the world, replaced by blue sky which filled the windshield. Grimacing, he saw the white needle zoom across the tachometer, dangerously crowding the red line. But *Yonaga* was in danger. Nothing else mattered, not his engine, not his flight, not his life.

After watching the altimeter needle wind to 6,000 meters, he leveled off, glimpsing the horizon climb back under his cowl. Gently, he banked the aircraft until settling on a compass heading of one-four-zero—a heading that pointed the A6M2 at the growing storm on the southeast horizon.

The storm. Those crazy Arabs must be closing through the killer drafts of the thunderhead. Probably Sabbah—insane assassins. Would Kadafi never learn? *Yonaga*'s airgroups had destroyed most of the mad dictator's aircraft at Al Kararim, Misratah, and Tripoli. Yet radar reported aircraft closing. He stared at the swirling ashen mass of the thunderhead that soared ominously like a great *Fuji-san*, and his mind raced on. If radar was not playing tricks, where did the enemy come from? Dakar was 1,300 kilometers to the east. But Portugal's Cape Verde Islands were less than 300 kilometers on the same bearing. Easy range for the enemy's bombers and fighters, too. Had the Portuguese capitulated to the Arabs? He shrugged. It made no difference. If an enemy was there, he would kill him. A familiar tingling warmed his groin. His lips pulled back, baring perfect white teeth. Better than a woman, he thought. He hunched over the stick. Within seconds he detected a glint low in the storm where there should not have been any. More reflections as airfoils and perspex caught the sun. Squinting through his goggles, he finally saw a strange collection of Libyan aircraft charging out of the storm low on the water; four Heinkel-111 medium bombers, three Douglas DC-3s, a pair of twin-engined civilian aircraft Brent Ross called Cessna, three North American AT-6s and most remarkable, a venerable Junkers-(JU)52 trimotor transport. The trimotor was the only plane without Arab markings. Instead, a Swissair was emblazoned on its fuselage and wings in bold letters. Escorting were twelve Messerschmitt 109s and a single ME 110, all flying slightly ahead and above the bomber swarm.

"Stupid!" Yoshi snorted, staring ahead and down, running the tip of his tongue over his suddenly parched lips. "What a waste of fighters. They should be up there," he shouted into the slipstream, glancing skyward.

Ignoring his radio, he waggled his wings and punched a balled fist upward three times, releasing his wingmen to individual combat.

A hard pull on the stick and kick to left rudder brought the nose of the fighter back and dropped the horizon like an express elevator. Then, he rolled into a dive, overboosted Sakae, shrieking, his blood pulsing with the engine, throbbing in his temples and bringing a tremor to his hands.

In the corner of his eye he could see *Yonaga* headed into the wind and launching fighters. Late! Late! he thought, knowing first contact was his and the survival of the carrier rode with his Orlikons.

Pushing the stick forward, he steepened the dive, sending the white needle spinning around the speed indicator and passing 350, then 400, to finally crowd the slower red danger line. He felt a flutter. Then shaking that sent dust flying. His wings were vibrating. Now the whole airframe shook like a Kyushu earthquake. He cursed. Clutched the control column until his hands ached. Felt his arms tingle with the

21

vibrations as he watched the altimeter unwind backward, needle spinning crazily like a watch with a broken spring.

"Get the bombers! Get the bombers!" he growled, pounding the instrument panel with a gloved hand.

But the Messerschmitts were climbing on a collision course with the Mitsubishis. A little right rudder brought the leader, the ME-110, into the first ring of the bouncing range finder.

A thousand meters! Too far! But the enemy was winking at him, and white smoking firebrands fell off beneath him. Yoshi snorted. Too far! But at the combined closing speed of perhaps 800 knots, a thousand meters was only a blink. Quickly, the enemy filled two rings of his range finder. He punched the red button. The commander hunched his shoulders and grimaced, baring white teeth as he felt his two 20 millimeter Orlikons and pair of 7-point 7 millimeter machine guns stutter and bark to life, new jolts jarring and slowing the fighter. A two-second burst. That was all, leaving him with fourteen seconds of firepower.

They were hub to hub. Was the enemy Sabbah intent on his own kamikaze mission? With a shout to Amaterasu, Matsuhara pulled back hard on the stick and felt the little fighter buffet like a leaf in a monsoon. As the enemy flashed beneath him, coolant spattered his windshield and he caught a whiff of smoke.

Feeling a familiar warmth spread through his groin, he pushed the stick forward, resuming the dive. A glance in his rearview mirrors told him Takamura and Kojima were both trailing abreast his elevators and the ME-110 was turning toward the sea, leaving a trail of smoke from its port engine, while a 109, minus a wing, tumbled crazily to its grave.

Now he concentrated on the bomber swarm which spread beneath him like a gourmet meal. The bombers were in the usual Arab "box" of four rows of three with trailing rows stepped up at hundred-meter intervals. In this way the enemy hoped to cover each other with defensive fire much like the overlapping fields of fire provided by well-spotted pillboxes. But an old bomber was not a pillbox.

Pulling back gently on the stick, Yoshi brought a Heinkel-111—the left-hand bomber of the leading three—into his gunsight. There were flashes, and hundreds of tracers looped toward him. But suddenly the ancient JU-52 slanted across the formation and into his rings. He thumbed the red button, squirting three short bursts.

At 200 meters, even the shaking Zero could not miss the lumbering giant. Cannon shells smashed into the JU's back, bursting in brilliant flashes and sending chunks of aluminum slaking into the slip-stream. A little right rudder sent the hammer blows marching up the fuselage, ripping off more aluminum, finally exploding the windshield and sending a cloud of shattered perspex flying like sparkling confetti. He pushed the stick forward.

Plummeting past the staggering JU, Yoshi caught a glimpse of white as a dozen Zeros streamed up from *Yonaga*. Screaming, "Banzai!" and bracing his feet, he pulled back on the column with all his strength. Six gs. At least six gs. He felt the blood drain from his brain, and the horizon began to spin. The Mitsubishi bounced like a gull in a typhoon, groaning its objections, threatening to shed its wings. His head became a boulder, bending his back and pressing him down into his parachute pack while leaden arms bent elbows despite his efforts to straighten them.

Mercifully, he felt the little fighter's dive flatten, and finally the horizon was above his cowl and then below it as he began to climb. His wingmen trailed in line at a stern with perhaps a dozen more Zeros climbing hard on their rudders. He shook his head clear.

But at least ten ME-109s were diving, some through their own bombers. One with a checkered nose zigzagged into his range finder. Again, the enemy fired at long range. Half rolling on his back, Yoshi held fire until his target filled two rings of his gunsight. Then he squeezed the button. But the enemy lost his nerve, pulled back hard on his stick, giving the Japanese his belly. Yoshi exulted as his Orlikons' shells smashed into the Arab's air-scoop, blasting it like a piece of trash into the slipstream. Spraying glycol and belching orange flame like a blowtorch, the 109 tumbled toward the sea.

A Zero out of control and burning pulled up sharply out of the melee, clawing for the sky like a wounded bird fleeing death. In a millisecond it vanished into a great rolling ball of flame, smoking wreckage raining through the battle like burning tentacles.

Cursing, Yoshi worked his controls until his gunsight ringed the fat fuselage of a DC-3. There was a great orange flash at the waist of the transport, and hundreds of tracers glowed past him. Gunship!

Gatlings! Leading the transport for a full deflection shot, he punched the button for a long burst. Saw his shells smash the Gatling then march the length of the fuselage, finally shattering the Douglas' tail. Lazily, the stricken transport rolled and then streaked for the sea, engines at full throttle.

"Banzai!"

Throwing quick glances from side to side, he caught glimpses of two other flaming bombers plunging toward the sea. Takamura and Kojima had scored!

"Banzai!"

Leveling off above the bomber swarm, Yoshi searched for fighters. Finally he caught sight of four 109s low on the water, streaking eastward for the cover of the storm with a swarm of Zeros in pursuit. But a half-dozen bombers survived, bored in toward *Yonaga*, which flashed with AA fire. Despite the ugly brown smears of exploding 127 millimeter shells erupting around them like a virulent pox, the bombers bore on, quickly approaching the 50° bomb release angle.

Yoshi grabbed the microphone, "This is Edo Leader! Engage the bombers! The bombers! Follow my lead!" He pushed the stick forward. More orange flashers and tracers streamed past. He felt the fighter vibrate, and a pneumatic drill suddenly drummed wildly on his wings, scattering bits of aluminum. He brought a Cessna into his range finder, punched the button and heard the hiss of compressed air. Out of ammunition! Cursing, he punched the instrument panel.

When Commander Yoshi Matsuhara made his attack, Brent Ross was staring skyward through his glasses, counting aircraft and bracing himself as the great carrier swung to her new course. "A dozen bombers, Admiral Fujita," he said in a carefully modulated voice that masked gnawing flutterings in his suddenly empty stomach. "And a full staffel of fighters."

"Types?"

"ME-one-oh-nines and maybe a single one-ten. The bombers are a mixed bag—HE-one-elevens, DC Threes and maybe a couple Cessnas."

"Very well!" The old man leaned over the windscreen where the dozen ready Zeros gunned their engines and strained at their tie-downs like hungry hawks scenting blood.

"Steady on one-two-zero, speed twenty-four, one-hundred-twenty-eight revolutions, sir," came from the voice tube.

"Launch! Launch!"

There was a flurry of yellow and white as handlers released tie-downs and chocks and raced for their catwalks. With its Sakae roaring hungrily, the first Zero roared down the flight deck. Then one after another, the gleaming white fighters raced down the short runway and climbed into the sky.

"A trimotor! A trimotor, admiral!" Brent said, leaning into his glasses.

"That's a JU-fifty-two," a new voice said behind him.

In a moment Adm. Mark Allen stood at Fujita's other side, adjusting his helmet strap with one hand and raising his binoculars with the other. A white-haired veteran of twelve WWII carrier battles, scholar and expert on Japan, the admiral—along with Brent Ross—was on liaison from Naval Intelligence and served as Fujita's adviser at general quarters.

"The JU has Swissair markings, Admiral Fujita," Brent said.

"I can only judge her by her company, ensign. She will die with the others." The old sailor turned to the talker, saying, "Radar! Range to the nearest enemy aircraft!"

"Fifteen kilometers, sir."

"All ahead flank!"

"You still have three fighters to launch, admiral. In this wind, you'll blow them off the deck."

"They will take their chances, Admiral Allen."

Brent felt a new surge as the ship's engines strained at the load and eighty-four thousand tons of steel smashed into the swell, exploding spray into glistening rainbows, hull booming its objections with hollow reverberations.

There was a cheer from some portside gunners.

"Our CAP has shot down a pair of fighters, admiral, and the JU's going in."

"Very well."

The flight deck reverberated with the blasts of radial engines at full throttle, and two more A6M2s clawed for altitude. One remained.

"Range?"

"Six kilometers, admiral."

"Main battery, stand by to engage aircraft to port—local control." The old Japanese leaned over the windscreen impatiently. "Launch that last Zero-sen!"

With an uneven roar, the last fighter leaped as its

27

pilot released his brakes. Brent saw a flash of white, then heard a backfire. In horror, he watched as the Mitsubishi faltered, then lifted in a sudden gust.

"Too short! Too short!"

Tilting to its left, the little plane caught the flight deck with a wing tip and catapulted crazily over the port side, shedding a wing and smashing into the nine man crew of a 25 millimeter mount.

"No rescue!" Fujita shouted at the talker as the little plane crashed into the sea and began twisting into the depths in *Yonaga*'s boiling wake.

"Admiral," Mark Allen said suddenly, "I would suggest your destroyers form a tighter screen. They must be ranging at least five hundred yards. We need those five-inch thirty-eights in closer, sir."

"Very well." The old man turned to the talker. "Radio room—bridge to bridge. Escorts close on me to two hundred meters."

Thunder rolled as the two American destroyers to starboard began firing. Brent had always been amazed by the speed of each ship's five, five inch, thirty-eight caliber cannons—cannons which could fire over twenty rounds per minute, turning the *Fletchers* into volcanos that belched flashes through clouds of brown smoke.

"In range, admiral."

"Commence firing!"

Like a thunderclap, twenty 127 millimeter guns fired as one. Groaning, Brent twisted his head but kept his glass on the approaching raid. The smell of cordite, the excited shouts of gunners, and the clang of brass casings on steel froze his stomach, and he felt his heart pound like a war drum, the hum of blood in his ears. His glasses trembled as they brought the carnage close; enemy fighters and bombers were being ripped by Zeros from above and below, yet at least a half-dozen bombers bored in toward the carrier while the bulk of *Yonaga*'s CAP engaged and pursued five or six ME-109s. Brent knew some of the enemy bombers would get through. Then he saw the two long cylinders.

"Torpedoes, admiral," he said sharply. "Slung under the AT-sixes."

"They'll try to distract us with the high level and sneak in their fish while we're looking up," Mark Allen said.

"Put us on the anvil with their two torpedo bombers," Fujita mused. "We shall see!"

Ignoring the ugly brown smears of AA filling the air, the surviving enemy planes wheeled slowly toward *Yonaga* and into the precise focus of Brent Ross's glasses. Every detail became clear: two HE-llls with glazed noses armed with 20 millimeter guns, twin Jumo-211A liquid-cooled engines, slender fuselages and high rudders like shark's fins; two Douglas DC-3s powered by huge Pratt and Whitney engines with landing gear tucked into the nacelles like double chins, round, pregnant fuselages and bombbay doors cut into their bellies; and a pair of North American At-6 Texans with Pratt and Whitney engines, high canopies and rear-pointing machine guns and huge, glistening torpedoes slung under their bellies. Brent choked off a gasp as the torpedo planes dived suddenly, once circling far ahead of the carrier.

"Torpedo planes beginning their runs, admiral," the young American said through tight lips.

"Very well."

"Don't change course yet, Admiral Fujita."

"I know, Admiral Allen. Let them committ themselves."

The old American nodded into his glasses.

A new ripping sound drifted across the water as the *Fletchers* opened fire with scores of 20 millimeter and 40 millimeter guns. There were staccato blasts from *Yonaga's* foretop, and then the galleries leaped with fire as triple-mounted 25 millimeter batteries exploded to life, spraying the approaching planes with garlands of smoking tracers.

The At-6, circling ahead of the carrier, was caught by Captain Fite's fire and blasted from the sky like a swatted fly. A Heinkel lost a wing and dropped into a tight spin, crashing into the sea in a hundred-foot column of water and debris. A DC-3 exploded, then a pair of Zeros pounced on the other, killing its crew with long bursts. Another Japanese fighter put a burst into a Heinkel's wing, breaking it off at the root. It was so close, Brent could see it spill entrails of colored wires and fuel lines as it twisted into the sea.

Now one HE-111 remained, making its run close to the water from port while the AT-6 was coming hard on the starboard bow.

"Right full rudder!" Fujita screamed. "Steady up on two-two-zero."

"Good! Good!" Allen said. "Give him the bow."

Recklessly, the Henkel bored in, ignoring the storm of tracers and pursuing Zeros with the intensity of a man bent on suicide.

Brent dropped his glasses to his waist, stared upward with both hands gripping the windscreen with

30

white knuckles. There was nausea and sour gorge rising. But he choked it back. Squared his shoulders as the same terrifying thoughts that crowd the minds of all men caught in combat filled his. They were coming for him, Brent Ross. These strange men in those old bombers wanted his blood — his alone. Again he felt the urge to run. To hide. The same panic he had known off Tripoli. But, again, he stood up to himself. Choked it back, presenting the cold visage of the samurai.

Not more than 200 feet high, and with one engine streaming smoke, the bomber was on them. Suddenly, six shiny black cylinders dropped away and arced toward Brent. But the bombardier had waited a split-second too long. Five of the bombs whistled over the deck and exploded in the sea off the port quarter. There was a sharp blast and shriek of tortured metal as the sixth struck a 127 millimeter mount, blowing the cannon into the sea, followed by its crew that rained into the water like broken mannequins.

As the bomber flashed overhead, its burning engine ripped out of its nacelle and tore away with most of the wing. Shedding pieces of aluminum like a reptile flaking skin and trailing ganglias of wires and fuel lines, the dying Heinkel flipped onto its back and smashed into the sea, cartwheeling crazily across the surface, revolving, flinging pieces and finally coming to rest in a great spray of water.

"Torpedo dead ahead!" rang from the foretop.

"I have her," Fujita said, moving forward, followed by Brent, Mark Allen, and the talker.

Brent studied the approaching streak. "We may take in on the port bow, admiral."

"Left one point."

A voice from the tube repeated the admiral's command.

"If she's a 'homer,' we'll eat it, admiral," Allen said.

"You mean either magnetic or turbulence."

"Correct! Even acoustical, admiral."

Fujita turned to the talker. "All stop!"

Brent felt the vibrations of the great engines come to a halt.

"Helmsman is to let me know the instant he begins to lose steerageway," Fujita shouted to the talker.

Hypnotized, Brent watched the approaching streak, not even noticing the At-6 plummet to its grave. In seconds, the torpedo passed to starboard and was soon lost astern."

"Banzai! Banzai!"

Brent felt a sudden deflation, a draining of emotion. "I'm alive," a little voice said. "It's over and I'm alive." The ensign smiled to himself.

"Cease fire, all ahead standard, steady on one-two-zero," Fujita said. "Bridge to bridge—Captain Fite, pick up survivors, resume one-two-zero, speed eighteen, standard cruising formations." The talker repeated the commands into the mouthpiece while Fujita's narrow black eyes moved around the bridge like glistening ebony, pausing on Brent Ross. The power there brought a surge of pride. The young man's back was suddenly steel, and he squared his shoulders which felt a yard wide.

"Swimmers in the water! Swimmers, bearing two-eight-zero, range fifteen hundred!" rang from the foretop.

Raising his glasses, Brent saw part of the fuselage

and tail of the JU-52 still above water with survivors clinging to the rudders. A *Fletcher* moved slowly toward the wreckage.

"Bridge to bridge," Fujita shouted. "Transfer all survivors to the flagship immediately." And then in a thick voice: "To all hands, you showed great *yamato damashii!* Banzai! Banzai!"

"Banzai!" reverberated through the ship again and again, accompanied by the rumble of thousands of boots struck sharply on steel.

The ancient Japanese turned to the Americans. "In your own tradition, Admiral Allen and Ensign Ross—well done! Well done!"

Despite a thickness in his throat, Brent managed a deep, "Thank you, sir."

Then side by side, the Americans saluted.

After a hasty response, Fujita turned back to the talker. "Secure from general quarters. Set the sea watch, condition two of readiness. Department heads will meet with me in Flag Plot at fourteen hundred hours."

The old man turned and walked slowly from the bridge.

Chapter Two

When Brent Ross entered Flag Plot, Adm. Mark Allen was speaking. "The Russians aren't giving Kadafi their latest torpedoes, Admiral Fujita."

Quickly, Brent seated himself in his usual place next to Allen while Fujita nodded from his chair at the head of the long oak table. Located between the flag bridge and the admiral's quarters and furnished with a single table, a dozen chairs, bulkhead mounted charts, blower, speaker, communications equipment bolted on a corner table manned by a rating, the long room boasted a large equestrian picture of a youthful Emperor Hirohito fixed to the bulkhead behind Fujita.

"Yes, Admiral Allen," Fujita said, nodding agreement. "That seems to be the consensus of the staff."

Brent suppressed a chuckle with difficulty. Staff! What a strange melange of age, race, and nationality clustered around the table; he and the elderly Mark Allen were both graduates of Annapolis, experts on language and on loan from Naval Intelligence (NIS); on liaison from Israeli Intelligence, Col. Irving Bernstein with sparse white hair, deeply lined face, and a neat mustache, was a tattooed survivor of Auschwitz and expert on codes, ciphers, and cryptanalysis; Executive Officer Capt. Masao Kawamoto, graduate of Eta Jima — Japan's Annapolis — nearly seven decades before; he was shriveled and thin as a bamboo stalk, as though the flesh had been burned from his bones by the mid-Atlantic sun; Scribe Lt. Kenji Hironaka, also an Eta Jima graduate, who showed his age in a face fallen into a desicated ruin of crisscrossing lines and pockets of sagging flesh, a permanently curved spine hunching him over his pad where he brushed ideograms with a trembling hand while giggling sporadically at private jokes; incongruously youthful Gunnery Officer Commander Nobomitsu Atsumi with black hair and eyes bright and dark as polished onyx, showing only a few lines at the corners of his eyes and mouth to hint at his sixty-two years.

The flight leader Commander, Yoshi Matsuhara, was not in the room.

Admiral Fujita tapped a pad with a single gnarled finger. "We lost two Zero-sens and their pilots. Also, eight gunners entered the Yasakuni Shrine, and twelve more were wounded. However, the single bomb hit did not damage our hull or impair *Yonaga*'s ability to fight. Eighteen of the enemy planes were destroyed and the rest put to flight! Our ETA, Tokyo Bay, remains unchanged."

"Banzai! Banzai!" Hironaka and Kawamoto sputtered, spraying saliva and staggering from their chairs. A wave from Fujita sent them toppling back.

"The prisoners, sir?" Brent Ross asked.

"Four, ensign. They are being examined by our medical staff and will be sent to us immediately."

36

There was a knock. A nod from the admiral sent a rating to the door. The flight leader commander, Yoshi Matsuhara entered, followed by a pilot Brent recognized as Lt. Nobutake Konoye who had commanded the ready Zeros. Both men, wearing swords and still in their brown flight suits and clutching helmets, goggles and *hachimachi* headbands, stood at attention facing Admiral Fujita.

Unusually tall for a Japanese, Commander Yoshi Matsuhara had a very un-Japanese visage with large eyes, aquiline nose, and sharp chin. His black hair appeared bleached in silver-white streaks from years of salt and sun. By contrast, Lt. Nobutake Konoye was short and squat with narrow eyes and a strong square jaw to match his massive physique, which appeared to be made of roughly hewn boulders. Burning pinpoints, his eyes were sheltered beneath massive black brows and a valance of coal-black hair.

Both men still wore the outline of their goggles on their faces.

"Fine interception, Commander Matsuhara," the old admiral said. "You broke up the bomber swarm."

"Thank you, sir."

"Your losses?"

"Lt. Tamon Kajioka and NAP First Class, Heijiro Abe both honored their *hachimachi* headbands, dying for the emperor with geat *Yamato damashii*, admiral."

"Their spirits dwell in the Yasakuni Shrine," Hironaka shouted suddenly.

Ignoring the scribe, Fujita moved his eyes to Konoye. Brent noticed a warning glint smouldering in the depths. "You led the ready Zeros!"

37

"Yes, sir," the pilot answered in a crater-deep voice.

"There were bombers in the air—making their runs on *Yonaga* while you chased fighters," Fujita spat, voice stinging like a whip.

"I have no excuses. I made the choice, feeling it was tactically correct and giving Commander Matsuhara—"

"Enough! You made the decision agreeable to you." The old admiral leaned forward, fists clutched on the desk like old roots. "The *Hagakure* teaches that a man who chooses only what is agreeable to him is useless."

They lapsed into silence so that the whine of the blowers and hum of the turbines intruded like whispers.

The deep voice, suddenly flat and dead, broke the silence. "With your permission, sir, the *Hagakure* also teaches to attack first and kill or be killed even if you face a thousand enemies."

"The bombers! The bombers! Always the bombers!" Fujita shouted, pounding on the polished oak with a bent fist. "They were your thousand enemies."

Again silence filled the compartment.

The square jaw worked slowly, neck cords bulging. "Sir," Konoye said, "with your permission, I will commit *seppuku* immediately."

The mention of ritualistic suicide sent an electric shock pulsing through the room. A dozen spines stiffened.

"Splendid and honorable thing you would do," Fujita acknowledged, respect softening the anger in his voice, "But no, I cannot give you permission. At

38

this moment, the emperor is in far more need of live pilots than dead heros."

"I cannot drink gall, sir."

"Said like a samurai! Then remember your priorities. Always the bombers!"

The pilot continued tensely: "Please, admiral— remember my request."

"Of course. But you should remember, too, Lieutenant Konoye, I contemplated the honorable exit at the sharp end of a *wakagash*, when we lost all the hostages at Tripoli. I and I alone was at fault. But I made the same decision for myself that I have made for you. The emperor needs us both!"

"Banzai," Hironaka and Kawamoto shouted.

Konoye's implacable face showed no emotion as he spoke. "Thank you, sir, I understand."

The reference to the hostages jolted Brent's memory. Over a thousand hostages had been taken by Kadafi's terrorists when a band of thugs captured the Japanese liner *Mayeda Maru* and steamed her triumphantly into Tripoli Harbor. Everyone remembered the uproar in Japan, the emperor's unprecedented personal plea to Admiral Fujita, the CIA's secret acquisition of seven *Fletchers*, the Arabs' *jihad* against Israel, the long voyage around South America that avoided the Suez Canal and Arab eyes. Then the massive, costly air battles over Misratah and Al Khalil where Fujita's veterans destroyed Kadafi's fighter strength. And the horror of the surface engagement when *Yonaga* was caught by the *Brooklyn* class cruiser and her escorts. Only Fujita's uncanny grasp of tactics, and the suicidal bravery of his pilots, saved the great carrier.

Capt. John Fite's brave run into Tripoli Harbor was perhaps the most courageous act of the campaign. Disguised as an Arab destroyer, Fite had taken his ship alongside the *Mayeda Maru* while *Yonaga*'s air groups savaged the harbor. Here, the American captain had found the ultimate horror; every passenger and crewman was dead, long dead. Killed slowly by garroting and dismemberment.

Brent recalled the rage and hunger for vengeance when Fujita had hurled his "avenging eagles" at the Arabs who threatened to drive Israeli forces into the sea at Al Khalil. A terrible revenge was exacted, and the Arab armies broke and fled before the combined power of the Israelis and Japanese.

But Admiral Fujita had blamed himself personally for the deaths of the hostages, which in his samurai's mind was a betrayal of the emperor. According to *Bushido, seppuku* was the traditional way to regain honor. But the Arab carriers were rumored at sea, waiting to ambush *Yonaga*. Grimly, Fujita declared he would never die while the depraved Libyan dictator commanded the means to destroy *Yonaga*. Plans for *seppuku* were put aside.

Brent's thoughts were interrupted by a knock, and two prisoners, dressed in green fatigues several sizes too small, were ushered in and pushed against a bulkhead by a pair of burly seamen guards armed with holstered 6-point 5 millimeter Rikushiki pistols.

The prisoners were a contrasting pair. One was quite old with a bald pate that reflected the light of the overhead fixture, a square jaw covered with white stubble, and a massive neck that brought memories of the old actor Eric von Stroheim. In fact, the man's entire demeanor — rigid posture, Prussian neck, baleful, sparking blue eyes, haughtily set jaw — was reminiscent of the German actor. With an effort, Brent suppressed a grin.

With brown hair and watery green eyes, the younger prisoner was tall and slender, bent slightly at the shoulders and obviously frightened. He huddled against the wall, cowering as if he had just entered a cave full of dragons.

"You," Fujita said, nodding at the older man, "step forward!"

Snapping his wet boots together with a dull thud, the man came to attention and saluted smartly. "*Oberst* Heinrich Wittenberg," he said in a thick Teutonic accent, voice strident enough to fill the hangar deck.

"We Japanese do not salute below decks, colonel," Fujita said. "We consider this area below decks." He waved idly.

"*Ja, kapitan.*"

"I hold the rank of *admiral*!"

"*Ja, Herr* Admiral."

"You are German?"

"*Jawohl.*"

"English, please — if you can speak it. Every officer on this ship speaks English."

The German nodded.

Fascinated, the staff stared silently like spectators at a tennis match as the admiral continued the exchange.

"Why did you attack me?"

"I am an officer in the Libyan airforce — a *staffelfeuher*. I was ordered to attack you," Wittenberg said in a thick accent.

"Staffel — twelve planes."

"*Korrekt*" the colonel said, lapsing back into German. "Fighters."

"You flew the twin-engined Messerschmitt?"

"*Ja*, admiral." He gestured to his young companion. "The lieutenant was my gunner-radioman."

Fujita waved at Matsuhara airily. "Meet Commander Yoshi Matsuhara. He shot you down."

The two men eyed each other. Matsuhara grinned slowly. "It was a pleasure, colonel."

"Perhaps," the German said slowly, "we will meet again under different circumstances."

"I am at your disposal," the Japanese pilot answered in a soft voice. "But next time, I would suggest you hold your fire. At a thousand yards, you were throwing away good twenty millimeter ammunition."

The German stiffened like a man splashed with ice water.

After silencing Matsuhara with a raised hand, Fujita continued. "Your base, Colonel Wittenberg?"

"According to the Geneva Conventions, I am not required—"

"Japan did not sign the Geneva Conventions."

"Savages!"

"We had no Auschwitz," Fujita shot back.

Brent detected a stiffening of Bernstein's back, but the Israeli remained silent while Fujita drummed the oak with bent fingers. The German used the respite to move his eyes over the strange tableau of officers filling the room. He stopped on Bernstein, eyes moving curiously over the Israeli's uniform. Suddenly the blue eyes widened with astonishment.

42

"Israeli! *Juden!*"

"Ja, oberst," the Israeli said, nodding. "And a member of the Auschwitz alumni association."

"I had nothing to do with that," the German said quickly. "I was in the *Luftwaffe.*"

"Only Adolph Hitler knew," Bernstein said casually. "All the rest of you merely followed orders with your eyes closed and ears plugged."

Fujita hunched forward like an old bird, an intent, fascinated look on his face. Watching, Brent knew the old Japanese loved to sit back and watch others caught in the heat of conflict. And here was a golden opportunity. Two men representing the most hideous crime ever perpetuated on humanity. But the roles were reversing—giving added flavor.

"Ja! You *Juden* blame every German ever born or who will ever be born for *endlosung.*"

"Who else, *oberst*?"

"Why not yourselves?"

The two men looked at each other as if they were trying to destroy each other with the force of their stares. No one was prepared for Wittenberg's next words. "You crowded into the chambers like sheep. Why didn't you fight?"

"Sweinhund!" Bernstein growled, half rising. But Mark Allen restrained him.

Ignoring the warning on Bernstein's face, the German pilot rushed on as if he were releasing long-festering thoughts. "There would be no Israel without Adolph Hitler. Hitler twisted world opinion in your favor, *Juden*. He made the state of Israel possible as a refuge for European Jews. Without him, you would still be wandering in the desert."

43

"Ja, oberst. But you reduced my tribe by six million."

"Enough!" Fujita snapped. He turned to a guard. "Seaman Ishimina, take this officer to the brig." In a moment, the German colonel was pushed to the door."

"Erzahle ihm nichts, Guenther!" Wittenberg shouted as the door slammed behind him.

Fujita glanced at Brent Ross. "He told him not to tell you anything, admiral," Brent said.

Every man in the room sensed the old Oriental's tactics: concentrate on the young frightened gunner; the pilot could not be intimidated. Fujita's voice cracked harshly. "Come to attention!" The young man came erect, jaw working. "Name?"

"Lt. Guenther Mueller," the young man said in a thin voice almost free of accent.

"Unit?"

"Elfter Jagerstaffel, Dritter Geschwader."

"English!" There was exasperation in Fujita's voice.

"Eleventh Fighter Squadron, Third Group, admiral."

"Are there so many Germans in Kadafi's employ that you would use old German designations?"

"Yes, admiral. Germans and Russians."

"Of course, Russians," Brent heard Bernstein mutter.

Admiral Allen spoke. "Many old *Luftwaffe* officers? Correct?"

"They are the cadre, *Ja!"*

"Do you have many Libyan pilots?" Fujita asked.

"A few. But they are *dummkopfs,* admiral."

Everyone chuckled.

"Your base?"

"We were carrier based, admiral."

Fujita nodded to a guard. A blow to the stomach sent the German crashing against the bulkhead, clutching his abdomen and retching.

"Come to attention!"

Slowly, the young gunner straightened, never taking his moist eyes from Fujita.

"I am not a *dummkopf*, lieutenant. You are lying."

The German looked at Mark Allen and Brent Ross. "Your General Doolittle did it with medium bombers a long time ago—during the war," he said, catching his breath.

Brent was surprised by the man's knowledge. Mark Allen responded, saying, "Sure. But only sixteen B-twenty-fives. An unusual aircraft with short takeoff capability. You threw over thirty aircraft at us." Hands flat on the polished oak, he leaned over the table. "There is absolutely no way a loaded DC-three could take off from a carrier's deck—not even *Yonaga*'s."

The young German turned slowly to Admiral Fujita. "The Cape Verde Islands."

"That is what we assumed, lieutenant. You could have saved yourself a lot of pain by telling the truth from the outset." His fingers began to drum on the desk. "What do you know of carriers?"

The man's face was suddenly that of a frightened, trapped animal. "The *oberst* will kill me . . ."

Fujita moved a hand. "He will not kill anyone. You will have separate quarters and a guard." The tiny fist impacted the table. "You were quick to lie about carriers, now tell me the truth!"

45

The young man gulped. "Two," he said softly. "I have heard of two, admiral. That's why I made up that—"

"Have you seen them?"

"No."

"Where are they?"

"I do not know, sir." He looked fearfully at the guard. "I am telling the truth, admiral."

"Big-gunned ships?"

"Perhaps two cruisers. Maybe more."

Fujita glanced at Bernstein. "Confirms our intelligence, admiral," the Israeli said.

Fujita turned back to Mueller. "One more question, lieutenant. Why do you fly for Kadafi?"

The gunner dropped his eyes. "For one million dollars American," he said in a barely perceptible voice.

Disgust crossed the faces of every Japanese in the room. Fujita spoke. "What has happened to the quest for glory, honor? We samurai believe that if a man faces his enemy and dies striving for his objectives, he will enhance his karma, and his spirit will dwell in eternal glory." He leaned forward. "But a mercenary fights for money. Where is the glory? Where is honor? How can a man die for the American dollar?"

For the first time, the German seemed to relax, and a tiny smile played at the corners of his lips. "Thousands of men have found that easy to do, admiral."

A long, awkward silence filled the room.

Bernstein's hard voice broke the silence. "Don't you fly against us because the Japanese are allied with Israel and you wish to kill Jews?"

46

The last vestige of fear drained from the young gunner's face as he lashed back. "Why do you Israelis feel all Germans hate you? I was born in 1960. Over half the Germans alive today had not even been born when you," he paused, waving a hand, and continued, "were killing each other. What do I know of your hates? Of your prejudices? I learned of *Zyklon B* on television. What do I know of Jews, of anti-Semitism? I am a mercenary, true. I work for money, true. But money is a clean reward, uncluttered by prejudice, hatred, and foolish ideas of honor and glory." He stopped abruptly, like a man who knew he had talked too much.

Every man stared at Guenther Mueller, stunned by his sudden bravado. Brent expected an eruption from Fujita. Instead, the old man stared at the German with a benign, almost respectful expression. The old Japanese spoke calmly. "You are dismissed, lieutenant." He nodded to a guard. "Take this man to his quarters and bring in the Arab."

In a moment, Mueller was gone, and a short, dark, wiry man with black hair and shifty eyes was pushed into the room. He had the disconcerted look of a street gang member who suddenly finds himself alone on enemy turf. With his eyes downcast, arms at his sides, the man showed apprehension, yet the straight spine and set of the jaw hinted at steely resolve, too.

"You are an Arab," Fujita began.

"Yes. My name is Tam Ali Khalifa. I am—ah, I was a gunner on a Douglas."

Fujita continued. "You flew from the Cape Verde Islands!"

The man raised his head, sneering. "I will not

47

answer that. Do your best. Allah *akbar!*"

Fujita nodded. Two guards swung simultaneously, one blow catching the Arab on the side of the face, the other in the stomach. Grunting explosively, Ali Khalifa stumbled against the oak table and slid to the deck, spitting blood.

Brent half rose. "Admiral . . ."

Fujita waved at the young American impatiently, and Brent felt Admiral Allen's hand on his shoulder, pulling him back into his chair. As the admiral pressed on, the Arab was pulled to his feet. "If you ever speak to me in that tone of voice again, Tam Ali Khalifa, your spirit will be dispatched to Allah at the end of a *wakizashi.*" He gestured to a long knife hanging at the belt of one of the guards.

Wiping blood from his mouth and chin with the back of his hand, the Arab moved his eyes to the knife and then back to the old Japanese. "You joined them," he said, waving toward Bernstein, "to drive us from our land—deny us our birthright. Why? Why?"

"I ask the questions, Ali Khalifa."

"Does the samurai fear the truth?"

Brent expected more violence. But Fujita surprised him again.

"The truth is, your mad master Moammar Kadafi killed over a thousand Japanese hostages, tried to sink *Yonaga* by ramming in Tokyo Bay, embargoed oil to Japan." The old man's eyes narrowed, and both bony hands became tight balls of roots as he hunched forward. "You are Sabbah!"

"Yes," was the quick, firm reply. "I serve in the spirit of Hasan ibn-al-Sabbah!"

The mention of the ancient assassin, ibn-al-Sabbah— "the old man of the mountain"— transported Brent back to a Tokyo alley and a pair of hashish-charged madmen attacking him recklessly, ignoring pain and stopped only by death. Involuntarily, his hand found his chest where a long slash still felt tender under his fingers.

"As surely as Allah is God and Mohammed his prophet, we will destroy you, admiral," the man said matter-of-factly. He gestured to the Israeli captain. "And we will drive the Jews into the sea."

"As you did at Al Khalil," the old sailor fired back sardonically. Then, obviously tiring of the questioning, he said, "Take this man to the brig."

"Death to the Jews! Allah be praised! Allah *akbar*!" the man shouted at Bernstein as he was dragged through the door.

"Bring in the last prisoner."

No one was prepared for the last prisoner—a Japanese woman of perhaps twenty-five or thirty. Tall and curvaceous, her sculpted buttocks flowed sinuously under the tight-fitting fatigues as she walked with a firm step, head high and erect, large rounded breasts jutting against the tight shirt. Her eyes were wide and flashed like chips of black diamonds, nose straight and well shaped, tapering to elegant nostrils, which gave her demeanor a haughtiness. And her hair was striking, falling to her shoulders in long lustrous folds, gleaming in the raw glare of the bulbs like fine lacquer.

The old Orientals had never seen a woman like this. Shocked, they ogled her with unabashed hunger.

Fujita spoke. "I am Admiral Fujita. What is your name?"

49

"Kathryn Suzuki," she answered in a surprisingly controlled voice. "You killed twenty-two innocent people on the Junkers, including my two best friends." Her voice caught, but there were no tears.

"You kept bad company."

"The Arabs forced us."

"What do you mean?"

Quickly she explained that the German trimotor had been leased to Swissair by the Swiss Air Force which had three of the ancient planes. Enroute to Brazil from Dakar, she had been scheduled to land at Natal and then fly to the United States on TWA and then on to Hawaii where she had relatives. But the JU had accidentally encountered the Arab bomber force and been herded along like a sheep to slaughter. "For cover," she spat, voice breaking for the first time. "That's all. Just cover. Stupid!" Breathing hard, she fell silent, eyes moving to the pilots.

She waved. "These men—these men, they shot us down."

Matsuhara nodded.

"How brave you are, mighty samurai," she said softly, voice cutting with a cold edge of sarcasm. "Do dead women and children improve your karma, too?"

Matsuhara smiled. "Next time choose your company with more discretion, madam."

"You are an American citizen?" Fujita asked abruptly.

"Yes. I was born in San Bernardino. I'm a Nisei."

"But you travel to Hawaii?"

"My only relatives live there. My aunt Ichikio Kume and two cousins. My parents are dead." She shifted her weight uneasily.

"What were you doing on the Junkers?"

"I'm a geologist for the Federated Oil Exploration Corporation. We have offices in Gambia, Senegal. I'm on my vacation."

"So you fly to Hawaii on vacation in these times — a time when open warfare has been raging in the Mediterranean and on the African continent?" Fujita asked, eyes birdlike, glittering with suspicion.

"Why not? The world doesn't stop turning because you mighty warriors decide to kill each other."

The Japanese eyed each other in shock. They had never heard a woman speak with such arrogance.

"Madam," the admiral retorted, "you are insolent. If you consider yourself equal to us, I will treat you as an equal. You will not find that pleasant — a Japanese should understand that."

"I'm not a Japanese. I told you I'm American," she shot back, giving no ground. "This is the twentieth century, not the sixteenth. And women do have rights and are treated as equals in civilized nations." She wheeled to Matsuhara, pointing, eyes flaming. "His bullets didn't discriminate. He killed both men and women with equal joy." Her lips pulled back from her teeth, eyes narrowed, nostrils flared as hatred seemed to ooze from every pore, replacing her beauty with the visage of a demon. The voice, suddenly dropped octaves, came from her chest. "You filthy, cowardly Jap shit!"

Commander Matsuhara's eyes widened and he opened his mouth as if to speak. But Lieutenant Konoye sprang forward, swinging a huge open hand that caught the woman squarely on the cheek, hurling her against a bulkhead with a crash and a scream of

51

pain.

Brent Ross reacted instinctively, propelled from his chair as if it were spring loaded. Swinging with all his strength, he caught the burly pilot in the stomach with his right fist while locking Konoye in a headlock with his other. The two men stumbled to the corner, knocked a communications man from his chair and then crashed to the deck in a welter of broken telephones, pencils, and a scattering of paper.

"Guards! Guards!" Fujita roared.

In a moment two guards, Mark Allen and Nobomitsu Atsumi pulled the combatants apart.

Coming to his feet, Konoye spat, "This will not be forgotten, barbarian."

"Enough!" Fujita shouted. "Out! Both of you are confined to your quarters." And then, glaring at Kathryn, he said, "Get her out of here."

Sobbing, Kathryn Suzuki was led from the cabin. But she turned her head, never taking her eyes from Brent until she was pulled down the passageway.

Chapter Three

Although Brent had been confined to his cabin for a week, he still stood watches on the flag bridge as junior officer of the deck. Fortunately, Lieutenant Konoye's "country" was the fighter pilots' ready room: a large compartment on the gallery deck, or the hangar and flight decks where he inspected and tested A6M2s or just tinkered with engines and weapons with dozens of other restless pilots and aircrewmen.

Despite the nearness of the equator, the second morning after the raid dawned magnificently with no hint of the heat to come. A light and fickle breeze — not even two on the Beaufort Scale — scratched dark patches on the surface of the placid deep blue sea, leaving the rest of it with satiny gloss. Surprisingly, there were seabirds working, their wings twinkling like flurrying snowflakes, huge flocks of them that stretched low across the horizon. Lowering his glasses, Brent stared down from the bridge at the pilots and mechanics who swarmed fondly over the next CAP flight of six Zeros. He heard a soft voice behind him. "Good morning, Mr. Ross," Kathryn Suzuki said.

53

Turning quickly, the young American moved his eyes to the lovely face. Although he marveled at the flawless flesh that glowed warmly in the morning sun with pearl-like lustre, a smile had awakened incipient lines at the corners of her mouth and eyes, hinting at years far beyond Brent's first assessment. Then silently and with unabashed candor, he dropped his eyes to the large breasts, tiny waist, and trim, flaring hips.

"You like what you see, ensign?" she said, a slight flush creeping to her cheeks.

"I approve of the distribution, if that's what you mean."

Her laughter did not hint at a trace of her previous haughtiness and anger. Brent wondered at the change in mood. Perhaps she was resigned to her long voyage on *Yonaga*. Or, possibly, hot food and sleep had altered her demeanor. Regardless, Brent liked her new mood and could not help thrilling at the presence of a woman in what had been a male desert.

Two lookouts turned from their binoculars for an instant, stared at the newcomer and then returned to their sectors. Kathryn moved close to Brent's side, leaned on the windscreen and spoke softly into his ear. "Thank you—thank you very much for what you did. That big brute could've killed me."

"That was nothing," he said grimly. And then with sudden curiosity, he said, "What are you doing on the bridge?"

"My cabin is there." She gestured to a door held in the open position by a steel pelican hook. "The admiral has said I can walk here once a day, but I've got to return to my cabin—even for my meals." He felt her hand on his arm. "I caused trouble between you and that pilot."

The hand brought a sudden warmth, and Brent could feel a familiar pulsing in his neck and then lower. He ached to move closer, but, instead, pulled his arm away. "No, Miss Suzuki . . . "

"*Kathryn*, please, Brent."

He nodded and pressed on. "No, Kathryn. It's been a long time brewing." He recalled Konoye's instant hatred the day the American boarded *Yonaga* in Tokyo Bay. Even during the bloody fighting in the Mediterranean, when it seemed they would all die together, the man's hatred for Brent had persisted unabated. It was certainly possible the forty-two years of isolation on the Chukchi Peninsula had broken the man's mind. Or, perhaps, when he discovered his mother, father, wife, and two children had been incinerated in the great Tokyo fire raid of 1945, he may have snapped. Maybe it was a combination of all these things. Certainly, the essence of the man's hatred was focused on Brent and not Mark Allen and the others. It was possible, in his samurai's mind, he was forced to select the biggest and strongest for his revenge—the revenge of the forty-seven ronin. Brent was certain of one thing: Someday, he would be forced to settle things with the burly lieutenant.

"You hate each other, Brent?"

"Not necessarily," he lied. "It's a shipboard thing. When you're cooped up like this, tempers can flare."

"He struck me."

"Of course. But watch your mouth, Kathryn. These are medieval men."

"The old school—women are for housekeeping,

55

childbearing, and sex," she spat. She stabbed a finger down at the flight deck. "They all have their geishas on the side." Brent laughed.

Before the American could answer, the woman continued. "It's hot — very hot." She gestured at the morning sun, which had climbed rapidly and glared down with hot rays despite the cooling effects of the freshening breeze. "It's hot in my cabin."

"We'll be crossing the equator soon. These latitudes are known as the doldrums. There's a lot of heat here."

"Doldrums?"

"Yes. We're between the northeast and southeast trade winds." He waved a hand in a semicircle. "Shifting winds, cyclones, unpredictable currents and calms. In fact, ancient sailors called these latitudes the 'horse latitudes.' "

She arched an eyebrow. Encouraged by her piqued interest, he continued. "Horse latitudes because a becalmed sailing vessel would run short of water, and if horses were in the cargo, they were thrown overboard."

"Then the slaves."

"They probably went before the horses."

Her eyes followed a flock of gulls. "It's still hot in my cabin."

"*Yonaga*'s not air-conditioned. You'll cool off when we round the southern tip of South America."

"Cool off, Brent?" she pleaded huskily, raising her eyes. "How can a girl accomplish that miracle with you around?"

For the first time in his life, Brent was at a loss for words. "Ah . . . Kathryn . . . I . . . "

Her laughter cut him short. "Sorry, ensign, that was brazen." Then with new seriousness she said, "I'm not a sailor, but it seems to me you're headed for the wrong ocean."

"Why?" he asked with a strange mix of both relief and disappointment at the change in subject.

"Why not round Africa and head across the Indian Ocean; it's shorter."

"Because," a new voice said from behind them, "we would be forced into narrow waters where a capital ship should never be caught."

Turning together, the couple found Adm. Mark Allen standing with his binoculars hanging at his waist. "I'm Adm. Mark Allen," he said.

"I know, admiral." Kathryn returned to her point, eagerly. "But it would be shorter, admiral."

"Yes. But Admiral Fujita is too smart to take this ship into restricted waters. We would be forced to navigate the Straits of Malacca, round Singapore and steam northeast into the South China Sea, skirting the Malay Peninsula."

"This is dangerous?"

The old American snorted. "Dangerous! Hah! The *Repulse* and *Prince of Wales* did it in 1941. They're still there; on the bottom where Japanese aircraft put them."

A shout of "Mark!" turned Kathryn's head, and she stared upward at the navigation bridge where Lt. Nobomitsu Atsumi stood, staring down at the vernier scale on his sextant while a rating read a stopwatch.

"Do they still navigate that way?" she said aghast. "I thought you had machines—computers."

The Americans chuckled. "Admiral Fujita hates

computers," Mark Allen said. "He feels they're taking the thrill out of life — warfare."

"I saw some. They're just outside my cabin."

"Yes, true," Brent said, entering the exchange suddenly. "But those are used for cryptanalysis and fire control." The ensign gestured upward. "The admiral had no choice. But he insists on navigating the old-fashioned way."

The girl nodded at one of the escorting destroyers. "I'll bet they use modern methods."

"True."

She moved curious eyes to Brent's face. "How can the navigator find stars in this bright sunlight?"

Both Americans laughed. Mark Allen said, "He's shooting the sun. He'll do it all day long and run up the sun lines, giving him an accurate, continuous fix. In fact, his LAN — ah, Local Apparent Noon sight will give him a precise latitude."

"Kathryn," Brent said. "LAN is an altitude taken on the sun when it's on your meridian. In a sense the only noon — true noon."

"But it won't give longitude," she said quickly, surprising both men.

"Right," the admiral conceded. "He needs his stars and planets for that."

She pointed to the horizon. "You must fuel somewhere. The Falklands?"

"No," Allen answered. "We'll meet a tanker."

"Oh," she mused, palming back her hair. "That's how you did it."

Brent felt an uneasiness as the girl's eyes suddenly chilled like chips of black ice.

"That's how," she repeated to herself.

58

There was a heavy step on the grating, and a seaman guard stood at quiet attention, holstered pistol at his side. "It's time for Anne Boleyn to return to the Tower," she said quietly, moving toward the door, her long delicately formed limbs and chiseled hips flowing and swaying under the tight fatigues. Watching the girl vanish through the door, Brent dampened his suddenly parched lips with the tip of his tongue. Slowly, he turned to the horizon, slitting his eyes against the rising sun.

At a steady 18 knots, the battle group steamed southward through the doldrums, leaving Ascension Island to port and finding the northeast trade winds gradually replaced by gusts from the southeast. Standing next to Brent — a position she took every morning as if she, too, were standing a watch — Kathryn said, "Funny how the wind's shifted."

"We're in the southern hemisphere, Kathryn," the ensign explained. "Actually, it's a simple thing. Just keep in mind, when winds and currents approach the continents, they are deflected by the earth's rotation. Clockwise." He circled a finger. "In the northern hemisphere. Counterclockwise in the southern hemisphere." He reversed the finger.

"Simple." She laughed, eyes tied to his. "Very simple."

He felt a compulsion to touch her. But his hands remained at his sides.

After crossing the Tropic of Cancer, course was changed to two-zero-zero, and as the days passed, Brent knew that far over the western horizon Brazil was slipping past and then Uruguay and Argentina. The air cooled, and the sun began to hang astern in a sky that slowly filled with high-cruising, stringy gray clouds. The sea became burnished slate, mounting combers taking the great ship on her port bow, punishing the 84,000 tons of steel, a constant reminder of *Yonaga*'s transient insignificance and the inevitable demise of men and man-made things while the sea rolled on infinitely. And *Yonaga* protested, creaking and groaning, shrugging off the seas, frames, plates, and rivets put to the test. Ten days after the attack, and with the Falkland Islands far to the west, *Yonaga* met her first tanker.

Speed was reduced, and flags and pennants whipped from the halyards as the gray tanker—low in the water with the chop frothing over her low freeboard like a great blue disporting herself on the surface—staggered through banners of blue water and white spray to a position directly ahead of the carrier and began to fuel in Japanese style: stern to bow. Impatiently, Fujita paced the deck, cursing the slow speed and haranguing the lookouts to increased alertness.

"We are cold meat for submarines," he shouted, gesticulating at the tanker. Kathryn Suzuki, who had been standing near the door with her guard, giggled quietly. Whirling, Fujita spat, "Return to your quarters, madam. Instantly!"

Muttering, the woman left.

Chapter Four

Eighteen days after passing the Cape Verde Islands, *Yonaga* entered the Drake Passage, splitting the Scotia Sea midway between Cape Horn and the South Shetland Islands. Dressed in a foul-weather jacket, heavy trousers, and parka, Brent stood on the bridge, gloved hands gripping the windscreen. Similarly dressed, Kathryn stood at his side in what had now become a morning ritual: a practice that was honored by every man on the watch. They maintained a discreet distance while the couple talked or merely stood side by side quietly.

Admiral Fujita had ordered course changed to two-seven-zero, a heading which brought the bow of the ship into a head-on challenge of the charging combers, which loomed one after the other in endless rows. Hard hit were the *Fletchers*. Top heavy with guns and narrow in the beam, they rolled deeply until gray water swept the decks, the sleek vessels sometimes vanishing into troughs to reappear again, rolling and shaking frothing seas from decks and upper works like lazy hounds caught by rainstorms.

"Gray, gray, everything's gray," Kathryn said, icy wind tearing the words from her lips in white ribbons.

Staring at the overcast above and the scudding dun-colored clouds that streamed from the horizon like terrified sheep fleeing the wolf of the wind, Brent nodded and winced as a particularly violent impact flung spray to sting his face like thrown needles.

"Where are the Zeros?" the girl asked, staring down at the empty flight deck.

"Struck below," he answered, bending his knees and following with the punch of a huge sea. "Not even a gull can fly in this."

"Jesus, it's rough and cold," the girl said, both hands on the windscreen.

"Sixty degrees south latitude."

"Almost to the Antarctic Circle?"

"About seven hundred fifty miles south of here," he said, sweeping a hand to port.

"Well, the crew should be used to it," she noted. "After all, *Yonaga* spent over forty years in the Arctic."

"Usual media inaccuracy," Brent snorted.

"The Chukchi Peninsula," she countered. "On a secret mission."

Brent laughed. "Is that what you heard?"

She nodded.

"The Chukchi is right, but south of the Arctic Circle."

She pounded the rail with a single, tiny gloved fist. "Tell me, then, the truth, Brent. I promise to stay silent."

After taking a deep breath, Brent stared over the bow and told the story of the great carrier: an incredible tale that began in 1935. Designed as a battleship—a member of the top secret *Yamato* class, which were 64,000 ton monsters with nine, 18-point 2 inch guns—*Yonaga*, along with *Shinana,* was converted to an aircraft carrier. But while *Shinana* remained in the *Yamato* configuration, *Yonaga* was lengthened, given a 1040-foot flight deck and sixteen Kanpon boilers instead of twelve.

"She was part of the Pearl Harbor task force," Kathryn said.

"True. There were seven carriers in that force— *Kido Butai* the Japanese called it—*Kaga, Akaga, Soryu, Hiryu, Zuikaku, Shokaku*, and *Yonaga,* which was so huge it was feared foreign spies would discover her."

Kathryn appeared hypnotized by the tale. Brent moved on slowly as if he, too, challenged the credibility of the 84,000 ton leviathan pitching and rolling under his feet. "To insure secrecy," he said, "an extraordinary thing was done: *Yonaga* was actually commissioned into the army's Unit Seven-Three-One."

"I didn't know that. Weren't they like the Gestapo? SS?"

"Correct! Killers. Even carried out medical experiments on POWs. They destroyed all Imperial Navy records of *Yonaga*, and she became a ghost ship. They went to incredible lengths. Early in 1940, Seven-Three-One moved her to an anchorage near Kitsuki on the island of Kyushu where she was covered with acres of camouflage netting—so much netting Admiral Fujita said there was a shortage of fishnets on Kyushu for almost a year. But it worked. From the sea she looked like another small mountain, and there wasn't a hint of her existence in western embassies, which the Japanese had correctly estimated as being filled with spies. But after the decision to attack Pearl Harbor was made, Seven-Three-One decided to move her to Sano-Wan, a secret base hidden in a gigantic cove on the southern coast of the Chukchi Peninsula."

"It juts into the Bering Sea from Siberia, Brent."

"Correct. And it's desolate."

"But why a base there? The media said—"

Brent interrupted. "The media talks a lot but knows little. Actually, Sano-Wan existed because Seven-Three-One needed a base to launch germ-warfare balloons."

"I didn't know that."

"Yes. Lethal strains of germs were developed, and they were afraid to attempt home island launches. So a Colonel Sano scouting in one of their big I-boats—"

"I-boat?"

"Submarines. Anyway, he found the cove, and the base was built." Then Brent explained how the planet's peculiar wind patterns send breezes down from the pole, past Sano-Wan, southwest over the Aleutians where the westerlies would pick up the balloons and carry them to the west coast of the United States. And the cove lay on the Pacific Ring of Fire with a steam vent that provided unlimited geothermal power.

"But *Yonaga* was trapped by a landslide."

"Not quite. An overhanging glacier broke loose. That's what trapped her, sank I-twenty-four and killed Colonel Sano." Brent moved on with the story quickly, telling of two tunnels cut through nearly a kilometer of ice and of how fishing parties took halibut, salmon, herring, cod, and even small whales from one of the world's great fisheries. Seaweed was cultivated in the cove, and for over forty years there was never a shortage of food.

"I still can't believe it. Even standing here — seeing it, feeling it; it seems like a dream. A bad dream, Brent."

Brent raised an eyebrow. "Bad?"

"They wrecked Pearl Harbor, sank the *New Jersey*. Isn't that bad?"

"Why of course, Kathryn. But we smashed Tripoli, destroyed Kadafi's bases at Misratah and Al Kararim and saved Israel."

"*We*? Ha, you're one of them, Brent. After Pearl Harbor they . . ." She waved a hand. "This crew killed your father."

The reference to his father, Ted "Trigger" Ross, stiffened the young man's back. Angrily, he turned to the girl. "My father killed himself."

"You're sure?"

"Why of course. Admiral Fujita gave me his word."

"And you were satisfied with that?"

"Naturally." Brent was incredulous. "His word of honor."

"You're one of them. Yes, you are. Another samurai." The words washed over him like acid.

"I can't find that reprehensible," he said, curtly.

"Oh, I'm sorry, Brent," she said, grasping his arm and looking up at him, suddenly, the contrite, wide-eyed young girl. "I didn't mean to offend."

Looking into the soft, moist eyes, Brent felt her look would melt the Antarctic ice pack. Again, he had the impulse to touch her. She seemed to read his

mind and whispered, "Someday we'll be alone Brent."
A roll of the ship swayed her toward him. With an
effort, he tore his eyes away and returned to the story.
"They practiced—"

"Who practiced?"

"The crew. For over forty years not only the fliers
but all members of the crew practiced in flight
simulators. Gasoline and oil tanks were sealed, and
they all entered rigorous physical training regimens.
Hundreds of senior officers died, but the rest of the
crew aged very slowly, and when the glacier broke
away, after forty-two years, over twenty-four hundred
men in splendid physical condition, manning a su-
perbly maintained ship, broke loose."

"And then the story began."

"Madam," a deep voice said behind them. "It is
time."

Sighing, Kathryn turned and faced her guard. "I'm
ready, warden. Back to the Tower."

Eyeing Brent and smiling her most dazzling smile,
the girl left the bridge.

The entire crew was relieved when *Yonaga* finally
doubled Cape Horn and altered course to the northwest where warmer, friendlier latitudes were to be
found.

"Where were you born, Brent?" Kathryn asked one
clear, calm morning, staring down at the flight deck
where a six plane CAP was being readied for the first
patrol in over a week.

"New York City," Brent said. "And you?"

"San Bernardino, California." She looked up at the

strong face. "Why the navy, Brent?"

"There was never a thought of anything else."

"Your family?"

"Yes. My father was a pro—came up from the ranks—a mustang. In World War Two he served on the *Enterprise*, was sunk on the *Hornet*, captured, escaped, was commissioned, served in Japan after the war with Mark Allen on Samuel Eliot Morison's staff. They helped write the *United States Naval Operations in World War Two*."

"But he was commanding a civilian ship, the *Sparta*, when *Yonaga* captured him."

Brent twisted uncomfortably. "True. He rose in the ranks quickly after the war, was sent as an attaché to embassies all over the world."

"Is this how you became a language expert?"

"Yes. I don't know if I'm an expert, but my father insisted I attend public schools and I picked up Japanese, German, French, Italian, and even a little Arabic in Saudi Arabia."

"You attended Annapolis?"

"Of course—what else?"

"Sorry, ensign." They both laughed.

"The *Sparta*—you didn't answer. Why was your father commanding it?"

Brent's mind went back to the painful memories of his high school years when his beloved, angelic mother died slowly, smiling through the pain as cancer ravaged her body. And his father's resignation of his commission, the years of bedside care and finally his mother's death, which she welcomed as the ultimate relief. But Trigger Ross did not. He stormed, railed and withdrew to the bottle. Only after a year of bitter withdrawal concluded by violence with his own son did Ted Ross pull himself from the depths and return to the cool catharsis of the sea. But, then, *Sparta* met *Yonaga*.

"My mother died when I was in high school," he said simply. "Father resigned his commission to care for her and then joined the merchant marine after her death."

She nodded. "My parents were *doho*."

"*Doho*—literally 'compatriot.' It applied to all Japanese immigrants; all Japanese living abroad," he said. "Japan never let go."

"Very good. 'Four-oh,' ensign." And then bitterly, she said, "Your—I mean the US never let go, either. My parents were interned at Manzanar from '42 to '45. They lost everything."

"Tragic. But they had dual citizenship. Consider the time—the panic, fear . . . "

"It was a Jewish plot!"

"Jewish?"

"Yes. Roosevelt plotted with the Jews to steal their property for pennies on the dollar."

"You sound like an Arab, Kathryn," he spat, anger flaring like a struck match.

A fleeting look of consternation crossed the girl's face, and she tapped her temple with a closed fist as if punishing herself. "I didn't mean that. I hate Kadafi as much as you do." There was contriteness in her voice.

Quickly, Brent curbed his anger and changed the subject. "You're a geologist?"

"Yes. I graduated from Southern Cal."

"Oh," Brent said slyly. "There's another member of

your alumni association on board."

She looked at him quizzically. "Who?"

"Admiral Fujita."

For a long moment silence gripped the platform, and only the thump of engines, the hiss of the sea sluicing past and the sigh of wind through the halyards could be heard. She finally managed an incredulous, "USC!"

Brent laughed so raucously a pair of lookouts turned their heads. "Yes, Kathryn. Many officers of his generation attended universities in Britain and the US. After all, the Imperial Navy was patterned after the Royal Navy. In fact, they even built their academy, Eta Jima, with bricks brought from England, and at the turn of the century, English was the official language of the fleet."

"I noticed they all seem to understand English," she agreed. Looking up, she narrowed her eyes. "Brent, how old is that man?"

"One hundred."

"One hundred," she repeated with disbelief.

"Yes. Admiral Allen and I debriefed him. He fought at Tsushima." Obviously confused, the girl raised an eyebrow. "Tsushima — in the Korean Straits, the Japanese annihilated the Russian fleet there in 1905," he explained. "Then the usual staff schools and war college where he helped develop the first carrier-borne aircraft."

"But USC?"

"After World War One, he got his Master's in English. Nineteen twenty-one, I believe."

"That's mind boggling."

"But not really unusual, Kathryn. Remember, Japan was dragged out of feudalism kicking and screaming in the nineteenth century. They had to catch up—pick the brains and technology of the western world. It was remarkable. They defeated Russia fifty years after Admiral Perry forced western contact on them."

A Sakae coughed to life, stuttered, almost stopped, and then after some faltering picked up as all fourteen cylinders began firing raggedly, gushing clouds of blue-gray smoke. Another engine burst to life. Then another and another until all six engines vibrated the tie-downs of the beautiful white fighters on the flight deck.

"I heard that a lot of these men haven't been off the ship in over forty years," she said, gesturing at the CAP.

"It's hard to believe, but true. Some went ashore at Tokyo and were disgusted by what they found."

"Their families?"

"Don't forget, this crew was MIA for over four decades. Wives remarried or died, and many were killed in American air raids. Admiral Fujita's entire family vanished at Hiroshima."

"Good Lord. Isn't he bitter?"

"At first, of course." He tapped the windscreen. "It's hard to understand the samurai mind." He pondered for a moment. "Kathryn, have you ever heard of *kokutai*?"

It was the girl's turn to ponder. "Ah, my father used that word. The emperor—we had his picture. He was Japan. Is that it, Brent?"

"In a sense, yes, Kathryn. The emperor *is* the embodiment of the national essence."

"That's passé."

"Not to these men. *Kokutai* is their basic drive."

"Still? You mean they're *still* warriors for their emperor. Now my father was an old Japanese at heart, but—

"Of course. I told you they were medieval with feudal loyalties. To them, Hirohito is still a deity, and his words are sacrosanct. Fujita answers only to him."

"Admiral on the bridge," Kathryn's guard shouted hastily.

Turning and coming to attention, Brent faced Admiral Fujita, followed by Captain Kawamoto and Lieutenant Hironaka. Fujita took his usual position next to the talker who stared from his oversized helmet expectantly while the two staff officers braced themselves against the windscreen.

"As you were," the admiral said, waving. "Maintain your watch."

"Aye, aye, sir," Brent said, glassing the horizon. Kathryn moved toward the door.

"You may remain, Miss Suzuki," the old Japanese said with unexpected cordiality. Smiling, Kathryn returned to Brent's side. The admiral continued with Brent. "Anything to report, ensign?" he asked, gripping the rail and staring down at the warming Zeros.

"Commander Atsumi is the OD of the watch, admiral. We are steaming as before on course three-one-zero, speed eighteen knots, all boilers on line, condition two of readiness as per your night orders, sir."

"Very well." The admiral seemed pleased. "We resume our CAP and training flights this morning." He turned to the talker. "Seaman Naoyuki, all

71

stations, pilots man your planes."

The command cracked through the PA system and a half-dozen brown-clad pilots ran across the flight deck and scrambled into their cockpits while crew chiefs stood on wings, leaning over their pilots like old birds over their young, fussing over belts, parachute straps, canopy locks, and oxygen bottles. Fujita looked at the battle ensign whipping at the gaff, glanced at a gyro-repeater and then turned to the talker. "Signal bridge, bend on the hoist, 'course one-three-zero.' "

Within seconds, flags and pennants snapped in the wind overhead like tiny whips. Raising his glasses, Brent moved to the front of the platform followed by the girl who clung to him like a security blanket. He saw answering signals at every yardarm. "All escorts answer our hoist, admiral."

"Very well. Execute!" With the snap of a powerful arm, a signalman jerked *Yonaga*'s hoist back down to the flag bag. Instantly, the *Fletchers* followed.

"Acknowledged, sir."

"Very well." The admiral turned to the voice tube. "Right standard rudder, steady up on one-three-zero." Heeling and leaving a curving white scar on the blue surface, the great ship swung in a wide arc, escorts maintaining their stations like wheeling dancers on the Bolshoi stage.

"He's turning around. Going back," Kathryn said softly in Brent's ear.

Brent chuckled. "Coming into the wind—the southeasterlies. A carrier can't ever launch with the wind astern. He'll probably increase speed, too."

"Steady on one-three-zero, sir," the talker said.

"Very well. Signal bridge, speed twenty-four."

Within minutes, more flags and pennants were raised and lowered, and Brent felt the rhythm of the four great engines pick up as throttles were opened.

"Why didn't he just call them on his radio, Brent?" Kathryn asked. "It would be simple."

"Yes. And it'd be simple for Arab radiomen to pick up our signals, too."

"Out here?"

"Out anywhere, Kathryn. Even off the Cape Verde—"

"You must use radios."

"Only when the enemy's in sight or in extreme emergencies."

Brent was interrupted by Fujita's command. "Two-block Pennant One." A triangular pennant with a red circle on a white background leaped to the truck.

Kathryn stabbed a finger upward at the bunting. "It's a signal to our escorts," Brent explained. " 'I am launching aircraft.' " Slowly, a *Fletcher* reduced speed and dropped astern. "Our lifeguard," Brent said, waving at the trailing destroyer. He brought his glasses to the cockpit of the lead Zero. Matsuhara stared back and waved. Brent raised a hand.

"Your killer's very friendly today," he heard Kathryn hiss.

"Belay that," he said harshly, without turning.

"The stripes back of the cockpit. What do they mean?" she asked quickly, trying to distract and ameliorate Brent's anger.

Brent accepted the ploy. "The green stripe means *Koku Sentai*—First Air Fleet. The blue stripe represents carrier *Yonaga*, and the three digit number on the tail identifies the mission of the aircraft and the individual aircraft itself."

Brent returned his attention to the flight deck where crew chiefs now stood clear of the aircraft, and he could see Matsuhara hunching over his instruments, gunning his engine, working his rudder, elevators, and flaps. Satisfied, the commander stabbed a thumb upward. Instantly, four handlers released wing and tail tie-downs, only two men at the chocks remaining.

All eyes moved to the yellow-clad director, standing on a platform mounted on the starboard side of the flight deck and holding a yellow flag high over his head. "Launch! Launch!" Fujita shouted at the talker. "What are they waiting for?"

Before Naoyuki could speak into his headpiece, the yellow flag dropped, chocks were pulled, and Matsuhara's engine roared. Then, with a snap, he released his brakes and the graceful fighter leaped forward, thundered down the deck, and clawed its way into the sky eagerly. One after the other the Mitsubishis raced down the runway and lifted into the sky to follow their flight leader into a counterclockwise orbit. Then, quickly, they formed the traditional Japanese Vs of three and climbed into the clear sky.

Fujita turned to Captain Kawamoto. "Now we have the sharp claws of eagles again." He stabbed a finger at the deck. "Where are our eyes of the hawk?"

"I have assigned two B-five Ns and a pair of Aichis to our air search, admiral," Kawamoto answered, pointing to the aft elevator, which ascended and locked level with the flight deck. With shouts, handlers wheeled a mottled green monoplane with an unusually long greenhouse forward to the ship's port quarter and quickly tied it down, locking its folding wingtips in place. Lost in the activity on the flight deck, Fujita, Kawamoto, and Hironaka moved aft on the platform, trailed by the talker who plugged his headset into a new receptacle.

"It's a very, very old airplane," Kathryn said with fascination, mouth close to Brent's ear. "I can believe anything now, Brent; especially after the Junkers."

"Well, believe this Kathryn; that's the Nakajima B-five N-two torpedo bomber, the first carrier-borne monoplane. It sank the *Arizona, Oklahoma, California, West Virginia, Tennessee,* and *Nevada* at Pearl Harbor.

"Even I know there were bombers there, too, Brent."

"That one," he said, indicating another mottled green monoplane with fixed landing gear being man-handled aft from the forward elevator. "The Aichi D-three A-one. It was used as a dive bomber and horizontal bomber throughout the war and sank more American ships than any other Axis aircraft. But at Pearl . . . " He gesticulated downward. "That little beauty did most of the damage with its torpedoes.

"Aren't you angry?"

"Why? I hadn't been born. In fact, my father didn't even know my mother, then."

"But you're an American, Brent."

"Let the old men carry those hatreds," he said impatiently. "I don't have time for it."

"Now it's Kadafi."

"Yes. He's certifiably mad."

"And you tried to kill him."

75

"We did our best. But he was hiding in his bunker in the desert." He tapped the rail. "Some century, Kathryn." She looked at him expectantly. He continued. "A century of madmen—Hitler, Stalin, Idi Amin, Kadafi, Khomeini. Attilla the Hun was a humanitarian compared to them."

"Perhaps," she said slowly, "one's viewpoint . . . "

An engine burst to life followed by another, and soon four radial engines roared as the patrol prepared to take off. "Madam," Fujita said, raising his voice over the roar and walking toward the pair. "It is time to return to your quarters."

"Yes, sir." She pursed her lips and suddenly became the poignant little girl. "Admiral, may I be shown your ship? Please, I won't destroy it. I'm going crazy in that two-by-four room."

Obviously in an expansive mood, the lined parchment of the old man's face creaked with a rare smile. "Madam, I am not in the business of offering tours of my command. But . . . " He moved his eyes to Brent. "if Mr. Ross will consent, he may escort you."

"I'll be relieved in a few minutes, admiral," Brent said, a flat expression concealing his excitement.

"Oh, thank you, admiral," Kathryn bubbled.

"Upper works and no lower than the hangar deck, ensign."

"An elevator Brent," Kathryn said as the door closed on the small car. "They must've installed it for the old men."

The pair had just completed a quick tour of the bridge where Brent had pointed out a magnetic

76

compass, gyro-repeater, and a battery of monitors giving readings on engine speed and propeller revolutions while ratings standing by the equipment stared at the woman with hard, piercing eyes. The officer of the deck, Commander Atsumi, had given the couple a cursory nod and then raised his glasses as the first Nakajima lunged from the deck and slowly climbed to port.

Walking with the girl close behind, Brent had pointed to VHF radiophones, a TBS (talk between ships) radio mounted above a chart table, and safe where lead-weighted code books were kept. Aft, between the wheelhouse and radio room, Brent showed the curious girl the ship's Combat Information Center: a compact space dominated by a large table reminiscent of a billiard table with a huge compass rose covering the center.

"*Yonaga* is the center of the rose," Brent explained as more curious heads turned. "Friendly and unfriendly aircraft and ships are designated by markers and moved by hand."

"There's the air patrol," Kathryn said, pointing at six red crosses on the periphery of the table. And then nodding at two luminescent tubes where glittering fingers swept through glowing green dots, dying and then reviving as the beams maintained their remorseless sweeps, she said, "The admiral believes in radar."

"The best," Brent had noted, turning the woman back toward the wheelhouse and the elevator.

After the elevator's door locked, Brent said, "All *Yamatos* had elevators. In fact, the battleship versions had two." He punched a button. The car began to descend slowly.

Looking up with black eyes suddenly gone velvet, Kathryn moved closer. "Brent," she said softly. "I've been alone, locked in my cabin." He stared silently as the points of her breasts pushed against his chest. A tingling began deep in his groin, spreading slowly like the beginnings of a bonfire. "But it's almost impossible for two people—"

"Two people," he interrupted, big hands grasping her thin arms, "almost impossible for two people to be alone."

"Yes." Head back, she swayed toward him, eyes swimming with desire.

He dropped his hands. "Kathryn! This is not the place."

"Where, Brent? Where?" Her voice was anguished.

He released his breath explosively. "Ashore, Kathryn. Ashore."

"You can't come to my cabin?"

"Unthinkable."

"Unsamurai. Isn't that why?"

The jarring stop of the car interrupted, and the door swung open on a half-dozen faces of curious plane handlers. They must have known the woman was on the car. But how? That mysterious ship's telegraph, Brent thought, leading Kathryn from the elevator.

"Against the island," he said, taking her arm and standing amongst the handlers who crouched and stared aft. "The last one."

With a blast of hot cylinder heads, the pilot of the last plane—an Aichi D3A1—opened his throttle. There was a flash of a yellow flag, and the big green monoplane lurched toward the bow. Brent had never stood on the flight deck during takeoff. The noise was overwhelming, gagging exhaust from the huge thousand horsepower Kinsei 43 engine blasted in their faces by a side-mounted exhaust pipe. As the plane thundered past, Brent saw details he had never seen clearly from the bridge: dull, nonreflecting paint on top of the cowl; telescopic external bomb sight projecting through the windshield; trousered fixed landing gear; crutches for bombs; under-wing dive brakes which could be rotated ninety degrees to steady near vertical dives; elongated rear canopy with drum-fed Type 92 machine gun pointed toward the tail and seated rigidly, the crewmen both helmeted, goggled and wearing *hachimachi* headbands.

Hands to ears, Brent and Kathryn watched as the dive-bomber raced past, rose from the deck, then dropped precariously low ahead of the ship and finally climbed away.

"Air search," Brent said, waving over the bow. "Four sectors are searched ahead of the ship roughly from beam to beam. Radar cannot replace the human eye."

She nodded. "Can we walk back there?" She pointed aft.

"Not during flight operations."

"Oh," she said with obvious disappointment.

"But we can go down to the hangar deck."

"But no lower."

"That's right, Kathryn. No lower."

"I might find a secluded corner and ravish your lilly white body. Isn't that what the admiral's afraid of?"

Brent laughed. "Yeah. The whole staff's virgins." He led her to the elevator.

Exiting on the cavernous hangar deck, the couple entered organized bedlam: row after row of aircraft swarming with mechanics and pilots, the reverberating sounds of metal striking metal, shouts, all punctuated with the staccato blasts of pnuematic tools. Awed, Kathryn stopped in her tracks, staring overhead at rows of floodlights and then from side to side at the frenzied activity.

Chuckling, Brent waved a hand. "About a thousand by two hundred feet — three football fields."

"Bigger than Rockefeller Center, the Metropolitan, Carlsbad Cavern all put together," she said.

He stabbed a finger upward at a partial deck jutting over their heads. "The gallery deck. Pilots' ready rooms." He pointed to the opposite side. "Ready racks, bombs, and torpedoes, which can be attached in minutes."

She gestured to a small tank mounted on a cart being pulled by two men. "That's primitive. Don't you have motorized carts?"

He shook his head. "The admiral insists on using the old methods — methods that are tried, true and understood by his men."

"Like navigation."

"Yes." He nodded at the cart as it rumbled past on iron wheels. "It's a bowser, used for fueling." He pointed aft. "They're gassing up the next CAP."

"Why don't they do it from the ship's tanks, directly?"

"Too dangerous, Kathryn. This way a fire can be localized."

"Carriers are volatile, Brent."

"Very. They're nothing but floating fuel and ammunition dumps."

He caught a fleeting smile that broke her face into hard lines. And her eyes glinted. He shifted his weight uneasily. "What is it, Kathryn?"

"Why nothing." Ignoring the stares of gawking mechanics, she took his arm and pointed to a wooden structure built near the bow. "What in the world is that?" She pulled him along.

"A shrine; the Shrine of Infinite Salvation," he said, stopping in front of a large square room built of unpainted plywood.

Kathryn pointed to the single doorway crowned by a gilded board. "A torii. It's probably a combined Buddhist temple and Shinto shrine."

"Right!" Brent pointed to flowers painted on both sides of the entrance. "Chrysanthemums."

"Of course, Brent. Sixteen petaled; they represent the emperor."

"Four-oh, for you, Kathryn." She laughed.

"This place is for honorable Japanese, not American sluts," a deep voice grated threateningly behind them.

Turning together, the pair confronted a glowering Lieutenant Konoye. Dressed in green stained mechanic's fatigues, the burly pilot stood in front of a Zero with its cowl removed, exposing the Sakae's fourteen cylinders. The booming voice turned scores of heads, and silence spread throughout the vast deck like a cold fog. Within seconds, hundreds of eyes focused on Brent, Kathryn, and Nobutake Konoye. There was the shuffle of rubber-soled shoes, and scores of pilots

81

and mechanics crowded around the trio in a silent circle, filling the compartment with a palpable aura of expectancy.

The line of Brent's mouth altered, eyes chilled to the hardness of pale sapphires, and he felt a familiar hot coiled spring begin to unwind in his chest, pressuring against his ribs, racing his pulse and shortening his breath. His mind was suddenly a computer, analyzing Konoye's blocklike stance, clenched fists, hard jaw, and menacing eyes. And his feet were spread, left before right, weight carefully balanced on the balls of his feet, clenched fists dangling casually at his sides. Every aspect of the man's demeanor spelled *killer*. Brent spoke softly. "If the lieutenant desires an early entrance to the Yasakuni Shrine, I'll be happy to open the door."

"My argument is with her," Konoye growled, stabbing a finger at the girl.

"Come on, you son-of-a-bitch," Kathryn hissed, grabbing a crowbar from the deck. "Find out about the equality of the sexes."

An astonished murmur swept the crowd, and the men pressed even closer.

Brent pushed the girl into the arms of an old chief, commanding, "Hold her, Chief Shimada." Instantly, the girl's arms were pinned by the chief, and a rating and the crowbar clattered to the deck.

"Let me go!"

"Quiet!" Brent shouted. "This is really my argument, and he knows it." He nodded at Konoye.

A mirthless grin cracked the stone of the pilot's face. "Have it your way, Yankee."

"It's not the girl, lieutenant, is it? It's really the fire

raid on Tokyo, your sunken fleet, destroyed air force, Hiroshima, Nagasaki, Curtis Le May . . . "

The pilot's narrow eyes became slits, glittering with hate. "Always! Always, ensign. It can never end."

"The vengeance of the forty-seven ronin."

"Of course. The way you avenged Pearl Harbor."

"Then come on, mighty samurai, improve your karma."

"I will fight you in your own style, Yankee. Fists against fists. I could kill you with my feet."

"That's generous of you," Brent said, instinctively raising his guard and dropping his right foot back.

Konoye raised a palm, smiling like a man who had suddenly stumbled on the idea of a lifetime. "Chief Shimada," he shouted without taking his eyes from Brent. "The crowbar—between us." His lips twisted, and his voice became acid with sarcasm. "An inscrutable Oriental touch. One weapon, two men." He laughed and two hundred men giggled. The chief slid the weapon across the deck, midway between them.

"Now!" Konoye shouted, leaping before the American could set himself. Cursing, Brent hurled himself, but the lieutenant snatched the weapon from the deck with one hand, fending the big American off with the other and came to his feet lightly, chuckling.

Brent found his balance and faced his enemy. "That was fair," he hissed, bitterly.

"As fair as your raid that incinerated my family." Giggling, the big Japanese waved the crowbar back and forth. An amalgam of fear and rage screwed Brent's guts into a ball and charged his veins with a rush of quick blood as he stared at the steel like a man hypnotized by a cobra.

83

At least twelve inches long, it was a fearsome weapon: curved claw at one end, sharp, flattened, knifelike edge at the other. And the look in Konoye's eyes was that of a madman. It would take insanity to use that weapon; a weapon that could crack a man's skull like an eggshell or open his abdomen, gushing blood and entrails on the user.

Konoye grasped the shaft just above the claw, bounced it in his palm, testing for balance. Then he advanced, holding it in front like a French duelist attacking with an épée, grinning confidently, circling the sharp edge.

Brent gave ground. Choked back his gorge as the Japanese circled the steel shaft and then thrust. But Brent leaped lightly to the side, the crowd bending away and closing behind, murmuring and chattering. But Brent was alone—alone with the steel point, moving his eyes constantly from his enemy's feet to the point and back. The young American had fought many times with his fists and had defeated two Sabbah assassins in a Tokyo alley. He knew enough to study his opponent's feet, not to be fooled by a man's eyes. Watching the movements of the leading left foot, the ensign could anticipate his enemy's tactics. The quick step, shift in balance and the lunge came again. Brent leaped to the side. The rod jabbed past his right side. Again and again the shaft flashed only inches away, but the American anticipated each thrust and avoided death with a quick sidestep. The crowd chattered gleefully.

Suddenly, Konoye tired of the game and grabbed the shaft with two hands. "I will kill you Japanese style," he spat, raising the crowbar over his shoulder in the traditional style of the Japanese swordsman. The crowd rippled with new excitement.

In a way, the change in tactics worked in the American's favor; the enormous advantage in reach was gone. But, the Japanese was on familiar ground, fighting in a manner taught by a lifetime of kendo and swordsmanship. Brent balled his fists, studied his enemy's feet as Konoye crouched and swayed. The attack came with startling suddenness. Leaping like a crab and with the bar raised above his head like an executioner's sword, the lieutenant swung with all his strength, trying for the samurai's quick kill.

Brent leaped backward and steel whistled past his ear, glittering sullenly in the gloomy light. The hiss of it was like a passing shell. Then a shift in balance, the swing at last, and the American's right fist brushed Konoye's left shoulder and crashed into his ear. Whirling and landing on the balls of his feet, Brent faced his enemy, who rubbed his ear while grinning with stunned surprise.

"Very good," the pilot said grudgingly. "Very, very good." He raised the crowbar and advanced slowly.

Again, an artillery shell fluted as the big Oriental swung with all his strength. But Brent gambled and charged forward inside the arc. He brought a huge fist upward into the man's midriff. There was an explosion of breath in Brent's ear. Then a thud — an impact that shot pain across his back; a blow so hard it jarred his spine, jerked his head so that his teeth clashed in his skull. But the crowbar clattered across the deck and thudded against the wooden side of the shrine. The crowd shouted and screamed with delight. The combatants bounced apart. Brent's breath was hard as he choked back the pain flaming across the small of his back. And Konoye was hurt, too. But he advanced, fists raised like a barroom brawler.

There was no boxing. Instead, Konoye tried to smother the American with a hail of blows. Lefts and rights rained off Brent's shoulders and arms as he retreated. He ducked. Weaved to the left. One wild swing caught the American flush on the jaw, spraying spittle, sweat, and blood. Pain shot from his neck to his knees. His nose ran. He felt as if someone had slammed a door behind his eyes, and his vision was suddenly narrowed and dimmed. Shaking his head, he tore the curtains away and shifted his weight forward. He bent his knees following the bobbing Konoye who stepped back, breathing hard, tired by his attack. Brent saw an opening.

The American exploded from his crouch like a loaded spring, swinging with all of his two hundred ten pounds concentrated in the knuckles of his left fist. He felt his fist impact, heard the gristle in Konoye's nose give with a crunch like teeth ripping a ripe apple. A fierce joy surged as mucus and blood sprayed. The Japanese stopped in his tracks. Quickly, Brent drove his right into the man's midriff, doubling him over. Then, clenching both fists into a massive boulder, he drove them with all his power into the back of his enemy's neck. Konoye fell like a steer struck by an executioner's sledge.

Brent leaped onto his enemy, rolling him over. Amazingly, Konoye was not finished. Rolling over and over through the blood-maddened crowd, the combatants punched wildly. Brent hit again and again, some of the blows dying in the air, others ripping his knuckles on the steel deck, and yet others cracking against bone and muscle. Brent knew he was hurt, blood running from his nose and salting his mouth. But he felt nothing — only the drive to destroy his enemy. Low sounds rumbled from deep in his chest. He was growling. Konoye snarled back.

Whirling like two crazed wolves, the pair crashed into the Shrine of Infinite Salvation. The Japanese took the brunt of the collision, bending his back around the entrance. Feeling sudden weakness in his enemy, Brent shouted triumphantly, pinning his opponent to the deck by sitting astride his chest and locking his arms down with his knees. He saw something glint against the plywood. Grabbed the crowbar.

Staring down, he saw no fear in the bloodied and bruised face — a face with a broken nose, missing teeth, blood running from the nose, mouth, the corner of one eye, and left ear. A strange compulsion to not only kill, but to completely obliterate his enemy overwhelmed whatever civilization remained. The crowd froze, and silence filled the compartment heavily like a viscous fluid.

"Enough, Brent! Enough!" He heard Kathryn's voice echo from a distant canyon.

"Never enough," he rasped, raising the claw while holding Konoye at the throat with his left hand.

"Go ahead, Yankee," Konoye said. "You owe me this."

Brent hesitated. Remembered that night in the Tokyo alley, goaded by fear and hate. On top of the Arab. The animal was loose in his veins, striking, driving shards of glass into the Sabbah's face, over

87

and over. Destroying eyes, nose, mouth, the flesh itself. Then, going for the jugular. And Matsuhara's voice echoing then, and now, again. "Brent! Brent Ross! Enough! Enough!"

He held the claw high. Turned slowly. And he was there. Matsuhara and Atsumi. Running through the crowd that parted like the sea before *Yonaga*'s prow. "No more! No more!" In a moment, Matsuhara and Atsumi pulled the American to his feet and pried the bar from his hand. Chief Shimada helped Konoye to his feet.

"You have no right—no right," Konoye shouted, blood running across his face and dripping from his chin. "I have been denied *seppuku*, and I have earned a samurai's death."

"You will earn it and enjoy it soon," Matsuhara shouted. "But not here." Then sweeping his eyes over the American, he said, "Both of you report to Admiral Fujita. Immediately!" And then to the crowd, he yelled, "Back to your duties!" The crowd melted silently like whipped dogs. "And you, Kathryn Suzuki. Back to your cabin."

Slowly, Brent and Kathryn, flanked by Matsuhara and Atsumi, walked to the elevator.

Glaring, Lieutenant Konoye stared at the American until he disappeared into the elevator.

Chapter Five

"The emperor needs you," Admiral Fujita barked from behind his desk, staring at the two blood-stained officers standing at attention before him. "Both of you." Brent stiffened at the oblique compliment.

"You denied me *seppuku*, sir," Konoye said, spitting *s* in a spray of blood and saliva through a bloody gap in his front teeth.

"Of course, you have been taught, 'There is a time to live and a time to die.' I have told you before, this is not the time to die, Lieutenant Konoye."

"With your permission, sir, I have also been taught, 'A warrior knows that death, though cold as ice, is a fire that purifies the body, and when in doubt, choose death.'"

"True. There is nothing more honorable than a warrior's death." Bony tendrils drummed the oak. "But carriers, submarines, and big-gunned ships lie in wait for *Yonaga*, lieutenant." Fujita moved his eyes to Brent Ross. "The American was to be your instrument of death?"

"If the gods so deemed it, sir."

"Respectfully, admiral. I challenged Lieutenant

Konoye . . ."

"It was the woman, was it not?" Fujita shouted, voice stinging like the tail of a scorpion. "We will drop her at the first opportunity," the old man added, pounding the desk with a tiny, bony fist. "Women do not belong on ships. Never! Never! Never!"

"Sir," Brent said. "It was more than the woman—"

Konoye interrupted. "It was Tokyo, my family. I have eaten stones, drunk gall, I will not sleep on logs, admiral."

"Enough!" Fujita shouted, hunching forward. "You can have your revenge, your *seppuku*, but only when I decide the time is right. I suspect our enemies know our route. Our destination. That raid from the Cape Verde Islands should have taught you something. They know we cannot steam the Indian Ocean, the Straits of Magellan. We can expect more attacks. At this moment we could be approaching a picket line of submarines or a secret base." He stared at the two officers facing him, but found their eyes focused on the deck like chastised schoolboys. "We must pull together or die together." He moved his eyes, which were like gleaming black beads to Konoye. "The samurai honors old scores, true. But if either of you challenges the other, I will have you both thrown in irons." Silence, a thing of weight and substance, filled the room. The admiral broke it. "And Ensign Ross, you must control your temper."

"I will, sir."

Fujita pushed on. "And both of you, your words as officers." He moved his eyes to the Japanese pilot. "And as a samurai—no more fighting. Avoid each other. That is a command. When we finish with these

90

Arabs, you can cut each other to ribbons. And remember, before this is over, we may all enter the Yasakuni Shrine together."

"I promise on my dead family, sir," Konoye said, staring enigmatically at the American.

Unflinching, Brent stared back. "And I on my dead father."

Although Fujita winced with a painful memory, he spoke with new calmness. "Both of you remember Emperor Hirohito has been on the throne for six decades. His is the reign of *Showa*." Konoye straightened like a man prodded by a spear.

"Enlightenment," Brent said.

"To be more precise," Fujita said, clipping his words as if his lips were scissors, "*Showa* means enlightened peace. Both of you are to leave this cabin enlightened as to whom your true enemies are and with peace in your souls for each other. Understand?"

"Yes, sir," the officers chorused.

Nodding, Fujita spoke with new harshness. "The woman is confined to the bridge! You are dismissed."

"Lieutenant Konoye is insane, Admiral Allen," Brent Ross said, securing the last button on a fresh green shirt. Brent had showered in his tiny cabin's lavatory and gingerly combed his hair, carefully avoiding tender spots on a skull that had battered the deck in a half-dozen places. And there was a bruise on one cheek, two cuts inside his mouth where his cheeks had been punched against his teeth. His lower lip was cut, and his jaw ached when he spoke.

"He did a good job on you," Mark Allen said from

91

the chair before the cabin's minute desk.

Wearily and slowed by sore muscles, Brent sank on the hard mat of the bunk, eyes running over the room as he unwound his huge frame carefully on his back. Formerly the cabin of a long dead senior staff officer, the tiny room was typically Spartan in the Japanese tradition: a single bunk, closet, sink, mirror, speaker, overhead light hanging in the inevitable maze of pipes and conduits, whining blower, brass clock, and the ubiquitous equestrian picture of a college-age Emperor Hirohito attached to the bulkhead over the bunk.

"Yes, he did," Brent said, turning his face toward the older man. "I almost killed him — had my chance with a crowbar."

"I know."

"I can't understand, admiral. When I'm scared, hurt, angry, I seem to go insane."

"Not unusual, Brent. Natural instinct to survive."

"It's more than that, admiral. I want to destroy — obliterate. It happened to me in Tokyo."

"I know. The Sabbah." Mark Allen sighed. "There's a streak that runs in your family."

"My father," Brent said, matter-of-factly.

"Yes. Trigger Ross, we called him. 'Trigger' because of his temper, you know."

The younger man nodded. "Yes. I know. I became quite familiar with his temper, admiral." Both men chuckled. Then Brent described the meeting with Admiral Fujita and the admiral's threats.

"And he told Lieutenant Konoye he could go for his vengeance at an . . . ah, appropriate time."

"How did you know, admiral?"

92

"Ha! Typically Japanese. Our friend Konoye lost face when you didn't kill him."

"Matsuhara stopped me."

"I know." The older man waved Brent off impatiently. "His karma was injured. But vengeance is sacred, and he can restore his karma by dying for it — can even attain nirvana."

"Doesn't do a thing for a Christian, admiral." The older man smiled.

Sitting up, Brent swung his long legs to the side of the bunk and braced himself with his hands on the steel frame. "I'll never forget the way Ogren, Warner, and Jackson made their torpedo runs on the cruiser."

"It was suicide."

"It was suicide, admiral, for American captains with American crews to save a Japanese carrier that had attacked Pearl Harbor. And Captain Fite's run into Tripoli Harbor to save Japanese hostages; the most courageous thing I'd ever seen. And they were Americans, not samurai."

Mark Allen began drumming a fist on the desk. "And you think the Japanese don't appreciate those sacrifices."

"Konoye is my case in point."

"He's one, Brent. And he's mad. Most of them appreciate American casualties — "

Brent cut in. "When we fought aircraft, the *Brooklyn*, those destroyers; when it looked like they were going to deep six us, there were no arguments, no hates."

Mark Allen nodded understanding; the fist stopped its pounding. "There was an old saying in the infantry in World War Two: 'The closer you come to the front, the friendlier people become.' "

"We were close to the front."

"Brent, we were the front."

"But admiral, the Arab *jihad* is still trying to kill us."

"True. But the danger isn't that grave. Old grudges can boil to the surface."

"Konoye is a stewing vat of hate."

"Do you wonder why?"

The young man released his breath slowly. "No. Not really. After forty-two years of entrapment up there, his entire family incinerated."

"But, Brent, give him credit. He has his priorities."

The ensign chuckled humorlessly. "And I'm second."

Allen moved on. "But we found this hatred in others, too."

"At first." Brent paused thoughtfully. "At first Commander Matsuhara was just as bad."

"True. It was obvious. He lost his family, too."

"The same raid on Tokyo, admiral." Ross knuckled his forehead with a massive fist. "But he changed."

"When did you sense it?"

"It started in that Tokyo alley after I decked those two Sabbah assassins. I was out of my head—going for the jugular with a broken bottle."

"Do you know why Matsuhara let him live?"

Surprised by the question, Brent looked up. "Why, I suppose—"

Allen interrupted. "You gouged the man's eyes out, tore off his nose, cut his face to a pulp with the bottle. In fact, he had no face left at all. In the samurai's mind, life was a far worse punishment than death.

Why do you think he had the other Arab's throat cut? I heard him discuss it with Admiral Fujita. They both thought it was a great idea."

Brent leaned forward. "I agree with them. Why not?" The young man straightened slowly. "Kawamoto, Hironaka, Atsumi, Takamura, Kojima, and the rest of the crew seem to accept us, admiral. In fact, they're respectful and I like them."

"True, Brent. They have risen above the old hates or put them aside because of Admiral Fujita."

"The admiral needs us to preserve his command."

"It's more than that, Brent. He's genuinely fond of you."

Brent waved at the overhead. "I'm an asset up there. I have the best eyes on the ship."

"I know. But it's still there. You're like a grandson."

"Great-grandson, admiral." For the first time, Brent laughed. He continued. "He'd sacrifice his great-grandson for *Yonaga*."

"True, Brent. He'd sacrifice himself."

Chapter Six

Steaming northeasterly at 18 knots, the weather changed dramatically. Within a few days *Yonaga* entered the horse latitudes, cruising the Tropic of Capricorn and entering the tropics on a hot, humid, oppressive day. Confined to the bridge, Kathryn spent her usual morning hours at Brent's side, seeking company with no one else. Aware of the attachment, Admiral Fujita ignored the woman when on the bridge, scanning the horizon with his glasses or fidgeting nervously when an escort wandered off station. Just after crossing the equator, excitement swept the bridge when word was received over the ship's radios of the explosion of several North Sea oil pumping platforms. Then, just after crossing the equator, word was received to be alert for a PBY Catalina, flying boat. The CIA man, Frank Dempster, was enroute to *Yonaga* with dispatches too sensitive to be put on the air.

It was early in the morning just after the first CAP had taken off and only thirty minutes north of the equator and six hundred miles northeast of the

Marquesas Islands when *Yonaga* met the PBY. Peering from the bridge, Brent had watched the sun reluctantly claw its way over the horizon, inflaming the sky with virulent reds and purples. The infinite cottonfield of tossing whitecaps were brushed with pale gold, wiping the shadows of the fading night from the short steep waves.

The talker broke bridge silence. "Radar reports an unidentified aircraft bearing three-zero-zero true, range three hundred twenty, closing at one hundred twenty knots, admiral."

"Very well. Fighter frequency, CAP intercept and escort."

Twelve pairs of glasses swung as one as if choreographed. But Brent, knowing the radio transmission was brief and that the admiral had no other option, felt sudden discomfort as he turned his focusing knob. Within minutes, the young American found three specks high to the west in the aching blue vault. Glassing the sighting, Brent found a seaplane escorted by two Zeros flying on either side and just behind and above her tail.

"Flying boat, bearing two-eight-zero relative, elevation angle twenty degrees, range twenty-five, admiral," Brent said.

"Very well," the admiral acknowledged, raising his glasses. Hironaka and Kawamoto leaned into their own binoculars while Adm. Mark Allen moved to Brent's side. The admiral had banished Kathryn to her cabin to make room for the staff officers on the narrow platform.

"I can't believe it," Mark Allen said. "A PBY. Five—operational in 1936."

"Interesting construction," Fujita said. "A wing like a parasol."

"True," Allen said. "Cantilevered with stabilizing floats that retract into the wingtips. Revolutionary for that time."

Silently the men watched as the trio of aircraft lost altitude quickly, swinging around the carrier out of range.

"He'll probably circle you once or twice to make sure you see his American markings."

"Wise, indeed," Fujita chuckled. "That pilot knows range is far more important to our gunners than identity."

The Japanese laughed. The admiral turned to the talker. "Seaman Naoyuki, signal bridge is to call our escort commander on flashing light and tell him to detach escort number three to pick up a passenger from the flying boat. Also, two-block Pennant Two over Able on the outboard starboard halyard." He drummed the rail of the windscreen. "Tell the signal bridge to try to raise the seaplane with flashing light. Order him to land off my starboard side." He turned to Mark Allen. "One transmission on our fighter frequency might slip by enemy RDFs, Admiral Allen."

The old American smiled. "I'm sure there are many curious ears waiting for our signals, sir."

Fujita said to Allen, "Flyers are terrible signalmen."

"True, admiral. But even if he can't read international Morse, he'll look for your hoist." He gestured at the halyard.

Within minutes, the drone of radial engines became a roar, drowning out the clatter of signaling searchlights as the tight group of aircraft swept close to *Yonaga*'s port side with the entire port battery swinging from bow to stern with them. With two great Pratt and Whitney engines, graceful cantilevered wing, two step hull flaring like an airfoil, retracted tricycle landing gear, four 50 caliber machine guns — two in blisters amidships — the PBY was a magnificent, elegant aircraft. There was a flash of light from the cockpit.

"He can read," Fujita said wryly. Everyone laughed at the admiral's joke. "She is a beautiful aircraft — beautiful," he added.

"Won the battle of Midway," Mark Allen said, before thinking.

"Won what?" Fujita asked sharply.

Obviously uncomfortable with his gaffe, Allen stumbled. "Ah, she did the early reconnaissance."

"Picked up our ships?"

"Yes, Admiral Fujita."

"Interesting," Fujita said in a flat voice. Brent smiled to himself.

Followed by his staff, Fujita walked around the front of the platform past the voice tube to the starboard side of the conning tower. The talker plugged into a new receptacle. Every man swung his glasses over the stern where the PBY dropped quickly toward the sea, stabilizing floats locked in the down position. The Zeros broke station and rocketed for altitude. "Soon our guest Frank Dempster will be aboard."

Spraying water from her hull and floats in blue sheets fringed with lacy white spray, the flying boat touched down, bouncing across the chop like a thrown rock skimming a pond. Then, quickly, slowed by the walls of water, the great aircraft came to a halt, bobbing and rolling gently in the chop like a tired migratory bird finding rest on a friendly pond. A destroyer approached her slowly.

Seated at the long oak table in Flag Plot, Brent Ross stared at Frank Dempster, who sat opposite. He had aged dramatically since their first meeting in Tokyo Bay a few months earlier. Tall, slender, fiftyish, with graying black hair, a sharp aquiline nose, cheekbones protruding through florid, veined skin, the man's tired hazel eyes roamed the table suspiciously as if he expected to find an assassin in every chair instead of Admiral Fujita, his staff, the two Americans, and the Israeli colonel, Irving Bernstein.

"You have made a long, dangerous journey, Mr. Dempster," Fujita said from the head of the table. "You must have important documents."

"I do, sir," he answered, his level of communication a whiskey-raddled rasp. "Information far too sensitive to be put on the air." Obviously tired and nervous after his long flight, he became strangely philosophical, voicing thoughts gnawing at every man in the room. "It's a strange world out there." He gesticulated. "Without the threat of the superpowers, terrorists have gone wild like rats pouring out of an uncovered sewer. Ironically, the US and the Soviets, in their bitter antagonism, imposed a kind of world government — unstable and even dangerous, true — yet, a kind of sovereignty over maverick states — the so-called third world — like Libya. But now, all men are equal, and Kadafi with his Arab friends and unlimited wealth is more equal than most." He sighed wearily. "He's really flipped since you mauled him."

"Flipped?"

"Sorry, admiral. Gone berserk." He pulled a half-dozen dossiers from a briefcase, thumbed through some documents, selecting one. "First, you copied reports of the destruction of the North Sea platforms?"

"Yes. A half . . ."

"All of them, admiral. The British haven't issued any official news releases, yet, but according to our sources, all eighteen North Sea rigs exploded this morning."

"Sabotage," Lieutenant Commander Atsumi said, incredulously.

Dempster took a deep breath, rushed on, spitting his words like a man who had bitten rotten fruit. "Kadafi's gloating—claims the oppressed people of the world have risen and the oppressed people of OPEC—I mean the Arab oil cartel—have raised the price of oil to five hundred dollars a barrel. They're awash in money."

Shouts of anger swept the room. "Insane," Fujita shouted. "Extortion!"

"Vengeance for sure, admiral. He's pledged revenge against Japan and *Yonaga*. And . . ." He looked up from a dossier, eyes sweeping the angry faces around him. "He knows where *Yonaga* is, course, speed, and destination—has sworn your destruction. I suspect Arab submarines have been tracking you. Don't forget, he hates Japan, Israel, and America, in that order."

102

"It would be degrading not to head that list," Fujita snapped.

"Banzai!" Hironaka and Kawamoto shouted.

Bernstein interrupted. "But Arab troops still attack Israel. I have the reports!" He pounded a pile of documents on the table. "Raids are launched from Syria, Lebanon, and by PLO units hiding in the Canaan Hills and the Sinai Desert."

"True, colonel," Dempster concurred, "but the Libyans are back behind their own borders, and the Iranians and Iraqis are back at their favorite past time, which is killing each other." A wave of humor swept the room. Dempster continued. "The Israelis are still hard put fighting off nuisance raids, but we— ah, I mean you broke the *jihad* and, anyway, as I have already said, Japan is the object of Kadafi's attention."

Fujita hunched forward, eyes as cold as a tomb. "Let him come for his vengeance, but let him dig his own grave first!"

Brent found himself shouting, "Banzai!" along with the Japanese. He stopped abruptly as Mark Allen broke into a broad grin.

Fujita silenced the officers with a wave, and Dempster cut in. "The British claim the platforms were torpedoed by Libyan submarines."

"How many does he have?" the Japanese admiral asked.

"Perhaps twenty-one or twenty-two."

Mark Allen spoke. "Old Russian diesels of the Whiskey class."

Fujita said, "This Whiskey Boat. We need all the information you have, Mr. Dempster."

The CIA man thumbed through a red catalogue, scanned several pages and looked up. "Length seventy-five meters." He glanced at the Americans. "Two hundred six feet and they displace just over a thousand tons. They're diesel electric, and their design is actually based on late German World War Two design concepts. You must understand, the Russians are reluctant to trust the Arabs with their more sophisticated equipment."

"Stupid simians, each with ten thumbs," Allen muttered.

Smiling, the CIA man continued. "The Russians built two hundred thirty-five Whiskies during the fifties. Some are still active in the Russian fleet, but most have been given to the friendly Arab states, Albania, Bulgaria, Egypt, North Korea, Cuba . . ."

Fujita waved impatiently. "Armament? Range? Maximum operating depth?"

"Six twenty-one inch torpedo tubes and, I understand, the Libyans have mounted two four-point six inch deck guns plus a half-dozen twenty-three millimeter AA guns on theirs. Range can vary with equipment, but up to eighteen thousand miles — twenty-eight thousand kilometers. Maximum operating depth is about seven hundred feet."

"Torpedoes?"

"Probably the Russian five hundred thirty-three-millimeter torpedo. We don't have much on it."

"May I be of assistance?" Bernstein inquired suddenly, rising and waving a single document.

Brent caught consternation crossing Dempster's face as the Israeli began to speak. He knew CIA men were often openly hostile toward Israeli Intelligence which somehow, without the men, funds, or exotic equipment, often outperformed every spy network on earth. In fact, it was joked that the Israeli budget wouldn't buy paper clips for the CIA. Yet, Bernstein reeled off facts that shocked every man in the room. "The five-three-three is eight hundred twenty-five-centimeters—ah . . ." He acknowledged the Americans. "Twenty-six-point eight feet long." He waved the document. "I have a sectional drawing showing warhead, detonators, air vessel, electric motor, silver-zinc-oxide battery power pack, control rod for depth vanes . . ."

"Please, Mr. Bernstein," Fujita shot impatiently. "We will copy it and distribute to staff. Confine yourself to performance data. If one is fired at *Yonaga*, we will not be interested in the control rod for depth vanes."

"Certainly, sir," the colonel said, stealing a sly look at an obviously disquieted CIA man. But his next words not only shocked Dempster, but brought Allen and Ross erect in their chairs, wide-eyed. "It is similar to the American Mark-forty-eight."

Mark Allen exploded. "Our most modern fish!"

Bernstein pressed on. "Like the Mark-forty-eight, the five-three-three is capable of attacking in both passive and active modes."

"Define yourself!"

"Sorry admiral. Like the American," he said, stealing a quick glance at the sunset-red Dempster, "in the passive mode, five-three-three acquires its target by processing target-originated noise with its own on-board computer. If a target is not acquired in this mode, it automatically converts to the active mode wherein it transmits an acoustic pulse and, again, its on-board computer analyzes returns. And finally, if both active and passive fail, there's always the wire."

Stunned and angry, the Americans stared at the Israeli. Mark Allen spoke. "You shouldn't know—that's top secret."

Fujita sputtered, "Sacred Buddha. Do you call this warfare?"

"I'm afraid so, admiral," the Israeli answered.

"Range? Warhead?"

"Range at twenty-four knots, seven thousand sixty-four meters or eighty-six hundred yards, warhead is two hundred sixty-seven kilograms of HE."

Silence. Then Fujita spoke slowly. "Our *Fletchers* do not have this type of equipment. They are armed with contact fuses only."

"That is correct, sir," Allen said. "But with your permission, I'll put in a request to have the new Mark forty-eight waiting for us at Yokosuka."

"You think your navy will send them?"

"There's a good chance, sir. Especially if I make the recommendation."

Fujita nodded. "Good, good. I dislike all your machines—your computers that take the chance; no, the joy of the hit out of warfare. A samurai's eye to the range finder, periscope, the web gunsight was all the computers we needed. But now . . ." He waved his hands in a gesture of futility.

"With wire guidance, even an Arab skipper can make his hits, admiral," Mark Allen noted. "And a truly effective acoustical torpedo will track all ship noises; not just the screws, but auxiliary engines, generators, blowers, even water sluicing off the hull.

106

Securing the main engines, as you did during the attack off the Cape Verde Islands, will not foil the five-three-three."

"Sacred Buddha! Your technology mocks the warrior."

Bernstein interrupted. "If the Russians trust the Arabs enough, sir. The Libyans lost six Whiskies in diving accidents alone. The word is two never even closed their main induction valves."

A chuckle swept tension away.

"I thought Kadafi hired German captains."

"Most are, sir," Dempster said, reestablishing himself. "But it only takes one Arab in the crew to sink a submarine."

Fujita moved on. "Radar?"

"Probably the HF Mast and Snoop Slab both of which can track you while submerged. As I said, we suspect a line has been established, and they're passing you along." Silence returned.

Fujita broke it. "Speed?"

"They can't fly like the SSNs."

The Japanese appeared confused. Fujita raised a hand.

"I mean," Dempster explained, "they're slow compared to nuclear-powered boats; six knots submerged, twenty-one or twenty-two on the surface."

Fujita turned to Commander Atsumi. "See to it this information is communicated to our escort commander and make certain all escorts are addressees. And beginning immediately, two Aichis equipped with one hundred twenty kilogram bombs will maintain anti-submarine patrols not more than ten kilometers ahead of *Yonaga*'s bows and at an altitude of five hundred meters."

While Atsumi grabbed a phone and spoke quickly, the old Japanese turned to Mark Allen. "A long time ago, when we were stalking Kadafi in the Mediterranean, you told me the British submarine *Conqueror* sank the Argentine cruiser, *General Belgrano* with two wire guided *gyos* off the Falkland Islands." He glanced at the Americans. "*Gyos*, torpedoes or fish to you."

Brent was surprised again by the old man's memory and insights.

"True, sir," Allen said. The old USS *Phoenix*, sister to the *Brooklyn* we sank in the Med."

"Then they can attack us from any quadrant." The ancient sailor turned to Atsumi who had just cradled the phone. "Nobomitsu-san, change the order to four Aichis patroling all four quadrants." Atsumi raised the phone.

Fujita moved back to the American Intelligence officer. "You said the British lost all of their North Sea platforms."

"True."

"And apparently the Libyans are responsible." The CIA man nodded. "But do the British have conclusive proof?"

"Our operatives report two subs sunk in the North Sea by British destroyers and perhaps four by accidents," Dempster said. "They may have their proof already. Anyway, they've reacted violently and they're mobilizing; no doubt about it — organized a task force and, according to our sources, the 'Iron Maiden' intends to attack Libya."

"Iron Maiden?"

108

"Sorry, admiral. Prime Minister Margaret Thatcher."

Fujita scratched his chin before speaking scornfully. "She is only a woman." And then grimly added, "Kadafi may be luring them in — inviting them into his cave of winds."

"We tamed the storm, admiral," Brent Ross said, smiling.

"True. But Amaterasu sat on our wings. I would not like to do it twice. And the British would follow in our wake. The Arabs learned from us." The old sailor turned to Dempster, saying, "Ships! You have said nothing of Kadafi's surface fleet. There were reports of two carriers." The timbre of the voice revealed anxiety.

The CIA man's jaw took on a hard set. He indicated a printout. "Three carriers," he said, glancing at the document. "Two *Colossus* class British World War Two carriers bought from Argentina and Brazil and an old American escort carrier, The USS *Cabot*, the Libyans bought from Spain." He explained all three were at sea accompanied by eight *Fletcher* class destroyers and a single cruiser. The battle group was last reported training in the Indian Ocean. The Libyans were scouring the world for pilots because most of their pilots had been killed in the recent fighting. "I would assume they are preparing a welcome for the British," Dempster concluded.

Hironaka looked up from his pad. "The Iron Maiden will lose her maidenhead." He giggled and drooled on the table.

Fujita ignored the scribe. "But if they defeat the Iron Maiden, they will be free to turn their attention to Japan."

"That's a big *if*, Admiral Fujita."

"We must assume we will be called on to engage this task force," the old Japanese said. "Specifics please."

"Frank," Bernstein said. "If you can't . . ."

"No thanks," Dempster shot back. And then smugly added, "I have it here." He thumbed some documents and spoke quickly. "Here's the specs on the carriers. The *Colossuses* are the *Minas Gerias* bought from Brazil—the ex-HMS *Vengeance*— and the one bought from Argentina is the *Veinticinco De Mayo*, which was formerly the HMS *Venerable*. Both were completed during World War Two." He raised a document. "Length six hundred ninety-three feet, beam one hundred thirty-eight, displacement about twenty thousand tons. Top speed is twenty-eight knots and range fourteen thousand miles at fourteen knots, seventy-two hundred at twenty-six knots." Smiling, he looked up, casting a quick look at Bernstein.

"Radar?"

"Unknown, sir."

"May I?" Bernstein said quietly, rising. Fujita nodded. Dempster's smile dissolved to a glare as the Israeli spoke. "Upon transfer to Libyan registry, both ships were equipped with LW-oh-one and WW-oh-two air search with V-one height finders; the DA-oh-two for target indicating and the ZW-oh-one for surface warning and navigation. Also, they were fitted with Ferranti CAAIS computers with Plessey Super CAAIS displays." He smiled benignly at Dempster. "This system is capable of direct computer-to-computer links with escorts. But, of course, the system

110

has been augmented with new Russian equipment—probably *Scoop Pair* and *Headlight C*, and we have reports that the Libyans have requested the new Russian ADMG-six-three-zero, Gatling action six barrel, thirty millimeter and quadmount forty-five millimeter AA guns in addition to twin mount seventy-six millimeter guns. But in the opinion of Israeli Intelligence, installation would require at least eight weeks, and the Arabs cannot spare the time with the British bearing down on them. Their principal AA is still the old twenty millimeter and forty millimeter plus five inch dual purpose." He stared at Dempster for a second and sat down.

Fujita drummed the desk restlessly, eyes roving over each man. "Aircraft! Aircraft! It takes a special type of aircraft to operate from carriers."

Kawamoto broke his silence. "Our Arab friends have been using many German and Russian pilots and technicians. How can either help with carrier based planes? Neither nation had a carrier during the Greater East Asian War."

"Not entirely true," Mark Allen responded. "The Germans had one. The *Graf Zepplin*. Two of the class were laid down."

"Yes. True, Bernstein said. "But never operational."

"Thanks to Herman Göring, interservice rivalry, and Hitler's stupidity," Mark Allen offered. A dozen pair of curious eyes prodded the American on. "By 1942 the *Graf Zepplin* was nearing completion. In fact, aircraft were ready; the JU-eighty-seven-C was an excellent dive-bomber and could take off and land on short runways. Also, Messerschmitt developed the

BF-one-oh-nine fighter which was one of the best. But, then, after *Bismark* and *Scharnhorst* were sunk, Hitler, in all his wisdom, decided surface ships were obsolete."

"But *Scharnhorst* was sunk late in the war, in 1943, in the Battle of North Cape," Fujita said, surprising no one with his knowledge.

"True, admiral. But enter Herman Göring who, from the very beginning, feuded with the navy over control of *Graf Zepplin*'s airgroups. He even had mock-up flight decks built and JU-eighty-seven-Cs and BF-one-oh-nines practiced taking off and landing. One hull was broken up in 1940, but the other, the *Graf Zepplin*, was actually being fitted out. But then Herr Hitler's order came down and fortunately for the Allies, *Graf Zepplin* was scrapped."

"So there were carrier-trained German pilots," Kawamoto said.

"Correct. And remember, gentlemen, as you know, most piston-engined fighters can be modified, and good pilots adapt quickly to carrier training."

"How many aircraft do you feel a *Colossus* class carrier can operate?"

It was Allen's turn to drum the table. "About fifty of all types."

Fujita punched the table and then turned to Dempster. "You mentioned an American escort carrier."

"Yes, sir," Dempster said, grabbing center stage. "The Libyans bought Spain's *Dedalo*—the old USS *Cabot*, CVL-twenty-six of the *Independence* class. She's a small ship of about seventeen thousand tons, six hundred and twenty-five feet long with a

112

beam of seventy-one feet. She can operate, perhaps, thirty aircraft."

"But she is slow."

"Not really. Last year she was re-engined with new GE turbines producing one hundred and thirty thousand horsepower. She can make twenty-nine knots."

Fujita nodded thoughtfully. "Then the Arabs can put up one hundred thirty aircraft from three fast carriers. The Iron Maiden had better tighten her chastity belt." There was no humor intended or taken, and a grim silence filled the room. The ancient admiral broke in, eyes flashing with new inquisitiveness as the canny mind moved to another gnawing question. "The Chinese satellites? Do you have any new information?"

Dempster explained that the orbiting Chinese laser satellite system was still effective. Neither the United States nor the Soviet Union had been successful in attempts to neutralize the killer beams which instantly destroyed any jet or rocket engine at the moment of ignition. Even communications and military satellites had been victims of the particle beams. "I explained this system to you five months ago during our first briefing in Tokyo Bay," the CIA man concluded. "Our early assessment still holds."

Tapping his temple and obviously dissatisfied, Fujita turned to Bernstein. "It seems that Israeli Intelligence — Capt. Sarah Aranson — said it was a chemical system; deuterium and fluorine."

Brent felt a tightening in his throat, and his skin warmed at the thought of Sarah Aranson and the passionate idyll they had enjoyed in her apartment in Tel Aviv just three weeks before. Self-consciously he stole a glance around the room, but all eyes were on the CIA man. "True. Twenty weapons systems in low, nine hundred and thirty mile orbits, while three command units orbit geosynchronously at twenty-two thousand, three hundred miles."

Captain Kawamoto spoke. "The chemicals should wear out, Mr. Dempster."

The American snorted. "Not true. No power dares launch a jet or rocket, and they've had no targets for months. They're loaded for bear."

"But their power?" the captain persisted.

"Fusion. We estimate the whole system is locked in place for decades. Orbits should start decaying in the next century."

The Japanese looked at each other. Smiling, Fujita said, "Then *Yonaga* remains the single most formidable fighting machine, or," he said, nodding at the white officers, "weapons system on earth."

Hironaka and Kawamoto staggered to their feet croaking, "Banzai!"

The admiral waved at the two officers impatiently. Brent helped Hironaka find his chair with a single palm to the bony back. Dempster continued. "The mad scramble for World War Two ships and planes is still on. In all, all over the world, there are one hundred and eight *Fletcher*, *Sumner*, and *Gearing* class destroyers in commission, over a hundred frigates, destroyer escorts, tugs, LSTs, transports, and auxiliaries. And the big powers are converting frigates and cruisers to gun platforms. The US is replacing Tomahawk, Harpoon, Seasparrow, Rim, and other rocket and jet-propelled missiles with the new Mark-forty-five, five inch, fifty-four caliber, and the Mark-seventy-five, seventy-six millimeter, sixty-two caliber fully automatic guns. And for close in AA, the Mark-fifteen Phalanx, which is self-contained with its own closed-loop radar. Fires three thousand rounds a minute." There was pride in his voice.

"Six twenty millimeter guns and very fast," Commander Matsuhara said suddenly. "The *New Jersey* mounted four when we attacked her in Pearl Harbor."

"She needed more," Hironaka giggled. An awkward silence stirred the men uncomfortably.

Dempster broke it. "The United States has developed a new three thousand horsepower Pratt and Whitney radial engine, and Grumman has designed a new airframe. Flight tests of a new fighter, the XF-one thousand, will begin early next year, and you can be assured the Russians are doing the same. In fact, we have word of a new piston-powered Yak fighter, and they're working furiously to convert their VSTOL carriers . . ."

He was halted by confusion among the Japanese.

"Very short take-off or landing carriers," he explained. "They have two, the *Minsk* and the *Kiev*. They're being converted to carry the new Yak fighter."

"Let them support their Arab friends," Matsuhara spat, pounding the table. "Our Zero-sens will tame their Yaks."

Dempster moved on. "Keep in mind the Arab oil cartel controls tremendous leverage with their oil reserves."

"But the US and Russia are big producers," Mark Allen said.

"True, Admiral Allen, Russia is the biggest in the world, but she can only take care of herself and her

115

European satellites, and the US is in an energy bind." Dropping his eyes to a new sheet, he spoke softly as if enemy ears were pressing to the bulkheads. "The US, with strict rationing, still consumes nine million barrels a day, and this is from only four percent of the world's reserves while the Arab states control fifty-five percent."

Fujita broke in. "Japan has none."

"True, sir. Indonesia is still your biggest source."

"She's OPEC," Bernstein said.

"No! Kadafi has been demanding that she stop oil sales to Japan. She broke away while you were in the Med, and already strange subs have been snooping around her oil ports," Dempster said.

An angry rumble swept the cabin.

Matsuhara said, "The US should help Japan. This is your war, too!"

Dempster sighed. "With our reliance on jets and rockets, we've found our capabilities almost cancelled. We're converting all thirteen of our carriers and even seven LPHs—helicopter carriers—to fixed wing capabilities. Yet, real offensive power is at least a year away. And keep in mind, we have our problems with the Russians in Western Europe, Cuba, and Central America. We can't even honor our commitments. And there's the matter of the moderate Arab powers, especially Saudi Arabia, which remained neutral during the recent fighting. American intervention would reunite Kadafi's *jihad* and bring the Russians storming across Pakistan, Iran, and even into Turkey into the heart of the Middle East. No," he said, nodding at Admiral Fujita, "I'm afraid you must handle this one alone. But," he added hastily, "the

116

CIA will give you all the assistance we can."

"Planes?" Fujita asked sharply.

The CIA man smiled. "Every old pilot who ever flew in World War—I mean, in the Greater East Asia War—is eager to fly for you, sir. We've patched together forty Zeros, twenty-three Nakajimas, and seventeen Aichis. They're training now at *Kasumi-gawa*. But half need engines."

Fujita glanced at Kawamoto. "We have them?"

The old executive officer nodded. "Yes, sir. Packed in petrolatum."

"Escorts?"

"We have seven *Fletchers* in Subic Bay. All are in mint condition with original five inch, twenty milli-meter and forty millimeter mounts and experienced American skippers and American and Japanese crews."

Reaching into his briefcase, the CIA man handed a single envelope to Admiral Fujita. "For your eyes only, sir."

Slowly, the old Japanese opened the letter. While reading it, he pushed himself to his feet. "It is from the emperor," he said, obviously moved by emotion. Every man in the room came to attention. After scanning the letter, he looked up. Haltingly, the admiral disclosed the contents of the letter: "Subma-rines have been sighted off Sumatra, Java, Borneo, and even the Malay Peninsula. It is feared the Arabs will attempt to bring Japan to her knees by staging a blockade. Self-defense forces are patrolling close to the main islands and are poorly equipped, and we all know they are useless anyway. Convoys are out of the question. We do not have the escorts. *Yonaga* is to

117

return to Japan at full speed, pick up more *Fletchers* and make a patrol in the South China Sea. Then let the Libyans meet our *Yamato damashii!*"

"Banzai! Banzai!"

"Sir!" Kawamoto managed over the bedlam. "We are low on fuel, and our escorts' tanks are almost empty. We will not meet our next tanker for two days and cannot steam over sixteen knots until we top off."

"Sacred Buddha," Fujita cried angrily. "We need more help." He turned to a paulownia wood shrine attached to a bulkhead under the emperor's picture, which contained a talisman of the Eight Myriads of Deities, a Buddha from Three Thousand Worlds, and a three inch gold Buddha of exquisite workmanship from Minatogawa, and assorted icons and good-luck charms from the shrines at Kochi and Yasakuni. Every Japanese clapped twice in unison. Fujita's voice took on reverential timbre. "Amaterasu, let us find hidden powers by contemplating the laws of the universe with reverence and introspection. In this way, we will be prepared to meet and conquer our enemy, or die facing him."

After a long silence, the old man turned to Commander Yoshi Matsuhara. "Yoshi-san," he said with an unexpected fatherly warmth. "You are a poet. Give us some of your *haiku*—a verse to inspire us to this new task."

Drawing himself up, the pilot stared at the overhead, finding another place, another time. He spoke slowly:

> There is no path returning
> To the spring of my youth

118

But my guns are young
And I will sow the sea
With the bones of my enemies.

Obviously pleased, the old Japanese stared the length of the table, black eyes hard, voice ringing like steel from a scabbard. "Yes, Yoshi-san. The bones of our enemies. Let any man who thinks he can attack *Yonaga* with impunity remember we have left the bones of hundreds in our wake." Knuckling clenched fists on the desk, he leaned forward as he reached back for teachings from his youth and spoke like a man quoting a favorite passage. "The bones of our enemies are not of this or that man, but the accursed bones of dogs."

"Banzai! Banzai!" the Japanese cried.

"Hear! Hear!" came from the Americans and Bernstein.

Fujita raised his hands. "With Amaterasu's help, we will kill them like animals."

Chapter Seven

Steaming on a northwesterly heading at a steady 16 knots, tanks almost empty, the task force finally met the tanker 500 miles southeast of the Hawaiian Islands. The CAP had been warned to be on the alert for American patrols, but none was sighted.

"Usual American alertness," Kawamoto snorted derisively early in the morning just before the launching of the CAP and the rendezvous with the tanker. Mark Allen and Brent had exchanged an uncomfortable look.

Dawn had found the flag bridge jammed with the usual group of officers, all searching the western horizon for the low silhouette of the oiler. Even Kathryn Suziki and her guard stood close to the bulkhead, staring at the horizon.

Over and over Fujita had had the same exchange with the talker.

"Radar!"

"Nothing, sir."

"Very well."

Brent had focused and refocused his glasses as if his

efforts would hasten the arrival of the tanker.

"Ninety-six revolutions, sixteen knots, sir," Kawamoto said to the admiral. "But we're making seventeen and one half."

Without lowering his glasses or glancing at a plotting sheet tacked to a small table attached to the windscreen, Fujita said, "We are at latitude twelve. The north equatorial current is giving us an extra knot." He waved a hand over his right shoulder. "Also, we are back in the northeast trades. They are making a sail of our freeboard."

"He never misses a thing," Brent said under his breath to Mark Allen.

"The best seaman I've ever met," Mark Allen acknowledged quietly.

The equatorial current brought moisture and moisture brought scudding patches of fog, dirtying the sky to the east where the sun climbed slowly out of a gray, lead sea. It was very red, rising like a mortally wounded warrior bleeding on the clouds.

Finally, the call everyone hungered for came. "Radar reports a target bearing two-seven-zero true, range three hundred. Closing at slow speed."

"Very well," Fujita said expansively, tension falling away like leaves from a tree in autumn. An excited murmur swept the platform, and even the sun brightened as it climbed slowly off the stern. But Brent felt none of it; instead, a mystic sense of pre-destiny filled him with ominous melancholy, a sense of unease and disquiet.

Fujita turned to the talker. "Standby to launch. CAP, search aircraft and antisubmarine patrol. Edo One and scouts Three and Four are to reconnoiter contact." He said to Kawamoto, "Provide the pilots with range and distance to target just before launch. Also, for their point option data, *Yonaga* will maintain this course and speed until fueling begins. Then we will reduce speed to eight knots."

"Aye, aye, sir." The old executive officer disappeared into the conning tower.

Just before noon, the tanker was sighted. "A giant," Lieutenant Hironaka said, staring through his glasses at the low wallowing hull. "At least twenty thousand tons."

"Ha!" Mark Allen snorted. "She's an old US Navy AO, twenty-three thousand tons, but little by today's standards. Some tankers displace over two hundred thousand tons."

Even Fujita was surprised, turning wide-eyed to the admiral.

"Oil from the Middle East, admiral," Allen said. "It's cheaper to transport in big hulls." The old Japanese nodded.

Fujita turned to the talker. "Seaman Naoyuki, signal bridge is to call the tanker on flashing light: 'Fuel escorts first' " And then into the voice tube with obvious distaste: "All ahead slow." Dropping his glasses, he turned to the other men on the bridge. "We must steam at eight knots until fueling is completed, an easy target for one of Kadafi's *Whiskies*. Stay alert!" Every man took new interest in his binoculars.

"Eight knots," came from the tube.

"Very well."

By late afternoon all escorts had been fueled and

the tanker moved ahead of *Yonaga*. "Fueling party, stand by," Fujita shouted at the talker. "We will take aboard fuel oil and high-test gasoline simultaneously. Two block 'Baker,' and the smoking lamp is out." Within minutes, four hoses were lifted from their floats and winched over the bow. Quickly, pumps began to throb, and the transfusion began.

But Fujita, upset by the slow speed, stomped around the bridge with the restlessness of a tortured spirit, urging everyone to renewed alertness. The dirty cloud cover closed in like a solemn gray shroud, the sea a flat dun-colored slate with only a hint of purple as a warning of approaching twilight.

Brent had hardly noticed Kathryn's disappearance at noon and reappearance just as the feeble sun died on the western horizon, smearing the sea with a long ruddy path of light and tracing silhouettes of hump-backed clouds with oranges and subdued reds.

The warning came not by light and not by radio, but instead, by the firing of John Fite's two forward five inch thirty-eight caliber mounts, and the burst of a red flare high over the destroyer. Two Aichis dove through the mists, firing and dropping clusters of bombs, explosions mixing with shell bursts.

"Submarine!" Fujita screamed, rushing forward to the voice tube. "General Quarters!" Claxons shrieked and men rushed to their stations.

"Splashes off the port bow of escort leader, bearing three-zero-zero, range ten kilometers."

"I see them," Fujita said. "He is marking a periscope."

"All stations manned and ready," the talker said.

"Very well.'"

124

A bridge-to-bridge transmission crackled through the loudspeaker. "This is Escort Leader. Periscope two-seven-zero true, range three kilometers." And then the most dreaded words a seaman at war can hear: "Torpedoes at two-seven-zero!"

"Bridge to bridge," Fujita shouted. "Tanker belay pumping! Fueling party, quick disconnect."

"Admiral," Mark Allen said. "There'll be fuel oil and gasoline all over the hangar deck."

Fujita roared at the talker. "Forward damage control party stand by with hoses and foam on the hangar deck forward. We will take the hoses with us." And then into the voice tube: "All ahead flank — left full rudder, steady up on two-seven-zero."

On the bow, two seamen pulled quick release levers, and *Yonaga's* bow swung as her engines pulsed under flank power. The great steel-wrapped hoses tore away, hemorrhaging fuel into the ocean.

The tanker had no chance. If the doomed vessel possessed any luck, it was that one of the oil tanks was hit first. But the tank was empty, filled with explosive fumes, which ignited like a hundred tons of high explosives, blowing plates, twisted frames, a derrick, winches, stacked fuel hoses, and a dozen men hundreds of feet into the air. Instantly, the stricken oiler stopped and began to settle by the bow. But her nearly empty tanks kept her afloat, burning oil spreading, the pungent smell gagging everyone on the bridge. Men leaped into the sea to be engulfed by flames, flopping like wounded seals.

Kathryn began to whimper.

Heeling hard over, *Yonaga* moved closer to the raging holocaust and the echoing thunder of explod-

125

ing tanks. Brent could feel the hot breath of the immolated ship across his sweating face, and his nostrils rebelled against the assault of burning oil and the sickly sweet smell of roasting flesh. "This turn's taking us close aboard the tanker, admiral," Brent managed, choking down bile. "We may breach some of her burning oil, sir."

"We have no choice." Fujita turned to the talker. "Fire and rescue party, drop rafts when we clear the burning oil."

A dozen great concussions turned Brent's head. Three of the *Fletchers*, moving at high speed, were dropping depth charges and firing K-Guns while three Zeros and a pair of Aichis skimmed low over the water.

"World War Two tactics and equipment," Allen said, "but effective."

With the dying tanker dropping astern, Fujita shouted into the voice tube, "Right full rudder."

"That sub's off our port bow, admiral," Allen warned. "You'll give him our beam."

"I know, Admiral Allen. But Captain Fite is keeping him occupied, and why did he attack the tanker and not *Yonaga*? He must be setting us up for an easy shot from another sub, which should be taking dead aim on us from out there." He gestured to the starboard bow. He turned back to the tube. "Steady zero-three-zero."

Just as the carrier began to pick up speed and steady on the new course, the fearsome cry electrified the bridge. "*Gyo!* Off the starboard bow, range, four thousand." The voice came from a lookout high on the foretop.

126

Then, as Brent swung his glasses frantically, and with the immolated tanker only a few thousand yards astern, a torpedo struck the oiler in a half empty gasoline tank. Thousands of gallons of high test gasoline and fumes ignited in a cataclysmic explosion that rocketed the entire superstructure and a pair of twisting derricks straight up hundreds of feet on the tip of a tongue of yellow flame like Fuji-san gone mad, painting the low-hanging clouds with a panorama of orange and yellow like the glare from a new sun, great chunks of wreckage raining and pockmarking the sea in a radius of at least a mile. Brent circled Fujita's bony shoulders with one arm while grabbing the handrail. Then the roar that deafened and concussion struck, jarring the 84,000 ton carrier like a small car ramming a cliff. Two great chunks of hull crashed close aboard, drenching gun crews with twin towers of water.

"Torpedo? Torpedo?" Fujita gasped, pulling away.

Brent focused, caught four white bubbling trails off the starboard beam. "Torpedoes. Range one thousand, bearing zero-nine-zero relative."

"Too late to comb them!" Mark Allen screamed.

"Right full rudder," Fujita shouted. "We cannot let them have our screws!"

Two more Aichis dove, dropped bombs and machine gunned, but with no effect.

Steaming at 32 knots and with her 45 ton main rudder hard over in the slipstream of the four huge bronze propellers, *Yonaga* heeled and turned slowly, so very slowly, toward the approaching doom. All eyes were on the quartet of approaching white streaks. Not one head was turned astern to the grave of the tanker where the oiler had vanished, leaving a great pool of burning fuel, and where a few men still swam frantically or clung to barrels, boxes, and other charred flotsam, screaming in high mindless keening sounds like steam from ruptured boilers as flames overtook them, searing flesh from their bodies and broiling their lungs.

Leaning far over the rail, Brent saw one streak pass close aboard, then another even closer. But he knew the next two would not pass. There was a shock like the ship had struck a reef and then another, and twin towers of water spouted higher than the bridge. *Yonaga* shook from truck to keel, explosions and the sound of wrenching, ripping metal boomed through her tortured hull like great temple gongs. Again, Brent held the admiral while Kathryn and her guard were hurled from the bulkhead, across the platform, finally sprawling on the deck in a heap with a pair of lookouts, Kawamoto, Hironaka, and Allen.

"Jesus," Mark Allen said, disentangling himself and coming to his feet, "the Russians have given 'em big warheads."

"All ahead standard course zero-nine-zero," Fujita said, gripping the tube, shocking every man on the bridge. "Those warheads were as big as our Type ninety-three, Long Lance," he added, awed.

"You won't stop?" Allen asked.

Fujita ignored the question and shouted at the talker, "Damage control—report!"

"Commander Atsumi reports damage, control panel shows red lights in starboard bilge fuel tanks five, seven, nine and eleven and the outboard starboard fireroom. No report from after damage con-

128

trol."

"Damn! Those *gyos* were set for at least seven meters—hit below our armor belt," Fujita snapped angrily. Turning his head to the stern where a large oil slick widened, he said, "We are leaving tracks." Blasts to port and starboard turned heads as four of the *Fletchers* made side-by-side runs off the carrier's bows, dropping clusters of 600 pound charges. *Yonaga* trembled.

"Admiral Fujita, you'll enlarge the torpedo damage at this speed," Mark Allen said.

"Perhaps, but if we stop . . . " He shrugged. "But remember, *Yonaga* has twelve hundred watertight compartments and a double bulkhead dividing her from stem to stem. She could take another dozen of those torpedoes."

The talker came to life. "After damage control verifies bilge fuel tanks five, seven, nine, and eleven ruptured and flooding in numbers eleven and thirteen outer starboard firerooms."

"Sacred Buddha—not the firerooms."

Suddenly, the rail moved away from Brent's hand. Leaning forward, he grabbed it.

"Commander Atsumi reports the clinometer shows a five degree starboard list!"

"Very well." Fujita turned to Kawamoto. "We must trim ship. Do we have any empty fuel tanks on the port side?"

"We never fueled eight and ten, sir."

"Very well. We will counterflood by pumping seawater into our port blisters. If we still list, flood fuel tanks eight and ten." Repeating the order, the executive officer turned to the talker.

Hironaka pulled a frantically ringing phone to his ear. Horror spread across his face like spilled oil. "The warrant officer in charge of number seven auxillary five inch magazine reports the cordite store is heating. The magazine is not on fire. The heat is coming from the bulkhead astern."

"Astern?"

"Compartment five-seven-one. Auxiliary steering engine."

"Flood the magazine and five-seven-one."

"The hatches are dogged, sir. Our men will drown like rats, sir."

"I know, I know!" Fujita punched the windscreen.

A tremendous blast to port turned Brent's head to where four great waterspouts crashed into the sea in a London-fog of spray, hanging over the tortured white eddies that swirled and crashed into each other in ever-widening circles. A great black cigar bobbed and rolled in the midst of the turmoil.

"Submarine! Bearing two-seven-zero, range two thousand," Brent screamed.

"Port battery open fire!"

With a crash and roar of vented anger and frustration, twenty five-inch guns exploded, the gun layers shouting with excitement and rage. Three Zeros swept low, guns blazing, leaving brown trails of burned gun powder. Men boiled from the submarine's conning tower and fore and aft escape hatches and began to unlimber a pair of deck guns. But *Yonaga's* fire and that of two destroyers struck the submarine with a typhoon of steel and explosives, blowing both guns from their mounts and hurling crewmen into the sea like torn rag dolls. In a moment, the stern dropped, and then the submarine made her final plunge stern first, bow pointed at the sky in a final defiant gesture. Heads bobbed in the usual gravemarkers of the sea; casks, barrels, planks, spreading oil, and face down corpses.

"Ship to ship and fighter frequency, no prisoners!"

The fighters flashed down, gunning survivors with 20 millimeter cannons and 7 point 7 millimeter machine guns.

More blasts off the starboard bow as another pair of enraged escorts sowed the seas with great explosions while Aichis and Zeros circled. But no black cigar bobbed. However, through his glasses, Brent saw great gobs of oil belch to the surface and spread in ever-widening flat blue-black pools.

"Escort number three reports second submarine sunk. He has spotted oil and has picked up ship breaking up sounds on his sonar." Brent shuddered. Breaking up sounds: compartments collapsing in a dying ship as she plunged into the black depths, water pressure tearing bulkheads from their flames and rupturing watertight doors, drowning fear-maddened men in a pitch-black hell that challenged the horror of the worst nightmares of every man who had ever warred at sea.

"They are only Arabs and Germans," Fujita said as if he had read Brent's mind. "Just drowning dogs." And then briskly told the talker, "Instruct Escort number three to square out from the oil slick. It could be a ruse, and those breaking up sounds could be the tanker." He waved at the black pall, which was not far astern.

After speaking into his mouthpiece, Seaman Naoy-

131

uki said to the admiral, "Commander Atsumi reports Escort number three has acknowledged on bridge to bridge."

"Very well." He turned to the voice. "Come left to two-eight-zero, speed eighteen." The great ship swung slowly, and Brent noticed the list slowly vanish as thousands of tons of seawater were pumped into the port blisters. Again to the talker: "Inform the damage control officer that I want to make at least twenty-four knots, but will not increase speed until I have his report."

The talker paled. "After damage control reports water in number three engine room."

"Sacred Buddha! Can we stay ahead of it with our bilge pumps?"

Every man on the bridge stared at the talker. "They are shoring and caulking, sir. And Commander Fukioka suggests you reduce speed to sixteen."

Cursing, Fujita agreed, and the pulse of the engines slowed as speed was reduced. "Instruct the officer of the deck to steam course two-eight-zero, speed sixteen and to make the hoist. All hands will remain at General Quarters. Escorts resume standard cruising formation. Department heads meet with me now in Flag Plot." The old man stomped off the bridge.

Chapter Eight

"Those were big warheads," Fujita said from the head of the table.

"At least three hundred kilograms, admiral," Mark Allen said. "Probably a new HE the Russians call Nytrolyte B—three to four times the explosive power of our old TNT warheads."

The old Japanese drummed the tabletop, skeletal hands corded with new blue veins. "Wire guided?"

"Two missed," Brent Ross said abruptly.

The fingers stopped. "If an Arab was on the periscope, that would be expected."

Despite the somber atmosphere, smiles appeared on the faces of the officers. Fujita turned to an enlisted man who sat at a table with a phone to his ear. "Radioman Ozawa. I want a report from after damage control."

Ozawa spoke over the mouthpiece, and his painful words struck with the force of javelins. "Commander Fukioka reports *gyo* hits between frames one-zero-two and one-two-zero and below the armor belt, blowing open the blister, original shell and shearing

133

bottom plates. Each explosion blew holes ten meters by four meters in the hull . . ."

"My God! Twelve feet by thirty feet," Mark Allen muttered.

"Fire rooms eleven and thirteen, number seven auxiliary five inch magazine, compartment five-seven-one, auxiliary engine room three, the starboard thrust block room and the next compartment inboard, the center motor room, are flooded." He listened intently, then continued. "Also, water in ventilation intakes is flooding the pump and dynamo room. Bilge fuel tanks five, seven, nine, and eleven are wide open to the sea and an eight inch fuel line was ruptured. We have a report of water in some of our fuel lines, but we have not isolated this damage as yet." There was a pause, and then the thunderbolt. "The bulkhead between number eleven fireroom and number three engine room is leaking in a dozen places." Gasps of horror and disbelief whispered through the room like the wings of death.

Fujita struck the table with an open palm, shriveled face drained of blood and withered like a yellow raisin. He shouted at Ozawo. "The bulkhead between number eleven fireroom and number three engine room should not leak—not from this damage. Tell Fukioka I want an explanation."

The enlisted man spoke hastily and fearfully into the mouthpiece while every officer in the room stared at him. He turned to the admiral. "Commander Fukioka says the armored box around our engine rooms and magazines has reduced flexibility in our plates, admiral. The explosions sheared revets in the armor plating and drove a reinforcing beam through the engine room bulkhead. He claims similar damage within thirty meters of the points of impact."

Brent Ross stared wide-eyed at Mark Allen. The Japanese had been immensely proud of the ship's armor, compartmentation, and especially the eight inch armored box that enclosed her vitals. But now the urge to produce an impregnable steel fortress inside the hull had worked against them. The ship had been gravely wounded by just two hits.

"Admiral," Mark Allen said, "it would be foolish to attempt to reach Tokyo Bay in this condition."

"We may have no choice. Keep in mind, Admiral Allen, we can lose number three engine room and still make eighteen knots. We have, perhaps, ten flooded compartments and have lost four fuel tanks."

"But our watertight integrity has been breached. You could lose an engine room, and the entire starboard quarter is weakened. More hits on that side could capsize us. And you have that longitudinal bulkhead running from stem to stern that won't allow the flow of water from starboard to port in your bilges. These ships are top heavy, anyway." Allen circled a single finger over his head. "That's how *Yamato* was lost — maybe a dozen hits on her port side, the water built up." He turned his palm up and shrugged. "And she rolled over."

A silence descended, so heavy it seemed to bend the shoulders of every man in the room. And new ship sounds were heard — the frantic heart-pump throb of pumps deep in the vitals of the ship. Allen broke the silence. "We're twenty five hundred miles from Tokyo Bay, but only three hundred from Pearl Harbor."

"You are suggesting putting into Pearl Harbor?"

135

"Of course, admiral."

"But all of you," Fujita said, gesturing at the Americans and Bernstein, "have repeatedly told me the United States is neutral."

Dempster spoke for the first time. "True, sir. But there is a huge graving dock . . ." He glanced at Mark Allen.

The American admiral answered the unspoken question. "The dock can handle *Yonaga.*"

The veined hands pressed on the table, and Brent could almost feel the force of the encyclopedic mind at work. Fujita spoke deliberately. "I remember in the Great East Asia War, December 1939, the British cruisers *Ajax, Achilles,* and *Exeter* caught the German pocket battleship *Graf Spee* off Uruguay. *Graf Spee* was badly damaged and docked in Montevideo — a neutral port. By international law, they gave her seventy-two hours. Her captain scuttled her in the River Plate." He turned to Mark Allen. "We would be subject to the same law."

"Of course! But, maybe, we can persuade the US to give us more time. And there is no immediate threat to Japan from the Arab battle group — not with an angry Margaret Thatcher charging down on them."

Fujita spoke with new animation. "We could weld patches over the holes, shore our weakened bulkheads, insure the watertight integrity of number three engine room." He punched the table. "Admiral Allen, have your cryptographer encode a message in a cypher we have never used."

"Zebra One," Brent Ross said abruptly.

"Very well. Addressee?"

"Principal addressee should be CINCPACFLT. I

136

would also suggest COMNAVBASE, COMNAV-
LOGPAC, NAVSHIPYD and NAVSECGUDET."

The old sailor threw up his hand in surrender.
"Please, admiral, you Americans and your acronyms
defy reason—logic."

"Sorry, sir. I meant Commander in Chief Pacific
Fleet, Commander Naval Base, Commander Naval
Logistics Command, Commander Naval Shipyard,
and the Naval Security Group Detachment."

"Why did you not say as much the first time?" A
chuckle relieved some of the tension. Fujita continued, eyes on Brent Ross: "Request immediate graving
dock availability for—ah, minor damage repair.
ETA," He glanced at Captain Kawamoto who scribbled on a pad furiously.

"Twenty hours at sixteen knots, admiral."

Fujita looked at a brass ship's clock on the bulkhead. "ETA, sixteen hundred hours, on Friday, thirteen March." He moved back to the American ensign.
"And Mr. Ross, request landing instructions for a
single Nakajima."

"One, sir?"

"Yes. We will send our bottom blocking profile and
related drawings to the dockmaster."

"Of course, of course," Brent heard Mark Allen say
to himself.

The black eyes flashed to Bernstein. "Colonel, we
will make use of your encryption box."

"Sir?"

"Send a signal to our escort commander in Subic
Bay. I want those seven *Fletchers* to make for Pearl
Harbor under forced draft. When we sortie, I want
twelve escorts!" Coming to his feet, he turned to the

paulownia wood shrine. Every man stood. The Japanese clapped twice. Then, the old man spoke slowly—reverent words that dropped from his lips like pebbles into a pond: "Amaterasu, help us show the courage of the great samurai Masahige Kusunoki who, one half a millenium ago, strove to restore the Imperial throne and when defeated by a cowardly ronin, shouted, 'Seven lives for the nation' as he committed *seppuku*. Let these words fall from our lips as we attack our enemies, remembering a man can be honored by the courage of his enemy." The line of his mouth altered, eyes chilled to the hardness of ebony, sweeping the room with anger that was a palpable thing: "But not by the bite of a mad dog!"

"Banzai!"

Chapter Nine

"Tangents on Koko Head and Barbers Point," Fujita shouted from his position at the front of the bridge.

"Koko Head bearing zero-four-three, Barbers Point three-two-zero, sir," a quartermaster said, staring through the sights of a bearing ring mounted on a gyro-repeater.

Furiously, Kawamoto worked a drafting machine and parallel rules on a chart tacked to the table attached to the windscreen. "Twenty-five kilometers to the main channel, sir. I suggest course three-four-eight."

"Very well. Radar verify range to harbor entrance." The talker repeated the command.

"Radar reports the range to harbor entrance twenty-five kilometers."

"Very well."

Kawamoto turned from the table, yellow parchment face broken by a triumphant grin.

"Come right to three-four-eight," the admiral shouted into the voice tube.

The unfamiliar roar of a dozen Rolls Royce Merlin engines turned Brent's head. Raising his binoculars, he found twelve American P-51 Mustangs flying in pairs, circling the task force. P-51s had appeared the day before with a pair of PBYs and a gull-winged Martin Mariner. From that moment on, constant American patrols had circled the ships, but well out of range. No surface ships had appeared, and the sea was free even of pleasure craft. Kathryn had been confined to her cabin since the torpedo attack.

Lowering his glasses, Brent turned with the rest of the staff as Mark Allen stepped on the bridge. "Berthing assignment, admiral," he said, waving a printout. "The graving dock is not ready."

"Not ready? We sent the request two days ago!"

"I know, sir. But they are still repairing damage you did to the *New Jersey*."

The Japanese looked at each other with mixed elation and disappointment.

Allen continued. "They're towing her out now. It will take them eight hours to pump out and set up, and we can enter tomorrow morning at zero eight hundred."

"That will leave us with fifty to sixty hours of availability."

"We could lay-to out here, admiral."

"I know, but it would be dangerous, and we are shipping more water in engine room number three."

Brent knew the admiral had no choice. The pumps had barely kept even with the ruptured bulkhead, and the ship had been slowed by thousands of tons of seawater, which flooded a dozen compartments on her starboard quarter. A like amount was pumped into her port blisters to counteract the list. Now she was on an even keel, but lower in the water, slower and less maneuverable.

"Docking instructions, Admiral Allen?"

Allen took a deep breath. "They want to isolate *Yonaga*, sir. We are to tie up to bollards just southeast of Ford Island."

"Numbers?"

"No numbers, sir. They are marked Tennessee."

A long, hard silence infected the bridge like a plague. Fujita spoke to Allen. "Anything new on the World Court and United Nations?"

"No, sir. The same. The Arab powers, Russia, and her lackeys insist that the US enforce international law. Seventy-two hours, sir."

"Criminals insisting on law enforcement," Fujita snorted. "Your nation's interests ride with *Yonaga*, too," the old Japanese added with unabashed bitterness.

"I agree with you, admiral. At this moment, I am not proud of my country. But remember, sir, democracies are highly sensitive to public opinion, and there is the matter of placating the moderate Arab powers, Russia . . ."

"It is called appeasement," Fujita snapped sharply. Before the American could answer, he turned to the talker. "By flashing light . . . " He stopped and grimaced, "No—bridge to bridge; everyone on earth knows where we are. *Yonaga* will stand in first. Escorts maintain a tight screen until I have cleared the channel. I do not want a torpedo up my stern post."

"All of that, sir?"

"That is correct!"

141

Allen broke in. "The escorts will receive berthing instructions by flashing light from the Aloha Tower."

Fujita snorted. "Aloha! They have 'aloha' everything. That is the most overused word on earth. Can they not think of any other?"

Yonaga, nudged by a pair of navy tugs, tied up to the bollards marked Tennessee. Craning his neck curiously, Brent could see the white bridge-like *Arizona* Memorial ahead, crammed with people staring at *Yonaga* through glinting binoculars. Rusting and still oozing oil, the tomb of over eleven hundred men could be seen clearly, lying beneath the memorial and at right angles to it. Fore and aft and marked with names of victims of the "Day of Infamy," bollards stretched like grave markers: *Nevada, Vestal, Arizona, West Virginia, Maryland,* and *Oklahoma* were all visible from the bridge. To the north, low-lying Ford Island showed thick green undergrowth along the shore and a cluster of neglected hangars in its interior. And here, too, hundreds crowded, studying the great carrier.

Behind Ford Island and in the distance the mountainous interior of Oahu loomed. Green escarpment mounting upon green escarpment soared upward behind Honolulu, Aiea, and the obscene sprawl of buildings and freeways, blending into the pristine grandeur of the Koolau Mountains where cane fields gave way to majestic buttresses and citadels of sheer rock. Dominating all like great silent sentinels, Mount Tanalus and Mount Olympus were wrapped with moisture-laden clouds driven by the northeasterly trade winds, swirling around the mountaintops like lacy nightcaps touched with apricot and gold by the slanting rays of the afternoon sun.

But Brent did not see the beauty. Instead, he stared with the other men directly south where the five escorts had tied up at the wharves at the Naval Supply Center of Kuahua Island—a mass of shops, derricks, and more staring people. Every man on the bridge was impressed by the massive facility. When they stood in, they had left the naval shipyard to starboard, made their turn to the east in the basin just south of Ford Island, skirted the shipyard's northern edge, passing three dry docks and finding the *New Jersey* tied up just outside the giant graving dock. From their mooring, they could stare south down the broad waters of Southeast Loch—the body of water the attacking torpedo planes had swooped over in making their runs on 7 December, 1941.

Bordering the loch were fueling docks, the submarine base, and acres of supply and repair depots. Off *Yonaga*'s starboard bow across the bay, Brent could see a large white ferry boat loaded with passengers making for the *Arizona* Memorial.

"These are navy waters, admiral," Mark Allen said. "You won't have the undisciplined flotilla of private boats crowding you the way they did last December in Tokyo Bay."

The old man nodded gratefully. He turned to Kawamoto, saying, "Put divers over the side. I want the exact dimensions of the holes before we go into dry dock." To Mark Allen: "I want you and Ensign Ross to be my liaison. We'll put a whaleboat over, and you can personally take our requirements to the dock

143

master."

"Sir," the talker said suddenly. "Communications reports a signal . . . He stumbled through unfamiliar ground: "N-a-v-c-o-m-s-t-a-p-a-c . . ."

"What in the name of the gods . . ."

"Naval Communications Area Master Station Pacific," Mark Allen explained.

"Thank you," Fujita said. He returned to the talker. "The rest of the message, Seaman Naoyuki."

"A repair officer is enroute to *Yonaga* now, admiral."

"Very well!" A dozen pair of glasses swung toward the vast repair facilities. Slashing through the broad waters, bow pointed toward *Yonaga*, was an admiral's barge, elegant with polished brass, gleaming paint, and a blue pennant with two white stars fluttering proudly.

Fujita turned to Kawamoto. "Prepare an admiral's side party and assemble the staff in Flag Plot! Summon Commander Fukioka. There will be no liberty, and the ship will remain at condition two of readiness." And then as an afterthought, he added, "Tell the woman to prepare to disembark as soon as we are on our blocks."

Dropping his binoculars into a canvas bag attached to the windscreen, Brent felt a hollow emptiness. As he turned for the door, he avoided the eyes of the other men.

Rear Adm. Taylor Archer was an elderly man and one of the fattest human beings Brent Ross had ever seen. When he entered Flag Plot, he towered over every man in the room except Brent, feet wide apart, moving in short jerky steps, body braced in the posture of a heavily pregnant woman to counterbalance his monstrous gut. His aide, a middle-aged captain named Wilfred Rhoads, actually helped the admiral into his chair, and Brent was surprised when the man was able to sit unattended in a single seat. Seated across from him, Brent stared at a pasty white face of vanilla pudding with chins hanging down to his chest like ripples of the sea. His mouth was a purple gash, loose, perpetually open as he labored for breath. "My aide," he said in a raspy voice, waving airily to the captain, "Capt. Wilfred Rhoads who is a naval architect and is in charge of Graving Dock Three where you will be repaired."

"You are not in charge of the dock, admiral?"

"Not an admiral, sir. I'm here to represent CINC-PACFLT—I am second in command," Archer retorted haughtily.

Fujita moved his eyes to Mark Allen. He spoke slowly, like a young scholar attempting a difficult word at a spelling bee. "Commander in chief, Pacific Fleet."

Smiling, Mark Allen nodded. Bernstein, Hironaka, and Kawamoto grinned at each other. Matsuhara stared, confused by the barely submerged humor while Commander Fukioka sat quietly, pouring over blueprints and reports.

Unaware of the subtlety in the exchange, the rear admiral moved his eyes to Mark Allen. "We've met, admiral."

"We graduated from Annapolis together."

"Why, of course—Mark Allen. You were captain of

145

the football team. The school hero." The timbre of the voice was derisive.

"That's right. You were team manager. I remember throwing you my dirty jockstraps."

Archer sputtered. Brent clapped a hand over his mouth while Bernstein giggled. The Japanese stared at each other, certain of an insult but unable to fathom American jests.

The pudding turned from vanilla to grape and Archer spat, "I didn't come here—"

"Please, gentlemen," Fujita interrupted. "We are here to serve the fate of *Yonaga*, Japan and, perhaps, much more than that."

Sighing, the fat man moved his beady eyes from Allen. "Your damage report—you refused to put it on our harbor circuit," he said.

"Of course. *Yonaga*'s condition is not to be broadcast to the world." He nodded at Commander Fukioka. "My damage control officer."

"May I record this, admiral?" Captain Rhoads asked, placing a small tape recorder on the table next to a notepad. Fujita nodded his assent.

Standing, Commander Fukioka described *Yonaga*'s damage in funereal tones. "And we have lost twenty-three known dead and forty-four wounded," he concluded. Then, moving moist eyes to Fujita, he said, "We must still open twelve flooded compartments—there will be more. Our muster shows sixty-three missing."

"Sacred Buddha," the old Japanese said. And then reverently, as if the room were a temple and he stood alone in the nave, he said, "They died with *Yomato damashii* and surely dwell in Yasakuni Shrine." A

146

long oppressive silence gripped the room.

Rhoads broke the silence. "We have one inch plates ready. As soon as you're high and dry, we can begin welding."

"Time?"

"We need the exact dimensions of the holes."

Fujita gestured to Fukioka. The damage control officer spoke. "Our divers are over the side now. But I only have two—the other two were killed when we flooded the auxiliary five inch magazine."

Fujita pounded the table. "Can you send us some divers, Admiral Archer?"

A smirk rippled through the chins. "We have a dozen divers, but they are all working on *New Jersey* and *Tarawa*. We must raise her; she blocks the channel south of the sub base."

"*Tarawa?*" The Japanese looked at each other.

"You should remember," Archer said with acid sarcasm. "You sank her."

Matsuhara spoke for the first time. "Admiral two of my flyers are qualified divers: Lt. Nobutake Konoye and NAPfc., Kiichii Mochazuki."

"Good. Put them over the side." He waved at the door. Matsuhara left. He turned to Archer and Rhoads. "We will relay our reports to you by couriers in whale boats."

"You could use flashing lights," Archer said.

"No! It is visible for miles. They could read it in Honolulu. And we need fuel, ammunition, stores . . ." He nodded to Kawamoto who handed a bundle of documents to Archer. "Our requisitions," Fujita said.

Scanning the requisitions, Archer muttered, "Je-

147

sus—you're getting ready for World War Three!"

"We've been fighting it for six months," Allen said bluntly.

"Very well," the fat American said. "We'll fill these at the dock." The Japanese grinned and looked at each other. Archer continued. "I would not suggest liberty for your crew or the crews of your escorts, Admiral Fujita. There are members of the crews of the *New Jersey* ashore, survivors of the *Tarawa*, an American Legion convention—"

"Admiral Archer," Fujita interrupted impatiently. "There will be no liberty and . . . " He waved at the Americans and Bernstein. "When I send parties ashore, these members of my staff will represent *Yonaga*. However, I reserve the right to protect them from Sabbah killers or any other menace with armed seaman guards."

"I have assigned a member of my staff, Lt. Loren Kaiser, to act as liaison with you and to provide transportation, guards, and protection for any of your personnel ashore. And please keep in mind, admiral, we have our SPs. I'll even send you a detail. They'll surround the graving dock, anyway. And there'll be marines."

"No! Your men are welcome at the dock, but ashore we will protect ourselves."

"But what business do you have ashore? I don't understand."

"You do not need to understand. These matters do not concern you, Admiral Archer."

"Whatever happens in this harbor concerns me."

"Not when you deal with me." A silence like a cold Arctic wind chilled everyone.

The lips compressed into a thin line, eyes cooled to the hardness of pale sapphires, and the voice quavered, "With your permission, Captain Rhoads and I will return to our duties." He began to push on his armrests in an attempt to rise.

But Fujita waved, indicating he was not yet finished. "You will maintain a CAP?"

"Six fighters from Hickam continuously over the harbor," he replied, sinking back into his chair reluctantly.

"Long range patrols?"

"PBYs and mariners." and then the rear admiral leaned forward. "Some of your guns are manned!"

"Condition Two—one half the ship's armament."

"It's not necessary. We are prepared."

"We know how alert you are, Admiral Archer."

The fat man's face twisted and contorted like a sheet of red-hot metal struck by a hammer. The livid lips managed, "With your permission . . . "

"You are dismissed!"

After the rear admiral waddled through the door, followed by Captain Rhoads and the amused stare of the staff, Fujita spoke to Bernstein, Allen, and Ross. "We need new codes, encryption boxes. The Arabs seem to know too much about us."

"If you approve, I'll call the Israeli legation," Bernstein said. "They should have new software we can use, but not an encryption box. The box ordered for us is waiting for us in Tokyo."

Mark Allen nodded. "And we can stop in at NIS. They should have some new programs we can use and possibly a new box."

"Very well. Tomorrow after we are secure in the

graving dock, take a detail of seaman guards and go ashore." And then quietly, he added, "Admiral Allen and Ensign Ross, please remain and the rest of you are dismissed." However, struck by an afterthought as the officers filed out, he added, "Take the woman with you, Colonel Bernstein."

"Yes, sir," came the voice from the door.

At the moment the door closed behind the departing officers, the riot broke out on the *Arizona* Memorial.

Lt. Nobutake Konoye felt responsible for the unfortunate events that took place on the memorial that afternoon. He had been checking his diving gear with NAP Kiichii Mochazuki on the starboard boat deck: 90 kilogram rubber suit, leather weight belt, threaded neck ring, helmet, air hose, and telephone line. He had just discovered the helmet's exhaust valve was stuck in the closed position when the call came from the repair party alongside on the diving platform, floats, and a single whaleboat. "Buoys away—they're drifting!"

Glancing down, Konoye saw a half-dozen red marker buoys attached together with a line drifting past the starboard beam, moving down on the *Arizona* Memorial. Cursing the inept seamanship that would allow the buoys to break loose and followed by Mochazuki, he had scampered down a Jacob's ladder and landed on a rolling thwart of the whaleboat moored alongside the torpedo holes. Despite the fact he had just been assigned to the detail, he was senior officer and responsible. There were four men in the boat besides Mochazuki and himself: the coxswain, Boatswain's Mate First Class, Shimei Futabatei, who was an original member of *Yonaga*'s crew and terribly eroded by time, leaving only wrinkle-riven flesh and stringy sinew and brittle bones; Engineman First Class, Kansuke Naka, who was also a 'plank owner' and as decrepit as Futabatei. The other two men, Seaman First Class, Soseki Natsumi and Seaman Doppo Kunikida had come aboard in Tokyo Bay five months before and were both young, strong men with fine *Yamato damachii*.

"Cast off! Cast off," Konoye had shouted, moving to the bow where he released the bow painter himself while pointing at the errant buoys, which were drifting toward the memorial's landing. "This is a disgrace to *Yonaga*'s seamanship!"

With the stern line cast off and a clang of the coxswain's bell, the engine roared, and the long gray whaleboat charged toward the *Arizona*.

Standing in the bow and slashing past *Yonaga*'s side, which looked like a steel *Fuji-san*, Konoye had a clear view of the buoys, which had become entangled in the pilings supporting the landing.

Within a minute they had cleared *Yonaga*'s bow, and *Arizona*'s rusty hull began to unroll beneath their keel. Only a single rusty barbette off their starboard bow and a half-dozen pipes projected above the surface.

He first became alarmed when he noticed they were headed for the center of the memorial where a bridgelike structure sagged, the American flag flew, and perhaps a dozen people stared at them through seven large openings in the white concrete. "Come right! Come right! The landing," he had shouted, gesturing and turning to the coxswain. Futabatei's shout was drowned by the engine as he brought the rudder over hard, swinging the bow sharply.

"No! No! The barbette! Are you blind, you old fool!"

There was a furious clanging of the bell and the rudder was put hard aport, but Futabatei's frantic efforts came too late. The sharp, rusty edge of the barbette caught them on the port side, just below the waterline. There was a crash, a ripping of wood, and a shock that staggered Konoye, and suddenly his feet were wet as water poured into a long gash that ran half the length of their port side. Immediately, the engine was flooded and the boat began to settle.

"I'll heave you a line," an American rating shouted from the landing, whirling a "monkey's fist" over his head. Two others clutched life rings.

"Our flotation tanks will keep us afloat," Konoye shouted. "Just pull us in."

Within a few minutes, the half-submerged boat was tied up to the dock and the six Japanese scampered out.

Staring at *Yonaga*'s bow, which loomed like a steel cliff over the memorial, Konoye was convinced no one had noticed the accident. Furiously, he waved his arms in the fashion of a man using international Morse. But there was no response from the bridge, flight deck, or anywhere else. And when they did notice his predicament, it would take time to man and lower another boat. Then he noticed two things: Coxswain Futabatei and Engineman Naka had disappeared, and the white ferryboat loaded with tourists was bearing down on the memorial.

After thanking the two American ratings and making certain the lines to the whaleboat were secure, he shouted, "Follow me," and entered the memorial with NAP Mochazuki, Seaman Notsumi, and Seaman Kunikada on his heels.

They entered a long, white, tomblike structure that sat squarely over the wreck. He heard excited voices and found the two old men standing at the far end before a huge marble plaque inscribed with over a thousand names. Hurrying the length of the gallery, the four men passed a few American tourists, who stared curiously and silently. They stopped before the plaque, which stretched from floor to ceiling and wall to wall. Near the bottom and centered in large letters, Konoye read, "To the memory of the gallant men here entombed and their shipmates who gave their lives in action on December 7, 1941 on the U.S.S. *Arizona*."

Konoye felt no compassion. Staring at column after column of names, he thought of Tokyo, the fire raid, his incinerated family, the cenotaph at ground zero in Hiroshima with its tens of thousands, the sunken ship's entombing the bones of dozens of his friends. No! He would not shed a tear here.

"Banzai *Akagi* Banzai *Kaga*!" Futabatei screamed suddenly, waving a fist at the names.

And Naka joined in, honoring the carriers in the Pearl Harbor attack, "Banzai *Shokaku*! Banzai *Zuikaku* . . . "

"What the fuck's going on?" roared someone behind them.

Whirling, Konoye found a crowd of tourists led by eight beefy men in late middle age and wearing ridiculous peaked caps emblazoned with "Post 109," closing in.

"What the fuck are you Nips doing here?" said a tall pasty-white man through thick red lips, with a huge stomach that hung over his belt. Adjusting his cap and leaning forward, he pushed the leering visage of a Hindu temple devil into Konoye's face.

The lieutenant spat back at the devil. "We are not *Nips*—we are on the emperor's business." He heard the familiar chugging sound of a whaleboat's engine approaching. "And we are leaving."

"The fuck you are." The eight men crowded close. "On the emperor's business, huh," the fat man growled. "We're legionnaires! We know about the emperor's business. Weren't you on the emperor's business when you murdered those men?" He waved at the names.

The lieutenant felt a surge of atavistic fury like a madness possess him—the same mindless rage that overwhelmed him when he faced Brent Ross on the hangar deck: no fear, no doubts, not even conscious thought. He opened his mouth, but someone else seemed to speak. "And whose business were you on when you destroyed Tokyo, Yokahama, Kobe, Hiroshima, Nagasaki . . ."

"They kicked Kadafi's ass, leave 'em alone," someone in the rear shouted.

"That don't mean shit!" the tall legionnaire groused over his shoulder. "They did that for Japan, not for us." He stabbed a finger at the names. "They murdered those boys!"

"And those are the fuckers who sank the *New Jersey* and *Tarawa*", another shrill voice shrieked.

"Banzai *Hiryu*! Banzai *Soryu*!" Naka and Futabatei shouted defiantly.

"Those are the carriers that did this," one of the legionnaires cried. "Get 'em!"

There were screams from the onlookers and the big man swung. But Konoye ducked easily and brought a fist up from the floor, burying it up to the wrist in the great, soft stomach that yielded like gelatine. The man's breath exploded in his ear.

"Fuckin' Jap!" Hard knuckles caught the Japanese officer on the side of his head, and he felt his teeth clash together in his skull, lacerating his tongue and bringing an instant salty taste to his mouth. The blow spun him, and he continued to pivot, bringing up his right foot and catching the fat man in the throat with a kick intended to kill. But his heel caught the man to one side, only partially impacting the windpipe. Clawing his throat and gasping like the victim of an executioner's garrote, the big man sank to the floor like a deflating balloon.

Now all the Japanese and the remaining legionnaires were locked in wild, screaming combat. Conditioned by years of physical training, even the old Futabatei and Naka were too wiry and quick for their heavier, out-of-condition opponents. With a shout, Naka ran, leaped and caught a retreating American with both feet chest high, knocking him through an opening and into the harbor.

But Mochazuki was down and two Americans sat on him, pounding with fists like hams. Konoye leaped, landing on top of the pile. Punched. Kicked while more bodies fell on him. There were screams. Curses. The flash of camera bulbs. Howls of pain.

155

And then Atsumi's voice echoed down a long dark tunnel: "Stop! Stop!"

A big American voice reverberated from the marble: "Belay that crap. I'll throw every fuckin' one of you in the brig!"

Big hands grabbed Konoye and pulled him to his feet. He was pushed roughly against a wall by Lieutenant Commander Atsumi, who waved a club menacingly. Behind him, Japanese seaman guards, American SPs, military police, and the crew of the ferryboat sorted out the combatants and pushed them roughly against opposite walls.

"A disgrace," Atsumi muttered. "A disgrace!"

Konoye could only stare at his feet.

Brent Ross moved to the far end of the table when the crowd of officers filed into Flag Plot. First Lieutenant Konoye and NAP Mochazuki were escorted in. Both were disheveled. Blood was caked in Mochazuki's black hair. One eye was almost swollen shut, and his green fatigue shirt was ripped as congealed blood streaked his chest. Konoye was not nearly as beaten, showing blood on his left ear and cheek, a bruised mouth, and a scratch across his forehead. Both men stood at attention against a bulkhead next to Admiral Fujita.

Then Rear Admiral Archer arrived, huffing, puffing and obviously distressed. "I picked it up on the Harbor emergency frequency," he wheezed as Captain Rhoads helped him into a chair. "The crew of the ferry thought World War Three had broken out."

"No!" Fujita snapped. "With some, the Greater

156

East Asia War never ended." He threw a scathing look at Konoye.

The flyer drew himself up. "I was fully and totally responsible, admiral," he said through his swollen lips.

"Ha! It's about time somebody admitted guilt," Archer said.

"Sir," Mochazuki pleaded suddenly, "may I make a report?"

"Proceed, pilot."

Hesitantly, the rating described the incredible series of events that led to the encounter.

"Well enough," Archer said. "But who started it?"

"That is unimportant, sir," Konoye interjected. "I was the senior officer present. I am responsible."

"Remain silent," Fujita commanded. "Continue with your report, Pilot Mochazuki."

"The Americans struck first! The Americans were the aggressors! We only defended ourselves!"

"My God," Archer exploded. "That's what you said after Pearl Harbor. I was an ensign on—"

Mark Allen leaped to his feet, face scarlet, fists clenched. "Christ, Taylor. You're just like the rest. You're still fighting the goddamned war!" He waved a hand. "These men bled in the Med fighting those Arab lunatics and saved our ass and our biggest ally from certain defeat. Doesn't anyone know? Doesn't anyone care? Doesn't anyone appreciate the sacrifices? We lost sixty-three pilots, seventy-two aircrewmen, forty-two gunners, and we're still counting the dead from those two torpedo hits."

Brent watched Fujita's eyes move craftily from Allen to Archer and then back. He was convinced the

157

old man was deriving pleasure from the exchange. Every man in the room stared intently as Archer retorted, but belligerence had given way to conciliation, "Of course we appreciate. We know your men died for us, too." He thumped the table with beefy knuckles. "But keep in mind, you're sitting on the bulls-eye of *Yonaga*'s target of last December. Of course there's resentment—no; hatred here."

"You heard Pilot Mochazuki's report. Our men were not at fault."

"Whose navy are you in, Mark? You keep talking in the first person, plural."

"He is a member of my staff," Fujita said simply. "I am convinced he has the best understanding of carrier warfare of any man on earth."

"With respect, admiral. This was not carrier warfare. This was a riot."

Allen leaned forward, clenched fists on the table. "It was an accident, Taylor. My God, you know the American Legion. Most of them never saw combat, and they make up for it with their big mouths."

Archer sighed. "There's truth in what you say. But CINCPACFLT will conduct a full inquiry." He turned to Rhoads. "You're getting this?"

"Yes, sir," the captain answered, indicating his tape recorder and pad.

Rage vented, Mark Allen sank into his chair. "We can't attend your hearing and you know it. According to International law, we've got to clear this port in less than sixty hours."

Fujita took over. "It is obvious my men were at fault despite the attitude of these so-called American Legionnaires." He turned his eyes to the two flyers.

158

"All of those involved will be heard at a Captain's Mast over which I will preside." He turned to the rear admiral. "But the disciplining of the crew of *Yonaga* is my responsibility, and you can conduct all the hearings you wish, but my men will not appear, will not accept your judgments or your punishments. These things will be done by me and at a time I deem propitious."

"Propitious?"

"Yes, rear admiral. After *Yonaga* is repaired and after we destroy any remaining Arab threat to the mikado."

"You'll do nothing!"

"Taylor!"

Fujita waved Allen to silence. "Are you challenging my authority, rear admiral?"

"Ah . . . " Archer sputtered, backing water. "Of course not. I would just like to report to CINCPACFLT that you have taken appropriate steps . . . "

"I will take *appropriate* steps," Fujita said in a mocking tone.

"Sir," Konoye said suddenly in an unusually high-pitched voice. "Please allow me to redeem my honor. My karma has been compromised." His baleful eyes found Brent Ross. He spat the words. "Twice now, sir."

"I have already told you, lieutenant. You will be given the opportunity. If the Arabs do not accommodate you, I will." Balled, rootlike fingers struck the oak irritably. "You are dismissed — all of you!"

Brent liked the feel of the 6-point 5 millimeter

159

Otsus pistol—"the baby Nambu," the Japanese called the deadly little automatic—which dangled against his right hip snugly in its leather holster. And he was in navy blues again, a single braid of gold glistening on each sleeve, his hat square and comfortable. Adm. Mark Allen, who walked ahead of him on the gangway toward the graving dock's rim, also wore his dress blues splendidly while Colonel Bernstein still wore the drab khaki of the Israeli army—but today he had a well-pressed look. Both were armed with Otsus. Behind Brent, Kathryn Suziki took long eager steps like a convict headed for the prison's gate on the final day of incarceration. Four seaman guards in blue jumpers, trousers with khaki leggings, and wearing flat hats emblazoned with ideograms, followed. Each carried an Arisaka Type 99, 7-point 7 millimeter short rifle slung over his shoulder and each wore a duty belt with a half-dozen ammunition boxes attached.

Stepping from the gangway, the party stopped as one, turned and stared at the beached behemoth silently. *Yonaga* was awesome. Eighty-four thousand tons of steel sitting high and dry on blocks. Her battleship genesis was obvious: side layered with sloping armor plate above a bulging torpedo blister. But it was the sheer size of her that overwhelmed. Staring hundreds of feet upward to the top of her yards where parabolic antennas turned in their perpetual search, Brent had the same awed feeling he had experienced when he first saw the Grand Tetons or stood in Times Square as a child. Size. Overwhelming size. Her stack was as big as an apartment house, and her flight deck umbrellaed over everything, supported by a forest of girders he had never seen from the bridge, and the muzzles of twenty five-inch guns could be seen, pointing skyward.

"Fujita. That's Fujita." Kathryn said. "That thing *is* Fujita."

Turning and walking toward the stern with two seamen leading and the other pair following, the party approached the torpedo holes. In only two hours a swarm of workmen had rigged scaffolding, and Brent's ears were assailed by the sounds of metal striking metal, shrieks of high-speed drills, and the machine gun bursts of pneumatic tools. Already a crane was lowering a great sheet of steel plating toward the damage where a dozen welders stood by on the planking.

Without command, the party stopped and stared down soberly at the two great wounds. "Jesus," Brent said to himself. "Each hole—maybe, thirty by twenty."

The torpedoes had hit well below the armor belt, opening the blisters like tin cans, bending jagged, blackened plates inward to scorched interiors. And black, ugly water streaked with oil poured out of the holes like puss out of open sores, splashing on the floor of the dock and sluicing to the drains.

"Powerful! Powerful warheads," Bernstein said.

"And shaped—shaped charges for better penetration," Allen noted.

"I'm Lieutenant Loren Kaiser," a voice said suddenly behind the group.

Turning, Brent found a young, squat, powerfully built young officer with chestnut hair stringing out from under his cap, a nose broadened and apparently flattened by impacts, square jaw fashioned from stone, and intense hazel eyes that glistened with latent hostility.

"Why the artillery? We gotcha covered," the lieutenant continued, jerking a thumb over his shoulder at two SPs close behind him with slung M-16s.

"We were expecting you but not your impertinence," Mark Allen shot back.

"Sorry, admiral," Kaiser said with forced contriteness. He gestured at the edge of the dry dock. "But we do have this area secured. There must be a platoon of marines on duty."

And there was, indeed, a large contingent of camouflage-clad marines clutching automatic rifles, posted at regular intervals. And a heavy machine gun had been emplaced behind sandbags at the lone gate.

"And no suicide truck can make it through those barriers." Kaiser said, pointing at a series of roadblocks leading to the gate.

"If you'll follow me, gentlemen, and . . . " His eyes moved to Kathryn and roamed her supple body, which was outlined provocatively by the tight-fitting green fatigues. "And madam, I'll take you to the two jeeps we have reserved for you just outside the gate."

"We'll need three," Mark Allen said. "Colonel Bernstein requires one, Mr. Ross and I need one, and Miss Suzuki will need a ride to—"

"To my aunt's," the girl injected, "at Laie."

"Sorry, admiral," Kaiser said. "Sorry about the foul-up. We didn't know you had the woman. Nobody told us."

"She's a survivor. I should have told you, lieutenant."

Kaiser looked around hastily and pointed at a

vehicle parked near a corrugated metal shed. "You can have that one, admiral. It's a work jeep, dirty, with a tool box instead of a rear seat, but it runs."

"Fine! Fine! And a driver . . . "

"Please, admiral, let Ensign Ross drive me," Kathryn said. "I won't ever see any of you again and . . . "

Brent felt a catch in his throat and a surge in his pulse. But never in his wildest fantasy would he have anticipated the admiral's reply. "Why of course," Mark Allen said. "I can complete my duties at NIS alone." He pointed at the shed. "But I can't assign you a guard. There's no rear seat in that jeep. There can be a Sabbah . . . "

"I'm sure we can manage," Kathryn assured him. "Don't you think so, Mr. Ross?"

"Why of course, Miss Suzuki. Of course." Brent was surprised by the steadiness of his voice.

Chapter Ten

Leaving the naval base with Brent at the wheel of the small windblown vehicle, Kathryn was stunned by the massive installation. "My family lived here, Brent, and we still have a place." She waved to the north. "But I've never seen this place up close."

"I know what you mean," he said, shifting gears and turning the wheel sharply, entering a wide road marked Avenue D. "I came here many times as a boy with my father and once after I graduated from the academy on NIS business. And I've only seen a small part of it."

As they passed row after row of buildings, Kathryn read the neatly lettered signs secured to the fronts: Post Office, Motor Pool, Chapel, Officers' Club. "Jesus, it's a city," she said.

After stopping at the Nimitz Gate and showing his identification, Brent was waved through by a guard who explained, "We know about Miss Suzuki, sir. Lieutenant Kaiser informed us." There was a quick exchange of salutes, and Brent pointed the small vehicle out into a wide avenue marked Nimitz Highway.

"Pull over to the first phone booth, Brent. I've got to make a call."

"Why didn't you call at the base? Your aunt must think you're dead. You know Fujita kept radio silence. There's no way—"

"Ah," she said, stumbling into his sentence. "This isn't official business, and Fujita let me out of my cabin only an hour ago. He's kept me locked up since *Yonaga* was hit. And you're right, they must think I'm dead. I've got to phone my aunt, Ichikio Kume."

"I don't even know where we're going."

"North Shore. I told you."

"But how? I've never been there." He waved. "I've never left the southern part."

"Most people don't. But don't worry, I'll show you, Brent."

"You have the con," he said, wheeling into a gas station.

After two calls, Kathryn reentered the vehicle. "Okay," she said, gesturing. "Nimitz Highway east until you reach H-One and then left."

"That's north?"

"Right!"

"No, no, Kathryn, say, 'that is correct,' not 'right'. *Right* is a direction."

"You're not steering a carrier, ensign," she mocked.

"Right!"

"You mean 'correct', Brent." They both laughed.

"Your aunt's home?"

"No, she didn't answer."

"But I saw you talking," he said, puzzled.

Again, the girl stumbled. "Ah, yes . . . I phoned the manager of a condo we own at Turtle Bay . . .

166

checking on a unit we have. Sometimes it's rented. It's available in case I can't find my aunt."

Brent felt uneasy. The girl's voice was too high and edged with tension. She was concealing something.

"Aloha Stadium," she said, pointing to the left at the huge bowl.

"Aloha everything." He chuckled.

"I don't get it."

"One of the Admiral Fujita's jokes."

"You mean that old killing machine has a sense of humor?"

"He's not a killing machine," Brent retorted hotly. "He's a brilliant tactician and the finest seaman on earth."

"Well, that fine seaman has left a lot of corpses in his wake. And he saved a lot of Jewish asses."

"What's this thing you have with Jews? The Israelis have saved our butts in the Middle East. Without them, Kadafi would control the whole area." And then harshly, he said, "Sometimes you sound like an Arab!" Shifting down, he jerked the wheel to the left and entered H-One, a six-lane divided freeway jammed with vehicles. Cursing, pivoting his head, he shifted gears, whipping the wheel and careening into the number one lane. The horrified driver of a 1967 Chevrolet braked, squealing tires and honking furiously.

"Easy, Brent! Don't finish here what Matsuhara started in the South Atlantic."

"I guess you hate him, too."

"He only shot me out of the sky." And before Brent could answer, she added, "And I'm not an Arab."

"All right! All right," he said brusquely, moving to

167

a slower lane. "What now? You're the captain."

"And I don't hate Jews. Just oppressors."

"Jesus! What now?" he repeated. "I told you I've never been out of Honolulu — Waikiki. Give me some directions!"

She pointed ahead. "Up there in a few miles make a right onto Kamehameha Highway. We'll pass Pearl City first."

He nodded silently. His anger kept him mute for several miles, wondering about this strange girl and the promise of the overt sexual advances she had made so casually on *Yonaga* — advances that could never be consummated on the warship. Now she seemed hard. Preoccupied. Especially after the phone calls. Maybe she had a lover. Had arranged a tryst. But, abruptly, his reveries were broken as she reverted back to her soothing little-girl's voice.

"You begin to see the beauty of Oahu out here. Back there," she said, jerking a thumb over her shoulder, "you're just in another urban sprawl."

"Slum," Brent said, anger cooling. And then added laconically, "The Paradise of the Pacific."

She laughed, and he was encouraged by her changing mood. She pointed at a beautiful stand of vegetation as the freeway passed over a creek. "Ginger, plumeria, orchids, lehu, African tulip, banyan, mango, and God knows how many more." And then she said quickly, "Here it is — Kamehameha." Brent turned the wheel.

As they headed north through some of the most beautiful country Brent had ever seen, the girl's spirits seemed to soar with the beauty. And she knew it all, reeling off names like a horticulturist: "Pride of

India, kapok, camphor, hau, algaroba, avocado . . ."

"Okay," he said in surrender. "It's beautiful. I didn't know Oahu could be so spectacular."

"Wait till you see the north shore, Brent. This is just a preview."

"We're entering a large, flat plain."

"Right, pineapple country." She pointed to the west to a majestic humpbacked range. "The Waianae Mountains . . ."

"I know, Kathryn." He gestured to the east to more majestic, cloud-shrouded peaks. "And those are the Koolau Mountains."

Within minutes, the road entered a vast red plain of thousands upon thousands of acres of pineapples. "That's a lot of *mai tais*," he quipped.

She laughed. "I'm getting hungry, Brent."

"Me, too."

"There's a nice place in Haleiwa. We'll be there in twenty minutes."

Suddenly, they left the pineapples, passed vast stands of sugarcane, bumped over a bridge that bottlenecked the road down to two lanes. "Things are changing," he observed.

"For the better, Brent," she concurred warmly.

"I agree with that."

From the secluded corner booth of Haleiwa's luxurious Konopopo Inn, Brent could see a broad vista of wind-swept sea, laced by feathery white caps stretching across the entire northern horizon. Clouds—smoky streams of altostratus, broken cumulus, and mountainous thunderheads driven south by

169

cool breezes from the northeast were caught by the declining sun, colored infinite hues of indigo and royal purple, brilliantly highlighted by striking shades of pink, gold, and vermillion. The sea broke on a curving coastline of sparkling sand as white as an Alpine ski slope while great porous outcroppings of volcanic rock added deep browns and scarlets in streaming heaps and isolated splashes of color on the sand.

"Beautiful. Beautiful," Brent said softly. "I never knew Hawaii could be so beautiful." He looked across the table at Kathryn. In the dim light her flawless skin appeared translucent, full lips soft and warm.

"Here's to the north shore," she said, raising an exotic rum drink the house called the "Mauna Loa Rumbler." Brent answered with his own scotch and soda, locking eyes with her.

"We may never see each other again," she said in a barely audible voice, eyes downcast.

"That's not true. Before I drop you off, give me the address of your home office, your aunt's home, and any other place where I can reach you. Here," he said, reaching into his coat pocket, "is my card. You can always reach me by addressing your letter to NIS, Washington, D. C." He handed her the card, but she dropped it, grasping his big hand in her velvet-soft palms, held it tightly, and searched his eyes with hers. He felt his heartbeat quicken and the blood begin to pound in his temples. The erotic Kathryn was back.

"I'll miss you. God, I'll miss you, Brent. You kept me sane all those terrible weeks on the carrier. I lived for those mornings with you. And you saved me from that animal Konoye. I owe you — owe you. How can I ever repay you?"

"You are now, Kathryn. Just by being here."

"No." She leaned forward, tightened her grip, eyes hot and moist under curved black brows. "No! That's not enough. Not nearly—"

She was interrupted by the waitress, an exquisite Polynesian with skin of gold and tar-black hair swept back severely into a bun. Her perfect body rippled under a tight-fitting lavalava, colorful with printed orchids and hibiscus. "Your salads," she said, smiling and placing large bowls of fruit salad filled with slices of mangoes, guavas, papayas, kiwifruit, pineapple, coconut, and bright yellow apple bananas.

"Been at sea a long time, ensign?" The beauty smiled down. Kathryn stirred uneasily as Brent stared back. "Sailors always order our fruit salads when they've been on long voyages. It's something they miss."

"That's not all they miss," Kathryn snapped, "but I can take care of that!"

The sharp words brought Brent's eyes back to Kathryn and sent the waitress scurrying for the kitchen. The promise in the rebuke had fanned a new hunger deep within him, and suddenly the gourmet salad in front of him held no interest. "You meant that, Kathryn," he managed, reaching across the table and recapturing her hand.

The black eyes burned into his. "Let's get out of here, Brent. We can eat later."

The drive to Kathryn's condominium at Turtle Bay was interminable. The road was narrow—so narrow a driver played Russian roulette when passing. "A military road. That's all this is. An old military road."

171

"Pillboxes," Kathryn said, gesturing to the sharp barrier of hills crowding the road.

Stealing a glance, Brent glimpsed two low concrete structures sited high on successive ridges. "I'll be damned, left over from World War Two."

Kathryn became talkative, pointing and chattering like a tour guide. Waving at the beach, she said, "The Banzai Pipe Line, greatest surfing on earth." Then passing through a thickly forested area, she added. "Waimea State Park, magnificent falls inland." After a silence, a sudden animation followed, and a finger stabbed at a huge luxurious villa, high on a bluff. "Elvis Presley's old place." Then the beach again. "Sunset Beach — they get twenty-one foot waves here."

"How many feet to your condo?" Brent demanded impatiently.

Kathryn laughed. "We're almost there."

Brent grunted and gripped the wheel tighter, narrowing his eyes in the failing light.

"Here! Here," she cried excitedly as they approached a wide double drive that led to a vast area of magnificently landscaped grounds. "Turn left! Turn left!"

Entering the grounds, Brent saw a parklike setting with row after row of graceful buildings leading to the luxurious tower of the Hilton Hotel.

"Golf course, tennis courts, swimming — everything you could want." She paused. "Well, almost everything." Her laugh was high, shrill and nervous. "In here — turn right and park." She pointed to a paved, shrub-shrouded parking area in front of a two-story building.

Braking to a jarring halt against a low curb, Brent

172

fumbled with the door handle, cursing before he finally stepped onto the asphalt. As his foot came down on the pavement, a single overhead light came to life, spreading its weak rays into the gathering gloom. There were only two other cars in the lot.

"This way," she said, indicating a narrow path leading to a dark house. "The key is hidden."

Kathryn had insisted on a shower. "Jesus," she said as she vanished into a bathroom. "I've been getting my baths out of a basin. I can't wait." Then she had handed Brent a scotch and soda and closed the door. Soon the sounds of rushing water could be heard, and Brent stared around anxiously from a wide couch in the living room of the two-story luxury apartment. From where he sat, he could glimpse a modern kitchen through a door left open when Kathryn mixed the drinks, a stairway to the second floor, a short hall leading to the downstairs bath, and another door, which he assumed led to a bedroom. Behind closed drapes to his left, a sliding glass door opened onto a golf course. The place was furnished with modern, tastefully selected furniture.

"Coming! Coming!" her voice called from a small dressing room adjacent to the shower. Brent was not prepared for what he was about to see.

Kathryn, smiling, eyes dancing with fire as if backlighted, stepped into the room wearing a hula skirt and flimsy halter, which covered only a small part of the large mounds of her breasts, leaving white half-moons heaving with her fast breathing. Like purplish dagger points, her swollen nipples stabbed through the diaphanous cloth. Then, flicking strands of her skirt, she jarred Brent with a glimpse of a slender marble thigh. "Shredded ti leaves," she explained, watching the hunger spread across his darkening face. "I've gone native." She began to sway her hips, move her hands gracefully like two love birds courting but never touching each other. "The missionaries didn't like this," she said, moving about the room. "They thought it was sinful, suggestive." The trim hips moved with new vigor; thighs broke through the ti leaves, and Brent felt a pounding in his temples, a tightening in his throat. He drained his glass. She moved toward him and held out a hand.

Unsteadily, he came to his feet, took her hand and moved closer. "That's right, big man," she cooed. "Just do what comes naturally." He felt her hips against his groin, pelvis moving.

Looking down into the black eyes, Brent was incapable of thought, a surge of fiery sensation spreading from his groin, overwhelming his consciousness, contracting his chest and lungs, leaving him breathless. He could feel the prickling of the hair on the back of his neck like scurrying insects, and lava poured through his veins. "My God," he said, taking her into his arms. "My God, what are you trying to do to me?"

She came to him hungrily, mouth open, arms circling his neck. The warm, wet crush of her lips was a physical shock, and their tongues met like dueling reptiles, darting and slithering. His hands cupped her swollen breasts, moved down her hard back, gripped her sculpted buttocks, pushing and twisting in the timeless motion of the aroused woman. A hand found her panties. Pushed under them to the stiff hair. Searched and plunged into her.

"No! No!"

"Why? Why?" He was frantic.

"In there, darling," she gestured down the hall. "In there." He followed her into the bedroom.

Before the door had closed, the skirt was on the floor and the halter thrown into a corner. She remained standing, wearing only her panties as he undressed. And her eyes swept his thick neck, broad chest, and muscular arms as he cursed and grappled clumsily with fingers of clay. Finally, he stood before her, dressed only in white boxer shorts. Why he had in his anxiety and passion left this one garment on was beyond the comprehension of his numbed mind. Perhaps the lone remaining garment they both wore represented the ultimate barrier they had to cross together—ceremoniously. Was he drunk? Was he irrational? Insane with desire? Following the impulse as old as humanity, he gripped the elastic top of her panties and she his boxer shorts. Then they pulled down together.

"Oh," she murmured, looking down at his arousal. "You're magnificent." She led him to the bed.

Almost two hours later, Brent lay exhausted, the nude young woman curled against him like a kitten sleeping after gorging itself. He had never known such passion. She had been insatiable. The first time had been quick and violent, the banked fires of weeks of yearning exploding into a raging forest fire that brought them to quick completion. Then the lovemaking became more leisurely, and Brent walked a high plateau of sensation like a lotus eater climbing to the sun. But the sun burst and he sagged back, tired muscles going soft.

"Tired, Brent?"

"Happy. Very happy." She had kissed the pulse in his neck. Ran her fingers through the hair on his chest, finding a hairless diagonal scar running from shoulder to diaphragm. "Accident?" she asked.

"Sabbah. In an alley in Tokyo. I killed one, left the other with no face."

He felt her tremble. "Horrible. Horrible." Then the lips moved through the hair, and a hand came up the powerful muscles of his thigh, finally taking him in a warm palm.

The flickering flames found new fuel, and he turned to her, pushing her onto her back.

This time fatigue had captured them both, and after the last frantic thrusts he heard her shout, "My God," and relax suddenly, hands slipping across his sweat-covered back and dropping to the bed as if she had been suddenly drained of the last spark of life. Slipping his hands down her slender arms, he covered her limp hands with his, not moving, breathing into her ear and still feeling the hot liquid essence within her. He had never known such peace. He slept.

Her voice had awakened him. "Brent! Brent! Please—you're heavy." Shaking the blanket of sleep from his eyes, he had come to life, still locked between her legs. She moved. "Please, Brent. It's been wonderful but I want to go the girls' room!"

Rolling from her, he felt her leave the bed. Exhausted and very, very hungry, he drifted off again.

But before drugged sleep returned, he heard her moving about and then the clicks—the snapping sounds of a child's toy tin cricket repeated two or three times. Then blissful darkness.

He awoke with a start, Kathryn's body curled close to his. Reaching to a nightstand, he switched on a lamp. "Jesus. It's late," he said, looking at his watch. "I've got to get back to the ship!"

Shaking her head, she sat up. She gestured to a phone next to the lamp. "And I've got to find a phone—this one's disconnected until the tourist season."

They both dressed quickly.

Walking to the jeep in the dimly lighted parking lot, Brent felt light-headed not only from the frantic lovemaking, but from the lack of food. He realized he had not eaten in almost eleven hours.

Walking at his side, Kathryn was strangely silent, moving her head restlessly as if she were looking for someone. And, indeed, she was. Just as they reached the jeep, Brent's wide peripheral vision caught a movement to his left and slightly behind him. Whirling, he saw a man step from the bushes. Short and husky, he was a swarthy man with a sharp aquiline nose and the eyes of a hawk that sparked in the lamplight ominously.

Taking Kathryn's arm, Brent stopped in his tracks, hand on his holster. She pulled away, turned, spoke mockingly. "Meet my friend Mana Said Hijarah. You met his brother in a Tokyo alley a few months ago and removed his face with a bottle. He'd like to discuss

177

that matter with you." Her giggle had the dust of insanity on it. The man remained silent.

Looking at the low crouching figure in front of him, Brent felt he was in the midst of a nightmare, back in the condo in bed with Kathryn. But the warm moist breeze on his face and the pounding of his heart in his ears and hollow emptiness in his stomach, which seemed to be dropping out of his body, told him he was wrong. This was reality. She had set him up—classically, with no food and weakened by sex. He unsnapped the holster and gripped the butt of the Otsus.

Kathryn moved to Hijarah's side. "Hungry, Brent? Weak, Brent?" she taunted. "Of course I'm Sabbah. We had a five hundred pound egg in the Junkers for you. I hope I didn't drain you of your strength back there." She waved at the condo. "And, oh, by the way, while you were sleeping, I unloaded your pistol."

He pulled the automatic, ejected the magazine— empty. Worked the action—nothing. "Bitch! Bitch!"

Kathryn mocked. "And when you feel that cold, hard steel sliding into your guts, think of me, you Jew-loving, imperialist pig." She turned and moved toward a path through the bushes. "Too bad! You were a terrific piece of ass!" She vanished into the darkness, shouting a final taunt: "And remember, you fucked yourself to death."

There was a glint in the Arab's hand and he stepped closer, speaking in a soft, low voice like wind through dry reeds. "I have something for you, Yankee."

Brent knew Sabbah always killed with the knife. It was part of the tradition dating back centuries to Hasan ibn-al-Sabbah, the ruthless Persian killer called "the old man of the mountain." Brent also knew Hijarah was probably high on hashish, making him even more reckless and dangerous.

Brent needed a weapon and, leaning into the jeep, groped in the toolbox and gripped a pipe wrench. He stepped away from the vehicle, balancing himself on the balls of his feet, pistol in one hand, heavy wrench in the other, every sense acutely tuned. He could even hear the assassin's hard breathing as he stepped forward. Chest high, the man held a long knife, point circling slowly like an approaching cobra.

"Come for it, asshole. You were going to stick it in my back. Now let's see what you can do face-to-face," Brent hissed.

The man lunged. Brent leaped aside, hurling the pistol, which glanced off the Arab's forehead, leaving a long oozing cut.

"Infidel dog. I will make sausages of you—kosher sausages for your Jew friends." He giggled at his own wit as he wiped blood from his forehead with a sleeve.

Again the slow advance resumed, and Brent looked into the mad, pitiless eyes of a fierce bird of prey, talons extended for the kill. But fear eroded, washed away by tides of fiery rage rising from his guts. He stepped back, anger breaking from his lips in sarcasm. "There is no God but Allah, and Mohammed is his prophet," he goaded.

Howling, "Allah akbar!" and charging with short choppy steps, the man leaped, bringing the knife down in a hard arc. Jumping aside and swinging the steel wrench, Brent heard the sharp fluting sound like the flight of a great insect pass his head. Then something ripped his new blue coat, left shoulder to

179

right waist. The wrench impacted something hard but yielding. Howling with pain, Mana Said Hijarah gripped his left shoulder.

"Get ready for your *hegira*, you son-of-a-bitch! I'm going to send you all the way to Mecca!" Brent jeered, hoping to anger the man to recklessness.

Shrieking, the man took the bait. He charged, calling on Allah, face contorted. This time Brent did not step aside. Instead, he brought the wrench down, felt bone crack as the heavy wrench broke the Arab's wrist and sent the knife clattering.

Howling with pain, the man crashed into Brent, and they both stumbled against the Jeep, arms wrapped around each other like drunken lovers. The man punched with one hand. Bit Brent's cheek. Pain shot down the American's neck all the way to his fingertips. Fury drove him, and he attacked like a killer shark rising to the smell of blood. A blow to the Arab's back bowed him. Knocked the wind from his lungs. Brent twisted away. Found room for the wrench. With all his strength, he brought it down in a vicious arc, missing the man's skull but smashing into the shoulder again. Something popped like a branch pulled from a tree. The collarbone.

Moaning, the man staggered backward. Leaned against the hood of the jeep, eyes dull, arms at his sides, gasping, spittle running from his chin.

The strange primal urge to kill—to obliterate—took command of Brent again as it had in the alley in Tokyo so long ago, and with Konoye on the hangar deck.

He raised the pipe wrench high over his head and brought it down again. This time, it did not miss.

There was a sound like a dropped melon as the American drove the heavy tool into the Arab's skull. Hijarah dropped heavily, twisting like a maimed serpent and rolling to his back.

Straddling the assassin, Brent swung the heavy weapon again and again. It was the alley all over again. No fear. No pity. No conscious thought. Just the impulse to destroy.

The bone became soft and the face was no longer a face. Finally, arms aching, the ensign came erect, wrench clattering to the pavement. "Now, Sabbah prick," he growled, "you and your brother are twins."

Then he noticed the lights. Red and amber lights revolving as they approached.

Releasing Brent from the Laie police station had been a simple procedure. After Brent's phone call made under the watchful eye of the duty sergeant, Commander Matsuhara and four Arisaka armed seaman guards commandeered a truck and drove to the station. With his holster strap unsnapped, Matsuhara led the four guards into the small but brightly lighted police station. Instantly, the sergeant was convinced Brent was innocent of any wrongdoing and his story of the attack by an unknown assassin was accurate. The ensign was released to the custody of the commander.

"But," the sergeant warned in a tremulous voice, "a full investigation will be made and a report made to your commanding officer. You understand the Arab is gravely injured—has no face."

"No face! No face," the commander said thoughtfully, looking at Brent Ross. And then he said, looking back to the sergeant, "Admiral Fujita will be happy to study your report and cooperate fully in any further investigations." Matsuhara secured his holster.

"Of course, commander. I know Admiral Fujita must be an honorable man."

"A very honorable man, sergeant."

Now after a bad night's sleep that lasted until ten hundred hours and a change back into his number two green battle dress. Brent stood in front of Admiral Fujita's desk. Commander Matsuhara, Col. Irving Bernstein, and Adm. Mark Allen were seated. Brent felt as if he were on trial.

Admiral Fujita, the commanding officer of the greatest warship on earth, spoke. "Another fight, Ensign Ross?"

"I defended myself."

"You were careless?"

"Perhaps with the woman, admiral, but not the assassin."

"He was Sabbah?"

"Yes. He made a knife attack. Attempted to kill from behind."

Brent tried to read the old man's face. But the flat, implacable visage defied anaylsis. He knew there had been embarrassment over Konoye's incident on the *Arizona* Memorial. And now a member of the staff had been arrested and, perhaps, released by force; at least with Matushara's thinly veiled intimidation. But samurai exalted the good fight, hated Sabbah and wallowed in vengeance.

Matsuhara interrupted, quoting a passage from the

182

samurai's bible, the *Haga Kure:* "When confronted by an enemy be first to attack and if you are killed, die facing the enemy."

The words brought the Mediterranean back, and Brent remembered Fujita's use of them before sending him into battle.

The old Japanese appeared unmoved by the words. "I understand he has no face," he said. "The woman—were you with her?"

Brent felt his throat tighten. "Yes, sir."

Admiral Allen interrupted, stretching the truth slightly. "I ordered the ensign to drive Kathryn Suzuki to her aunt's home, admiral."

"I know."

"Admiral, the woman was Sabbah," Brent said anxiously.

"I know that, too, ensign. We spent the morning investigating her."

"The Junkers were armed," Brent went on. "They were trying to sneak in with their civilian markings. They probably did run into the raid by accident." Everyone nodded. "She lied about everything, admiral."

Fujita spoke. "She was safe in her lies as long as we were on the high seas. She knew we were on radio silence and would not reveal the presence of prisoners or survivors in any event. No, she was clever and she knew how to handle men." There was an awkward silence.

"She phoned," Brent continued. "Contacted her assassin friend, Mano Said Hijarah. But her aunt, Ichikio Kune, doesn't exist."

"Not true, Brent," Bernstein objected. "I inter-

183

viewed her this morning."

"I'll be damned. There is an aunt? She told the truth?"

The Israeli chuckled. "Not quite. There is an Aunt Kume who lives in Mililani, not Laie, and the condo does belong to the family." Brent felt heat fan his cheeks. "But Ichikio Kume hates Kathryn. Says her real name is Fukiko Hino. She was kicked out of USC in '74 for revolutionary activities — she only threw a bomb into a synagogue — went to France where she met 'Carlos the Jackel' — Ilich Ramirez Sanchez, the Al Capone of terrorists. She lived with him for years, helped gun down three policemen and an informer named Michel Morikarbal in Paris. Then they fled to Kadafi's bosom when things got hot and disappeared for a couple of years except for one brief incident when a woman answering Hino's description threw a grenade at Anwar Sadat's limousine."

"Jesus," Brent mumbled, "she's a lot older than she looks."

"Thirty-four. And as far as Israeli Intelligence knows, and we do have an extensive file on Fukiko Hino, she spent several years in Libya living with a variety of Marxists, dissidents, and terrorists, and training at Al Hamra where she became an expert with the Kalashnikov, Makarov, RPG-Seven bazooka, SAM-Seven, and plastiques. Then in 1980, she took part in the *Demetrios* incident — "

Brent interrupted with a confused stare. *"Demetrios?"*

"Sorry, ensign. A bunch of *fedayeen* loaded the Greek steamer *Demetrios* with dynamite and rockets, pointed her at the beach at Eilat on Rosh Hashanah when they knew it would be jammed with Israelis celebrating the new year, set the automatic pilot and went over the side. Fortunately, it was intercepted by the Israeli navy."

"She did that?" Brent mumbled in disbelief.

"She was second in command to her new lover, Muhammed Abu Kassem. We call him Nader."

"Then what?" Brent mumbled numbly.

"We have reports that over the past five years she has been seen as an instructor in Cuba, El Salvador, Chile, Lebanon, Greece. She also helped plan the attack on the marine barracks at the Beirut Airport."

Fujita interrupted. "Thank you, Colonel Bernstein." His eyes focused on Brent Ross. "She was clever—she fooled us all, ensign. And a wise man learns when in the classroom; does not go home with an empty head."

Matsuhara spoke to Brent. "You got some revenge for us back there in the parking lot. And we will remember Kathryn Suzuki—Hino, or whoever she was."

"True," Fujita agreed. And then, face grim, Adm. Hiroshi Fujita, samurai, spoke. The words brought a sigh of relief to Brent. "We Japanese exalt vengeance—the vengeance of the forty-seven ronin. We must remember one cannot demand that hate last forever. How can one answer for the moment when life is nothing but a succession of moments? No, only duty to the mikado can prevail immune to the onslaught of time—clean, pristine, and eternal. Let us put this unfortunate incident behind us and look to the future—a future dark with the clouds of new dangers." The black eyes flashed to the pilot. "But

185

Yoshi-san, if the opportunity presents itself . . ." The two Japanese smiled at each other.

Brent sighed, feeling a great weight of anxiety lifted from his shoulders. There was a knock at the door, and the admiral nodded at the ensign. Opening the door, Brent ushered in Capt. Wilfred Rhoads, followed by a yeoman carrying a large briefcase. "I'm sorry to interrupt. It's a financial matter," the dock master said, eyes moving around the room.

Fujita spoke. "These are members of my staff. We may discuss any matter you wish. Please be seated."

Seating himself, the captain removed a large bundle of documents from the briefcase. "The bill for repairs, dock use, ammunition, and fuel comes to twenty-two million, four hundred and fifty-six thousand, two hundred thirty-four dollars and twenty-one cents. And I understand we will be expected to fuel seven more escorts. Our PBYs have picked them up."

Mark Allen, with an elfin twinkle in his eyes, asked softly, "What's the twenty-one cents for, captain?"

"It's just part of the bill, admiral," Rhoads retorted heatedly.

"You'll be paid," Admiral Fujita said. "Just forward your bill to the National Parks Department, Tokyo."

"Not the Self-Defense Force?"

"No, captain. *Yonaga* violates Article Nine of Japan's constitution. We were declared a national monument," Fujita explained. "*Yonaga* is in the Register of National Parks. Send them the bill."

"Well, I'll be damned. I'll be damned." And then, tapping the briefcase, he said, "I brought itemized printouts for your inspection."

"Very well. I will have my executive officer study them. You may return to your duties, captain."

"And admiral," Rhoads said, rising. "Those escorts should be here tomorrow."

"I know. That would be in accordance with my orders."

Chapter Eleven

The next day, the plates had been welded, dock flooded, and *Yonaga* eased back to her moorings south of Ford Island, while from deep in the bowels of the ship the sounds of hammers and pneumatic tools could be heard as Commander Fukioka's crews shored damaged bulkheads and replaced reinforcing beams. Engine room three was secure.

"We can make flank speed again," Fujita had muttered from the bridge as he watched the ship's lines secured. At that moment, the first of seven sleek, gray-clad *Fletchers* rounded Hospital Point and made for the pier at the naval shipyard just south of *Yonaga*'s berth.

"Signal bridge," Fujita said to the talker. "Make the hoist. Escort captains report aboard flagship." He left the bridge.

Flag Plot was so crowded Brent Ross and Yoshi Matsuhara were forced to stand. From his position at the end of the table opposite Admiral Fujita, Capt. John Fite sat. A huge bearlike man with a shock of white hair over dark brows, he had close-set blue eyes that glowed with good humor, yet held a promise of steely resolve if provoked. Brent liked the man. He had shown courage in the fight with the *Brooklyn* and had even entered Tripoli Harbor at great risk in the fruitless attempt to save the hostages. He recognized Wright, Lucy, and Kozloff. But faces were missing, too: Ogren and Warner who died hideously with their crews, charging the *Brooklyn* on their gallant torpedo runs. And Jackson was gone, blown to bits when a broadside exploded his magazines.

Fujita opened the meeting. "Please introduce your new captains, Captain Fite."

Coming to his feet, the escort commander spoke in a deep, sonorous voice. "I handpicked each one," he said proudly. "They are all Annapolis graduates and experienced destroyer skippers." Then as Fite introduced them — Haber, White, Marshall, Fortino, Thompson, Philbin, Gilliland — each stood as their commander gave a brief biography. They had much in common: they all wore three stripes, had fought in three wars, and had personal reasons for fighting the Arabs. For most, it was the humiliation of seeing America placating sneering dictators; for others, it was hatred for Kadafi and terrorists. In fact, Gilliland's wife had been murdered in the hijacking of a TWA DC-10. All refused pay and all wore at least five decades on their faces. Nevertheless, there was strength and resolution in the eyes and the set of the jaws. These were fighters, Brent thought. Like Ogren and Warner.

Fujita spoke. "You are taking on fuel and provisions, Captain Fite?"

"Yes, sir."

"Condition of your command?"

"Each vessel is armed with five, five inch, thirty-eight main batteries, twenty millimeter and forty millimeter secondaries in their original configurations."

"Torpedoes?"

"Mark Fourteens."

Fujita tapped the table. Turned to Admiral Allen. "Our Mark-forty-eights?" The destroyer captains muttered excitedly.

"I've been told they'll be waiting at Yokosuka, sir," Allen said.

"Great! Now we'll have a real fish," Fite said.

"You know we were hit by the Russian five-three-three," Fujita said, restoring his dialogue with Fite.

"Yes, sir."

"From a Whiskey!"

"We know that too, sir. It's a vicious fish, and even an Arab can wire-guide it."

"We can defeat it with a new cruising formation." Hunching forward, the old admiral described an array of escorts divided into outer and inner screens. The outer screen would be led by the escort commander who would patrol 15 kilometers ahead of the carrier's bows. Then 3 more to port and 3 to starboard, 5 kilometers from the flagship and 3 kilometers between ships so that not only *Yonaga*'s bows and beams would be protected, but her stern as well. And the remaining five *Fletchers* would steam in the usual formation: one leading — ahead of *Yonaga* and astern of Fite — and the remaining four patrolling in pairs 500 meters from the carrier's sides. "And," Fujita concluded, "my executive officer will give you printouts of this formation." Captain Kawamota staggered to his feet and distributed the perforated sheets.

Eyes still fixed on Captain Fite, Fujita continued. "Number your ships from one to twelve and paint the number on your bows. You will remain number one, captain." Fite nodded. "Divide your command into divisions One, Two, Three, and Four."

"For torpedo attacks, sir?"

"Yes. And for command flexibility. Choose your own division leaders and inform me of your choices by sixteen hundred hours."

"Yes, sir."

"In the event of sonar contact, fire your main battery and fire a single red flare." Twelve heads nodded as one. "There will be strict radio silence unless the enemy is in sight. Then use bridge to bridge and FM ten. All communications will be by flashing light or flag hoist." Again the nods. The admiral's eyes roamed the expectant faces. "Your crews — you are satisfied with your crews?"

"Fine crew," Marshall volunteered. "American and Japanese."

"I've never seen such dedication and determination, sir," Gilliland added.

A rare smile stirred the wrinkles at the corners of Fujita's eyes and mouth into new patterns. "Good! Good! The tasks ahead will call for brave men, indeed." His eyes moved back to Fite. "We sortie tomorrow morning at ten hundred hours. My executive officer will give each of you a packet explaining codes, hoists — which will be standard international signals — our fighter frequency and calls, CAP, and search patterns." His eyes moved back to the new faces. "Questions?"

"ETA Tokyo, sir?" White said.

"Sometimes it is best that certain things remain in one man's head." There was a rumble of laughter. White nodded, smiling. Fujita looked at Brent and gestured to the door. Brent turned the knob and two attendants entered, each carrying trays, bottles, and cups. Soon each officer clutched a white cup filled with sake. Slowly, the old admiral stood. Then with a scraping of chairs, every man followed, holding his cup chest high.

Fujita smiled at John Fite. "Do you remember the toast we made before we pulled the tiger's teeth in his own jungle, captain?"

"Indeed, sir," Fite said, smiling back. "Here's to good hunting!"

"Hear! Hear!" sprinkled with "Banzai!" roared back. The cups were drained and quickly refilled.

"And in the Japanese tradition," Fujita said, setting his cup down. Every Japanese mirrored his movement and then clapped twice. Turning to the paulownia shrine, Fujita spoke reverently yet quickly like a chanting priest: "Oh, Izanagi and Izanami, whose love gave birth to our islands, earth, sea, mountains, woods, nature herself—the god of fire, the moon god, the sun goddess, Amaterasu, who ascended to the supreme place amongst all gods on the Plain of High Heaven, join with us and your descendant, Emperor Hirohito, in showing us the way to lay waste our enemy and remove the shadows of fear from the face of our nation."

Silently, the cups were drained.

Chapter Twelve

After clearing Pearl Harbor, the task force steamed due west at 24 knots. By noon, Oahu had faded astern and the vast blue wasteland of the Pacific stretched endlessly to every horizon. Although the repairs had been made hastily, there were no leaks, and the great warship drew her normal thirty-two foot draft as she bit through the mounting rollers that greeted her west of the land mass of the Hawaiian chain.

The sea watch had been set, and Brent was off duty; still he remained on the bridge standing next to Admiral Fujita long after the Special Sea Detail had been secured. A sense of exhilaration filled the ship. *Yonaga* was well, answered the helm with her usual quick obedience. And the throb of engines was strong like the heartbeat of a young athlete. High above, the CAP was at work again, circling the widely spread task force—Mark Allen had said Fujita's deployment over hundreds of square miles of ocean was like that of a modern battle group. The anti-submarine patrol had increased to eight bombers, all low on the water, new depth bombs armed with the most modern sonar homing and acoustic fuses visible under their wings and fuselages.

Two familiar faces were missing: Frank Dempster, who departed the day they entered Pearl Harbor, ostensibly for CIA headquarters, but Brent was convinced the man found the nearest bar first; and Kathryn Suzuki. Brent was grateful that not one man had mentioned the woman since the meeting in the admiral's cabin. He knew he should hate her, but found difficulty focusing that emotion on her. Perhaps once you've been to bed with a woman, feasted on her passion and spent your longings within her body, hatred for her became an impossibility, yet he knew if he ever saw her again he would kill her. He shuddered, thinking of the coldly diabolical act that he would perform without the help of hate, rage, and all of the other emotions nature so conveniently provides a man in danger, making violence not only easier but sometimes mandatory. He would kill her because she had tried to destroy *Yonaga*. He would kill her because she warred against his country. He would kill her because she had led him into a trap—a trap he should have sensed, but did not because his desire for her blinded him to warning signals that should have been obvious to a schoolboy. He had been a fool.

Fujita's voice shocked him. "The deep sea can be fathomed, but who knows the motives of men and women," the old sailor said, staring through his binoculars over *Yonaga*'s bow.

Brent was stunned. The old man seemed to climb inside his mind. "I would kill Kathryn Suzuki, if that's what you mean, admiral."

"Yes, ensign. We would all welcome that opportunity, indeed." Dropping his glasses, he looked up at Brent, mind flying to another topic with an abruptness that never failed to startle Brent. "Your navy has been lying about *Arizona*." Brent's inquisitive stare encouraged the old man. "You know I have done a little reading about the Greater East Asia War."

A little reading. The phrase brought a smile to Brent's lips. The admiral's library—the cabin of a long dead flag officer next to his own—was crammed with histories written by historians and combatants of all nations. It was so congested, younger members of the crew claimed it was easier to fight your way on board a Japanese railroad car than to shoulder your way into the admiral's library. Whenever free of the bridge and his frequent meetings, the old man pored over the books; sometimes smiling, sometimes pouting, and sometimes a tear would find its way down a ridged and creased cheek. He missed nothing and retained details like a computer.

"Your first histories reported an unlucky bomb dropped down her stack, exploding her boilers and setting off her forward magazines—virtually impossible."

"I know, admiral, but later the official histories claimed a bomb penetrated six decks and set off the magazines. In fact, the tour guides tell this version to the tourists."

"They are lying," the old man said matter-of-factly. "I studied her, ensign. I stood on our bow and studied her."

"You couldn't see much, sir."

"Enough, ensign. No Japanese ordnance did that."

"How can you be so sure?"

"I planned the attack."

The admiral had to be joking. But Brent knew the subtle wit *never* joked about naval matters. The young man pulled his thoughts together. Recalling a scrap of history, he said, "But I read a man named — ah, Kuroshima . . ."

"A sake-sodden *shiran-kao*. Sorry, ensign," he explained, "a drunken know-nothing. I did the planning with Kameto Kuroshima and Minoru Genda. Genda was the one who thought of using finned fourteen-inch AP shells for bombs. And I designed the wooden fins for the torpedoes. You know the harbor was only forty-two feet deep, and an aerial torpedo can plunge to a hundred feet when dropped."

"Kuroshima plotted the course, didn't he, admiral?"

"Any *shiran-kao* could do that. It was a simple great circle route across the North Pacific. There was no other choice for a surprise attack."

"Then what destroyed her?"

"Since none of our bombs could penetrate six armored decks and a torpedo inflicts only outer hull damage, *Arizona* must have had powder stored on one of her upper decks — number two or three by the looks of her."

"Why, admiral?"

"Carelessness. Or her gunnery officer was just lazy and, of course, your navy would be embarrassed by the truth."

"So after all these years, they are lying still?"

"I believe so, ensign." He gestured over the bow,

continuing in his unusually talkative mood and moving to a new topic. "We will stay on this heading until free of those snooping PBYs. Then we will come to two-seven-five, splitting the waters between Wake and Midway Islands. This heading will carry us northwest on our own great circle and well clear of Taongi, Bikini, Rongelap, and other atolls in the Marshall Islands."

"No problem there, admiral. The Marshalls are American."

"You conducted atomic bomb tests there."

Brent began to wonder about the new path taken by the canny mind. "At Bikini and Kwajalein."

"Uninhabitable?"

"Parts, true, admiral. The radiation levels are very high."

"High enough to kill, ensign?"

"Of course—over a period of time."

"Would Sabbah care?"

Brent stared with amazement. "You don't think a base could be established."

"The commanding officer of a warship must consider every contingency; especially when dealing with suicidal fanatics led by a madman." He tapped the windscreen. "Before the Greater East Asia War, we developed submarines with aircraft-carrying capabilities. I'm sure the Russians have built submarines capable of transporting planes. They could even be disassembled."

"Of course, admiral." Brent returned to his glasses.

The great carrier had just crossed the Tropic of

Cancer and the International Date Line, had Midway Island 300 miles off her starboard beam and Wake Island the same distance to port when Fujita called Brent Ross and Mark Allen to his cabin.

"Our pilots have disturbing reports about Kwajalein," Fujita began from his chair behind the desk. He waved Brent and Mark Allen to chairs facing him.

"Lord," Mark Allen said, seating himself. "Kwaj must be five to six hundred miles south of us."

"Our D3As and B5Ns have the range."

Brent remembered the admiral's concern about air bases in the Marshalls. "Then we've scouted Bikini, Rongelap, Wotje—"

"All of them," Fujita interrupted impatiently. "But at Kwajalein they discovered a very disturbing structure—a great circular concrete dome, perhaps three hundred meters in diameter, and the stern of a sunken warship jutting from the water."

"The ship is the *Prinz Eugen* . . ."

"The German cruiser?"

"Yes, admiral. She was used in atomic bomb tests. She didn't sink immediately, but was under tow and foundered in the anchorage."

"The circular dome? A base?"

"No. Radioactive waste disposal."

The old Japanese tapped the desk. "Don't you mean storage, Admiral Allen?"

"What do you mean?"

"You conducted tests on the islands."

"Yes."

"The soil, rocks, trees, junk from your tests will be radioactive for thousands of years."

"True."

200

"Then you cannot dispose. You can only store."

"You can look at it that way."

"What have you done to this planet, Admiral Allen?"

Sighing, Allen hunched forward. "There were military pressures immediately following the war. We had to show the Russians . . ."

"I saw Kwajalein many times during my naval career. Its anchorage was a crystal clear lagoon so vast a man could not see from one end to the other. There was a fringe of coconut trees growing from the narrow white islands surrounding the anchorage." He moved his eyes to the overhead and stared into the past while the Americans looked on silently. "I would dive off the ship, pull myself down the anchor chain, could see fish and plants on the bottom like they were in glass. I would swim to the island and crack coconuts open on the rocks." He moved his eyes back to Mark Allen. "And now it's an obscenity."

"You don't understand."

"Yes, I do understand, Admiral Allen. Women are raped by monsters, too."

A knock interrupted the hard silence. Obeying Fujita's gesture, Brent opened the door. A glowering Lieutenant Konoye in full flying kit entered the room. Brent moved to his chair, but did not seat himself. Instead he stood behind it while the pilot became a ramrod in front of the admiral's desk. "Another of the huge, circular structures at Bikini Atoll. I saw it myself and made several low level passes." With the terrible loss of bomber pilots in the recent fighting, fighter pilots often did double duty, flying reconnaissance and anti-submarine patrols in the bombers.

201

They despised the clumsy, slow airplanes. Konoye continued. "I saw no aircraft, just a few fishing boats far to the south, and there were no visible entrances or exits from the circular structure. That is why I maintained radio silence."

"A wise choice, lieutenant. They mount no threat to *Yonaga* but could inflict terrible casualties on mankind for generations to come."

"I do not understand, sir."

Quickly, the admiral explained the origins of the structures and their function.

"You did that?" Konoye said, shifting his fatigue-rimmed eyes to Brent Ross as if the young American was personally responsible.

Brent felt the usual tight spring begin to uncoil in his chest, and his senses sharpened. "Yes," he said, eyes flaring. "My nation tested in those waters. The tests were actually mandated by the Kremlin."

"I thought you did your testing over Hiroshima and Nagasaki. Certainly you had hundreds of thousands of guinea pigs there to work with — to incinerate — to vaporize."

"See here . . ." Mark Allen began.

"Please, sir." Brent said, waving the American admiral to silence. "This is directed at me." Angrily, the admiral sank back while Fujita again assumed the attitude of spectator at a sumo match. Brent knew the old man derived a kind of twisted pleasure in watching others thrash out differences. Now he was one of the performers. Nevertheless, there was no anxiety, just anger and resentment at the unjust attack. Konoye hated him virulently, not only as a symbol of the defeat of his nation and the burning of

202

his family, but for the degradation Brent had inflicted on him on the hangar deck as well. Such hatred could not pass or be dimmed by time. It must be settled, somehow. Perhaps here and now.

"We still have something to settle, ensign."

"No!" Allen shouted, half rising.

"Please, sir," Brent pleaded, "allow me — please." Sighing resignedly, Mark Allen sank back. Fujita continued his implacable stare. Perhaps in his wisdom he knew this thing must be resolved.

"I have nothing to prove to you or any other man, lieutenant."

The pilot stabbed a finger at the deck. "You denied me an honorable death that day on the hangar deck. Injured my karma. Denied me my place in the Yasakuni Shrine."

"No. I obeyed the order of Commander Matsuhara."

"Liar! No hand restrained you. You yielded to his voice!"

"My God. Of course I yielded to his voice. We're trained to obey. Our lives would have no meaning . . ."

He was halted by the staggering impact of a gloved hand that cracked across his cheek so quickly he had no time to duck or even roll with the blow. Instantly, lights flashed in his eyes, and a salty taste came to his mouth as the blow lacerated soft tissue against his teeth. Staggering backward and to the side, he went into his crouch and brought up his fists, the fires of rage welling and wiping out all restraint.

But Mark Allen was between them, pushing on their chests while Admiral Fujita shouted, "Enough!

Enough! Come to attention or you will both be in irons."

Turning slowly to the admiral, Nobutake Konoye asked, "We can settle this matter, admiral?"

"Yes, lieutenant. It must be settled for the good of *Yonaga*."

Rage dictated Brent's response. "Yes, I agree."

The baleful eyes moved to Brent. "With the admiral's permission, I will meet you in the Shrine of Infinite Salvation at fifteen hundred hours."

"A pleasure, lieutenant."

"You are dismissed," Fujita snapped.

"May I remain for a moment, sir?" Konoye requested as the Americans filed out.

After the door closed, the flyer made a request that shocked even Adm. Hiroshi Fujita.

Brent entered the Shrine of Infinite Salvation alone. Because there had been a flurry of signals from Tripoli, Benghazi, Cairo, Tel Aviv, Rome, London, Moscow, and Washington, Colonel Bernstein and Adm. Mark Allen had rushed to cryptography to assist panicky cryptologic technicians, promising to come to the shrine as soon as the mystery of the avalanche of signals was solved. "The British—the British—they must be in the Med," Allen had shouted as he ran down a passageway past Brent. "Sorry, Brent! Sorry!"

Now it was 1500 and the ensign had made his way alone from the elevator across the hangar deck. Scores of mechanics laid aside their tools the moment the elevator doors opened. They had been expecting him.

The shrine occupied a large part of the hangar deck forward on the starboard side, enclosed by unpainted plywood. Its interior was unlike any place of worship Brent had ever seen—he had been in it once before to claim his father's ashes for shipment to Arlington. There was no nave, no chairs, and no altar. Instead, there were shelves against the walls where the ashes of the dead were kept in white boxes covered with ideograms. Here and there, gold Buddhas and other icons were placed between the boxes. The deck was covered with a fine white cloth, and the center of the enclosure was dominated by a raised platform also covered with white cloth. There were over a hundred officers standing in rank behind Admiral Fujita, Capt. Masao Kawamoto, Commander Matsuhara, and Lieutenant Commander Atsumi. The entire assemblage was silent as were the mechanics who had been working on their aircraft. But all work ceased, and a heavy oppressive silence descended the moment the American officer walked to the shrine. The mechanics followed, but remained outside—a large silent group that listened mutely with the discipline of decades. There was a figure dressed in flowing white robes with wide hempen wings kneeling on the platform and obviously praying. His hair had been knotted at the back. It was Konoye.

Shocked, Brent stopped in his tracks.

Before Brent could speak, Konoye's strident voice boomed, filling the hangar deck. "Welcome, Yankee," he said, coming to his feet. "We shall soon see if you are a man."

"I'm here. What else do you want?"

205

"Courage! Resolution!"

"No man has ever sneered at my back."

"Spoken like a samurai," Konoye acknowledged. He extended a hand. "Come forward, ensign. Come forward." There was no threat in his voice. Brent stopped at the platform. "Up here." Carefully Brent mounted the platform, fists balled, muscles tight. He could feel the cords in his neck pulse, and he was suddenly thirsty.

"You denied me my destiny as a samurai."

"You've told me several times."

"My karma can be redeemed and my spirit can find its place with my ancestors."

"If we fight and you kill me, or if we fight and I kill you. You really can't lose either way."

"Or by *seppuku*."

The word shocked Brent. *Seppuku*. Americans mistakenly referred to ritualistic suicide with the knife as hara-kiri—Japanese slang for belly-slitting. Was this why the man wore the white robes? Certainly, in the samurai mind, *seppuku* was justified. Konoye had invoked Fujita's wrath when he ignored bombers and pursued fighters off the Cape Verde Islands. And the humiliation in his fight with Brent. It, too, would be cleansed in the bloody wash at the end of a knife. Finally, the incident on the *Arizona* Memorial. Konoye had been senior officer and took the blame. In Brent's mind, it was not justified, but he knew in the Japanese way of thinking, Konoye was responsible. He had heard Admiral Fujita reject earlier pleas by the flyer for suicide. But now *Yonaga* had found a new security. The British had Kadafi tied up in the Mediterranean, and the well-protected carrier seemed

206

free of threats in the Pacific. And even Fujita could not stand in the way of the code of Bushido indefinitely. After all, were they not all cut from the same cloth?

"You don't need me for this," the ensign said, beginning to turn.

"Yes, I do. You will be my *kaishaku*."

"Your what?"

"In your tradition, my second. You will be given a sword, and if I falter . . ."

"Oh, no. No way." He began to turn again, and again Konoye stopped him.

"You said no man has ever sneered at your back." Brent stared at the black eyes that burned like coals in dark hollows. "Yes! That's true. And—"

"And this would be more of a test of your courage than mine. I am a Japanese. I can accept this—no, rush to it joyfully—but you, you would be put to a supreme test."

Brent whirled to Admiral Fujita. "It is his right, and he does this only with my permission," the old admiral said. "In our way of thinking, you defeated the lieutenant and owe him his death. It would purify his karma if you were to act as his *kaishaku*. Keep in mind, the *kaishaku* is not expected to kill."

"But if he falters?"

"You know Lieutenant Konoye. Do you find any lack of strength there? Resolve? He will complete the disembowelment."

"Please, ensign. As an officer—as a man of honor, accept this duty," Konoye pleaded.

"But I must use the sword."

"At the end. When I am finished with my work.

207

And here . . ." He fingered the knot of hair at the nape of his neck. "I have given you an aiming point."

"Banzai! Banzai!" came from the crowd, and Brent felt the excitement begin to infect him. The man was beginning to make sense. He opened his mouth, but someone else spoke like an illusion brought on by a high fever. He could not believe his own words. "All right," he finally conceded. More "banzais."

The burning in Konoye's eyes became feverish, and he gripped the ensign's hand with a firmness born of desperation. He spoke with genuine gratitude. "Thank you, Ensign Ross. Thank you. You show the *Yamato damashii* of a samurai. Your duties are simple." He gestured at Captain Kawamoto who held a white silk cushion on which a knife at least ten inches long glinted. "After my prayers, you will hand me the *wakizashi*."

"The knife?"

"Yes. Then Captain Kawamoto will give you his sword. Stand at my right side until I am finished."

"How will I know?" Brent felt like a man who had slipped into the middle of a dream while awake. Had he really consented to do this? What had he become? Maybe they were all lunatics and he had joined the patients.

"I will start here." Konoye indicated the left side of his abdomen. "Bring the blade across horizontally to release 'the seat of the mind,' and then upward on the right side. When you see the blade come up, you must decapitate me with one clean stroke." His eyes moved to the young American's broad shoulders. "One reason I picked you was because of your great strength. Now, take the *wakizashi* from the captain

208

and I will pray."

While Konoye prostrated himself on the platform, head resting on a small silk-covered pillow, Brent turned and accepted the knife from the executive officer. Standing and holding the small cushion, Brent waited patiently in a silence that seemed to amplify the throb of engines and whine of blowers. Finally, the supplicant came to his knees, facing Admiral Fujita. He gestured to Brent to kneel before him. Brent complied.

Konoye spoke. "I and I alone was responsible for the tactics of the ready fighters off the Cape Verde Islands. I and I alone was responsible for the disgrace *Yonaga* found on the *Arizona* Memorial. Now I disembowel myself and implore all present to be my witnesses." He reached into his belt, removed a small piece of paper. "My death poem," he said to Brent softly. Then he read in a loud voice:

> To the river of life
> That has no end
> I consign my spirit
> For eternity.

"The knife," he said softly. Brent offered, Konoye accepted reverently. "Now the sword and stand to my side."

Standing, Brent took the curved killing blade from Kawamoto and was surprised by its weight. Like a hypnotized man, he stepped to the condemned man's side and gripped the leather-wrapped handle.

"Hold it over your right shoulder and remain in that position until I complete the ceremony or falter.

209

You understand?"

"Yes," Brent said in a disembodied voice, raising the blade.

Quickly, Konoye stripped his upper garment and placed the point of the knife to the left side of his abdomen. A hundred men held their breaths.

With agonizing slowness, the blade was pushed in, parting flesh and squirting blood that ran down the white robe to the platform. Then the pull to the right while gouts of blood and gray intestines poured and tumbled to the platform like live snakes. Watching Konoye's face, Brent saw muscles twitch, and the narrow eyes had become saucers. Perspiration beaded on his forehead and ran down his cheeks. But resolve did not dim. Finally, the knife turned up the right side; and suddenly the pitch forward, exposing the nape and the bull's-eye knot of hair.

"Now!" Fujita's voice commanded.

The command wiped out any hesitation, and the ensign swung with all his strength, bringing the great killing blade humming through a vicious half-circle that impacted the knot squarely. But Konoye had miscalculated with the knot. When he bent his neck forward, the knot crept upward to the base of the skull. There was the butcher-shop sound of steel cleaving bone and flesh, and Brent felt a jar as the blade thudded into solid bone instead of a cord of vertebrae. Nevertheless, with all his weight and strength behind the blade, the sword slashed through, severing the head just below the lower jaw, sending a spray of teeth, mucus, blood, and a half-severed tongue flying. The body, with still part of the lower jaw attached, pitched forward on the platform, sliced

210

jugulars hosing blood from the still beating heart. The severed head rolled across the platform like a kicked ball, leaving a trail of gore and stopping at the edge, eyes staring at Brent.

"Banzai! Banzai!" reverberated through the deck like cannon shots.

The young ensign turned and vomited.

Chapter Thirteen

"The British have been clobbered," Colonel Bernstein said from his seat in Flag Plot. "Radio Tripoli
has been gloating all afternoon. They claim all three
British carriers sunk, a frigate sunk, two frigates
damaged, and four destroyers damaged. Also, they
claim over a hundred British aircraft destroyed." He
looked at Fujita. "They walked into it," he anguished.
"They were hit by both carrier-based and land-based
aircraft."

Brent had had time only to return to his cabin and
change out of his bloodstained clothes into fresh
number two greens when the voice of Captain Kawamoto summoned the staff over the P.A. system. The
blood madness had cooled, congealing into revulsion
and disgust, and an acid bitter gorge still fouled his
mouth when he entered the conference room. Every
Japanese officer had greeted him with nods and faint
smiles. Matsuhara had even grabbed his hand and
muttered, "Well done." But Brent yearned to be alone
in his cabin with a bottle of Chivas Regal. He was
incapable of assembling his thoughts and making
precise judgments in what appeared to be a critical
meeting.

"Jesus," Allen said. "Thatcher should have known better. My God, they lost dozens of ships there to aircraft and subs during World War Two. *Barham, Ark Royal* . . ."

"What do you expect of a woman?" Fujita asked rhetorically. "She should be home minding her kitchen, not world affairs." He turned to Mark Allen. "We can only find grim prospects in this news."

"Sir," Commander Atsumi said with an angry edge to his voice. "Kadafi has called us yellow monkeys . . ." A shock rumbled through the Japanese.

"True, admiral," Allen confirmed. "He promises to 'train those little yellow monkeys.' "

"You think he will send his task force to the Far East? He has no bases, Admiral Allen."

"True," Allen agreed. "But we know he has at least ten tankers and a half-dozen replenishment vessels. And," he added, his face clouding over grimly, "we have reports that two pumping stations on the Alaska pipeline blew up this morning."

Fujita's agile mind responded. "Then that means if he can neutralize or destroy the Indonesian fields — you said Indonesia bolted OPEC — the Arab powers will be in a position to dictate — no, to enslave the world to the great god oil."

Allen nodded. "But as I pointed out, sir, and even without Alaskan oil, the US can manage with strict rationing, and the USSR is in the same boat. But most of the rest of the world . . ." He shrugged and turned his palms up in a helpless gesture.

Fujita moved to Bernstein. "You expect an Arab move against us?"

The Israeli fingered some documents, but kept his eyes on Admiral Fujita. "As an Israeli, I have grown accustomed to Arab attacks. After all, we've been at war since 1948." He glanced at a document, and Brent felt more trouble was on the way. The Israeli continued. "It's true the *jihad* dissolved, and the Ayatollah Khomeini and Saddam Hussein have pulled back Iranian and Iraqi forces, and they are busy killing each other again. But all of you know Kadafi has three aims: to kill all dissidents at home and abroad, become the leader of a united Arab front, and to destroy Japan and Israel."

"But Hosni Mubarak won't allow his troops to cross Egyptian soil—they drove the Libyans out, Irv," Allen said. "Israel's frontiers are secure. The Israeli Air Force is still the strongest in the Middle East."

"True, Mark. The IAF is the strongest air power in the region, and the Arabs' unbroken army front is gone, but now Kadafi's power is in his surface fleet."

"And he has won a great victory, and Arabs will flock to a leader who can win," Fujita observed.

"Throughout history this has been true," Bernstein acknowledged. "We know Kadafi has the unwavering support of Syrian president, Assad, King Hussein of Jordan, King Hassan of Morocco, the Druze leader, Walid Jumblatt of Lebanon, the smiling butcher, Yassir Arafat of the PLO and, of course, Russia and every old 'Nazi' supports him." He glanced at Mark Allen. "I would expect the Arabs to avoid a war of attrition with the IAF."

Fujita spoke. "As I have already suggested, a strike at the Indonesian oil fields to destroy Japan's only source of oil and then Israel."

215

Bernstein and Allen both nodded agreement. Allen said to Admiral Fujita, "I can assure you both NIS and Israeli Intelligence are keeping a close watch on the situation. We should have confirmation within days—even hours. And there are American submarines posted on all possible routes the Arabs would take."

Fujita rose slowly and moved to one of four charts attached to a bulkhead. "*Yonaga* is the greatest carrier on earth, and *Yonaga* defends a nation Kadafi despises. *Yonaga* stands in the way of Arab domination. I do not feel, gentlemen, that an attack on Indonesia and even our own home islands is an option—no, indeed, it is inevitable." He turned to the chart. "I would expect them to assemble here while keeping the Israeli Air Force occupied with the land-based aircraft." He moved a short pointer to indicate the eastern Mediterranean. "Transit the Suez Canal, the Red Sea into the Gulf of Aden and then steam southeast across the Indian Ocean." The pointer swept downward. "To the Straits of Malacca into the Java Sea and then turn northeast into the South China Sea and make for Japan." He dropped the pointer. "While steaming the Straits of Malacca and the Java Sea, oil installations on Sumatra and Borneo would be in easy range. In fact, surface ships could bombard the complexes at Balikpapan and Tawitawi. He can save his aircraft for us." His eyes flashed to Mark Allen. "But, Kadafi must have his tankers . . ."

"Verified, sir."

"Then let us assume they are coming," the old admiral said, returning to his chair. Everyone stared silently for a moment. Fujita broke it with words to

Kawamoto. "Increase speed to thirty knots!" The old executive officer picked up a phone. Fujita turned back to Bernstein. "Encrypt a message to the admiralty — ah, National Parks Headquarters via your Israeli Intelligence officer in Tokyo: 'Replacement aircraft and pilots as ordered in previous request to be assembled at Tokyo International . . .'" He glanced at his navigator.

"At thirty knots we'll make our landfall." He looked at a pad. "In forty hours."

Fujita returned to Bernstein. "'In forty hours. Our ETA, Yoksuka graving dock fourteen hundred hours on Friday.' Repeat the message, colonel."

The Israeli read the message back.

"Very well. This meeting is closed." Fujita turned to Brent Ross. "Please remain. You, too, Admiral Allen and Commander Matsuhara."

As the staff filed out of the room, Mark Allen and Yoshi Matsuhara eyed each other while Brent Ross stared at a bulkhead with dead eyes. The ensign expected to hear more of tactics and options but instead, Fujita's mind was elsewhere. The voice was soft, warm. "You did well today, Brent-san."

The use of the familiar *san* (honorable) stirred Brent out of his lethargy. "If you refer to what I did in the shrine . . ."

"Yes! You did a great service for Lieutenant Konoye."

Mark Allen spoke. "I heard, Brent. I couldn't believe —"

Matsuhara interrupted. "He performed magnificently. You would have been very proud, Admiral Allen."

217

"You released him from his agony, and his spirit has flown to the Yasakuni Shrine," Fujita said.

Brent opened his palms. Stared intently. "They're covered with blood, sir. I didn't feel this way after the Arabs. I fought them. I beat them. But with Konoye, I was an executioner."

"No! He was his own executioner as it should be with a samurai. Your blow was ceremonial."

"You should have used one of your own," Allen said bitterly.

"Brent-san is one of our own," Fujita retorted.

"You've put the young man under hideous pressure, Admiral Fujita."

"You cannot undertand us — cannot understand Bushido, can you? Most of you think Bushido is related to the martial arts." Obviously irritated, Mark Allen opened his mouth as if to speak. Fujita waved him to silence with a gesture of impatience like a professor piqued by a slow student. "It is not a fighting technique, but a way of life, as we would say, 'the way of the warrior.' " The voice rose. "It dictates everything from early rising, cleanliness, dress, courtesy in manner to strict obedience to one's superiors and, also, care and protection for those below. In the old days, a samurai served by honoring his ancestors, obeying his mother and father, by his loyalty to his daimyo, who, in turn, obeyed his shogun, who served the emperor. Today, the loyalty is still there — he obeys his superior officers who serve the emperor. A break in this chain, failure of any kind, leads to dishonor and death." He tapped his desk. "The good samurai perceives his own death and meets it joyously and quickly. As we would say, there is nothing else worth

218

recording."

"I know. I understand Bushido, admiral. I was raised in Japan; had my early schooling in Japan."

"Then you should understand. There were no options, and Ensign Ross was only an instrument in Nobutake Konoye's mind."

"But you should be aware," Allen pleaded. "Be aware of the western mind, admiral. My aide has had a shattering experience."

Brent came to life, saying in an anguished voice, "I couldn't even do a decent job of it!" He turned to Mark Allen, the blue of his eyes heightened by moisture. "I botched it. Hit him too high . . ." He choked on the rest of it.

"Not true. You hit your aiming point. The knot was my idea," Fujita said.

"My God! My God!"

Matsuhara spoke with deep concern. "And Brent, your great strength did it — you did it cleanly." Silence wrapped the room, covering everyone with its heavy blanket.

Brent spoke to the bulkhead. "It's not just that." His eyes found Matsuhara, flashing with new energy. "It's the woman, too. I was stupid — allowed her to fool me — endangered us all."

"Not true," Fujita said. "We were all misled — believed the lies. And you defeated the assassin."

"Yes," Matsuhara joined in. "That was superb. His face was a thing of beauty."

"Brent-san," Fujita said. "We Japanese have a long history of wise men, and we preserve their words. One of the wisest was Shotoku Taishi who lived over a thousand years ago. He said. 'While only few are

219

born wise, it is open to many through earnest endeavor to become wise.' You are gaining in wisdom; you are a valued aide, have the best eyes on the ship, know a dozen languages, and are an expert cryptographer. So learn from these experiences. Try to understand the ordeal to which Lieutenant Konoye subjected you and remember *Yonaga* needs you now more than ever."

Brent staightened his spine, felt a new spirit creep through his body.

"Yes, Brent," Allen sighed. "You must."

Fujita moved on impatiently. "And there is a tradition we observe. The man committing *seppuku* always bestows a gift on his *kaishaku*." He reached down behind his desk and brought up a samurai's sword, which was encased in a magnificent scabbard and inlaid with gold and silver ideograms. But the most startling decoration was a sixteen-petaled chrysanthemum done in diamonds, rubies, and other precious stones.

"My God," Allen breathed. "Beautiful."

Fujita caressed the sword with his eyes and spoke reverently. "With the sword, the samurai defends the honor of his realm, his emperor. If he fails, he defends his honor by taking responsibility and committing . . ." His eyes moved to Brent Ross, then to Mark Allen. "You invented the rifle, which is nothing but a killing machine. But this . . ." He raised the weapon. "Represents life. This is a samurai's soul," he finished.

Staring at the jeweled scabbard transfixed, Brent spoke in a deep voice. "It's Lieutenant Konoye's, isn't it?"

Lowering the sword to the desk, Fujita spoke slowly. "Yes. It is, or was, his. Lieutenant Konoye belonged to a distinguished samurai family." He gestured. "The sixteen-petaled chrysanthemum represents the emperor, and these ideograms are the names of some of the lieutenant's most renowned ancestors and identify places where they performed heroic deeds." He pointed at the scabbard. "Daishi Konoye who died using this sword defending the Shogun Tokugawa against ronin assassins in the shogun's own palace in Edo. And this name is Yoritomo Konoye who single-handedly dispatched a dozen garlic-eating Korean pirates, and here," he said, caressing an ideogram, "his grandfather Nurano, who was gravely wounded leading a charge against Russian positions at Port Arthur in 1904, and," he said in a trembling voice, "this represents his uncle, Enshu, who in 1912 committed *seppuku* as Emperor Meiji's funeral entourage passed his home." He sighed. "So you see, ensign, you have only helped preserve the destiny and tradition of a great family." He offered the sword. "It is yours."

Silently, the young American stood, accepting the blade.

"Please understand, ensign," Fujita said smiling, "although we have our Bushido, our rigorous codes of warfare, we are humanitarians first — value life and preserve it."

"Of course, admiral," Brent said, staring at the scabbard.

One of the phones in a jumble of communications equipment in a corner rang. Quickly, Matsuhara took a message and turned to the admiral. "One of the

221

prisoners is very ill, admiral," he said, cradling the phone. "He is in the sick bay."

Confusion crossed the old man's face. "Prisoners?"

"Yes," Mark Allen said. "The two Germans and the Arab."

The old eyes brightened with remembrance. "Oh, yes. Of course. Execute them!"

Chapter Fourteen

Steaming at 30 knots with a stiff following breeze, *Yonago*'s lookouts high in the foretop first made the landfall of Honshu's mountainous coastline in the morning. It was a blustery day with the wind quivering and breaking the surface into frothing whitecaps, sending spray streaking like long veils of bridal lace. Humped by the wind, a big following swell from the northeast as high as the hangar deck had taken the carrier squarely on the stern since the mid-watch began, driving her head-on into the troughs where her great bulbous battleship bow thundered into the back slopes of the swells, exploding curtains of blue water and spray, only to pitch back and rise again, readying herself for the onslaught of the next pursuing mountain of water. The sun was dimmed by a cover of clouds that rolled close to the sea, here and there the cover torn open by the jaws of the wind, revealing the sky's blue vault. And the gulls were there in huge flocks, wheeling and planing into the wind on widespread pinions.

Despite the weather, the airgroups took off at dawn for the flight to Tokyo International Airport where they would be put through maintenance checks and training flight with new pilots. But most important, CAP flights over *Yonaga* would be maintained from the airport. Matsuhara remained aboard and would split his time between the carrier and the airport.

High on the bridge with the admiral, Mark Allen, Commander Matsuhara, and the usual crew, Brent Ross felt comfortable in his heavy foul-weather jacket. Radar had been reporting bearings on islands. Aoga Shima, Hachijo Jima, Mikina Jima, and Muyake Jima had all been called out and cut in by Commander Atsumi on his charts. Then the mainland itself was traced by the glowing green fingers, and the excitement began to mount. Brent was gratified, too, that the prisoners had been spared beheading. But only after hard pleading by Bernstein, Allen, and himself. Grudgingly, Fujita had conceded that there might be some information remaining to be extracted, but refused to keep them on board. They would be turned over to the Self-Defense Force immediately upon docking at Yokosuka. "The charge will be piracy," the old man said. "And pirates are executed." Then he smiled.

Now through his binoculars the ensign saw the outlines of the two peninsulas, Isu Hanto and Boso Hanto and their tips flanking the channel—Iro Zako off the port bow and Nojima Zaki off the starboard bow. Hundreds of crewmen gathered on the flight deck and, crowding the foretop, began to cheer.

"Quartermaster," Atsumi said to a petty officer. "Bearings on Iro Zaki and Nojima Zaki." The rating complied. After a flurry of activity with his parallel ruler and drafting machine, the navigator turned to the admiral, saying, "Suggest course three-zero-five, sir."

"Very well." Fujita spoke to the talker. "Signal bridge make the hoist; course three-zero-five, speed sixteen, execute to follow." There were shouted commands on the signal bridge, and within minutes pennants and flags snapped in the wind like whips.

Brent swept his glasses over the escorts which had moved in closer to the flagship as land was approached. "All answer, sir."

"Very well," the admiral said, moving to the voice tube. "Execute!" Then to the tube: "Come right to three-zero-five, speed eighteen."

The vessel heeled and the pulsations under Brent's feet slowed. "Steady on three-zero-five, speed eighteen, ninety-six revolutions, sir." The voice came from the tube.

"Very well."

As the crew shouted and gesticulated like men returning to a long-deserted mistress, Brent stared through his glasses at this strange enigmatic land that seemed filled with paradoxes: guests removed shoes, not hats; wine was heated, fish eaten raw; bathers scrubbed themselves clean before entering a bath; mourners wore white; taxis had no door handles, but the doors sprang open on springs that could cripple the unwary; an emperor who was a man and would die was the direct descendant of an immortal god; two separate religions practiced with equal fervor—birth celebrated by Shinto rites, death by Buddhist; a language with no alphabet but more then two thousand Kanji characters, borrowed from the Chinese, with multiple meanings depending on context. And the Japanese were polite, ceremonial with their courtesy until you entered a railroad car with them—then they would casually break your arms and legs to beat you to the door. "Strange, he sighed to himself. "Strange." And it was here he had met Sarah—Capt. Sara Aranson, in Bernstein's office in the Israeli Embassy. He remembered the strong yet attractive face, which showed its thirty years with softly etched lines crinkling at the corners of her wide brown eyes, glowing with intelligence. Her skin was tanned and healthy, brown hair coiffed smartly about her ears. Despite a loose-fitting blouse and slacks, Brent recalled the excitement of her full-formed body, pointed breasts, and rounded hips showing through the khaki. They had had dinner together in a private little house at the *Kobayaki-ya* restaurant. They drank too much. Sarah drank far too much. Talked of the holocaust. Her grandparents, aunts, uncles, all roasted for the glory of the Third Reich. Of Israel's desperate plight with the *jihad* closing in on all of her borders. She spoke casually of her dead lover, Ari Weitzman, the pilot of a Mirage fighter, who, failing to elude a SAM missile, had been blown to pieces over the Bekaa Valley. And Brent had felt the attraction between them from the start—a fierce attraction that remained unconsummated until *Yonaga*'s attack on Kadafi and Brent's mission to Ben Gurion Airport to pick up a new encryption box. Then, thirty-six hours with Sarah in her Tel Aviv apartment seared the hot blood from his veins and left him drained, in a state of peace he had never known before—or since. He stirred uneasily as Kathryn's face awoke in the dark recesses. Pushing her back, he sighed and returned to Sarah.

Would he ever see her again? He knew she had served all over the world and expected an assignment in Washington. But the world was such a mess. So many obstacles.

He was shocked from his reverie by the talker's voice. "Radar reports many targets exiting the channel."

"Very well."

Refocusing his glasses, Brent spotted a small shape tossing in the waves and bearing down on *Yonaga*. Then another and another loomed.

"Many small craft," he said, turning to the admiral. "Off both bows, sir."

"Sacred Buddha — and in this wind." Shouted commands reduced the great warship's speed to 10 knots.

As *Yonaga* made her regal way into the sheltered waters of Sagami Nada and the main channel, the wind lessened, and hundreds of gaily decorated boats jammed with cheering thousands crowded close by, forcing further reductions in speed and very careful piloting.

"Fools. They are slowing us," Fujita growled with unconvincing pique.

"They're glad to see us, Allen said softly into Brent's ear. "They'll have gas for their Toyotas as long as *Yonaga*'s afloat." Brent smiled.

"Sir," the talker said, "bridge to bridge reports a message from the commander, Self-Defense Forces — proceed to dry dock, Yokosuka."

"Very well." The old Japanese turned to Mark Allen and Brent Ross. He was obviously in an exuberant mood. "COMSELDEFOR," he said with satirical relish.

The three men laughed.

That same afternoon *Yonaga* was carefully eased into the great graving dock at Yokosuka by four tugs that scurried about her like peasants fawning over a great *daimyo*. By nightfall, the dock had almost been pumped dry and the behemoth settled on her blocks, frames and plates groaning their displeasure with the unaccustomed stresses. Immediately, yard workmen began stripping the temporary plates from the torpedo holes. And Frank Dempster came aboard, carefully clutching the lifeline on the gangway as he weaved unsteadily toward the quarterdeck, and the meeting Admiral Fujita had already convened.

"They flew me in," the CIA man said, blowing a gust of alcoholic fumes into Brent Ross's face from his seat in Flag Plot. He drank from a cup of black coffee that Admiral Fujita had ordered for him and then ran his eyes over the staff before speaking to the admiral. "I have some news for you, sir." He patted a dossier. Then removed a single sheet. "The Arabs have broken Alpha Two and our Zebra codes. They've been reading your transmissions since you left the South Atlantic."

Bernstein said, "We have a new encryption box waiting for us at the Israeli Embassy."

"And at NIS," Mark Allen added.

"Good," Fujita said.

Sighing, Dempster selected another document. "We confirmed the defeat of the British. They lost all three carriers." There was an angry rumble. "And we have reports that an Arab battle group is, at this moment, gathering in the eastern Med. Kadafi is riding high on his victory, and he's getting new support. He has pledged to teach 'those maverick Indonesian dogs a lesson,' and 'to tame those little yellow monkeys.'" There was a roar of anger. The CIA man raised his hands. Silence. "Also, we have word that the Arabs have two big-gunned ships we thought had been bought for scrap." He picked up a sheet. "Two of the British carriers were sunk by aircraft, but the third was shelled and sunk by two cruisers. We have identified them as the Indian cruiser *Mysore*, formerly the British *Nigeria* of the *Fiji* class. Ten thousand tons, nine six inch Vickers in triple mounts, eight four inch secondary guns, and forty millimeter and twenty millimeter AA. She can do thirty-two knots and has a range of forty-five hundred miles at twenty knots. The other is the Pakistani *Johangir*, ex-HMS *Diadem* of the *Dido* class, seven thousand five hundred sixty tons, eight five-point-two-five inch guns, fourteen forty millimeter secondary, speed thirty knots, range four thousand miles at eighteen knots." He dropped the sheet. "We have word both vessels are manned by combined German, Russian, and Arab crews. Their shooting was fair to good. Both ships are well equipped with radar—Type two-seven-four fire control."

"Their aircraft?"

"Primarily the ME BF—one-oh-nine T and the JU-eighty-seven C, as we suspected. They're actually building the airframes in East Germany. They're using a variety of engines—the Jumo and Damlier Benz both being built also in East Germany."

Matsuhara spoke suddenly. "We can beat them. The Messerschmitt is too heavy."

Bernstein added, "There are reports of a few Grumann F-four-Fs."

Matsuhara snorted, "The flying sake bottle. Target practice."

"Pilots?" Fujita asked.

"German, Russian, and Arab — mostly Syrians and Libyans."

"Mercenaries — no match for the *Yamata domashii* of our samurai," Matsuhara added, eyes gleaming. "Banzai! Banzai!"

"Mr. Dempster," Fujita said, ignoring the shouts. "We expect the Arabs to attack, and I would expect this task force — or battle group as you like to call it — to be underway within five weeks; unless some of their heavy units received serious damage in the recent fighting."

"No, sir. Some bent plates from near misses on one *Colossus* and forty-two planes destroyed or damaged. Nothing they can't repair and replace in Tripoli and Benghazi."

"Very well, Mr. Dempster. But *Yonaga* will be ready for sea in four weeks. We will prepare a reception for them."

"Banzai! Banzai!" the Japanese shouted.

There was a knock, and a rating ushered in two Japanese officers in the dress blues of the Maritime Self-Defense Force. Brent recognized one, Capt. Takahashi Aogi, who had been the first representative of the Japanese government to board *Yonaga* when she first entered Tokyo Bay in December. Gray and

230

lined, he was a tall slender man with wide un-oriental eyes. Brent remembered the look of awe in his eyes when Aogi first saw Admiral Fujita. It was still there.

"Welcome," he said softly. "All of Japan is grateful."

"And the emperor?"

Aogi removed an envelope from an inner pocket of his tunic and handed it to the admiral, saying obsequiously, "From the emperor."

Quickly, Fujita tore open the envelope, placed steel-rimmed glasses on his nose and read.

"He is pleased! Pleased," he exulted, looking up. "I meet with him tomorrow!'

"Banzai! Banzai!"

Brent knew the importance of imperial approval. Holding the Self-Defense Force in contempt, disgusted with the hedonism rampant in Japan and appalled by the loss of ancient values and virtues, Fujita and *Yonaga* answered to no one except the emperor who, everyone knew, was a deity, descended in a direct line from the sun goddess Amaterasu-omikami.

Aogi turned to his companion, a short, roly-poly man of about fifty with shifty, nervous eyes and a frightened look turning down the corners of his mouth. "Admiral, Lt. Comdr. Yoshiki Kamakura. He is the dock master and is in charge of repairs and of filling your requisitions."

Admiral Fujita fired his first question at Lieutenant Commander Kamakuro. "From my bridge I saw a fence and one gate with a small guardhouse. Two guards were lounging there smoking and talking."

"I can assure you, sir. Security is adequate," the

231

lieutenant commander pleaded in a scratchy, breathless voice.

Fujita turned to Brent Ross. "Once, long ago, you told me of Arab attacks with car bombs on Americans in Lebanon."

Again the puzzling memory of an old man. Fujita had forgotten about his own prisoners, yet remembered a scrap of information casually mentioned during a bridge watch in Tokyo Bay, six months earlier. "Yes, sir," Brent answered. "In April of 1983, a car bomb killed over sixty people at the American Embassy in West Beirut. And then, maybe, six months later, another suicide bomber destroyed the American marine barracks at the Beirut Airport. Over two hundred American marines were killed."

"Two hundred forty-one, to be exact," Mark Allen added.

"Sabbah?" Fujita asked.

Colonel Irving Bernstein spoke. "Perhaps, admiral. Probably recruited from the Shiites."

"A Moslem sect," Fujita said. "I have heard of them but I had the impression the Druze and Sunni were the most powerful."

"Until recently," Bernstein responded. "Shiites are basically an impoverished, rural people. They split from the Sunni over doctrines concerning descendants of Muhammad and other basic tenets of Islam. They are ruthless, known for their brutal acts, and in the last few years have earned their reputation for suicidal attacks which, of course, can lead to eternal life in heaven. Shiites make the best recruits for Sabbah."

Fujita removed a richly bound volume from his

232

desk and began to read. Shocked, Brent realized the old man was reading a description of heaven from the *Koran*: " '. . . an oasis of paradise and silk attire, reclining therein upon couches. Naught shall they know of sun and bitter cold . . . its fruits shall hang down. Vessels of silver are brought round for them and goblets like flagons made of silver. There they are to drink of the cup . . .' " Brent moved his eyes down the table as the voice droned on. " ' . . . their rainmant will be of green silk and gold brocade. With silver bracelets they will be adorned and the Lord will give them drink of pure beverage . . . ' Need I read more?" Fujita asked. "My staff has experienced their suicidal attacks." He eyed Kamakura. "We will provide our own security."

"But, sir . . ."

Ignoring the dock master, the admiral turned to Capt. Masao Kawamoto. "Beginning now, the officer of the deck will maintain his watch at the head of the accommodation ladder as usual. But move the junior officer of the deck to the guardroom at the gate . . ." He paused thoughtfully. "No, the petty officer of the watch at the gate with four seaman guards." He fingered a single white whisker on his chin. "None of the ship's armament can depress enough to cover the gate, so place a Nambu in a sandbag, emplacement between the gate and the foot of the accommodation ladder." He turned to Kamakura. "Your fence is sturdy. If the Sabbah attempt an attack with a truck bomb, I would expect it to come through the gate. The Nambu would have a zero deflection shot."

"Sir," the chagrined dock master implored. "We have security—twenty men. There is no need for machine guns."

"Enough! You have heard of the battle cruiser *Amagi*. She was knocked from her blocks by an earthquake in this graving dock in 1923 and lost. A truck loaded with explosives could do the same to *Yonaga*." The old admiral turned to Kawamoto, gesturing to a phone. "Give the orders, captain."

Kawamoto put the instrument to his hear and spoke hurriedly. After cradling the phone, he spoke to the admiral. "Your orders are being carried out, sir."

Kamakura fidgeted with irritation. But Fujita's next statement brought shock to his face. "Half the ship's armament is to be manned and ready as ready guns." Kamakura released his breath like a high-pressure boiler.

"You have a CAP, sir."

Brent expected an explosion. It came. Bringing a tiny fist down on the oak, Fujita shouted. "Enough! This vessel's security is my concern. Take care of your dock, repair *Yonaga* and see to it my supplies are delivered."

Sinking back, the dock master spoke in a subdued voice. "I did not mean to presume, sir." He lifted a document with a trembling hand. "According to this report sent to me by your damage control officer," he said and nodded at Commander Fukioka, "you had flooding in fire rooms eleven and thirteen, number seven auxiliary five inch magazine, compartment five-seven-one, auxiliary engine room three, the starboard thrust block room and the center motor room. Bilge fuel tanks five, seven, nine, and eleven were ripped open, and," he said, looking up, "the bulkhead between number eleven fireroom and number three engine room has been damaged."

"That is correct."

"And I understand you expect this damage to be repaired and new plates welded over the holes in four weeks."

"The fate of Japan . . ." The admiral glanced at Bernstein. "Israel and perhaps what remains of the free world is in the balance."

The dock master placed open palms down hard and flat on a schematic of *Yonaga* taped to the table. He spoke in a hushed, barely audible voice. "You have been underway under combat conditions for three months."

"That is correct, commander."

"Then, admiral, you were not able to secure boilers for routine maintenance," the dockmaster noted.

"Correct."

"Then your boilers should be descaled, water tubes checked for deterioration and burn-through." Fujita nodded. Kamakura pressed on: "You must have condensed seven hundred thousand gallons of water a day."

"Sometimes nine hundred thousand."

Kamakura stabbed the schematic with a single finger. "Your evaporators should be descaled, the mineral deposits—"

"Commander," Fujita interrupted sharply. "I know these things. This is my ship."

"I know, sir. I would not challenge that." The man's professionalism pushed aside his trepidation. "But if you add the lack of routine maintenance to your torpedo damage, you are asking for the impossible. I need four months, not four weeks."

Fujita hunched forward, anger replaced by determination. "You can repair the hull? Clean the boilers and the evaporators?"

"Yes. It's the inboard compartments. They can't be completely restored."

"The watertight integrity can be—"

"Yes."

Fujita turned in his thin lips. "I need the five inch magazine, the rest of it is redundant."

"I can give you clean boilers, tubes, evaporators, the magazine, fuel tanks, and a hull as good as new." Everyone sighed and there were smiles.

"My escorts?"

"Members of my staff are inspecting them, admiral."

"Mark-forty-eight torpedoes? My destroyers were to be equipped with them."

"I know nothing of Mark-forty-eight torpedoes, sir."

Fujita turned to Mark Allen. "You said we would have them waiting for us!"

Allen swallowed hard. He glanced at Brent Ross. "According to our last transmission from NIS," he answered. Brent nodded.

"But they are not here?"

"I can contact the navy department through our attache at the embassy."

"Do it personally."

"Now?"

"Sunday. I want the entire staff on board for the next forty-eight hours." He turned to Bernstein. "You can pick up your new encryption box then." The Israeli nodded. Brent watched with fascination as the

236

nimble mind opened still another critical subject. "Captain Aogi, we lost sixty-three pilots, seventy-two aircrewmen, forty-two gunners, and eighty-three dead to the torpedoes."

Aogi smiled as he answered. "Admiral, we have thousands of pilots eager to fly for you. One hundred fifty are training at Tsuchuira and Tokyo International. Hundreds of gunners and seamen are awaiting your call at Sasebo."

"Aircraft? Engines?"

The smile turned to a broad grin. "Nakajima is building a new twelve hundred horsepower Sakae, and Mitsubishi's engineers have studied old museum A six M twos, and the plant has begun producing new airframes."

"We lost twenty-two Zeros."

"We have the planes and the pilots."

"Banzai! Banzai!"

Fujita raised his hands slowly in sudden languor. Silence. "Have them assemble at Tokyo International. My flight leader," he said and gestured at Matsuhara, "will select the replacements."

"Yes, sir."

Captain Kawamoto spoke. "Admiral, there is a question of liberty for the crew."

The old admiral sank back, obviously tiring. "I know. Last December only half chose to go ashore and most of them returned in disgust. That is not the Japan we left." He waved. "They do not revere the emperor as we do. They have their television sets and sit in front of them like vegetables. Music is gone, replaced by singers who screech and cannot read music or carry a melody and call themselves artists.

237

Cars race over broad acres of concrete fouling our air. Buildings of cold concrete soar hundreds of meters into the sky like ugly, sterile forests. This is not our Japan. This is not what we left."

"But Hirohito is our emperor, sir. And this is the land of our birth."

Fujita nodded slowly. "Yes, Masao-san. It has been over four decades for our men—four decades of serving this ship."

"They do not complain, sir."

"I know, Masao-san. The blood in our veins keep our bodies alive. So is it with our crew. We cannot bleed them."

"They would not desert us, sir."

"Of course. I know. Offer liberty to those who will take it—port and starboard sections. But readiness status two must be maintained."

"Yes, sir," Kawamoto said, scribbling a note on a yellow pad.

Fujita stared with weary eyes the length of the table at the intent faces. Then he swept a palm over his riven cheek as if fatigue were a mask he could strip from his face and discard. He spoke slowly. "Our tasks are heavy, and great perils face us. But if we remember the words of the great warrior Takeda Shinge, who emblazoned on his banners the virtues of the samurai, 'Fast as the wind; aggressive as fire; quiet as the forest; and immovable as the mountain,' nothing can stop us!"

"Banzai! Banzai!"

"Hear! Hear!"

The old man sat back, folded his hands on his chest and smiled. Then he said slowly to the overhead,

"Return to your duties, gentlemen."

Quietly the officers filed out, leaving the admiral sunk in his chair, half-closed eyes staring. There was a look of contentment on the old face. "Home," he said slowly, reaching into a drawer and removing a large folio. Sighing, he opened the album and stared at a faded, brown-tinted formal photograph of a slender dark man with a severe, haughty look in his eyes and a short beautiful woman whose lustrous skin and hair that glistened like lacquer glowed even from the ancient photograph. The man was in western garb, complete with waistcoat, cravat, and stickpin, while the woman wore an elegant traditional kimona with a white obi wrapped around her tiny waist and tabi on her feet. Two young boys, also in western dress, stood between them. One was perhaps nineteen, tall and slim as a reed with the distant look of the aesthete in his eyes. The other appeared to be about sixteen years of age, short, husky, with deep intelligence glowing from the wide-set eyes.

Turning the photograph over, Fujita saw the words, Seiko and Akemi Fujita and their sons Hachiro and Hiroshi greet the year 2561 — the twentieth century to the English. Banzai Emperor Meiji.

The Fujita home, where Hiroshi Fujita was born and grew to manhood, was located in Sekigahara, a suburb of Nagoya where Seiko Fujita held the post of professor of mathematics at Nagoya University. Typical of houses built in a society terrorized by frequent earthquakes, the home was of wood and paper construction, with cypress posts and cedar planks chosen with care, fitted with precision and polished with devotion. Compared to its neighbors, it was large and opulent, reflecting the past glory of a great samurai tradition that was broken but not destroyed in the bloody Meiji restoration of 1871 and the Saigo rebellion of 1877.

Hiroshi and Hachiro had their own rooms: Hiroshi's a large "three mat" room with an *amado* that slid open on the garden. In fact, all the rooms opened onto the huge grounds with no trace of a dividing line between house and nature. Here, man seemed to be part and parcel of nature. There were carefully crafted paths winding through irregularly shaped lawns, scattered rocks, a stream, bridge, shrubs, beds of azaleas, jasmine, gardenias, all framed by a blurred boundary of pines and maples, concealing neighboring houses in the distance and perfecting the harmony of the whole.

In their early years, the boys raced through this wonderland, shrieking and shouting with their playmates, playing samurai and clashing wooden sticks together in mock combat. Later as they grew bigger and stronger, the hard staves of kendo were substituted for the sticks, and the blows became swifter and painful despite protective pads. The boys loved archery, sumo, soccer, and a new game called *beisuboru* — an American game played with a ball and a bat that led to many arguments.

Oka-san would scold and sometimes chase noisy playmates away, but Akemi could never conceal the twinkle of affection and good humor that always sparkled in her eyes.

Each evening the entire family would remove personal dirt, which was considered an affront to the gods, by the purificatory rites of *yuami*. This was done by filling their large tub with hot water, washing themselves thoroughly and then entering the tub in an unalterable order: first Seiko, second Akemi, then Hachiro, and last Hiroshi. It was a time of purification for the soul as well as the body, and Seiko would discuss every samurai's duty to the emperor and speak of the heroic deeds of their many distinguished ancestors.

He would say wise things as all listened solemnly: "The whole world searches for God, but only Japan has the true God, Amaterasu, who shines in the sky and who gave birth to our imperial order. Japan is the divine country and the emperor is the key." He deplored the westernization of the country and had loved to quote his favorite poet, Tachibana:

> It is a pleasure
> When in these days of delight
> In all things foreign
> I come across a man who
> Does not forget our Empire.

The Fujita house had two altars, one honoring Buddha and the other dedicated to the mystic *kami* (gods) of Shinto. Through Shinto, the young Hiroshi learned to acknowledge the countless *kami* associated with the heavens and the natural wonders of the earth.

Shinto taught that the sun goddess Amaterasu's direct descendant, Emperor Jimmu, was the first mortal ruler of Japan and that Meiji was one hundred and twenty-second in this unbroken line. The family even made a pilgrimage to the shrine at Kumano-Nachi, built on a mountainside on the coast near Katsuura. At least 120 meters high, the Nachi Falls were enclosed by the temple, and the family climbed the stone steps notched into the hillside next to the roaring, spray-shrouded torrent. Finally, they stood tired and happy in the main hall under a great camphor tree. Here Hiroshi felt the spirit of the sun goddess as a palpable force that brought "Banzai Emperor Meiji," bursting from his lips. His mother clutched him while his father and brother stood proudly by. At that moment, Hiroshi knew he was destined to serve the emperor with his sword.

Buddhism was not neglected. Standing before the altar in the main room in their house, eyes focused on a small gold Buddha, which had been blessed at Naru's Todajii Temple where the fifty foot Daibutsu sat—the great Buddha of bronze and gold—the family listened daily as Seiko spoke of the four truths: Existence is suffering; suffering springs from desire; desire can be extinguished; purification can only be attained by following Buddha's path of truthfulness and chaste behavior.

Both boys were fine students, leading their classmates in every subject. On *Tango no sekku* (Boys' Day) the Fujitas flew the usual carp banner high above their house. However, theirs was larger, made of brighter-colored material and flew with more hauteur than any of their neighbors. Knowing the carp was the most exalted fish—a symbol of strength, determination, energy, and willpower—Hiroshi and Hachiro would stare upward, filled with pride.

The new century was not a year old when trouble began to brew with Russian designs on Manchuria and Korea. Immediately, Hachiro joined the army and Hiroshi watched enviously as his father presented his older brother with the family sword as Hachiro left for officer's training. Within a month, Hiroshi had joined the navy and been sent to Eta Jima where, if he could survive the rigorous regimen, he could earn a commission.

On February 10, 1904, war broke out with Russia. Within weeks, the army was heavily engaged in Korea and Manchuria with fighting especially bloody around Port Arthur and Mukden. The war was not six months old when Hachiro was killed leading a charge against the Russian works at Mukden. Hiroshi, now a newly commissioned ensign, would never forget the homecoming for his brother's ashes, contained in the usual white wooden box with ideograms describing his heroic death

The box was brought to his home by Hachiro's captain who handed it to his stony-faced father who stood next to Akemi, wide-eyed, jaw quivering. At least a hundred neighbors stood outside shouting, "Banzai!" Then Seiko, followed by the captain, his wife, son, and mourners walked around the house to the garden where a new shrine stood on a small plateau behind the stone bridge. The steps, lantern, and torii were all stone matching the polished granite of the shrine. On either side of the low entrance were the usual lion-dogs. However, these had been painted white. Reverently, Seiko Fujita laid his son's ashes to rest while a Buddhist monk chanted and rang his bell. Before Hiroshi turned away, he noticed that there was room for one more box in the shrine.

The war climaxed with a shattering victory over the Russian fleet in the Korean Straits. As control officer in the after turret of the battleship *Mikasa,* Hiroshi had had the thrill of finding the enemy in his range finder and of firing the great twelve inch guns himself. He killed hundreds. He was very proud.

After the war ended, Japan annexed Korea and gained concessions in Manchuria. Hiroshi Fujita was ecstatic. For the first time in history, an Asian nation had defeated a European power. But *oka-san* spent long hours in the garden, kneeling before the granite shrine. Refusing her food, she withered and became an old woman almost overnight. The black lustrous hair became streaked with silver, the face lined, bright eyes dimmed.

"Hachiro is with the gods. His spirit dwells in the Yasakuni Shrine! You should be happy," Seiko pleaded one day when Hiroshi was home on leave.

"Yes, I know, *Seiko-san,*" Akemi answered. "I am overjoyed." In 1907, her withered body — little more than a skeleton — was found stretched between the two lion-dogs. Her wide sightless eyes were on the white box and her clawlike hands were reaching for it.

After a suitable grieving period, Seiko returned to his post at the university, finding solace in the arms of a local geisha whom he established in a small house on the outskirts of Nagoya. Hiroshi returned to his own geisha, the Imperial Navy, where he rose quickly to full lieutenant. In 1912, a week after Emperor Meiji's death, Seiko Fujita died. Everyone said it was grief — the same shattering sense of loss that led to the *seppukus* of General Nogi and Col. Enshu Konoye on the day of the funeral. But there were snickers, too, when the rumors spread that the old man expired from exhaustion between the heaving loins of one of Nagoy's most famous geishas. Nevertheless, Hiroshi — with chants and chimes ringing in his ears — laid his father's ashes to rest next to his mother's in the Fujita crypt outside the great *Ohara no Sanzen-in* (Temple of the Absolute) near Kyoto. Then, returning to the empty family home, he stood outside the shrine, staring at the vacant shelf next to his brother's ashes for a long, silent moment. Then he prayed — an invocation to the gods to be worthy of that space.

In 1914, Japan declared war on Germany and by 1918, Japan had captured German bases in China and all of her island colonies in the Pacific. In 1919, Hiroshi was a full commander.

Because the Japanese navy was modeled after the British, her first four battleships built in England and English the official language of the fleet, hundreds of officers were sent to England and the United States for advanced studies. By the end of 1919, Commander Fujita was enrolled in the University of Southern California as an English major. Fast rising, bright and a bachelor, he was an ideal candidate. Observant and with an infallible memory, he soon learned to respect the latent power of this country and the great war-making potential dormant in her big, strapping young men. He took many trips on the Southern Pacific and Union Pacific Railroads, finding a land so vast it challenged the great emptiness of the plains of southern China. He even took a trip to Mexico and met his friend and classmate from Eta Jima, Isoroku Yamamoto, who had hitchhiked from

Harvard. Someday, Isoroku would command the combined fleet. They drank tequilla, made love to Mexican girls, and laughed boisterously over reminiscences. Both knew Japan could never defeat America.

After Hiroshi's return to Japan, his bachelorhood became a heavy burden. Forty years of age, time was growing short, and he was the last Fujita. He fell in love twice the same year. His first love was the airplane and he consummated the courtship at the Kasumigaura Air Training School when he earned his flyer's patch in June of 1924. Then, after his assignment as flight operations officer to the new carrier *Akagi*—a battle cruiser hybrid of the despised Washington Naval Conference—he met Akiko Minokama who lived in Hiroshima where the carrier was based.

Small, with skin of burnished ivory, she was a polished jewel of a woman whose eyes swam with love for him the very first moment they met. Although she was seventeen years his junior, her father, a well-to-do rice merchant, was delighted with the union. Hiroshi sold the family home in Nagoya and had the shrine and his brother's ashes moved to a lovely flower-strewn glade in the garden of a house he bought in Hiroshima. Then the couple settled down to an unusually blissful marriage in a country where unions were usually pledged by families at birth and consummated by near strangers just after puberty. Hiroshi never sought out a geisha as so many of his fellow officers did. Isoroku Yamamoto, happy in his marriage and madly in love with a geisha he kept in Kobe, often chided Hiroshi about his "abnormal attachment." But Hiroshi just smiled. His son Kazuo was born in 1926 and Makoto in 1928.

The next decade found Fujita and Yamamoto viewing the army's growing ambitions in China with alarm. In 1931, the Kwangtung Army, acting as a state within a state, seized Manchuria, and the puppet state of Manchuko was established. The Chinese dragon turned to lick its wounds but the Russian bear growled angrily, massing new divisions of armor and artillery along its 2100 mile border with Manchuko. Knowing a war against Chinese and Russian manpower was unwinnable, the navy advocated expansion to the south—a push to the Dutch East Indies and the priceless oil fields of Sumatra and Java.

By the middle of the decade, Fujita had risen to rear admiral and was a key officer on the staff of Isoroku Yamamoto, who was a full admiral. The navy watched uneasily as a variety of political figures who opposed the army's expansionistic ambitions in China were murdered.

"Government by assassination," Isoroku called the killings angrily.

Then in 1936, the *Kodo-ha* action took place when the First Infantry Division rebelled, left its Tokyo barracks and murdered some of the nation's most prominent politicians. By pure chance, the prime minister escaped. Although the mutiny was suppressed and the leaders executed, the army emerged with control of the cabinet, and the march toward war accelerated.

Fujita and Yamamoto not only feuded with the army, they found themselves at war with a clique of old admirals within the navy as well—the so-called battleship sailors who, in 1935, wangled funds from the government for four monstrous new battleships of

247

the *Yomato* class. The fight was hard and tenacious and finally, in the Japanese tradition of compromise, three hulls would become battleships while the fourth, hull number 274, would someday become known as *Yonaga*.

The war on the mainland enlarged, and the stalemate Fujita feared enveloped Japanese divisions as they confronted a quagmire of inexhaustible Chinese manpower. The Americans imposed sanctions, and Roosevelt and Hull shouted angry words. American pilots even flew against them in China. Then the naval general staff sent word to Yamamoto to draw up plans for an attack against American forces. Angrily, the admiral shouted, "This is insane! A war we cannot win!"

But Isoroku was a professional, and despite his knowledge of the power of the great slumbering giant far to the east, he called in Kameto Kurashima, Minoru Genda, and Hiroshi Fujita, who was just forming the air groups for the new carrier *Yonaga*, and the planning for Plan Z—the Pearl Harbor attack—began.

At the first meeting aboard the battleship *Nagato*, Yamamoto's flagship, Hiroshi had said to the admiral, "Eighteen months. We can have our way for eighteen months. Then the Yankees . . ."

"Nonsense," Kuroshima had argued, cigarette dangling from his lips. "The barbarians will have no chance."

In November of 1941, Adm. Hiroshi Fujita knelt before his brother's ashes for the last time and then stood rigidly while Akiko, Kazuo, and Makoto bowed, clapped and implored the gods to walk with husband and father. Then Hiroshi held Akiko briefly, clasped his son's hands, turned and left. Glancing back for a last look at the family, which had followed him to the roadside where an Imperial Navy staff car waited, he paused. His eyes lingered for a long moment on his eldest son, Kazuo, a giant for a Japanese at six feet and perhaps 170 pounds with short-cropped hair, steady eyes, and a square jaw. Decades later, long after Kazuo had been reduced to swirling radioactive dust, he would meet a blond American giant who would bring Kazuo back with his strength, courage, and intelligence.

The old man's head sagged and the tip of his chin dropped almost to his chest. The narrow eyes were closed and the breathing was slow and deep. Hirosho Fujita slept for the first time in twenty-seven hours.

Chapter Fifteen

The next day as junior officer of the watch, Brent Ross stood his duty at the position designated by the admiral, midway between the main gate and the foot of the accommodation ladder. Crossing the accommodation ladder, he had been halted by Bernstein's excited voice. "Brent! Brent!" the Israeli called from the quarterdeck. "Sarah Aranson's at the embassy. She brought the encryption box from Tel Aviv."

"Great! Great!" Brent enthused, smiling broadly.

"We'll see her tomorrow," Bernstein said. "We'll pick up the box together—admiral's orders."

"Aye, aye, sir," Brent said with mock servility. "I always obey orders." Both men laughed. Brent crossed the ladder with a new spring in his step and a glint in his eyes. "Sarah, Sarah. I'll see Sarah tomorrow," he sang to himself.

Then he was overwhelmed by the noise—the usual cacophony of shouts, bangs, and riveting pneumatic tools. Gawking silently, several groups of workmen and Maritime Defense Force guards stood on the dock and stared at the leviathan. Blocking up such a colossal mass seemed a violation of the laws of physics. Certainly it appeared that nothing could hold her, and the great steel behemoth should crash from the supports, crushing everything that stood in her way. And how could one man bend such a giant to his will—command her to run, to stop, to turn, to fight, and kill? Brent remembered Kathryn Suzuki's remark. "That's Fujita. That thing *is* Fujita." Yes. She had been right.

Walking from the foot of the ladder to the gate and guardhouse, he passed the sandbagged machine gun position manned by a single gunner wearing the badge of a water-tender. The man was struggling with a belt of ammunition, forcing it into the block of an air-cooled Type 92, 7-point 7 millimeter Nambu. The same model Brent had used to shoot down an Arab plane on his flight to Tel Aviv.

"Not that way," Brent said, stepping into the position and squatting down behind the tripod next to the water-tender.

"Water-tender second class, Hidari Jingoro," the man said, stopping his fumbling and saluting.

"This is a two-man mount," Brent said, answering the salute.

"Yes, sir." Jingoro gestured to a small building next to the gatehouse. "The gunner is Chief Gunner's Mate Shikibu Mushimaro. He's ill—ran to the head." He looked at the weapon helplessly. "I have spent a lifetime in the engine room, sir. I know nothing about these aircraft weapons. The chief said I would only have to feed the belt and he would teach me."

252

"Well, Water-tender Jingoro, Chief Mushimaro taught me, and there's not much to loading one of these," Brent said. "Now just hold that first brass-tag holder on the belt."

"Yes, sir."

"Now, I'll open this shutter." Brent lifted the shutter on the side of the breech. He turned to the water-tender. "Pass the tag loader through the block." The man followed instructions. "Watch carefully. I'll load one." He jerked back the crank handle on the opposite side and let the spring drive it home. "The gib at the top of the extractor has engaged the first round."

"I see, sir. But we are not finished," Jingoro observed. "We need a round in the firing chamber."

"Very good. You're right," Brent said, impressed by the usual intelligence found in members of *Yonaga*'s crew. He gripped the crank. "Now we'll load two," he said, pulling hard against the handle, the feed block clattering as the first round was driven smoothly into the breech. "Now she's loaded and cocked." He threw a small lever to the left until it pointed at a green dot. "And, it's on safe."

"I see, sir. Red to fire."

"Correct."

As Brent rose, the water-tender settled down behind the weapon. "Can you handle it?"

"Yes, ensign." Jingoro waved at a thin figure approaching. "And here comes Chief Mushimaro."

"Very well." As Brent walked toward the gatehouse, he answered the chief's salute and stopped the petty officer with a raised hand. "Are you well enough to stand your watch, Chief Mushimaro?"

"Yes, sir," the gunner's mate answered. "Just a little upset." He patted his stomach. "Too much rich food. None of us are accustomed to it, Ensign Ross."

Another exchange of salutes, and Brent continued his walk toward the gatehouse. Warehouses that had been loaded with stores and ammunition months in advance stretched to both sides. Swarms of fork lifts and electrically driven carts moved pallets laden with supplies directly up ramps into the ship's bowels or to cradles to be winched aboard. Only a few trucks were to be seen. One, a ten-wheel ragtop with *Yonaga* in both English and ideograms emblazoned on doors and canvas, almost ran Brent down as the young man made for the gate.

"Careful!" he shouted as the truck passed him headed for the gate.

"Sorry, sir," the driver shouted back contritely. Recognizing the huge bulk of Chief Aviation Mate Shimada behind the wheel, Brent waved back good-naturedly.

"He went out alone?" Brent said to the petty officer of the watch as he arrived at the gate.

"Yes, sir," the petty officer said. "He logged out to the administrative offices." He gestured to a tall, modern concrete building jutting up among the warehouses about a half mile to the west.

Brent looked around quickly; besides the petty officer who was armed with an Otsu automatic just like the one on his own hip, four Ariska-armed seamen guards stood alertly behind a white wooden barrier that was raised to permit traffic in and out. In the guardhouse, two young Defense Force ratings sat by communications equipment. To the left and right a

254

heavy, tall wire fence supported by closely placed steel posts gave added security. Satisfied, Brent turned and walked back toward the machine gun position where he could see Jingoro and Mushimaro squatting behind the weapon. The gun was pointed at his chest.

With an empty feeling in his stomach, he moved to his right to a stack of empty pallets. Carefully, he climbed up the stack, which was about six feet high, and sat down, facing the gate, legs dangling.

The hours passed. A rating brought him coffee and sweet rolls while the others received their tea, raw fish, and cucumbers. Often trucks passed, and Queen *Yonaga* continued to devour supplies as fast as the worker ants could stuff her. While yawning, Brent spotted Chief Shimada's ragtop returning. The good old chief. He had tried to stop that terrible fight with Konoye on the hangar deck. A competent man with a sweet nature. But even from this distance, the chief looked smaller. Brent straightened. Reached for his binoculars. Cursed. Of course he did not have them. Not for this watch. Then he saw the passenger. An alarm rang in his brain.

Leaping to the ground, he shouted at the machine gun crew, "Machine gun—the truck! The truck!"

Chief Mushimaro shouted. "Aye, aye, sir," and squinted through his sights, tightening his hand on the pistol grip.

Racing toward the gate, Brent saw the truck suddenly gain speed. He pulled the Otsu from its holster, screaming, "The truck!" It disappeared behind a building.

For a few horrifying moments, the guards seemed not to understand. Then the truck reappeared, charging the gate at at least fifty miles per hour. The passenger was on the running board holding a stubby weapon, the driver huddled low behind the windshield and the protective mass of the engine.

There was a shot, then another and another as the guards opened fire. Then flame leaped from the running board, and there was the sound of a machine gun firing so fast the shots sounded like a ripping sheet. The guards were swept from their feet by a blizzard of slugs, Arisakas clattering on the hard asphalt.

"Uzi! Uzi!" Brent shouted. The truck crashed through the barrier, crushing the screaming wounded, swerving and bringing half the gatehouse with it in a a hail of splinters, ripped timbers, and smashed siding.

Hurling himself to the ground, Brent turned, shouting, "Machine gun! Machine gun!" Then he squeezed off two quick rounds and saw a body tumble from the running board, and the Uzi stopped firing just as the Nambu chattered to life.

Hundreds of slugs slammed into the radiator, shattered the windshield and blew out both front tires. Jerked to the left by a shot-out steering gear, the truck crashed into a warehouse, slid along the side, shearing off big chunks of galvanized iron, lurched toward Brent, and then came to rest, steaming radiator buried in a small mountain of bagged rice not more than ten feet from the ensign. The driver's door flew open, and a slender figure tumbled to the asphalt.

Slowly, Brent came to his feet, Otsu in one hand, the palm of the other turned to the Nambu. "Cease fire! Cease fire! The truck must be loaded with

H. E."

He moved to the driver who lay on his face and moaned quietly into his own blood. Holding the Otsu on the man's head, the young American rolled the driver over with one foot. It was not a man. It was Kathryn Suzuki.

Blood welled from a chest wound, and a trickle ran from her mouth. "We almost did it," she gasped. "Twelve tons—we had twelve tons for *Yonaga.*"

Looking over his sights at the beautiful face now distorted with pain, Brent could hear screams coming from the crushed bodies at the gate, scattered like bloody green sacks. And there was a trail of destruction in the truck's wake, the shattered guardhouse littering the roadway, the bodies of the two young communications men covered with splintered lumber and broken furniture. Only the petty officer was on his feet, clutching his Otsu and walking toward Brent.

Brent felt a rage begin to swell and grow—an atavistic urge feeding on the hot blood of combat.

"Brent . . . " Kathryn was stopped by a cough that scattered congealing blood like small bits of chopped liver. "You were the best, Brent. I liked you, Brent. It's too bad . . . "

Brent could hear shouts behind him. Many booted feet running.

A tear ran through the blood on the woman's face. "Am I going to die, Brent?"

"Isn't that what you want?"

"No. Not here. Not like this. Not now, Brent. I was going to jump."

"I'm afraid you're dying, Kathryn."

The girl's brow wrinkled with confusion. "You

257

can't be sure—how can you be sure?"

"Because I'm going to pull this trigger."

"No!"

He pulled the trigger. The Otsu bucked, and a small blue hole appeared between the woman's eyes. There was the usual involuntary jerks of arms and legs, and Kathryn Suzuki lay still, eyes wide and fixed on Brent Ross. Holstering his pistol, he turned and walked away.

Rage crisscrossed Admiral Fujita's face with a new web of lines and the sallow flesh was actually tinged with crimson. "Two seaman guards dead, two wounded, two Self-Defense Force ratings dead, twelve tons of H.E. . . ." Brent Ross, Mark Allen, Irving Bernstein, Captain Kawamoto, Lieutenant Hironaka, Lieutenant Commander Atsumi, and the dockmaster Lieutenant Commander Kamakura all stared silently from their chairs as the admiral's anger washed over them like the waves of a tsunami.

The flaming eyes moved to Brent Ross, and the ancient sailor continued, the angry timbre of his voice softened by respect, crimson cheeks fading. "And it was Brent-san who saved us. His quick thinking."

"Thank you, sir," Brent answered. "Chief Mishimaro and Water-tender Jingoro stopped the truck with the Nambu."

"You were in command. If they had succeeded, you would be to blame. But you thought fast and fought well in the best tradition of Bushido."

Brent was happy with the compliment, but felt awkward in the stares of Bernstein and Allen. He managed to say, "Thank you, sir." And then quickly, added, "I would suggest more Nambus, barriers . . . "

"Sir," Kamakura said. "I am bringing in two hundred more men, machine guns. There's no need—"

"No need!" Fujita shrieked incredulously. "We could have lost the ship!"

The lieutenant commander bit his lip. "This facility is my responsibility."

Brent feared Fujita would suffer an apoplexy. "Enough! My staff will see to security. You repair my ship! Do you understand?"

Red-faced, the plump little man sank back. "Very well," he muttered through tight lips.

Glaring at the dock master, Fujita came to his feet. Pointing at a plan of the entire Yokosuka facility taped to the table, he said, "Our own men will stop all traffic here." The finger moved to a point a half mile from the ruined gatehouse. "We will establish eight machine gun posts here." He ran a finger in a line outside the fence. "Eight more here." The finger traced a line inside the fence and a few feet from the foot of the accommodation ladder. "We will park a maze of trucks here." He indicated the road leading to the gate. He stared at Kamakura. "Not a silk worm will get through."

"Sir," Captain Kawamoto said softly. "We've found Chief Shimada." Brent felt cold fingers on his spine. "We found him in a warehouse with his throat cut." There was a rumble of anger and horror.

"Which warehouse?" Kamakura asked suddenly.

"Number seven."

The man's pudgy fist struck the desk. "Damn! We lease half our warehouses. We leased that one to an oil company. Ah, I think it was Federated Oil —"

"Federated Oil Exploration Company?" Brent asked.

"Yes. That was it."

Fujita's eyes returned to the ensign. "That was Kathryn Suzuki's company?"

"Yes, admiral."

"She drove the truck."

"Yes, sir."

"And you killed her."

Brent bared his teeth in a mirthless smile. "Much too quickly, admiral." For a long moment the two men stared at each other.

"Yes," Fujita almost whispered. "She deserved something prolonged and inventive." The old man returned to the diagram. "Then they stored their explosives in your warehouse," he said, throwing a look as cold as thrown ice at a wincing Kamakura, "intercepted our truck, drove it in, killed our chief, loaded the truck, and made their attack." The man nodded. "But why no explosion? The truck hit the gatehouse, bounced off a warehouse, and rammed a pile of rice bags."

"I can answer that," Lieutenant Commander Atsumi said. As gunnery officer, Brent knew Atsumi had the responsibility to investigate the truck. In fact, Mushimaro, the most experienced rating in the gunnery department, had climbed into the vehicle only minutes after the truck crashed to a stop. "They had a clever arrangement, admiral. They must have anticipated impacts, crashing through barriers, and per-

260

haps even hitting traffic bumps at high speeds. Their H.E. is a new, highly unstable plastic, and without a doubt armed contact or impact fuses would have set it off when it crashed into the gatehouse. But they had rigged a contact fuse just behind the radiator."

"It should have gone off!"

"No, admiral. It was electrically activated, but the circuit was broken in the cab. The driver had to throw a switch on the dashboard to arm the bomb."

"Clever! Clever!"

"Sir," Adm. Mark Allen said suddenly in a tense, high voice. "I have been in touch with the Navy Department concerning our Mark-forty-eight torpedoes." Everyone stared expectantly. Brent anticipated more bad news. Allen provided it. Staring down at the table, the American admiral rifled through some papers and then looked up. "There will be no Mark-forty-eights!"

There were shouts of anger, and every Japanese officer came out of his chair.

"Please! Please!" Mark Allen said, raising his hand. "The Arabs will not have the Russian five-three-three, either." The Japanese returned to their chairs.

"I do not understand," Fujita hissed, controlling his voice with an effort.

"Bargaining chips, sir," the old American continued.

"We do not fire bargaining chips from our torpedo tubes."

"In a sense we do, admiral. Both the USSR and the US are concerned about arming the world's powers with their latest weapons. Both countries have been discussing these matters for years in talks in Geneva. From the beginning, there was an agreement to trade off their ADMG-three-zero, six-barrel, thirty millimeter AA mount for our Mark-fifteen Phalanx six-barrel, twenty millimeter AA system. And the Ruskies denied the Arabs their new seventy-six millimeter dual purpose gun as long as the US refuses to provide *Yonaga* and the Self-Defense Force its new Mark-forty-five, five inch, fifty-four caliber completely self-contained automatic system."

"And now the torpedoes?"

"Yes, admiral. We will retain our Mark-fourteens."

"And the Arabs, they used the five-three-three against us."

"Not any more, admiral. Only two subs were armed with them, and we sank them both. The Russians refuse to supply any more five-three-threes to the Arabs."

"What can we expect instead?"

Allen glanced at another sheet. "The Model sixteen which is similar to the best German World War Two fish with the same pattern running. It's twenty-one inches in diameter and twenty-three feet long and can make up to forty-seven knots on short runs. It has a two hundred fifty kilogram warhead cast into a shaped charge."

"Very well," Fujita said with surprising alacrity. "I do not like your automatic systems that duel each other unmanned while computers do the thinking instead of warriors. The best fire control is a samurai's eye to a web sight or adjusting the prisms of a range finder. At Tsushima I personally fired twelve inch shells into Russian battleships. How much of a thrill would a computer get out of that?" No one answered the rhetorical question. He continued. "There is death and pain to be found in warfare, true. But a man's highest honors, his greatest achievements are found on the battlefield. And death on the battlefield is the supreme glory." His eyes moved over the silent faces. "What glory is there to die in a hospital bed with tubes stuck in every orifice?" The men squirmed. "And how do computers die? Do they expire slowly, spilling their chips and transistors on the deck? Is there an electronic nirvana they seek?" The men snickered.

Bernstein spoke up for the first time. "But, sir, we need ours for enciphering and deciphering."

"I know, colonel."

"And, sir, with your permission, I will make a trip to the Israeli Embassy to pick up our new encryption box."

The old admiral drummed on the desk. "Take a dozen seaman guards."

"Sir," Kawamoto said. "With sixteen machine gun posts, two hundred guards, five hundred men repairing damaged compartments, and three hundred men on liberty—"

"Only three hundred?"

"Yes, admiral, the other four hundred men in the section refused to go ashore." Fujita smiled as Kawamoto continued. "We do not have the men to spare."

"Sir," Matsuhara spoke up. "I can serve as a guard for the colonel. Lt. Tetsu Takamura and NAP first class Kojima are doing an excellent job with the new pilots at Tokyo International and Kasumigaura."

"The CAP?"

"I am not scheduled to fly until Monday, sir."

"And you, Ensign Ross?"

"I would be happy to serve as a guard, admiral." Brent felt a wave of joy at the prospect of seeing Sarah Aranson. He managed an impassive look as Bernstein grinned at him.

Fujita glanced at the clock. "Gentlemen, the Son of Heaven expects me at sixteen hundred hours."

"Banzai! Banzai!"

"I must prepare myself." Hands on the table, the little old man pushed himself to his feet. "You may return to your duties."

Brent could feel the excitement when the admiral left *Yonaga*. Standing at attention between Mark Allen and Irving Bernstein in front of rank after rank of officers and men, all in dress blues, Brent watched with pride as the little admiral walked stiffly past. Only on one other occasion, when Admiral Fujita made his first call on Emperor Hirohito in December — the only time he had left the carrier in over forty years — had Brent seen the old man dressed so splendidly. He was resplendent in a single-breasted blue tunic with stand-up collar and slash pockets, hook and eye fastening in front. Rich black lace trimmed the top and front edge of the collar and the front and skirt of the tunic as well as the pockets. More heavy folds of lace layered on the cuffs designated admiral's rank. Shoulder straps with four cherry blossoms and four more on his gold-braided peaked cap also identified flag rank. His long sword hung from his left side and his tiny hand pushed down firmly, holding the blade at the precise parade-ground angle.

"Nineteen-forty," Allen whispered into Brent's ear. "That uniform is vintage 1940."

As the old man reached the top of the ladder, 200 booted heels snapped together as seaman guards in dress blues and flat hats presented arms. Then the tweet and squeal of boatswains' pipes, the low beat of ruffles as a pair of drummers working their sticks like distant thunder were joined by the flourishes of a quartet of trumpeters whose instruments blasted so close to Brent's ear that he winced.

Before stepping on the ladder, the admiral exchanged salutes with the officer on the deck and then saluted the colors. Then led by two guards and followed by two more, the old man walked slowly, stiffly, and unaided down the ladder to a waiting limousine with imperial logos on its sides.

As the limousine pulled away, it was led by a Tokyo police car and followed by another with red and amber lights flashing. But before the entourage had passed the demolished gatehouse, two Nambu armed jeeps with four of *Yonaga*'s guards in each joined the escort, one leading, the other following.

There was thunder in *Yonaga* as thousands of boots struck the deck, and the blue-clad side party's cheers were joined by those of hundreds of deckhands and AA gunners who stood by their weapons screaming, "Banzai Fujita!" and waving their helmets. As the limousine vanished into the maze of warehouses and buildings, the cheering faded and the ranks melted away.

"Brent," Mark Allen said. "I'd like to talk to you."

"Aye, aye, sir." The ensign followed the admiral to

his cabin.

Befitting his rank, the admiral's cabin was much larger than the ensign's with a large oak desk, wide bunk with a real American mattress instead of a flat pad, two upholstered chairs, two telephones, maps of the Pacific and Indian oceans on one bulkhead, the youthful Hirohito astride the usual white horse on another, and the inevitable maze of pipes and conduits overhead.

Sitting at his desk and toying with a pencil, Mark Allen opened the conversation. "I'll pick up our new encryption box Monday. You know we're having trouble breaking that new Arab cipher."

"Scimitar Three?" Brent said from his chair facing the desk.

Allen nodded. "Yes. It's a bitch."

"But, sir, the boys in Washington with the main frame, Micro-Vac fourteen hundred, can chew on it. Our CBC sixteens don't have the capacity."

"Tomorrow afternoon I have been given permission to access Micro-Vac fourteen hundred on our new optical-fiber data link from NIS Tokyo from thirteen hundred hours to eighteen hundred hours."

"You'll need me?"

"No, Brent. You'd better go with Bernstein. I have cryptographers Pierson and Herrera. They're competent. Any more cooks would get into each other's way." He drummed the pencil. "Pierson has some good ideas on coding sequences and coding keys he picked up from a scrap of plain text. Now we can throw out the garbage and use our old program for

Scimitar Two, load our variable sets—"

"But, sir, you only have five hours."

"I know. But, I believe fourteen hundred can chew through it in our allotted time." He dropped the pencil. Brent saw the clouded look on the older man's face and knew there was much more than ciphers troubling him. "Brent," he said, looking up. "Admiral Fujita is a strong influence—on all of us."

"Of course, sir. He's our commanding officer."

"With some of us, Brent, he commands more than just military obedience."

"What do you mean?"

Allen picked up the pencil and drummed the eraser. "He has an insidious way of penetrating and controlling men such I have never seen before. He's a Svengali—I've felt it. And you saw the men when he left. That was more than loyalty, more than love, that was allegiance to a deity."

"The same thing they feel for their emperor."

"Yes. They call it *kakutai*."

"My father talked about *kakutai*, admiral. The emperor and Japan are one. In fact, they believe the national essence is embodied in Hirohito. Correct?"

"That's right, Brent. But his men had added Fujita to the equation."

The young man nodded, mind moving ahead of the admiral's. "And you think I might be slipping into the same pattern of thinking."

The blunt statement surprised the admiral. He recovered quickly. "You beheaded a man."

"Yes."

"I blame myself. I should've been there."

"It would have made no difference."

267

"Why did you do it?"

"It was the right thing to do."

"Not in Kansas City."

"We're not in Kansas City, admiral."

"No. But we bring it with us."

Brent knuckled his forehead, felt perspiration. "I can't understand my actions. I can only tell you it seemed right at that moment."

"You were commanded?"

Brent punched the armrest. "Admiral! Please. This is not the third degree."

"Answer my question, ensign."

The younger man's breath exploded in a deep sigh. "Yes. By Admiral Fujita. But you must understand, Konoye pleaded, begged. He was convinced I was the only instrument that could restore his lost face—deliver the coup de grace as he believed I should have on the hangar deck."

"Yes, Brent, I can understand the samurai's mind. You know I grew up in Japan."

"Yes, sir."

"But I'm concerned about you, Brent. You can't take their values back home with you."

"I don't intend to, sir."

"You killed the woman."

"Yes."

"Did you feel sorry?"

"No."

"Elated?"

"No."

"That's what worries me."

Brent came erect. "Sir, I've killed two Sabbah, one with my hands, the other with a pistol. You weren't

268

concerned then."

"You were angry."

"And scared, admiral."

"But with Kathryn Suzuki you were nothing."

The young man threw his head back and stared at the pipes overhead. "I felt anger and fear when the truck charged us, admiral."

The eraser moved across the desktop making a large X. "But when you had her forehead in the sights of your Otsu—when you squeezed off that round, what did you feel?"

The big, clear blue eyes found the admiral, and the two men stared at each other in silence. Brent spoke slowly. "I felt the same emotion I feel when I step on a cockroach."

When Admiral Fujita returned aboard, the expected staff meeting did not materialize. Instead, Brent was resting on his bunk, hands clasped behind his head, wondering about his words with Admiral Allen and the strange, sometimes unbelievable things he had experienced in the past six months. He remembered long ago, when he had first met Admiral Fujita, the admiral had told him how highly he had respected his father, Ted "Trigger" Ross. How Trigger had taken his own life. Died like a samurai.

The young man stirred uneasily. Was there some of the samurai in all fighting men? Had Bushido merely codified the feelings and conduct of all men who put on uniforms and picked up arms? Certainly, if asked, he was sure Admiral Fujita would make that claim. Yet, the samurai was more dedicated, formal, and

269

sought death eagerly and joyously. He wasn't taught that at Annapolis.

He punched the thin mattress. But he had thought that way—fallen into their pattern that day in the Shrine of Infinite Salvation when Commander Ko-noye bared his neck. He remembered the moment of impact. Fujita's shouted command. And the feeling of joy—of completion, and of a great void in his life which had been suddenly filled. Filled with what?

Cursing, he sat up as Fujita's voice suddenly interrupted. Tinny on the speaker, it was still forceful.

"Men of *Yonaga*, I have met with the Son of Heaven, and he is pleased with *Yonaga*."

Because Fujita held the Maritime Self-Defense Force in contempt, considered the Diet a zoo peopled with monkeys, he answered only to the emperor. Only the emperor's orders would be obeyed. And obviously, the old admiral was pleased with what he had heard in the imperial chambers.

"His Majesty said only *Yonaga* stands between Japan and her enemies. He has ordered us to do the thing we all knew had to be done—meet our enemies who are gathering now on the other side of the world and destroy them. With the support of the gods from which the mikado has descended, we cannot fail." There was a pause and the voice began to sing. "Corpses drifting swollen . . . "

Brent recognized the old anthem *Kamigayo*—the song the crew sang before going into battle in the Mediterranean. And thousands of voices joined, pouring through the vents, the door, the steel itself. The ensign sang along with the few words and phrases he remembered.

" . . . in the sea depths, corpses rotting in the mountain grass. We shall die, we shall die for the emperor. We shall never look back." The speaker snapped off amongst the shouts of "banzai!" and the stomping of boots. Then silence.

Brent sank back, hands again behind his head. "Definitely not 'Anchors Aweigh,' " he said to himself. Then he laughed. And laughed. And for a long time he could not control it. When he finally stopped, he was weak and tears had streaked his cheeks. He rolled over, eyes wide open, staring at the bulkhead where Konoye's sword rested on a pair of brackets.

Chapter Sixteen

Because Col. Irving Bernstein had had five years of duty at the Israeli Embassy in Tokyo, he drove the unmarked Mitsubishi staff car to the capital from Yokosuka — a journey of about thirty miles — with Commander Matsuhara at his side and Ensign Ross in the back seat. All three men carried Otsus concealed in shoulder holsters.

"If Mitsubishi built this sedan as well as the A six M two, she should outmaneuver every car on the road," Matsuhara quipped in a rare display of humor.

Bernstein and Ross were pleased with the flyer's good spirits. Although Matsuhara had indicated his intention to split his time between *Yonaga* and Tokyo International Airport, he had managed to delay going ashore, sending his wingmen and most trusted fighter pilots, Tetsu Takamura and Hitoshi Kojima, to the airfield to coordinate training. Bomber training was under the old reliable bomber leader, Commander Yamabushi who had moved his staff to Kasumigaura.

"You will have enough pilots and machines?" Bernstein asked as he wheeled the small sedan through the outskirts of Kawasaki onto a broad expressway.

"Yes, Colonel, Takamura and Kojima report more volunteers and machines than we can handle."

"Are you receiving new aircraft?" Brent asked.

"A few, but most are old, rebuilt machines."

"Engines?"

"Nakajima has delivered a half-dozen new twelve hundred horse-power Sakaes."

"Is that all? What will you do for engines?"

"You must remember *Yonaga* was built to operate one hundred and fifty-three aircraft."

"I still can't believe it," Brent said.

Matsuhara smiled. "Every aircraft on the ship was designed to use the Nakajima Sakae twelve engine. Each aircraft was backed up with a spare engine."

"Then, originally, you had one hundred fifty-three spare engines in your holds."

"We still do."

"I don't get it."

"Whenever an engine was pulled, it was sent to the shops, rebuilt and placed in storage. We still have one hundred fifty-three Sakae twelves. We will have no problems with engines."

As the small car approached the great sprawl of Tokyo, Yoshi fell silent, staring wide-eyed at the tall concrete buildings, wide highways, and crowded commuter trains that flashed by at one hundred miles an hour speeds on a right-of-way that paralleled the road.

"Sacred Buddha, what has happened to Japan?" the flyer asked himself.

"It's been over forty years for you," Irving Bernstein remarked.

"Yes. That is correct." He looked around. "A

274

different world." He turned to the driver. "You will pass through the Shimbashi?"

"That's the district south of the palace, near the harbor?"

"Yes. My home was there. Just a kilometer from the Sumida River."

Brent felt uneasy, knowing the story of the great fire raid of 1945 and the devastation of the entire area surrounding the harbor. Even the imperial palace had flared up in the great fire storm.

"We'll stay on this road, the Aoyami-Dori, until we reach the Kasuga-Dori and then north to the Bunkyo-Ku District. The Israeli Embassy is just north of the Koishikawa Botanical Gardens," Bernstein said.

"There are so many cars!"

"Hah! There's a fuel shortage. You should've seen this place before the oil embargo — we'd be crawling."

Matsuhara waved to the north. "Those buildings — I saw New York City once when I was a boy. Now we have the same."

"True. Eleven million people live here, Commander. Those towers are the Keijo Plaza Hotel, Center Building, Nomena Building, the Sumitomo Building, and over there, the World Trade Center and more I don't remember."

The pilot pivoted his head to the south. "From my home I could see Fuji-san."

"Smog," Brent said bitterly. "It plagues the world. It would be much worse if we weren't short of oil."

The car climbed a low hill and swung to the left as Bernstein entered the Kasuga-Dori.

"I can see the harbor," Matsuhara shouted, pointing. "My home was over there!" His voice thickened.

"My wife Sumiko, sons Masahei and Hisaya—" Choking, he turned away from his companions. A tense silence gripped the men.

Brent broke it. "When I debriefed you, Yoshi, you said you had an uncle, aunt, and three cousins living in Beppu on Kyushu."

"Do not patronize me, ensign!"

"Commander," Brent retorted. "I'm not patronizing anyone. You do have roots. All of you have roots here. Why cut them off? We all regret the losses you have had to that war and to time itself. We had ours, too."

"I do not need the lecture, Brent." The voice was hoarse, but not hostile. Brent remembered their first meeting; the distilled hatred Matsuhara vented—a malevolence to match Konoye's. But, thankfully, as they put their lives on the line, side by side, the antagonism faded, replaced by mutual respect, and finally there had been flashes of genuine friendship. Brent knew the commander was exercising care in his choice of words.

"Perhaps," Matsuhara continued. "When we have finished with Kadafi, I will find them. And there are probably many more cousins and second cousins by now."

"Koishikawa Botanical Gardens," Bernstein sang out, wheeling the car off the thoroughfare onto a side road.

After skirting the eastern edge of the sylvan grounds, dense with blossoming cherry trees, elm, birch, and pine, interspersed with streams, ponds, and beds of gaily blooming flowers, Bernstein turned right on a narrow road and stopped in front of a low concrete, fortresslike building. "Here we are," he announced, reaching for the door handle. "Time to go to work."

But only thoughts of Sarah Aranson filled Brent's mind as he slammed the door. His step was light as he followed Bernstein and Matsuhara up the long walk.

She was more beautiful than he had remembered. Standing tall in the middle of the office, she was the soldier in her khaki shirt and tight slacks, but the irrepressible female was there, too: pointed breasts peaking under the shirt, rounded buttocks outlined by the tight-fitting pants. The well-formed nose and perfect flesh covering the high cheekbones were tanned, showing a conspiracy of new white lines at the corners of the brown eyes that were soft and warm as they probed Brent's with a long look that brought his heart to his throat. Nevertheless, the female did not exclude the soldier—a presence that was more than khaki. There was steel in her spine, and the hard metal glinted deep in her eyes—a look that told all: "I am a soldier! I am an equal!" Brent had believed the arcane male comraderie of war was a bond that could never be shared by a woman or anything female. But as Sarah had told him so long ago, she was an Israeli, and Israeli women learned to fight alongside their men.

"Shalom," she said, standing in front of her desk and extending her hand, ignoring Bernstein and Matsuhara in spite of military protocol.

"My name's Irv Bernstein," the colonel said in obvious good humor.

Dropping Brent's hand, she laughed. "Sorry, colonel," Sarah said, grasping both of his hands in hers. "Shalom."

Bernstein turned to Matsuhara, who stood awkwardly just inside the door. "This is Commander Yoshi Matsuhara, *Yonaga*'s fighter operations officer."

Again the warm smile and the extended hand. "Yes. We've met."

Matsuhara took the woman's hand, face slightly flushed. Then Brent realized that instant—that moment of contact—was the first time Matsuhara had touched a woman in over forty years. "You've met?" Brent asked. "When?"

"Last December after you played games with those Sabbah in the alley by the graving dock. They were sewing you back together in the sick bay, and the commander was kind enough to give me an impromptu tour of *Yonaga*." Again, the brilliant smile. "Please be seated." She gestured to a group of plump leather chairs clustered around a cluttered desk, which was placed to one side of barred french windows. Snipers, Brent thought. Always the chance.

Bernstein was all business. "You have the new encryption box, captain?"

"Yes," she said. But Brent's eyes were not on Sarah. Instead, he watched Yoshi, who stared at the woman with narrowed eyes, his face the visage of such intense concentration the man appeared hypnotized. Brent moved his eyes back to the lovely face as Sarah continued. "We have a few surprises for our Russian and Arab friends." Rising, she walked to the corner of the room to a small strongbox while Brent and Yoshi followed the tantalizing sway of trim hips. She's built for slacks, Brent thought to himself.

Bernstein spoke to Matsuhara, who tore his eyes from the woman with an effort as she leaned over the safe, revealing even more of her body, pants molded to her flesh. "You know the encryption box has its own software and automatically encrypts messages using predetermined key generating systems, priming keys, nulls . . . "

The Japanese nodded. "Yes, colonel. I have seen ours. We have two in the radio room hooked to computers."

"Right. One from NIS and the other from Israeli Intelligence. They do our enciphering electronically, but . . . " He shrugged.

"But, our enemy has broken our codes."

Sarah returned with a small leather carrying case complete with shoulder strap, chain, and handcuff. Seating herself and placing the case on the table she said, "We've seeded this little jewel with a new pseudo-random sequence." Brent grinned at the look of bafflement on Yoshi's face.

"They'll expect that, Sarah," the American said.

"Of course. But we've added a little kicker."

"You've screwed around with the frequency," Bernstein said.

"Yes, colonel. You remember." Patting the box, she looked at Brent. "We've added frequency agility."

"You mean random frequency hopping?"

"That's right, Brent." She turned to Bernstein, eyes glinting. There was pride in her voice. "We'll time hop, too, colonel."

Completely lost, Matsuhara remained silent.

279

"You have been busy," Bernstein laughed.

"Then it has the capacity to transmit in random bursts," Brent said.

"Correct. Some transmissions will be completed in milliseconds and at random intervals, and at the same time, it will change frequencies at random."

"That should slow them down," Bernstein said.

Matsuhara broke his silence. "But not stop them?"

Bernstein shook his head. "Eventually they'll break it."

At that moment the door opened and a short Japanese woman of about forty entered, carrying a tray with a silver service. Beautiful, she had features as delicate as the brush strokes of a Heian artist. Her eyes were the same shiny color of chipped black diamonds that shone from her hair. Slowly, they moved from Sarah to Bernstein, to Brent, finally lingering on Yoshi Matsuhara, who recoiled as if he felt a shock like a blow to the chest. Her skin had the silken texture of a Kyoto doll, well-formed body lithesome under her tailored business suit.

As the woman placed the tray of tea and cakes on the table, the men stood. "This is Kimio Urshazawa," Sarah said. Smiling, the beauty nodded briefly to each man and turned toward the door.

Eyes on Matsuhara's working jaw, Sarah added, "Please stay, Kimio." And then to the men she said, "Mrs. Urshazawa is my executive secretary and has top secret clearance."

"Oh, yes. I remember," Bernstein said. "We hired you last November. Good to see you again, Kimio."

"You, too, colonel," the woman said in a soft voice. Seating herself, the secretary crossed her legs, slender calves like marble through the hose.

"Mrs. Urshazawa's husband was the first mate on the *Mayeda Maru*."

The horror of the murder of the entire crew and all of the passengers of the hijacked liner by Kadafi's killers in Tripoli Harbor brought hard looks to the eyes of the men.

"I'm sorry," Brent said.

"Please, gentlemen," the woman said with downcast eyes. "Have some tea and cakes."

They talked casually of Tokyo, the new Japan, and the effects of the oil shortage, carefully avoiding *Mayeda Maru*. But time was short, and Brent glanced uneasily at his watch.

"We'd better return aboard soon or the admiral will send a platoon after us."

Bernstein laughed his agreement, but Matsuhara was lost in Kimio's eyes. Reluctantly, the men rose.

As Kimio, Bernstein, and Matsuhara filed through the door, Sarah locked the handcuff on Brent's wrist. Quickly he slid the strap attached to the carrying case over his shoulder. "Colonel Bernstein has the key," she said, holding his arm. She moved close, hand tightening.

Despite an aching hunger, he managed to say, "I know, Sarah."

"Brent," she said softly, lips close to his. "Tomorrow night?"

"Yes. Port section has liberty. I'm due."

"And Yoshi Matsuhara. Can you bring him? Kimio is a widow and . . . "

"I think he showed a slight interest," Brent answered.

They both laughed.

"I'll ask Kimio—phone tomorrow on our leased line." And then with her warm soft eyes searching his she said, "Shalom aleichem."

"Shalom aleichem to you, Sarah."

The next day, Brent sought out Commander Matsuhara on the hangar deck. Dressed in green fatigues splotched with oil and grease, the officer was lost in a gaggle of mechanics carefully lowering a huge 14-cylinder, 1200 horsepower Sakae into place on the front of his fighter. Yoshi smiled and waved at the American and returned to his work, supervising the connecting of fuel lines and the securing of engine mounts bolted to the fire wall. Impatiently, Brent waited for nearly a half hour.

"Now," Yoshi said, stepping back from the Zero. "Sorry you had to wait."

"Something private, Yoshi."

The pilot gestured upward to the gallery deck.

Matsuhara's cabin was as small and Spartan as Brent's. Following Yoshi's gesture, the ensign sank on the hard board of the cot while the pilot sat in a chair behind a small desk. "Staff meeting, Brent-san," he quipped.

Again the familiar *san*, first used by Fujita, jolted Brent, leaving a deep, warm feeling. "That's right, commander," he said, matching the pilot's warmth. "Some tactics for this evening."

"You have a campaign in mind?"

Brent laughed. "Not really, Yoshi." He tapped his forehead. "I'm going to see Sarah this evening and Sarah just called. Kimio Urshazawa would like to see you — have dinner with you — maybe we could all go to a Kabuki first."

The humor vanished and the pilot straightened. "I have not been in the company of a woman for over four decades, Brent."

"I know."

"We are warriors."

"Warriors have women — families. I'm not suggesting we take Sarah and Kimio with us when we tangle with Kadafi's task force," Brent chided.

"I would like to talk to a woman. You know, Brent, when you are on a ship, working with the same men year in and year out, conversation is exhausted."

"Yes. Even in the few months on *Yonaga*, I felt it."

"Think of what it has been like these past decades. We became silent, read all the books over and over, lost ourselves in our aircraft, simulated problems in our trainers, dismantled and reassembled engines and weapons endlessly, fought time with daily exercise."

Brent knew of the cloistered, monastic existence and hard workouts that kept *Yonaga*'s men amazingly youthful. Mark Allen said he had noticed this phenomenon in Soichi Yokoi when he emerged from the jungles of Guam, and Lt. Hiroo Onoda, who was debriefed by the admiral in 1975 after Onoda's thirty-year holdout on Lubang in the Philippines. Staring at the flyer's black hair, unlined face, and solid physique, Brent knew that Yoshi had probably entered flight training at age fifteen and had probably not yet reached his sixtieth birthday.

"I am almost sixty years of age," the flyer said as if Brent's mind was open to him. "Perhaps Mrs. Urshazawa is not interested . . . "

"Yoshi! She asked for you. She's interested in you."

The pilot smiled broadly like a lost traveler who had suddenly found an oasis in the Sahara. "I would be delighted to go, Brent-san."

Sitting cross-legged on a *zabuton* in a box under the balcony of the Kobayashi-za, one of Japan's oldest Kabuki theaters, Brent felt uncomfortable on the thin cushion, hoping the performance would begin. Legs cramping from the unaccustomed strain, he shifted his weight and leaned toward Sarah, who smiled, covering his hand with hers. She was dressed in a tight silk blouse that seemed to wrap itself around her breasts, and her short skirt was tight, long perfectly formed legs folded beneath her.

Kimio was spectacular, dressed in a traditional kimono of deep purple with embroidered camelias, orchids, and hibiscus wrapped about her tiny waist with a narrow yellow obi fringed with gold lace. Even her hair was done in traditional style with willow sprigs and gold pins scattered in the lustrous folds.

Yoshi sat next to her, eyes feasting with unabashed hunger. Staring at the curtains, Kimio leaned toward Brent. "Have you ever seen Kabuki?"

"No, Kimio."

"The Kobayashi-za is a very old theater—dates back to the early seventeenth century. It is said a Shinto priestess and her troupe danced Tokyo's first Kabuki performance here in about 1610."

284

"Women?" Brent interrupted. "I thought there were no women."

Kimio's smile flashed perfect white teeth, and she spoke a little louder as the conversations of the restless crowd grew in volume. "That's true," she agreed. "Women started Kabuki, but later too many performers were linked to prostitution and they were banned." She shrugged. "Now it's all male—but the female impersonations—*onnagata*—are very convincing."

"Indeed they are," Yoshi said suddenly. Sarah giggled.

Kimio continued. "The title of this evening's performance translates literally as *The Forty-seven Seek and Find.*"

"Vengeance," Brent said.

"Sacred to us, Brent," Yoshi said with sudden grimness. "Every schoolboy is—was taught this true tale of classic vengeance."

"Watch carefully as the story unfolds, Brent," Kimio said. "The actors talk very fast, and the action is highly stylized. But there is Lord Asano who will be tricked by a scoundrel named Kira into unsheathing his sword in the imperial palace, which was a capital crime. Asano commits *seppuku*, his lands will be confiscated, and his forty-seven samurai become ronin—vagabonds, drunks."

"Yes," Brent nodded. "Admiral Fujita told me this story. On the anniversary of Asano's death, the forty-seven rise—they have faked their debauching—and cut the villain Akisa to pieces."

"Then they commit *seppuku*," Yoshi said.

"Of course."

"That is the Japanese way, Brent."

A clack of hard wood *hyoshigi* silenced the audience and a stagehand cloaked in black hauled back the curtain revealing paper cherry trees along a river made of tin. A vast estate crowned by a fortress was on one side of the river while a large paper and paste rice field occupied the other. Musicians crouching at one side of the stage began to pluck the three strings of their samisens, and a narrator opened his chant.

Brent's eyes widened when the actors stormed onto the stage. Deathly white-skin makeup highlighted by eerie black lines of mascara, garish mouths concealed by heavy white paint and replaced by tiny painted lips of vermillion were grotesque. Ponderous costumes seemed ludicrous with wings, horns, and even spider legs radiating from one actor's neck. Speaking in squeaking falsettos, the *onnagata* were extraordinary in mimicking female mannerisms. In fact, one young *onnagata* who had the female lead was quite lovely. Gradually Brent realized a *Romeo and Juliet* subplot had been woven into the tale, but the two lovers were never allowed to meet, separated by a cardboard bridge over the tin river.

Fascinated, Brent watched as the action spilled over onto the *hanamishi* — auxiliary aisles that extended in the audience. The American could not restrain a chuckle as a butterfly fluttered across the stage, the insect dangling from a stick and line carried by a stagehand dressed and hooded in black. And then another black-garbed assistant worked a stuffed fox. Groups of these phantoms rushed out periodically to straighten the magnificent but cumbersome costumes. With the exception of the American, nobody noticed them.

Then came the denoument with the forty-seven dying in a heap in front of the fortress while the lovers disemboweled themselves at opposite ends of the bridge.

"Magnificent! Magnificent!" Yoshi said softly, rising and taking Kimio by the elbow.

"Yes," Kimio sighed, brushing a tear from her cheek. They stood for a moment, close to each other.

But Brent's attention was on Sarah, who rose to him almost from the force of his stare alone. "It's over, Brent," she said with no meaning whatsoever.

"I know," he answered just as inanely.

They moved toward the aisle.

The restaurant, Tanamma-Ro, was as classic as the theater. Fenced, it was an enclave of small huts built around a manicured garden. A little wizened man ushered the four diners into a large, private "four-mat" hut with a low table, *zabutons*, and walls hung with exquisite sepia ink drawings and classic calligraphy. A *tokonoma* was in an alcove — a piece of *haniwa* sculpture on a mahogany stand and a Heian vase with a cunning flower arrangement.

"You are the guest of honor, commander," Kimio said. "Please sit with your back to the *tokonoma*." After exchanging bows with the woman, Yoshi squatted slowly and ceremoniously in the place of honor. Quickly, the others settled on their *zabutons*.

"Now the surprise," Sarah said. The women giggled.

At that moment, the door opened and two women

287

entered with tiny, mincing steps. They were dressed in kimonos of rich silk, coifs exquisite with sprigs of cherry blossoms and jeweled combs. Their faces were painted starch white, lips carmine red, eyes dark as a cloud-covered night. One carried a samisen.

The leader and older of the pair spoke. "I am your geisha, Miyume." She glanced at the American with a coy, little-girl's smile. "Miyume means 'beautiful dream' and geisha means 'cultivated person.'"

"Sarah retained me and my *maiko*, Kojiku—my apprentice, 'Little Crysanthemum'—to serve and entertain you tonight." She nodded to Kojiku, who sat in a corner and began to pluck the three strings of the samisen and sing softly.

Quickly but with studied grace, the geisha distributed white porcelain cups and filled them with hot, spiced sake. "*Saka-zuki*," she said.

Brent correctly surmised that his ensign's uniform and youthful face had misled Miyume into believing he knew very little of the Japanese culture. He smiled to himself as he watched the lovely woman set aside the sake server and step back demurely, fan raised as she swayed into a delicate yet sensuous dance. He was watching an ancient, fading tradition designed to relax the daimyo, shogun, or business executive in an ambience stripped of wives and responsibilities. The geisha would ply her clients with sake, play games, tell jokes, dance, and sing. Although she did not market her body, she was ever alert for the wealthy patron, hoping to retire someday as the courtesan of a wealthy man. She was not accustomed to women and was not trained to entertain them. However, Sarah and Miyume were obviously friendly, and the geisha

288

seemed completely at ease.

The fan was dropped on a small table, the samisen went silent and the cups were refilled.

Yoshi raised his *saka-zuki*. "To the emperor." They all drank.

Brent offered his own. *"Yonaga."*

Again the cups were filled, and Brent felt a mild glow begin to spread. He knew Japanese did their serious drinking before eating, and it was late. He was very hungry and knew he would feel the effects of the hot, spiced wine quickly. "Ah, what the hell," he said under his breath. "Maybe in four more weeks . . ."

"You say something, Brent?" Sarah asked.

"Ah, no," the ensign answered. "Just that this sake is perfectly spiced." He looked down and miraculously the cup was filled again. He took another sip.

"Never let the cup be empty, never let it be full," Miyume said over his shoulder. He could feel her warm breath on his neck. Sarah threw a quick, hard glance.

Kimio held up her cup. "May Watatsumi-no-Mikoto smile on you." She glanced at Brent. "The sea god."

They all drank, but Matsuhara held his cup just inches from his lips. He quoted an old samurai maxim. " 'There is a time to live and a time to die' — may we sow the sea with our enemies' corpses."

"But return! Return!" Kimio pleaded, eyes moist.

"Of course," Brent injected. "We are led by the finest seaman and naval tactician alive." He glanced at Sarah, who appeared fuzzy and slightly out of focus like an aging Hollywood actress photographed through gauze. "Admiral Fujita," he managed to say,

289

without slurring his words. They all drank.

There was the flash of kimonos, and a black lacquered box was placed in front of each diner. Opening his, Brent found sliced eel layered on white rice.

"*Shimagawa*," Matsuhara enthused with delight. He picked up his *hashi* and attacked the food with relish. All the other diners except the American showed the same enthusiasm. Slowly, Brent raised his sticks and began to eat. Heavily spiced, the eel was pleasantly tasteful.

Then the dishes came one after another; "*Cha-wan-mushi*," Miyume announced, placing a superb steamed custard filled with vegetables and fish in front of Brent. And there were ginkgo nuts, baby crabs, cherries, peas, noodles, and more sake. He remembered vinegared carrots and *um-abo-shi*, pickled plum seeds, or was it pickled cucumbers? Anyway, it was pickled something.

"Better than *Ma-ku-do-na ru do*," Miyume quipped.

Kimio and Sarah roared with laughter while the men looked at each other in bewilderment. "McDonalds! McDonalds!" Sarah finally said.

Yoshi shook his head, but Brent laughed.

Finally the sated diners sat back while the geisha and her *maiko* cleared the table. Then Kojiku sat with her samisen on her lap, and Miyume moved to the center of the room. Her hips began to move provocatively, and the black eyes roamed from one man to another, never to a woman. "As my last offering," she said, still affecting the traditional little-girl personality of the geisha, "I would like to perform the Geisha

290

warutsu." She looked long and hard at Brent while Sarah squirmed. Miyume smiled. "The Geisha waltz, ensign." Brent smiled back.

Kojiku plucked and Miyume swayed, her voice, deep and rich and obviously trained, filled the room. Moving with tiny graceful steps, arms extended, hands continuously in motion like feathers in a breeze, she sang, eyes ignoring the women, challenging the men who stared back:

> You guide my footsteps in the dance
> And my hair is loosened in your
> Embrace. I catch a glimpse of a
> Fleeting love; I am perturbed
> And at the same time happy.

She bowed. Kojiku stood and bowed. Applauding, the guests stood and all four bowed.

Smiling, Miyume and her *maiko* left. As the geisha passed Brent, she brushed him, and he felt a small pressure against his tunic. Reaching into his pocket, he found a card. He smiled.

Kimio and Yoshi seated themselves and began to sip tea from a service that Miyume had left on the table. But Sarah stared at Brent. "I hate to tell you this, but something came over just as I left the office. It's been deciphered, but I would like to go over it — should go over it." She looked at Brent, pleading. "I'm sorry, Brent. You can stay. I'll catch a cab . . ."

"No, you won't," the ensign said. "We'll go together." He turned to Kimio and Yoshi. "Will you excuse me?"

"Of course," Yoshi said. Kimio nodded.

"We'll leave you the staff car."

"Fine," Yoshi said. "I think my driver's license has expired, but I can manage." Everyone laughed.

As Brent and Sarah stepped into the garden, Sarah asked softly as she clutched Brent's arm, "Do you think anyone believed me?"

"Absolutely no one!"

They were laughing as they entered the cab.

After Brent and Sarah left, the two Japanese sat quietly, sipping their tea. And then self-consciously, Yoshi said, "You wanted to show me 'Dai nippon' still lives, Kimio."

She smiled. "I think that was obvious, Yoshi." She tabled her cup. "As obvious as Sarah's excuse for leaving." He laughed. "Are you convinced, Yoshi-san?"

"No. But I was happy you tried."

"It has been a long time since you talked to a woman."

"I had a conversation in the ship's elevator last December with Sarah Aranson."

"That is all?"

"Yes. You know *Yonaga*'s history. You know we were isolated—trapped in Sano-wan for over forty years."

"Sarah told me you lost your family."

"Yes. My wife Sumiko and my sons Masahei and Hisaya in the great fire raid." He drummed the table. "I was filled with hate, thirsted for the revenge of the forty-seven ronin. Insulted Brent Ross."

"Ensign Brent Ross? But you are friends. Anyone

can see . . ."

"Not at first. I insulted him — goaded him. Chose him as the instrument of my revenge. But he stood up to me like a samurai, has fought like a samurai, with courage and intelligence. And Admiral Fujita depends on his eyes of the hawk and treats him . . ." He stopped in mid-sentence, struck by a new thought. "I met the admiral's family when I was first assigned to *Yonaga*. He had two sons. One, Makoto, was big, strong, intelligent —"

Kimio interrupted the thought. "They are all dead?"

Yoshi nodded. "Hiroshima."

The woman toyed with her cup. "Yoshi-san, you speak with an accent."

The commander laughed. "I was born in Los Angeles, California."

"A *nisei*," she said, wide-eyed.

"Yes. My father and mother were *doha*, loyal to the mikado."

"But you are an American citizen?"

"Of course. There were thousands of *nisei* who served the emperor."

"You still do."

"*Kokutau* still lives in *Yonaga*. Gives us a reason for existence."

"But the gods still reign. Amaterasu . . ."

"True. But this," he said and waved a hand, "is not our Japan."

She lowered her moist eyes. "I am sorry, Yoshi-san. We tried."

She reached across the table, covered his hand with hers. It was soft, warm, and there was electricity there

293

that fanned a long dormant heat to life. Suddenly distressed, he pulled his hand away. "Your family?" he asked huskily.

"You know my husband Kiyotaka was first mate on the *Mayeda Maru*."

"We tried to avenge him. Piled Libyan corpses—"

"Please!" she choked. "I do not want that."

"What do you want?"

"Peace. To see my children grow into a free, happy world with no hate."

He sighed. "Yes. Something mankind has wanted since time began but could never find. Instead, they give men like me endless work." He hunched forward. "You have children?"

"My son Sadamori is away at Fukuoka attending the university. My daughter Shimikiko is married, lives in Kobe and will make a grandmother of me in four months."

"You look so young."

"Thank you, Yoshi-san. I was born in 1944."

"Your parents?"

"My father flew for the emperor. He vanished over Saipan two days after I was born. My mother died a few years ago." She held his eyes riveted for a long moment. "You are the one with eternal youth. Your hair is black, skin clear, and you have the physique of a young man." She shook her head. "It seems a miracle."

He felt his face heat up. "Thank you, Kimio. It seems men who have existed as we; austere lives with no tobacco, alcohol, eating plain food, exercising daily, have maintained better health."

"Maintained better health? Why, you have defied

time!"

"No man defies time. Perhaps, a few can endure it with a little more grace."

"You said you did without many things, Yoshi-san."

"Yes." He blushed, knowing where her mind was.

"All those years with no women."

"Yes."

"You could have taken 'pleasure girls.' The army did. Everyone knows that."

"No. It was impossible. We were destined for the Pearl Harbor attack. We were the flagship of *Kido Butai*."

She shook her head. "You have not had a woman for over forty years."

Strangely, he was not shocked by her bold remark. He had this woman for himself, and she was interested in him. She devoured his words and challenged him at the same time. His response was as blunt as her appraisal. "Isolation does not corrupt a samurai. Men will not love men because they are deprived." He squirmed uneasily. "And the warrior will not abuse himself."

"Your release?"

"There was none until I could kill." Her eyes widened with shock, but he seemed to look beyond her into the past with eyes narrowing and the hint of a smile toying with the corners of his mouth. "First there were three over China, then a giant Russian jet when we broke loose from Sano-wan, autogiros at Pearl Harbor, an AGI, an observation plane. But the best was at Al Kararim and Misratah. We shot them out of the skies like slaughtered game. Then the Cape

Verde Islands; we killed them all . . ."

"Please, Yoshi-san. Please. This is your woman? War? Killing. Is that how it is with all men?"

"I cannot speak for all men."

"Then you have the wrong *kami*—you have been tricked."

"Tricked?"

"Yes! You have been bedding a whore. She took my father, my husband, so many . . ."

"The samurai does not think that way." He leaned forward. "The *Haga Kure* teaches, 'Having received the word of the emperor, one must act upon it.'" He pounded the table with a closed fist, eyes flashing. "What would you do with Kadafi? Let him have his way?"

"There are always Kadafis. History is filled with them."

"He killed your husband. Do you know how he died? How long it—"

"Please! Please, commander," she pleaded hoarsely. "Take me home." Covering her eyes with a palm, she turned away.

Yoshi felt despair. Leaning forward, he almost touched her hand. This woman, this exquisite woman, was lost to him. It had been so long, and he knew his words had been harsh—offensive. But he had to see her again.

"Do not think of me as a butcher, Kimio," he said, voice softened with deep concern.

"I do not—I know *Yonaga* has taken terrible losses, and you stand between us and those madmen, Yoshi-san."

"May I see you again, Kimio?"

"Oh yes. Yes. Come to my house on your next liberty. I will cook you a meal that would please the gods." She smiled and reached across the table.

"Tuesday — next Tuesday." This time he clutched her hands and held them for a long moment as his eyes locked with hers. His heart pounded in his chest and the deep, strange warmth spread.

Sarah's apartment was on the ninth floor of a new building in the Shinjuku-hu district. Completely modern and westernized, it boasted a large living room, dinette, kitchen, bath, bedroom, and a huge window overlooking the city. From a luxurious sofa in the living room, Brent could see the lighted grounds of the imperial palace just three miles away and the garish neon glare of the Genza in the far distance.

"Chivas Regal and soda," Sarah announced as she backed through the kitchen's swinging doors holding two highballs.

Handing the ensign his drink, she sat close to him, raising her glass, she said, "*L' chayim.*"

"To your health, too," he said quickly.

"You remember," she said, obviously pleased.

"How could I ever forget thirty-six hours with you?"

She laughed and spoke with lowered eyes. "I think we set records, Brent." Tabling her drink, the soldier crept back into her voice. "You were attacked off the Cape Verde Islands; torpedoed three hundred miles from Pearl Harbor."

"It's been in the media. There's no secret."

"You took prisoners."

"Yes. But that's been reported, too." He began to wonder about the surprising turn in the conversation.

"You released both prisoners to the Maritime Self-Defense Force."

"No. There were three, two Germans and an Arab. For some reason germane only to himself, Admiral Fujita released the two Germans to the Maritime Self-Defense Force. He's kept the Arab on board — I would guess for further interrogation."

He sipped his drink and, wrapping a hand around Sarah's, he caught a glimpse of smooth knees as she pulled her legs up on the couch and leaned close to him. "You picked up a survivor."

"Why, yes. Kathryn Suzuki. But that — ah, information about her has been classified by the admiral. There has been no public release . . ."

"I know. Her name is Fukiko Hino and she is a terrorist. She and an Arab, Abdul al Kazarim, tried to bomb *Yonaga* yesterday. Right?"

"I didn't even know his name."

Sarah took a long drink. "You were close to her, weren't you, Brent?"

"Bernstein!"

"Not really — only as far as he functions as part of the intelligence apparatus. He's very closemouthed."

"You have agents in Hawaii — at the graving dock, here."

She smiled. "As an intelligence officer, you couldn't expect me to answer that."

It was Brent's turn to take a deep drink. "So, what's on your mind, Sarah?"

"You went to bed with her."

He felt more than just alcohol burning in the pit of

his stomach. "This is beneath you, Sarah."

"Why?" The soldier was gone and she was all woman. "You're the most important man in my life."

He pulled his hand away. "You're important to me, too, Sarah. But we made no commitments—no promises. You weren't betrayed." There were traces of sarcasm in his voice.

"Do you feel attachment to her? Could you—would you see her again?"

"See her again?" He was stunned. "She's dead! They're both dead. You didn't know?"

"No. Only that there was an attempt on *Yonaga.* Our informants told us Hino and Kazarim were the only Sabbah in Tokyo. It was easy to add up even with Fujita's tight lid on it." She moved a little closer. "How did she die?"

"I shot Kazarim off the running board of a truck they loaded with H.E."

"And Kathryn?"

He drained his glass. Sighed. "She was on her back, wounded." He stopped.

"And?"

"And I put one between her eyes."

"Oh, Brent," she said, shocked.

"You wanted her dead, didn't you?"

"Yes. All Sabbah. But it must have been hard on you."

"Not really. They cut Chief Shimada's throat, were trying to destroy *Yonaga.*" He held up his empty glass.

Quickly, she disappeared into the kitchen and returned with recharged highballs and sat close, breast pressed to his arm. He took a long drink.

299

"Maybe I'd better leave, Sarah."

"I didn't mean to offend you, but if you feel you should, Brent." And then added softly, "I've missed you so—so terribly much." She brushed her lips across his cheek. He tabled his drink and sought her lips. Her mouth was open, wet and hot, tongue hungry. She pulled him down on the couch, and he could feel her hard body tremble under his hands. "You're not angry with me?" she gasped between kisses, running her hands over his broad back.

"God, no, Sarah. I've waited so long for you. So long." He ran his hands over the swollen breasts, waist, hips, to the hem of the skirt, then upward over burning flesh.

She pushed hard against his chest. "Not here, darling." Slowly, they came to their feet, trembling for each other. For a long moment they stood close, running their hands over each other. She sought his neck, bulging muscles of his arms, flat stomach, narrow hips, finally his throbbing manhood, while his hands slipped down her back to her firm buttocks, then he pulled her against him hard. "God," she groaned, taking his hand. "This is torture." She led him to the bedroom.

Chapter Seventeen

The next day the announcement blared over *Yonaga*'s PA system suddenly, taking Brent by surprise just as he came off watch. It was Kawamoto: "All officers not on duty report to the Shrine of Infinite Salvation immediately for a special ceremony."

When Brent entered the shrine, wondering about a "special ceremony," he found perhaps two hundred officers headed by Admiral Fujita and his staff standing at ease in ranks. Many of the officers were new young replacements, and again Brent was struck by the youthful appearance of *Yonaga*'s original crewmen who stood side by side with the replacements. Brent took a position in the front rank between Adm. Mark Allen and Commander Matsuhara. Matsuhara greeted him with a smile.

"What's up?" the ensign asked. Matsuhara shrugged.

Suddenly two ratings entered, one carrying a large wooden block and the other a basket. The block was placed on the platform in the center of the shrine and the basket next to it.

"I think I know," Mark Allen said ominously.

Kawamoto shouted, "Officers—attention!" Hundreds of booted feet thudded together. Then two seaman guards entered, dragging the bound and terrified Tam Ali Khalifa between them. They dragged the Arab onto the platform. Fujita nodded and Atsumi stepped onto the platform. Hissing like a snake leaping from ambush, he pulled his long killing blade from its scabbard.

"So that's why he kept him," Brent said to himself.

"Your comrades have killed three of my men. You will die in return. A dog for three samurai. A terrible trade, indeed, but better than no barter at all," Fujita said.

"No!" Khalifa screamed. "No trial?"

"As much of a trial as your friends gave Chief Shimada." Fujita nodded, and the guards threw the Arab down roughly on the block, securing his hands to cuffs at the base and tying his feet together tightly.

"Admiral Fujita," Mark Allen shouted. "There is no honor in what you do. This man should be turned over to the authorities."

"He will soon be turned over to the ultimate authority, Admiral Allen. They can judge him."

"This is wrong, sir. Unjust, inhuman . . . "

"We are dealing with a dog, not a human. And please, Admiral Allen, do not attempt to remind me of my responsibilities." The voice was surprisingly cordial.

"Let me pray, admiral. Please, sir. One last prayer."

Fujita gestured and the guards untied the Arab's hands. "A rug—please, a rug."

Fujita waved to a rating. The man rushed forward and spread a *tatami* mat on the platform. With his feet still bound, the Arab wriggled onto the mat like a

302

young seal. "East? East?"

Gesturing with his sword, Atsumi said quietly, "Mecca is in that direction."

Khalifa bowed to the east with his forehead touching the floor and began to chant, "There is no God but Allah and Mohammad is his prophet." He repeated the prayer a half-dozen times and then looked up at Fujita. "I am ready for my *haj*, you yellow monkey!"

"Behead him!" Fujita shouted.

The Arab struggled up onto his knees, swinging. Brutally, a guard smashed him to the platform with a blow to the neck. In a moment, the hands were tied down again and the basket waited. "Proceed, Commander Atsumi," Fujita barked.

"Allah akbar! Allah akbar!" the doomed man cried over and over. Atsumi raised his sword and paused, and the world paused with him. No hammers, tools, blowers, engines, or anything else made a sound. Then there was a flash of steel, a hum like passing wings of death, a thud of steel crunching through flesh and bone and the cries ceased, the head crunched into the basket and blood spurted onto the platform.

Fujita spoke to the corpse. "Death, though cold as ice, is a fire which will purify your body." He turned to Kawamoto. "Place him in that box." He indicated a crate in a corner. "Address it to the Libyan Embassy."

"Deliver it, sir?"

"No. Place it outside our perimeter, phone them and tell them to pick it up. If they do not, he can go out with the garbage." He moved his eyes over the rigid ranks. "You are dismissed!"

As Brent left with Mark Allen, the admiral said softly, "Barbaric, Brent. It's still there."

"But, sir," Brent said just as softly, "what could he do?"

"What could he do?" Allen repeated incredulously.

"Yes, sir. He had no choice. They must be shown."

"My God, Brent. My God. What's happening to you?"

But Brent did not wonder at the words. It had been right. It had been just.

Work on *Yonaga* proceeded rapidly, and there always seemed to be at least twenty Zeros circling the warship as new pilots practiced with the veterans. There were no intruders, but early Monday a JAL Constellation wandered too close to *Yonaga*'s airspace and a dozen Zeros pounced, one firing a burst ahead of the transport. In haste born of panic, the pilot of the big Lockheed wheeled her into a sharp bank and fled for the airport. Hundreds of *Yonaga*'s seamen pointed and laughed.

Yoshi Matsuhara spent all of Monday and most of Tuesday at the airport. Brent noticed a new gleam in the pilot's eye and spring to his step when he left the ship.

"Got a date tonight, Yoshi?" Brent whispered to the commander late Tuesday afternoon as the flyer returned, passing Brent's station next to the Nambu at the foot of the accommodation ladder.

Matsuhara's smile was warm. "Come to think of it, I do have some plans. And you?"

Brent chuckled. "I might get away for a little while,

Yoshi."

They both laughed.

Kimio Ursazawa's home was a large traditional wood-frame structure in Shibuya-Ku district of Tokyo. After removing his shoes, Kimio ushered Yoshi into the main room, seating him on a *zabuton* placed in front of the *Tokonoma* — a vase with an artful arrangement of cherry blossoms in front of an exquisite pen and ink sketch. Kimio was dressed in a tight kimono, and her hair again was done in classic style. After filling his cup with hot sake, she sat opposite him.

"It is generous of you, Yoshi-san, to find time in your busy schedule to honor my humble home."

He smiled at the time-honored, self-deprecatory opening of the Japanese hostess.

"No, indeed, Kimio," he said, following the ancient script. "It is I who is honored — a mere sailor invited into such a splendid dwelling by such a lovely hostess." He emptied his cup. She filled it.

"We almost forgot," he said quickly, raising his cup. "The emperor."

"The emperor," she echoed. They drank, and surprisingly the cup was empty again and Kimio recharged them both. "You leave soon?"

"That is classified."

"Everyone will see you leave. You cannot hide *Yonaga*. She is as big as Fuji-san. And there are rumors that an Arab force is gathering. Perhaps to attack Indonesia and then Japan."

"Rumors," he said cautiously. "I am only a flyer

305

who follows his orders."

"Yoshi-san," she said suddenly, lightening her voice. "Let's shut out the world tonight. Just you and I and nothing else." She held his eyes with hers, and again he felt that strange feverish feeling.

"Yes, Kimio, I have never had that luxury. Yes. Let us try."

She rose slowly. "I have prepared a meal for you." As she walked to the kitchen, Yoshi felt a physical jolt as he watched the smooth flow of her buttocks under the kimono.

In a moment she returned and served the meal fit for the gods: sushi, exquisite eels in rice and soya sauce, tempura dipped in a thin batter and fried with mushrooms, sweet potatoes and green beans, bowls of steaming rice and soba. And his *saka-zuki* was kept filled.

Sighing as he finished the gourmet meal, Yoshi relaxed, sipping more sake instead of tea. Kimio returned after clearing the table and sat toying with her own *saka-zuki*. He felt content and the sake was warm, adding a glow to everything. Kimio appeared even more beautiful. "You are a stunning woman," he said with simple sincerity.

"Thank you, Yoshi. You are an extremely handsome man." He felt heat on his face. Reaching across the table, she took his hand. "You have not been with a woman for many, many years."

"You know that." He captured her other hand. It felt like warm velvet.

"You think I am attractive, Yoshi-san?"

"You are beautiful. You have the body of a goddess."

306

"Would you like to see it?"

Not believing his ears, he caught his breath as if someone had punched him in the solar plexus. "You do not owe me that."

"Would you like to see my body?" she repeated.

His lips trembled and he felt a million tiny needles pressing against his face and neck. Incapable of forming the word, he nodded mutely.

Slowly, she stood, moved to the center of the room and locked eyes with him. Hypnotized, he watched as she leisurely pulled the sprigs, combs and pins from her hair. Shaking her head, she sent the gleaming mass tumbling about her shoulders like a cascade of black silk. Then she untied the obi, released the fasteners and let the kimono fall open, revealing amber-tinted flesh and delicate white undergarments. The kimono slipped from her shoulders and slithered to the floor. Yoshi had trouble breathing, and his eyes, wide and unblinking, drank in the sculpted body clad only in fragile silk brassiere and narrow, lace-trimmed panties. He felt a force in the room—the power of her sexuality—that brought him to his feet like metal drawn to a magnet. Extending her hand, she said, "I am not doing this because you are a samurai who serves the emperor."

"Why, then? Why for me?"

She looked at him, eyes glazed with passion. "At this moment, Yoshi-san, I serve myself." She reached behind her and the brassiere fell away, releasing the mounds of her large pointed breasts.

Yoshi raised his hands, cupped the breasts, caressing the areolas and nipples. She gasped and moved closer. The frustration of decades overwhelmed him,

307

and he crushed her to him, kissing her mouth, eyes, neck, breasts, stomach, as she twisted and moaned. "The last is for you," she hissed.

At first he did not understand. Then she placed his hand on the elastic band, and he pulled down hard, ripping the silk of the panties as he tore off the garment, shaking like a man with palsy. There was thunder in his ears as he stared at the dark triangle of hair covering her sex. And her hands were busy, too, unbuttoning his tunic.

"A pistol," she said.

"Yes. Orders." Then, despite shaking, numbed fingers, he discarded the Otsu, and the rest of his uniform soon followed, strewn on the floor like old rags.

Her eyes moved over his shoulders, small waist, muscular legs and turgid manhood. "You are magnificent, Yoshi-san."

Taking his hand, she led him to another room with a large futan. Slowly, she lay on her back and raised her hand to him. He lowered himself between her legs, and she raised her hips as he finally found the hot, liquid depths of her. She gasped and clawed his back, and the room seemed to turn like a carousel.

Again and again he took her, frenzied and untiring until the early hours of the morning when he finally slipped from her and fell into a deep sleep—a rest of contentment and peace he had not known for over forty years.

Chapter Eighteen

Work progressed quickly and the five inch magazine and the damaged bulkhead of engine room three were completely repaired within ten days. Another week found the outer hull patched and the fuel tanks repaired. But there was ominous news from the Mediterranean.

Three weeks after entering dry dock, Admiral Fujita called a staff meeting. Frank Dempster, who had been ashore for a full week, stood in front of a chart attached to a bulkhead and said, pointing, "As you know, there is always a lot of tanker traffic here in the Gulf of Aden and especially here." He moved the pointer northwest. "In the Gulf of Oman."

"Exiting the Persian Gulf," Fujita suggested.

"Yes, sir." He turned back to the chart. "The US Navy has SSBNs on station here and here." He stabbed points in the Arabian Sea just off the Gulf of Aden and the Gulf of Oman.

"SSBN?" Kawamoto queried.

"Sorry," the CIA man said. "An SSBN was originally designed as a 'boomer'—missile boat; that is, before the Chinese laser system went into orbit. Now they are used as modified attack boats and for reconnaissance. I understand the boats on station are *Ohios*, both nuclear, nineteen thousand tons submerged, and they can stay there for months."

"Your report," Fujita said impatiently. The CIA man's face was flushed and his smile crooked. Brent, seated at the far end of the table with the junior officers, wondered if Dempster had been drinking.

"Yes, sir. Three days ago, two two hundred thousand ton tankers exited the Gulf of Oman and headed southeast."

Fujita interrupted. "But ships of that size would not be fleet oilers."

"True, sir. But we have reports they're headed for the Nicobar Islands." The pointer slid to the west across 40° of longitude to a point north of the northern tip of Sumatra.

Mark Allen spoke up. "The Nicobars are Indian."

"And India is under Kadafi's heel," Bernstein said.

"I can't believe that," Mark Allen shot back.

"It makes no difference, Mark," Dempster said. "According to our information, the Arabs are setting up a floating base there—in the Nicobar Islands. Just the way we did at Kwajalein, Ulithi . . ."

"I know, I know," Allen said.

Fujita seized the issue. "What is the registry of the tankers?"

"Liberian."

"Convenience?"

"Correct, admiral. They are Arab owned and Arab

310

manned."

"Then they can anchor anywhere they like—in any neutral port. Your argument is academic."

Allen and Dempster stared at each other. "Of course," Dempster conceded, reddening.

Fujita pushed on. "And what about the fleet replenishment vessels? The fast twenty to thirty thousand ton tankers?"

"Three exited the Gulf of Aden last night. All ex-Russians. Two thirty-five thousand tonners of the *Berezina* class and one twenty-five thousand ton tanker of the *Boris Chiliken* class."

"Then the large tankers can anchor anywhere, the smaller vessels can refuel their task force and off load more oil from the larger vessels."

"There's nothing illegal about that, admiral," Mark Allen agreed.

"And the Russians and Arabs own your United Nations and the World Court?"

"In my opinion," Dempster said, "that is an accurate assessment, admiral."

Fujita's eyes flashed to Bernstein. "Colonel, before the meeting you told me the Arab task force was underway."

"Yes. We just got the transmission. The Israeli Air Force reports three carriers, two cruisers, and perhaps twelve destroyers have made a transit of the Red Sea and should be entering the Gulf of Aden now. Our agents tell us they are headed for Indonesia."

Every back in the room stiffened, and the old admiral's eyes roamed the table. "Now, with the movement of the tankers, we can be assured it has started." He raised the pointer. "They should steam

311

southeast across the Arabian Sea and pass south of the Maldive Islands and north of the Chagos Archipelago. Then due east across the Indian Ocean to a point west of Sumatra and south of the Nicobar Islands. That is a run of almost six thousand miles. They must refuel here." The pointer struck the chart again west of Sumatra. "Then, if they wish to destroy the Indonesian fields and attack us, they must enter the Straits of Malacca." He traced the pointer southeast through a narrow neck of water flanked by Malasia on the north and Sumatra to the south. "And then into the Java Sea before they make their turn north to attack Japan." He thumped the pointer on the deck thoughtfully. "A terrible place for heavy ships. Terrible!" The astonishing encyclopedic mind of the insatiable reader went to work. "During the Greater East Asia War, the British lost the *Prince of Wales* and *Repulse* here." He stabbed a point off the Malay Peninsula. "The *Dorsetshire* and *Cornwall* here." He indicated a point off Ceylon. He moved the pointer north of Java. "And that stupid Dutch admiral, Karel Doorman, lost *Kortenaer, Electra, Jupiter, Java, De Ruyter, Houston,* and *Perth* here, in confined waters." He tapped the chart. "Here, in this graveyard of stupid seamanship, we will catch them!"

"Banzai! Banzai!"

The old admiral traced a line southwest from Tokyo through the Philippine Sea west of the Ryukyus, then north of Luzon and south into the South China Sea. "We have a run of fifteen hundred miles to intercept," he said almost to himself. "We can engage them first and then refuel." He spoke to the CIA man. "Mr. Dempster, you have permission for our tankers to

312

anchor in Subic Bay?"

"Yes, sir. They are underway from Valdez—should anchor in Subic Bay within forty-eight hours." The CIA man glanced at a document. "The Philippine government has been deeply concerned about threats to the Indonesian fields. We have been negotiating for permission to use an old American strip at Puerto Princesa on Palawan in the event *Yonaga*'s flight deck is damaged. The Filipinos will not rearm or refuel our aircraft. However, they may allow them to land."

Fujita thumped the chart. "Good, good. You have done well, Mr. Dempster. Let us hope we do not need Palawan." He stared thoughtfully at the American Intelligence agent. "But we still do not have their permission?"

"Right, sir. But we expect it, and we should have their decision come over a NIS transmission from their ambassador in Washington tomorrow."

"They have as much at stake as we do," Fujita grumbled. He turned to Kawamoto. "I want to put to sea by zero-eight hundred tomorrow morning."

"But, sir, the work is not finished."

"Our liberty parties will be back, we have restored watertight integrity to engine room three and the auxiliary five inch magazine."

"Yes, sir. But the bulkhead between fire rooms eleven and thirteen is holed. And we have not restored watertight integrity to compartment five-seven-one, the starboard thrust block room, and the center motor room. I have calculated one hit on the starboard side aft would admit two thousand tons of seawater. Also, we have not completed provisioning . . ."

Turning to Matsuhara, Fujita cut off Kawamoto

with a wave. "Your fighters?"

"Ready, sir."

To Commander Yamabushi: "Your bombers?"

"Ready, sir."

To Captain Fite: "Escorts?"

"Ready, sir!"

"Engineering?"

"All boilers are serviced and ready. Auxiliary engines are standing by and can take over as soon as we disconnect from shore power, and our fuel tanks are topped off."

"Light off all boilers now and tell Lieutenant Commander Kamakura to start flooding the dock." The commander lifted a phone to his ear. Continuing, Fujita moved his eyes to Lieutenant Nobomitsu Atsumi. "Gunnery?"

"All weapons and fire control are ready—magazines are full."

Fujita moved to Admiral Mark Allen. "Our encryption boxes, radar, radar detectors?"

"All ready, sir. We have a new ESM—Electronic Support Measures—sensor that can record radar signals, classify frequency data, pulse repetition, power, and even 'fingerprint' the transmitter."

Despite confusion among the Japanese officers, Fujita returned to the executive officer. "But you are short of stores."

Kawamoto fidgeted nervously. "Yes, sir."

"Load as much as you can, especially rice, until we leave the dock, which should be in seven or eight hours." He fingered a single white hair on his chin. "If necessary, we will go on half rations. But, regardless, we sortie tomorrow morning."

314

"Banzai! Banzai!"

Dempster interrupted the shouts. "Sir! Sir! With your permission, I would like to remain aboard for this operation." Silence.

"There are grave dangers."

"I'm aware, sir."

"Very well. Welcome aboard."

Although excitement was running high and *Yonaga* began to stir to life with the rumble of auxiliary engines and the roar of oil-fed boilers, Brent Ross found little to do. Not having the watch and with liberty cancelled, he walked to Yoshi Matsuhara's cabin, mind filled with thoughts of Sarah.

Smiling, the flyer ushered Brent into his cabin. Relaxing in a hard-backed chair, Brent noticed nail clippers, scissors, paper, and an envelope in front of Yoshi. Seeing the question in the American's eyes, the flyer said, "We samurai believe in preparing for all eventualities." He gestured at his littered desk. "I am writing Kimio and enclosing fingernail and hair clippings."

"Fingernails and hair?"

"Yes. If I die and my ashes are not returned to Nippon, she can cremate these." He tapped the envelope. "And this will aid my spirit in entering the Yasakuni Shrine."

Brent nodded. He had just written Sarah Aranson, pledging his love and promising to return. He told Yoshi of his note, adding, "But I didn't include any hair or fingernails."

"Well, Brent-san, she is a Jew and you a Christian,"

315

Matsuhara said earnestly.

"Correct, Yoshi-san." The use of the familiar address was involuntary, but surprised neither of the men.

"Well, then, you will have two of the more powerful religions on earth pushing your spirit. Certainly, your soul should have no trouble making its way to heaven." The dead serious expression belied the absurdity of the statement. Matsuhara was actually trying to console him. Brent nodded his gratitude gravely.

"Brent-san," Yoshi said with unaccustomed shyness. "Do you like poetry?"

Surprised by the question, Brent answered, "Why, yes, I have enjoyed Burns, Byron, Sandburg, Frost . . ."

"Haiku?"

"Why, yes. My father was quite fond of it."

The pilot moved his eyes to a sheet of paper on his desk, and his face reddened slightly. "I am very fond of Kimio Urshazawa and I am grateful to you."

Brent was shocked. A samurai was actually baring himself. "I'm pleased, Yoshi-san. A man is not complete without a woman."

The commander sighed. "For most of my life, I flew to fight and to die not thinking of women, family, especially after the fire raid. But now there is Kimio and I still fly for the emperor, but I would like to return, Brent-san." He looked into the American's eyes, surprising Brent again with his next question. "Do you think this will lessen me as a warrior?"

"Recklessness creates corpses, not heroes for the emperor," Brent said.

316

Yoshi chuckled. "Sometimes you sound more like a samurai than a Japanese." And then he added seriously, "During those long years in Sano-Wan, I read every book on board—I can read English, French, and German, too," he said with pride. He moved on. "Have you ever read *Moby Dick*, Brent-san?"

"Why, yes. It's a classic."

The Japanese drummed the table. "Do you think we are all Ahabs pursuing our white whales?"

The ensign shrugged. "The biblical Ahab pursued false gods. But I think Melville might agree with you."

"Then my white whale is honor, tradition, and dying for my emperor."

"And *Yonaga* is our *Pequod*, Yoshi-san?" Brent was fascinated by a side of Matsuhara he had never suspected.

"Why not? And your quest is really the same as mine: honor, tradition and—"

"But I would live for my country." The ensign hunched forward. "I don't measure my manhood, my fate, with the calculus of death, Yoshi-san."

"That is where you are wrong, Brent-san. Dying well on the field is the ultimate goal of all samurai. We find eternal life through death."

"Of course—I know, Yoshi-san. And you know I would not turn my back on it."

Obviously pleased, the pilot returned his eyes to the desk and tapped the single sheet of paper. "I have written a poem to Kimio. I would like to read it to you."

"Of course, Yoshi-san. I would be honored."

317

The flyer read:

Like a kite
Torn from its string
By the winter's storm
My heart has tumbled
To Kimio's feet.

"It's beautiful, Yoshi-san."

"It's haiku and you lose the meter in English. In Japanese, it consists of three lines of five, seven, and five syllables. That is where you find its true beauty."

"No, Yoshi-san. The true beauty is in the thought, not meter or syllables."

"You are wise for an American of such few years," Yoshi said with a broad grin. He was interrupted by a slight motion detectable by only men who spend their lives at sea. "We are afloat, Brent-san."

"Time for the last act, Yoshi-san."

"Yes. I can hear the *hyoshigi* calling us." Quickly he folded the letter and sealed the envelope.

Chapter Nineteen

Preceded by her charging escorts, *Yonaga* stood out the Urago Suido early the next morning. Clearing point Nojima Zaki to port and Oshima Island to starboard, Fujita set a course of one-eight-zero, speed eighteen. From his usual station on the bridge, Brent Ross experienced a resurgence of confidence, feeling the thump of the four great engines in the steel grid under his feet. *Yonaga* was free of the beach, her umbilicals cut, her skin patched and her heartbeat strong again.

The morning was dark and foreboding with a large swell from the southwest taking the carrier on her port bow, lifting her and rolling her 84,000 tons gently as she crunched valleys in the endless combers, shearing off tons of gray water and flinging spray as high as the hangar deck. And the CAP could be heard but not seen in a solid overcast that was gray, too, like the flesh of day-old corpses. Shuddering, Brent plunged his hands deep into the pockets of his foul-weather jacket.

Fujita called him to the chart table. "We are on the one hundred fortieth meridian and will steam one-eight-zero until we reach the thirty-second parallel.

Then we will change course to two-two-seven and enter the Philippine Sea here." He ran a finger down the chart. Brent nodded and returned to the windscreen. He was off watch, but remained with the admiral, sweeping the horizon with his binoculars.

By noon the sky had cleared and the sea calmed. Bathed in brilliant sunlight, the carrier slashed through the flat sea like a knife through blue velvet. Everyone's spirits buoyed with the weather.

The talker, Seaman Naoyuki, turned to the admiral. "Radar reports large formations of aircraft approaching from three-five-five, range three hundred kilometers, sir."

"Very well. Our new airgroups," Fujita said. "All ready guns track aircraft bearing three-five-five. CIC vector in the CAP." Brent smiled to himself—the old man never took chances. After the passage of a few minutes, a deep rumble could be heard high in the sky and astern of the carrier. Raising his binoculars, Brent found echelon after echelon of aircraft flying in the usual Japanese formation of three threes of three. There were "banzais" from the flight deck.

"Stand by to take aboard aircraft," Fujita shouted at Naoyuki. Commands were shouted, hoists made and executed and the great carrier swung slowly into the wind.

Brent sensed a new presence on the bridge. It was Yoshi Matsuhara who leaned anxiously over the windscreen, staring at the flight deck as the first aircraft, an Aichi D3A, made its approach.

"Damn, Brent," the flyer said, pounding the rail. "I should have led them in."

"Why, Yoshi?" Brent asked, gesturing high in the

320

sky where gleaming white Zeros wheeled like restless sea birds. "Takamura and Kojima are the best. You said so yourself."

"I know, I know, but I do not like being here while they are up there."

Brent chuckled. "Join the club."

"The club?"

Brent laughed, "I mean, that is all we know."

The pilot smiled understanding.

After all the new aircraft landed, Matsuhara rushed to the gallery deck while Fujita shocked everyone with his next command. "Course two-two-seven, speed thirty."

"Thirty?" Mark Allen said.

Fujita turned slowly to the American admiral. "I will discuss this decision with you in due time, Admiral Allen."

"Of course, admiral. It was not a challenge."

At 30 knots, the task force penetrated the Philippine Sea quickly, leaving the Bonin Islands over the eastern horizon and Okinawa far over the western horizon to starboard. The next day Brent was called to the radio room by Cryptographer Pierson. Pushing his way into the crowded room, filled with green-glowing cathode ray tubes, computers, and bank after bank of electronic equipment, Brent finally stood behind the young cryptographer, who also stood watches at the ESM console. The young man was listening intently on his earphones and staring at the scope of a radar sensor. He glanced at the ensign with dark intelligent eyes, and his voice was hesitant as he slid an earphone from his right ear. "I think someone is out there and they're curious, Mr. Ross."

The man had an uncanny knack for detecting and interpreting signals. Knowing Pierson was on to something, Brent leaned forward.

"There it is again, sir." Pierson clutched his earphone. Brent gestured to a bulkhead-mounted speaker. The technician threw a switch and static rasped. But then a faint fuzzy beep—one only. Then several seconds later, it was repeated.

Because radar could be detected at distances far greater than it could generate returns, Brent knew the chances were excellent they were undetected. Anyway, when an operator picked up a target, he focused the beam on the blip, and sensors on the target vessel would emit a constant high-pitched sound. This strange sweep was making the standard search of the unalerted operator.

Pierson stared at his scope, changed scales, cursed, turned another knob. He gestured at the dark patches on the edge of the scope. "He's probably out there in that storm front—that's why our scouts haven't seen him."

The fuzzy beep came through again and again. "He's not targeting us," Brent observed.

"No, sir. He'd direct his beam right at us, and we'd get a steady hum." He turned a dial, threw two switches. "X-band, eight Gigahertz, maybe fifteen kilowatts, range about one hundred forty miles. Powerful, not a merchantman, Mr. Ross, but mounted on a small ship."

"How can you tell?"

"At this range, the curvature of the earth causes the

322

beam to pass over us." The speaker beeped again, a blurred, hazy sound. "Hear that, sir? His beam width is only about four degrees and we're getting the downside edge. That's why it's fuzzy, like not tuning a radio station's carrier wave in on dead center. If he were targeting us, you know we'd get a steady, clear sound."

Brent nodded. "You said it's a small vessel?"

"Yes, sir. With a four degree beam and at a range of maybe one hundred forty miles, his antenna is less than two feet in diameter. A large ship would have a bigger antenna on a high mast, and they'd be ranging us by now, sir."

A faint dot appeared on the edge of the scope, partially hidden by the storm. "There he is, sir. A sub or an AGI, I would guess, Mr. Ross."

"Good work, Pierson," Brent said.

"Report this to the OD?"

"No. I'll report it to the admiral myself. He's on the flag bridge."

Just minutes later, Brent had worked his way through the crowded radio room, to the pilot house and up the ladder to the flag bridge to Admiral Fujita, who listened to the report with intense concentration. He lifted a phone and shouted commands. After cradling the phone, he turned to Brent. "A camera equipped B-five-N will make a run over the target."

"It may be an enemy sub or AGI, sir. He'll know we're nearby."

"They know, anyway, Mr. Ross. The whole world knows we are at sea." He smiled slyly. "Let us hope it is an intelligence vessel. We will give him a good look."

Perplexed, Brent lifted his glasses to the clouds on the far horizon.

"It's a Russkie AGI of the *Primorye* class," Mark Allen said, seated in Flag Plot staring at the photograph. "Four thousand tons, top speed maybe fourteen knots. A real intelligence factory."

"Good. Good," Fujita said. He turned to Lieutenant Commander Atsumi and gave a command that baffled every man in the room. "Come to one-seven-three. Speed sixteen."

"Sir," Mark Allen said. "He'll pick us up for sure."

"I know, Admiral Allen, I know."

The next afternoon, steaming slowly, *Yonaga* passed within six miles of the small trawlerlike vessel laden with antennas. She was so close, two of the carriers' screening *Fletchers* actually passed outboard of her.

"She flies Russian colors," Brent said, staring through his binoculars. At that moment six Zeros banked sharply and 'ran the Russian's keel' from bow to stern, Sakaes at full throttle. Sluggishly, the little vessel turned away, showing *Yonaga* her stern. Everyone laughed.

Fujita turned to the talker. "Make the hoist, execute to follow, course two-two-seven." He moved to the voice tube, eyes on Brent Ross.

The ensign swept his binoculars over the far-flung escorts, who were still in visible range to permit signaling by flags, pennants, and flashing lights. "All answer, sir."

"Very well. Seaman Naoyuki, flag bridge execute." To the voice tube: "Come right to two-two-seven." He looked up at the fast disappearing AGI. "Now, Ivan, tell your Arab friends about our sixteen knot speed." He turned to Brent. "Your man manning the radar sensor?"

"Pierson, sir. The best."

"I want to know the instant we are out of Ivan's radar sweep."

"Aye, aye, sir." The old man was up to something — the keen tactical mind was grinding behind those glinting black eyes. But what? Why this deliberate contact? He shrugged. They would all find out soon enough. Maybe on the business ends of bombs and torpedoes. He returned to his binoculars.

The staff meeting was called immediately after Cryptographer Pierson reported the AGI's signals weak and finally vanished completely. Immediately, Fujita ordered speed increased to 30 knots.

Clutching a handful of printouts, Dempster entered smiling and excited. "Admiral," he said as the staff members seated themselves, "the Philippine government will allow us the use of the strip at Puerto Princesa on Palawan."

"Excellent."

But Mark Allen had grim news. "Cryptographer Herrerra just handed me this." He waved a sheet. "A US submarine spotted the Arab task force about two hundred miles, three hundred twenty kilometers,

325

southwest of Ceylon, or Sri Lanka, as it is called now." He looked down and read, "Longitude seventy-eight degrees east, latitude about three degrees north."

Standing, Fujita moved to the chart. "About here," he said, pointing. "They must be making about twenty knots." He fingered his chin. "They should be here off the northwest coast of Sumatra in about thirty-three hours, refuel and maybe enter the Straits of Malacca about forty hours from now—if they are good seamen."

"Sir," Mark Allen said. "They also know about us. We picked up that AGI's transmissions, and he told the whole world where we were."

"Good! And he told the whole world our speed was sixteen knots." The officers looked at each other.

"But, sir," Allen persisted. "They can expect us to change speed—design tactics—"

"But they do not really know, Admiral Allen." He turned to the chart, stabbed a pointer far to the south in the South China Sea. "We will be here, between the Malay Peninsula and Borneo, four hundred eighty-five kilometers—three hundred miles—from the Straits of Malacca when they exit." He turned back to the men. "We will even the odds."

Mark Allen was not satisfied. "You're assuming a lot, admiral. Poor reconnaissance, that they will arrive on schedule, that they will not detect our scouts . . ."

Fujita thumped the desk impatiently with the pointer's rubber tip. "Admiral Allen, I have been reading Morison's report of the Battle of Savo Island."

Allen flushed. "I know, sir. I interviewed survivors and helped write that volume."

"In that battle, you lost cruisers *Quincy, Vincennes, Astoria,* and *Canberra* in thirty minutes simply because your stupid Admiral Ghormley, who knew a force of cruisers and destroyers under an old friend of mine, Gunichi Mikawa, was bearing down on him, never anticipated an increase in speed by Mikawa, and was caught with his guns trained fore and aft."

"And you think you can emulate Mikawa? Catch them unprepared? It will take luck."

"Only a fool depends on luck, Admiral Allen." He turned back to the chart. "When they come into range, we will send in twenty-seven Zeros and twenty-seven Aichis at eighteen thousand feet."

"Their A-band radar will pick them up at two hundred to two hundred fifty miles out, admiral," Mark Allen said.

"Of course. They will intercept." He stabbed at the chart. "We will send in our B-five-Ns low—one hundred meters from the water, under their radar. While they are looking up, we will blow them out of the water with *gyos*."

"Banzai! Banzai!"

Chapter Twenty

The passage of three days found *Yonaga* steaming within one hundred fifty miles of the northern tip of Luzon and then southward, passing midway between Borneo and Vietnam until the Malay Peninsula was only a hundred miles over the southwest horizon and the Straits of Malacca three hundred miles in the same direction. Not a single merchantman had been sighted. Brent had a feeling of "High Noon," of cleared streets and empty shops before the shootout began. In fact, one afternoon standing behind Pierson while staring at the ESM, the cryptographer commented bitterly, "Nothing, sir. Not since the AGI. They're all afraid, aren't they, Mr. Ross, like the kids on the block all watching while one guy with guts takes on the neighborhood bully. They don't want to be involved, but they want to see the bully knocked on his ass."

"I'm afraid you're right, Pierson," the ensign answered with his own share of bitterness.

A continuous CAP of twelve Zeros was kept aloft and half a dozen Aichis and Nakajimas with auxiliary fuel tanks ranged in every sector, searching for the enemy. Fujita paced the bridge like a caged tiger while keeping the task force on first a two-seven-zero heading and then running the reciprocal zero-nine-zero. "They must come through! They must come through!" he muttered to himself in frustration. "We're burning fuel needlessly."

First word of the enemy came from the Indonesians, not *Yonaga*'s scouts, when the refinery at Banda on Sumatra was bombed to ruins by fifty JU87Cs.

Gleefully, Fujita jumped up and down, pounding his hands together. Then high-flying scouts spotted two cruisers followed by three carriers and at least a dozen destroyers entering the Straits of Malacca. Surprisingly, Fujita ordered a turn to the north, away from the enemy, before calling the staff together.

"We must open the range," he explained. "If we are to remain undetected." He turned to Mark Allen, "Once you told me the enemy's Messerschmitts and Junkers were designed for very short-range operations."

"Yes, sir. European distances, sir. Even with auxiliary fuel tanks, they have only half the range of our aircraft."

"Good." The old man moved to the chart, raising the pointer. He stabbed the Straits of Malacca. "They are here, probably with one eye on the oil facilities at Balikpapan, which is one thousand miles west of them and still out of range, while the other is looking for *Yonaga*. They should not expect us to be this close."

Bernstein spoke. "Sir. The Indonesian Air Force . . ."

"Air force?"

330

"Two DC-sixes, four DC-threes, and a half-dozen F-four-Fs made a raid on the enemy. They claim damage to one destroyer. It just came over."

"Losses?"

Bernstein grimaced. "They lost all of their aircraft. But they are repeating over and over in plain language that aircraft of any power fighting the Arabs are welcome at their airfields."

"A little late." Fujita glanced at Yoshi Matsuhara and Commander Yamabushi. He moved the pointer. "There are fields at Banjermasin, Balikpapan, and Pontianak." He stepped back. "But we still have Palawan." He pushed the rubber tip just south of Singapore. "Only a madman would attempt to negotiate the straits at night with darkened ships and at high speeds. If they steam all night at sixteen knots, they would hope to enter the Java Sea here at about zero-eight hundred, putting them about twenty miles south of Singapore and forty miles north of Sumatra. And look at these islands — Kapulauan Riau, Kepulauan Linagga, Singkep, and more on their DR track. Maneuvering will be restricted." He thumped the chart. "Just what we want." Turning to Yamabushi he said, "We will send your torpedo bombers in low under their radar."

Pointing, he continued with new vigor. "Use these islands for cover." He turned to Matsuhara. "Commander Matsuhara, as you know, will come in high with twenty-seven Zeros and twenty-seven Aichis. He should draw off their CAP, and he can vector you in on your fighter frequency; or we will do it from *Yonaga*'s CIC. In any event, this operation will require the ultimate in precise timing." He tapped the

331

pointer on the deck. "We will begin our run-in this evening at twenty hundred hours and begin launching our strikes at zero-six hundred hours tomorrow morning. We will keep eighteen A six M twos, nine D three As, and nine B five Ns in reserve. Take everything else that can fly."

"Banzai!"

"Sir," Mark Allen said, raising a hand. "Excellent plan — Midway in reverse. Turn their heads up and sneak in the torpedo bombers on the wave tops." The reference to the ignominious defeat at Midway, where the carriers *Kaga, Akagi, Soryu,* and *Hiryu* were all lost to dive-bombers, brought hard looks to the Japanese faces. Mark Allen pressed on to another point. "But you plan one strike — over a hundred aircraft. I would suggest two — ."

"No!" Fujita interrupted, rankled by the reference to Midway. "Hit them hard with everything!"

"But you can't handle all those returning aircraft."

"We may lose some — death is the way of the samurai. But we will hit them hard. Overwhelm them at a time and place of our choosing. Tactically, there is no other choice." Allen sat back in resignation.

Finished with Mark Allen, Fujita turned toward the shrine and the Japanese clapped. "Tenno Jimmu," he said, calling upon the spirit of Japan's first emperor. "Watch as your sons challenge the enemies of Dai Nippon and smile with Amaterasu as we destroy them. Let us fight with the true spirit of Bushido, remembering the ancient pledge, 'If my sword be broken, let me strike with my hands. If my hands be severed, let me attack with my shoulders. If my shoulders be slashed from my body, let me lay open

332

my enemy's throat with my teeth.' "
"Banzai! Banzai!"
"Hear! Hear!"
Mark Allen remained silent.

Chapter Twenty-one

Standing on a dais before a blackboard and a huge chart mounted on a stand, Commander Matsuhara let his eyes wander over the packed briefing room and the fifty-four fighter pilots crowding it. Sadly, there were many new, young faces amongst the old, but each new pilot was handpicked—the very best of hundreds of volunteers. Filled with *Yamato damashi*, every man wore a *hachimachi* headband, showing his determination to die for the emperor, and he knew most had wrapped a "belt of a thousand stitches"—a cloth made by one stitch and a prayer from a thousand strangers dedicated to helping the warrior find an honorable death—around his waist. All were dressed in brown flight suits, fur-lined helmets with earflaps up, rising sun patches on the left shoulder, and ranking patch on the right. Gloves, parachutes, and oxygen masks were piled at their feet. Each held a clipboard and stared at the commander expectantly.

Yoshi leaned on his sword. "As you know, we expect the enemy to sortie from the straits this morning at zero-eight hundred hours." Disdaining the

335

pointer, he pulled his sword from its scabbard with the ringing sound of steel on steel. Pointing, he continued. "We will approach the target at six thousand meters covering twenty-seven D three As at five thousand." He paused while the pilots scribbled on their clipboards. "We are decoys." There was a groan. "They will have us on their radar early and should intercept with every fighter they can get in the air. Every carrier sailor remembers Midway where we lost four carriers and the war to dive-bombers." There was a grim silence. Yoshi moved on. "Commander Kenzo Yamabushi will come in just off the wave tops, under their radar and, using islands for cover, will hit their carriers with twenty-seven B-five Ns."

"Banzai!"

Yoshi raised his hands. "Then we will dive-bomb them with the Aichis." He paused. "We have been over the rest many times, but it bears repeating, especially for the new pilots. As usual, *Yonaga*'s call is 'Iceman' and I am 'Edo Leader.' I am in command of top cover, and the sections are color coded as usual—Blue and Green with me." He pointed at a short, gray-haired pilot. "Lieutenant Ariga's Gold Section will cover Yamabushi's torpedo run, Commander Okumiya will command Orange and Purple—eighteen aircraft—and will remain with the carrier as CAP.

"As you know, we can expect to engage the Messerschmitt BF-one-oh-nine and perhaps a few other types of fighters. The ME is a fast aircraft with two twenty millimeter guns and two seven-point sevens—the same firepower as ours. But, no one can

336

turn with the Zero. Dogfight them but maintain flight discipline and stay with your wingmen until released to individual combat." He stabbed the desk with the tip of the sword. "I will personally shoot down any glory-hunting ronin who violates flight discipline." His eyes moved over the intent faces. Turning, he gestured to a yeoman who moved to the blackboard. "For your point option data, we will be launched here." He raised his sword to the chart. "At longitude one-zero-seven, latitude two degrees, thirty minutes north. We will be less than three hundred kilometers from the target." Surprised faces looked up as the yeoman scribbled.

"Too close, sir," Ariga said. "We have greater range."

"True, lieutenant. Admiral Fujita will open the range on zero-four-five at a SOA of eighteen knots for one hour. Then *Yonaga* will steam the reciprocal two-two-five for thirty minutes. Then back to zero-four-five." He paused while the men made notes.

When the pilots looked up, he went on. "Radio silence until I break it." He struck the chart with his sword. "Emergency landing fields are available to you here at Palawan, Pontianak, Palembang, Banaka, and any other Indonesian field, but not Singapore. Weather over the target is clear with a few scattered clouds, but thunderheads are reported to the south. Wind is from the west, gusting to eight knots. Your in course is two-two-zero, exit course zero-nine-zero; we do not want to vector the enemy back to *Yonaga*. Speed of advance one hundred forty knots on a lean mixture, of course. All good fighter pilots conserve fuel; you know we can double consumption when we go into overboost." He pointed his blade at the pilots. "You new men, remember you have only sixteen seconds of firepower. A disciplined fighter pilot fires burst of one to two seconds at ranges less than two hundred meters." He leaned forward. "Try for the fifty meter shot. It's a sure kill, and all great pilots of the past always fired at very close range. Let the enemy waste his ammunition."

He returned the sword to its scabbard, placed it point down on the deck before him, wrapped both hands around the hilt and leaned toward his men. "And now for something I have not said before. Those madmen are trying to strangle our islands. They are nothing but terrorists who would subjugate the world with their new power. Only *Yonaga* challenges them, and you are the cutting edge."

"Banzai! Banzai!" Every man came to his feet. Then the single door at the rear of the compartment opened, and two ratings carrying aluminum battle ration containers worked their way down the crowded center aisle to the dais. Working hastily and aided by two yeomen, they distributed a cup of sake and a single chestnut to each flyer. Every man stood.

Matsuhara raised his eyes, quoted the *Haga Kure*: "A samurai of courage may hope to do anything as if his body were already dead because in death he becomes one with the gods!" He drank and every man drained his cup. The ratings moved and the cups were refilled as the men ate their chestnuts.

The commander held his cup high, shouting, "Tenno heiko banzai!"

The salute to the emperor roared back, and again the cups were drained. "Pilots man your planes," blared through the speaker.

"Dismissed," Matsuhara shouted. As the pilots crowded through the door, each handed a waiting yeoman an envelope containing fingernail and hair clippings.

When Commander Matsuhara exited the island, he found the flight deck crowded with Zeros. Running to his A6M2, the lead aircraft, he waved to his crew chief, Shoishi Ota, who sat in the cockpit making his final check of canopy lock, oxygen, radio, hydraulics, safety belt, and instruments. By the time Yoshi rounded the wing, Ota was already lowering his big bulk to the deck while armorers and fueling crews pulled their carts to the side.

"She is ready, commander," Ota said. "And you have two hundred more horses." He gestured at the new Sakae.

Grinning, Yoshi reached up, grasped a handgrip and pulled himself onto the wing. Then, after stepping up on the single step, he eased himself into the cockpit — a narrow, coffinlike compartment not much wider than his body.

After locking his parachute straps and seat belts and checking to assure himself the canopy was locked in the open takeoff position, he released and then reset his brake. Quick movements of the stick and rudder bar told him ailerons, rudder, elevators, and flaps all responded.

339

Nodding with satisfaction, he switched on his magnetos. Instantly his instruments sprang to life, and his hand moved instinctively to the throttle, setting it ahead slightly.

He looked first to his left, to his port wingman Lt. Tetsu Takamura, who smiled back, raising a thumb, then to his right, to his starboard wingman NAP first class Kojima, who gave the same signal, and then finally, he glanced down and to his right, to Crew Chief Ota, who stared back expectantly. Matsuhara circled a single finger over his head. Circling his own finger, the crew chief stood well clear of the propeller.

Punching his fuel booster and starter, the big new Sakae came to life with a volley of bangs, hard coughs, and sputters that trembled through the airframe and jerked the three-bladed propeller stiffly, belching blue smoke into the wind. The reluctant engine continued to bark stubbornly, and Yoshi pounded the instrument panel in frustration. Almost as if chastized by the blows, the big engine settled down into the familiar uneven roaring sound of the warming Sakae.

Sinking down into the cockpit with the sudden release of anxiety, the commander checked his instruments: tachometer reading 2200 rpms, oil temperature 22°, manifold pressure 60 centimeters of mercury. He watched the tachometer reading drop to 800 as he throttled back to wait while the engine warmed. Anyway, the yellow-clad control officer standing on his platform on the starboard bow had his flags crossed and at his knees. The steam blown from the vent at the bow streaked straight back down the center line of the deck. The bow was in the wind, and he knew the life guard destroyer trailed. In his rear-view mirrors, he could see propellers turning on dozens of aircraft. But the engines were cold. They must all wait. He struck angrily at his oil temperature gauge with the heel of his hand. It showed only 25°.

Throwing back his head, he impacted his headrest, and Kimio was there, smiling, looking up at him from the futon. "This business does not include you," he said to himself. But she remained, her soft lips parted, body ready for him. "I will come back. I will! I will!" he shouted into the engine's roar.

He shook his head to clear away the hot memories and looked down at his instruments. Oil temperature 50. He stabbed both thumbs up.

A flash of yellow caught his eye. The plane director was waving. Then the flags were held rigidly over-head. Yoshi felt the fighter tremble as tie-downs were released from wing tips and tail, and three handlers raced for their catwalk. Now, only two men manned the chocks while two others held the wing tips, steadying and checking the folding wing tip locks.

The final check. Pushing the throttle forward, the pilot watched rpms climb to 4,000, manifold pressure to 80 centimeters of mercury. Satisfied, he throttled back and nodded to the men at the chocks, who crouched under the wings. With a jerk, the clocks were pulled, and the last four handlers raced for their catwalk.

A flag dropped. Yoshi pushed the throttle to the panel and released the brakes. Joyously, the little fighter leaped, pressing Matsuhara back. In less than

341

100 meters the powerful Sakae accelerated the Mitsubishi to over 100 knots. Pulling back on the stick, Yoshi felt the plane leap into the sky eagerly like a long-grounded hawk. Reaching under the seat, he pulled up on a lever and felt two thumps as the landing gear retracted into its wells. Then a quick motion locked the canopy and Matsuhara banked into a counterclockwise orbit followed by both of his wingmen.

Brent was amazed by the skill of the new pilots. Only one aircraft had been lost in the run south, and the accident occurred when an arresting cable snapped and an Aichi careened over the port side, killing a handler and the bomber's pilot and gunner. Standing on the flag bridge with the admiral, Frank Dempster, Mark Allen, Irv Bernstein, and Captain Kawamoto, Brent watched as Matsuhara and his wingmen—all flying with the more powerful engines—rocketed into the sky.

Brent disliked steaming in the tropics. Only 300 miles north of the equator, the sun was hot already and the humidity was over 80 percent, bringing perspiration to plague a man already burdened with binoculars, helmet, and life jacket. But at least the sky was almost vacant—just a few low stringy clouds stretched far across the western horizon—and the wind was surprisingly constant and from the east, the sea calm. But weather was unpredictable here; squalls and thunderstorms could strike with little warning.

He was staring at the last Mitsubishi as it streaked down the deck when the electrifying news came over the radio. Seaman Naoyuki spoke. "Admiral, the radio reports air raids in progress on Palembang, Jakarta, and Jambi."

"Oil installations," Mark Allen observed.

"Good," Fujita said. "Less aircraft for us to engage."

"Sir," the talker continued. "The oil installations at Balikpapan are being shelled by two cruisers."

"Cruisers? Shelled?" Allen gasped incredulously.

Fujita glanced at the chart tacked to the table. "Eight hundred miles due west of us." He scratched his chin. "They must have split their forces—sent their *Fiji* and *Dido* through the straits and the Java Sea at over thirty knots—good seamanship, but they are not an immediate threat."

"They must have re-engined them," Allen mused. "That's incredible speed for ships that old."

Fujita studied the chart. "They are on the other side of Borneo. If they want to engage *Yonaga*, they must steam north through the Celebes Sea into the Sulu Sea and west through the Balabac Strait, all the way around Borneo before they can enter the South China Sea."

"This could put them behind us."

"I know. But this is a thousand miles of hard steaming, and if we dispose of their carriers, they may turn tail."

"And may not."

"Let them come, Admiral Allen. We continue with our attack as planned." He turned back to the flight deck.

Gripping the windscreen with white knuckles, Adm. Mark Allen watched uneasily as the sky slowly filled with orbiting Zeros and the first Aichi took off. He turned to Admiral Fujita nervously. "We're launching over a hundred aircraft, sir."

"One hundred eight in addition to our CAP."

"We should send two strikes, admiral. We will have trouble recovering them," Allen insisted.

"We discussed this, Admiral Allen. One strike, the decisive battle the Japanese way." He waved at the fighters. "With their auxiliary tanks and on a lean mixture they can remain in the air for eleven or twelve hours. Combat may reduce that to six or seven hours. But we are only one hundred eighty miles from our target, with an abundance of friendly landing fields available within easy range."

But they were too close. Just as the last plane disappeared to the southwest and *Yonaga*'s course was changed to zero-four-five, Cryptographer Pierson picked up the first ominous pulse. He spoke into his headpiece, and on the bridge the talker turned to Admiral Fujita. "ESM reports strong incoming pulses on S-band air search."

"Ranging."

"Yes, admiral, he has us."

"Sacred Buddha. Range to intruder?"

"Four hundred kilometers, bearing two-six-three true."

"Break radio silence. One 'three' of the CAP to intercept. CIC to vector their interception on our fighter frequency. Inform the escorts on bridge to bridge." He moved to the voice tube. "All ahead full!"

As Brent stared upward and saw three Mitsubishis of the CAP streak to the southwest, he felt the rhythm of the engines accelerate, and a voice came from the tube. "Thirty-two knots, one hundred seventy revolutions, admiral."

"Very well."

Obviously confused by the proceedings, Frank Dempster turned to Mark Allen. "We have more planes — why not put them up?"

Allen waved at the sky. "We have nine fighters in the air, nine more in the hangar deck along with nine dive-bombers and nine torpedo bombers. They must be kept in reserve to give us striking power in the event we are attacked."

"The cruisers!"

"No, Frank. They're over a thousand miles away."

"But we have been spotted."

"True. But no raid has been — "

Before Allen could complete his sentence, Seaman Naoyuki shouted, "Admiral, radio reports many aircraft bearing two-two-zero, range three hundred twenty kilometers, closing at a SOA of one hundred forty knots."

"CAP engage! Bring up the reserve fighters. Ready fighter pilots man your planes." To the voice tube: "Right to zero-nine-zero, speed twenty-four." Back to Naoyuki: "Signal bridge hoist 'pennant one.' AA stand by to engage raid approaching from the port quarter." He pounded the rail, glaring at Kawamoto. "Where are our scouts?" Then pointing at the horizon he said, "That sector should have been covered."

"It was, sir. But we received no reports. They must have killed him quickly."

Every man stared down at the flight deck anxiously

as the Zeros were wrestled from the elevators and pushed to the flight line. Quickly, pilots tumbled into their cockpits and engines coughed to life. But now anxious glasses were turned astern and the talker shouted, "Range to raid two hundred kilometers."

"Their SOA is greater than one hundred forty." Fujita mumbled.

Although Brent knew the enemy was still over 100 miles away, he searched the horizon and found comfort in the glistening white wings of nine Zeros high in the sky, streaking toward the attackers.

Then, with a roar, the first ready fighter leaped from the flight deck. In less than three minutes all nine aircraft were in the air. But the ready fighters remained close to *Yonaga*, circling high around the task force.

Fujita shouted orders at Naoyuki and put his lips to the voice tube. Heeling in a sharp turn, the carrier resumed course zero-four-five, speed thirty-two.

Seaman Naoyuki spoke to Admiral Fujita. "Sir. CAP reports twenty-eight JU-eighty-sevens and twenty-four Messerschmitts closing at one hundred fifty knots, range eighty. Am engaging."

"They kept one carrier's airgroups in reserve," Fujita noted. "Smart."

"Probably a *Colossus*," Allen added.

Each man raised his glasses. Brent saw nothing for several minutes until a flash caught his eye. And then black smoke trailing into the sea. "Aircraft—many aircraft approaching from two-two-zero true, elevation angle thirty degrees."

"Radar confirm."

"Radar confirms, admiral."

"Very well."

Now Brent could see the approaching aircraft clearly: sleek Messerschmitts engaging the outnumbered Zeros in a tumbling, twisting dogfight high above the echelons of single-engined Junkers, some armed with bombs, others with torpedoes. The numbers had been reduced. Brent counted twenty-one JU-87s banking toward the carrier.

Chapter Twenty-two

From 6,000 meters, Commander Matsuhara had a panoramic view of thousands of square kilometers of the South China Sea. However, with the straits at least 100 kilometers to the south, the airgroups were still at least thirty minutes from the target. He knew his force must have been picked up by enemy radar and tracked for at least the last half hour. The enemy had excellent radar; even airborne radar. The Japanese had none on their aircraft. He disliked playing decoy — being bait. Wryly he recalled an old Japanese adage: "No one ever armor-plated a worm before putting it on a hook."

Below his fighters he could see the bombers led by old Commander Sako Gakki lumbering, engines straining with the weight of the 400 kilogram bomb each carried slung under its fuselage.

To the west he could see the humpbacked spine of the Malay Peninsula, while Borneo was far to the east, and the low ridges of Sumatra and its outlying islands crouched low on the southern horizon like predators lying in ambush. Looking down, he was unable to see the torpedo bombers, but from this altitude their camouflage paint would make them almost invisible. But the white wings of Ariga's nine escorting Zeros flashed far below, and Yoshi knew the torpedo bombers must be nearby.

Restlessly, he turned his head, looking into the sun. Nothing up-sun. Where were the Libyan fighters? Then down and ahead. Still nothing. Where was the enemy? He had three carriers, over 130 aircraft. Were they asleep?

Cursing, he freed himself from his parachute straps. Turned with new freedom. "The pilot who rests his neck soon rests with his ancestors," his old instructor at Tsushiura had warned.

His tachometer read 2,000 rpms. He pulled back slightly on the throttle, dropping the needle to 1,800 while boosting manifold pressure. The big new engine coughed its objections, backfired and then settled down to a slower but steady roar.

He looked at his watch, glanced at the small chart attached to the clipboard strapped to his left knee. Twenty minutes to target. A cough, spurting flame, and black smoke fired from his exhaust. A look at his fuel gauges told him it was time to drop his auxiliary tank. Leading the fighters in a broad, sweeping turn to the left away from the Aichis, he pulled a lever, sending the aluminum tank tumbling and fluttering with twenty-six others. Then a little right rudder and he led the protective umbrella of fighters back over the bombers.

A fearsome streak of orange flame attracted his eye down and ahead. A Nakajima was burning close on the water. And now he could see them. The stream of torpedo bombers lumbering to the south. But two dozen low-flying Messerschmitts were racing in with the Malay Peninsula at their backs, while Ariga's hopelessly outnumbered force of nine Zeros whipped through hard turns to meet them.

Then Kojima's voice in his earphones. "Many fighters—high at three-one-zero. Up-sun! Up-sun!"

So that was it. An ambush from above and below. On the anvil. His mind raced as he threw a switch and barked into the microphone in his oxygen mask. "This is Edo Leader. Edo Leader will engage fighters attacking our torpedo bombers. Blue and Green sections intercept fighters at three-one-zero high. Individual combat! Break!"

A kick of left rudder, a push of the stick to the left and down, and he split-essed into a power dive, overboosted Sakae thundering. Thumbing the safety ring on the trigger to Fire, he felt the torque of the big Sakae pull hard to the right, corrected with left rudder. Without looking, he knew Takamura and Kojima were hard on his elevators with two more threes trailing.

A panorama of battle was beneath him. Ariga's Gold Section was engaging at least twenty ME BF-109s—a stubbier shipboard version of the ME-109s he had fought over Africa. Far below two MEs trailing flame and smoke arced toward the sea. A Zero exploded, flinging pieces of smoking wreckage in every direction. A dozen MEs had broken through Ariga's cover and were shooting the slow bombers out of the sky like clay pigeons. Within seconds, three Nakajimas crashed into the sea. Then two more flamed and climbed wildly out of control.

Yoshi punched his instrument panel in fury. Ignored a vibrating airframe that shook and bounced the pilot up and down as the big new engine pulled the fighter past limits never intended by its designer, Jiro Horikoshi. The altimeter's white needle was spinning backward, tachometer at the red line, and airspeed indicator at 410 knots. Yet, Yoshi did not ease his throttle. Instead, he vised his teeth together and spat epithets as two more Nakajimas disintegrated into the sea.

Closing the range fast, he pulled back on the stick and finally reduced throttle as an ME, hard on the tail of a B5N, bounced into his range finder. Just as the bomber exploded, Yoshi fingered the red button, sending a ragged two second burst into and around the Libyan fighter. As he flashed past, the ME dropped off on its port wing and dove for the sea.

"Missed! Missed!" A diving Zero was a terrible gun platform.

At that instant, Takamura and Kojima both scored, one enemy fighter losing a wing at its root where the ME BF-109 was the weakest. The other flamed straight up like a rocket before turning into its final dive.

Now alerted to the new danger, the Arab fighters wheeled and turned to face their attackers, and the complete mad melee of the dogfight filled the sky with snarling aircraft spitting flame.

Pulling back hard on his stick, Yoshi screamed to relieve the pressure as g-forces pushed him down hard onto his parachute pack, and he could feel the wicker seat sag as his weight was multiplied by five. Despite clouding vision, he pulled the stick back between his legs with all his strength, filling all three rings of his

352

range finder with the bottom of an ME. A one second burst shattered the air-scoop, sending glycol spraying. Yoshi rolled off the top of his loop into an Immelmann turn, found Takamura with a 109 close on his tail.

Making a difficult full deflection shot at 100 meters, Yoshi gave the ME a three second burst that marched up the fuselage. Aluminum chunks flashed in the slipstream like storm-blown paper, and the hammer blows of 20 millimeter shells smashed through the cockpit, shattering plexiglass and exploding the pilot's head like a bursting melon.

"Banzai!"

A Zero with no tail whipped crazily into a loop and then spun like a top until it smashed into the sea. Still another Japanese fighter with a dead engine glided to the sea, pancaking in a great splash and spray of seawater. Banking, Yoshi could see the pilot tumbling into his yellow life raft.

A hammer pounding on his fuselage stabbed him with fear, a horrible paralyzing fright that turned his stomach to a block of ice, and his eyes caught the red spinner of a Messerschmitt in his mirror. Instinctively, and taking advantage of the enormous torque of his engine, he snap-rolled to the right and whipped into a spin. But the sea was close and he kicked hard left rudder, pushed the stick forward and then back, centering the rudder pedals. Holding his breath, he watched the hard blue sea fill his windshield. "Come up! Come up! Sacred Buddha, come up!"

With agonizing slowness, the horizon dropped into his vision and crept down to the top of his black cowl, the Mitsubishi skimming so low its propeller kicked up a plume of spray.

He looked around. No red spinner behind. Furious with himself for having been frightened, he pulled back on the stick and shot skyward where fighters continued to shoot each other to pieces.

A Zero with two MEs close on his tail flashed from left to right, and then the trio streamed skyward as the Japanese tried to escape with his superior climb. But the Libyans were close on his tail. Firing. But they were too intent on their kill. Neglected their own tails. With the 1,200 horsepower engine in overboost, Yoshi closed on the left-hand ME quickly, forming a murderous four-plane daisy chain.

The Zero was streaming smoke when the commander fired a two second burst from 200 yards. Twenty millimeter shells blew the cowl from the ME's Daimler-Benz, and instantly black smoke and orange flame streaked from the engine, enveloping the fuselage.

The cowl popped back.

The other ME broke to the right, rolling into a power dive while the smoking Zero banked toward a small cloud hanging to the south. Leveling off protectively above the Japanese fighter, Yoshi watched the burning ME as it reached the top of its climb, stalled, and then fell off on one wing. A figure fell from the cockpit, and a parachute opened instantly. But too soon. The canopy was caught by the flames and blazed up, shriveling to nothingness like the tip of a match. Trailing cords like tattered banners, the man plunged toward the sea like a dropped stone, turning and twisting, arms and legs flailing.

"Banzai," snarled Yoshi. "Think about it all the way to Mecca, Arab dog."

Miraculously, the sky was suddenly empty of enemy fighters. Then he saw them: a half-dozen MEs fleeing low on the water to the southwest. Easing himself alongside the damaged Zero, Yoshi recognized one of the new pilots, Lt. Hatsuhashi Omura. There were holes in the wings and cowl. Omura's windshield had been shattered, and smoke trailed like a black ribbon. Nevertheless, the pilot appeared uninjured and saluted as he stared back at Matsuhara. Answering the salute, Yoshi glanced at his map and clicked on his microphone. "This is Edo Leader. Lieutenant Omura, make for the island of Bintan and the airfield at Tanjungpinang—course two-six-five, range one hundred twenty kilometers."

Repeating the command, Omura glanced at his own chart and then banked the Mitsubishi carefully to the right and headed for the western horizon where banks of clouds marked the nearby island.

Looking around, Matsuhara counted twelve bombers and ten Zeros. The Nakajimas were forming up on Commander Kenzo Yamabushi, who still led despite a dozen holes in wings and rudder. Then, searching overhead, he found an air battle spread over the entire southwest quadrant. At least 5,000 meters above them and 70 kilometers away, the commander could see only vapor trails and the black streaks of burning aircraft descending. Reaching for his microphone switch, he mouthed a quick prayer to Amaterasu first and then threw the switch. "This is Edo Leader. Form up on me. We will escort the bombers into their runs."

355

Gracefully, the white fighters formed their sections and layered themselves 300 meters over the bombers.

Then Yoshi heard a scout's excited voice on his earphones. "This is Scout Four. Carriers! Carriers! Three carriers exiting the straits. Longitude—" An explosion, a scream, and the circuit went dead. All that training, Yoshi thought, for an eight-word transmission. But the man's life had been worth it.

Within minutes, they were approaching the eastern end of the Straits of Malacca and the island of Kapulanan Lingya, which should be between them and the enemy force. He brought his fighters down low with the bombers, using the island as a radar shield. Now beneath him, the coastline, surf breaking on white sand, the black strip of a coastal road, cars, bicyclists, and people staring up with white faces and pointing. Then there were farms, cattle, and they passed over a hamlet not more then 50 meters high, shaking every building with their thunder. Ahead was a ridge. But they hung low, almost scraping their fuselages with brush and scrubby trees as they roared over.

"They should be over that ridge! Please, let the enemy be over that ridge," Yoshi prayed, pulling back gently on the control as he cleared a rocky spine.

And suddenly they were there in the channel about 7 kilometers directly ahead. Two *Colossus* class carriers and the *Independence*. Steaming in a column, they were surrounded by seven *Gearing* class destroyers. The force was steaming at a high speed on a sea as flat as a blue mirror. And the channel was narrow with little room for maneuvering. A quick upward look assured Yoshi that the enemy's CAP had been drawn into the great air battle to the northeast — just as Admiral Fujita had predicted.

Immediately, the bombers broke, forming three groups of four, and began their runs.

The force reacted quickly to the threat. Yoshi had never flown into the teeth of AA like this. The destroyer cannons fired so fast they seemed to be burning. Then the carriers added their own cannon fire, brown puffs smearing the sky, shorts sending columns of water leaping. Then storms of 40 millimeter and 20 millimeter shells glowed toward them like firebrands. At the same time, all three carriers began launching ready fighters.

"The fighters," Yoshi shouted into his microphone. He pulled back on the stick.

A torpedo bomber exploded. Another lost a wing, flipped over and tossed its torpedo high in the air in a tumbling arc, and then crashed into the sea. A burning Zero slowly pulled up and exploded in a ball of flame. Two more torpedo bombers plunged into the sea, disintegrating as their 140 knot speed impacted the water like concrete.

Now the Zeros were above the storm that met the Nakajimas, which had passed the screen and veered toward the carriers. Desperately, the big ships turned toward the Japanese bombers. There were six bombers left, and swerving in pairs toward the carriers, they dropped their torpedoes.

But Yoshi had no time to watch. Two MEs were in the air. It was easy. Climbing slowly, he put a short burst into the leader's cockpit, sending it into the sea with a dead man at the controls before he could even retract his gear. A short burst from Takamura silenced the engine of the second. Slowly, the fighter descended for a dead stick landing.

But Matsuhara was over the leading *Colossus* and, looking down, he found the jaws of hell spouting flames. A trip-hammer pounded the airframe and as he pulled back on the stick, the right wing dropped awkwardly, and he pushed the stick hard to port to keep level. Then the smoke—reeking, choking smoke—filled the cockpit.

The carrier seemed to leap from the sea as two torpedoes struck her port side. But Yoshi was too busy to rejoice. As he banked cautiously, stomach tied into a frozen lump, he jerked the canopy back with its twin handles, mind numbed with every carrier pilot's horror of drowning trapped in his cockpit. The plane lurched to the right again and he jammed the stick to port.

The air cleared the cockpit, and Matsuhara realized he was not on fire. The smoke must have been cordite from exploding shells. Then with a shock, his eyes found his right aileron. Shot full of holes, it had been ripped from its mounts and hung from the wing, flopping in the slipstream. And there were holes in the right side of the cockpit. His instruments had been shattered, and there was a long rip across the front of his flying suit. But the Sakae roared as steadily as ever, and as he climbed and throttled back, the faithful Takamura and Kojima took position behind and above his elevators.

The dragging aileron and the torque of the Sakae forced Yoshi to keep the stick hard to port. And bits of aluminum peeled from the right wing. He would never make it back to *Yonaga*.

And looking down, he cursed. One *Colossus* was sinking, but the *Independence* and the other *Colossus* were steaming at full speed while more aircraft were brought to the flight decks. Not one B5N survived. But there was a way to disable the flight deck of one of the carriers. A sure way. The way of the samurai. Then Kimio was there, but he pushed her back as he banked cautiously toward the *Colossus*.

"Dive-bombers! Dive-bombers!" exploded from his earphones. Joyously, he watched as at least a dozen Aichis, diving, flaps down, plummeted. Shouting thanks to Amaterasu, the commander watched as D3As hit each carrier with at least three 400 kilogram bombs.

Exploding bombs, gasoline, and torpedoes made volcanos of the carriers. Great chunks of wreckage rained down, pockmarking the sea with huge splashes. Red fireballs roiled from the ships like incandescent balloons; black smoke spread its pall, and he could see crewmen leaping into the burning sea.

"Banzai! Banzai!" But more metal ripped from the wing in big strips like a reptile shedding skin, and he could not keep his trim. He was finished. He switched on his microphone. "Tenna heiko banzai!" he shouted. And then, with the switch off and his eyes on the sky he said, "I am sorry, Kimio."

Chapter Twenty-three

Stomach empty and sick, Brent Ross watched the enemy raid roar toward *Yonaga*, thinned by the CAP, but nevertheless well organized and commanded—"Probably German and Russian led," Dempster had shouted while staring through his binoculars. At least a dozen JU-87s broke formation; six climbing for dive-bombing attacks while the six remaining torpedo-armed planes broke into two groups of three and raced for both sides of the carrier.

Fujita shouted at Naoyuki, "Bridge to bridge. I will circle to my right at flank speed." To the voice tube: "All ahead flank, right full rudder!"

Brent, Frank Dempster, and Mark Allen were thrown against the windscreen as the great carrier heeled into her turn. Then it seemed every gun on the ship exploded at precisely the same instant with a concussion that deafened the ensign. Leaving curving white wakes, five of the escorts had pulled in dangerously close to the carrier, firing their guns, pockmarking the sky with drifting shell bursts and ripping it apart with tracers.

Above, a reduced number of CAP fighters dueled

with the stubby BF-109s, trying desperately to break through to the bombers. Throttle wide open, a 109 plunged into the sea like a fire arrow. Two more MEs, caught by quicker turning Zeros, spouted flame, leaving signatures of black smoke against the blue sky as they smashed into the sea.

AA tore a wing from a torpedo-armed JU, and it looped to its death. Two more, controls shot away, flipped, tumbled, and flew to pieces on the surface like toys thrown against concrete by a petulant child.

But the dive-bombers, climbing into the fighter melee, were more vulnerable. Two were shot out of the sky almost immediately, but the other four wheeled toward the carrier, dive flaps dropped to the 40° dive angle as *Yonaga*'s 25 millimeter triple mounts came into range.

With stuttering blasts, 120 guns came to life. Thousands of glowing tracers climbed into the sky in sheets or burned in horizontal streams, slashing long white bullet trails across the ocean swell as gunners on full trigger emptied their thirty round magazines in seconds, loaders working like madmen to keep the streams uninterrupted.

Caught by a cyclone of tracers, a dive-bomber's wings folded and then flew free like leaves in a storm, the fuselage pulled by the big Jumo engine plunging as if an alchemist had turned it to lead. Bomb ripped by an attacking Zero, a JU vanished into a great yellow-orange ball of flame, the explosion destroying both victim and attacker, smoking pieces of wreckage raining over miles of ocean.

But two JUs were in their dives and three torpedo bombers—two to starboard and one to port—were making their runs through a jungle of brown smears and thickets of splashes.

Gripping the windscreen, Brent waited, heart a mallet against his ribs. The cold liquid of fear had washed away his guts, and ice water coursed through his veins. The old horror of combat—wondering about the men who would try so desperately to kill him—was back. He watched the enemy pilots cleverly curve their approaches, trying to anticipate *Yonaga*'s position as she turned.

"Left full rudder," Fujita shouted. Responding to the steering engines like power steering in a sports car, the 45 ton rudder swung on its post 90°, throwing men against bulkheads, gun tubs, and windscreens.

Then Fujita reversed the order, almost running down a *Fletcher* that passed bow to bow within twenty feet of their port side. There were splashes under the torpedo bombers.

"*Gyos!*" a lookout shouted from the foretop. "Two to starboard and one to port!"

"We're clear of the one to port, admiral," Brent shouted.

"Very well." The old man pointed to starboard. "But we will eat two."

Despite the approaching streaks to starboard, the scream of two descending Jumo-211 engines turned every eye upward.

Brent looked up just in time to see two bombs drop from the dive-bombers, which veered to port as they tried to escape low on the water. To the ensign, the two black shiny cylinders were plummeting directly at him. Hypnotized, he watched as they dropped side by side as if tied together. One struck the stern elevator, penetrating at least four decks, blowing the 11 meter square steel platform and all of its hydraulic gear, except the pump, straight up and then over the stern and into the sea like discarded junk. The other bomb penetrated the armor of the flight deck like a knife through butter and exploded in gasoline stores on the hangar deck, hurling tons of flaming wreckage in a vast red, blooming circle of death.

Grabbing Fujita's shoulders with one hand while grasping a stanchion with the other, Brent, the admiral, and every other man except Dempster dropped to their knees as *Yonaga* bucked under their feet and chunks of debris ricocheted from the windscreen, concussion bulging the steel plating inward. The CIA man, seemingly fascinated by the bomb, lingered at the screen despite Mark Allen's frantic grasp and efforts to pull him down. Hearing the sound of metal striking metal and bone, and feeling a spray of blood and small bits of soft gray chunks on the back of his neck, Brent looked up in time to see Dempster turning slowly toward him, glassy-eyed and sinking, the top of his head severed neatly just above the brows, as if a clever surgeon had made a deft stroke with a giant scalpel. Sighing a last breath from his lungs, Frank Dempster twisted and fell, brains and blood spilling across the deck.

Ripped from its bolts, the chart table was hurled across the deck to shatter over the screaming lookout, Seaman Koshiro, whose ankles had been fractured by the heaving grating. The gyro-repeater flew from its gimbals and was smashed to junk against the bulkhead. High above, a lookout on the foretop shrieked as metal splinters ripped his arm and part of his chest from his body. Spraying blood in wide arcs and screaming over the din like a high-pitched steam whistle, he was hurled from his platform next to the forward gun-director into the tub of a 25 millimeter gun. Two searchlights and a half-dozen life rafts were blown from the stack while the after gun-director was jarred from its bearings by the impact of a huge strake of plating, tilting crazily to starboard, its panicked crew tumbling out of its single door.

Holding Fujita down with one arm and gripping the stanchion, Brent, numbed by fear and horror, felt *Yonaga* tremble and shudder. Just as the ensign and Fujita straightened and the other men peered over the windscreen at the holocaust on the flight deck, the torpedoes struck; one amidships to starboard, the other reopening the old wound at the starboard quarter. Luckily, Brent still circled Fujita's narrow shoulders with one arm while clutching at the windscreen.

Booming, ringing, sounds of tortured and bursting steel reverberated through the hull, and *Yonaga* leaped twice like a mortally wounded great blue, her agonized contortions lifting the steel grating from the deck under Brent's feet. If he had not kept a tight hold on the windscreen and the old man who was clinging to a loose voice tube that no longer had brackets, Fujita would have been flung across the deck like Allen and Kawamoto and heaped with them against the bulkhead with Dempster's corpse and the injured lookout. The mast snapped twice like gunshots, stays and signal halyards snapping and flopping helplessly in the wind while a colorful rain of shattered glass sprinkled the flag bridge as recognition lights disintegrated. Adding to *Yonaga*'s agony, heat rose from the burning hangar deck in waves, oily black smoke choking everyone on the bridge.

Fujita leaned close to Brent's ear. "Bring her left — west, west, the wind is from the north."

Pulling himself unsteadily to his feet, Brent called into the voice tube, "Pilot house!" Silence. He shouted, "Pilot house!"

"Pilot house, aye," a stunned voice responded hoarsely.

"Left full rudder. Steady on two-seven-zero."

Slowing and listing as thousands of tons of water poured into her, the great carrier turned to her new heading, the breeze from the north blowing the smoke and fumes over the leeward side to port.

"All stop! All stop, Brent-san."

Brent repeated the order into the voice tube as two orderlies carried the groaning lookout and Dempster's body from the bridge. The pulsing stopped beneath Brent, and a great empty feeling swallowed his heart as it seemed *Yonaga* was dying. But he felt a new thump beneath his feet as engineers deep in the bowels of the ship — some perhaps drowning already — started bilge pumps.

The amazing old admiral was on his feet, eyes again bright and shifting analytically over his command. He was faced with fire at sea on a ship badly holed by two torpedoes with astonishing explosive power. The fire first: He turned to Naoyuki who was straightening his oversized helmet. "Damage control, hangar deck. Foam out the fire and jettison all ready fuel, bombs, torpedoes, and combustibles. Command Center, I want a damage report."

"Commander Atsumi reports red light in starboard fuel tanks three, five, seven, nine, eleven, thirteen; fire rooms nine, eleven, thirteen."

"Auxiliary five inch magazine?"

"Secure, sir."

"Engine room three?"

"After bulkhead warped and leaking, and there are red lights now in storage rooms five-seven-one and five-seven-three, the after generator and evaporator rooms." He paused. "More red lights in the starboard thrust block room, center motor room, and the starboard steering engine room and auxiliary engine room three. The clinometer shows a six degree starboard list."

"We will counter-flood," Fujita said to Brent and Mark Allen. To Naoyuki: "Commander Atsumi, flood port blisters two, four, six, eight, ten, twelve, and fourteen. Fourth damage control, flood port compartments three-three-two to three-four-four, and does Commander Fukioka answer?"

"Yes, sir."

"Commander Fukioka is to personally command damage control on the hangar deck."

The talker relayed the orders, and Brent felt the list begin to decrease as thousands of tons of water poured into *Yonaga*'s port blisters and compartments. For the first time, he noticed that the gunfire had stopped. The sky was empty except for a handful of Zeros climbing and circling. Swinging his body in a full turn, he found all twelve *Fletchers* close to the wounded, stationary giant, protecting her with their own hulls.

A dazed, dull-eyed Mark Allen clinging to the

windscreen managed to say breathlessly, "Admiral. For God's sake give the order not to ventilate ship." He pointed down through the hole in the hangar deck and the greasy black smoke rolling in solid black clouds to port. "Gasoline fumes can make a bomb of us. That's how *Lexington* and *Taiho* were last — "

Fujita shouted at the talker. "All hands, do not ventilate ship." He spoke to his executive officer. "Captain Kawamoto, take charge of damage control on the flight deck."

"Aye, aye, sir." The old captain hobbled off the bridge.

Looking at the huge hole in the middle of the flight deck, Brent could no longer see flames, and the smoke had diminished as hundreds of men both on the hangar and flight decks poured tons of a new foam supplied by the Self-Defense Force on the conflagration.

Naoyuki turned to the admiral. "Commander Fukioka reports fire under control, combustibles have been jettisoned. Requests permission to go below to the starboard quarter."

"Lord, that was fast. Less than fifteen minutes," Mark Allen said. "Great crew!"

Brent knew the crew of engine room three must be shoring the twice weakened bulkhead not only to help save *Yonaga*, but their own lives as well. But there was an added peril from a hit amidships that had flooded outboard compartments, putting pressure on their starboard bulkhead, too. And Fukioka had requested permission to descend into the hell of ruptured compartments and hideous death.

"Permission granted." Fujita glanced down at the

flight deck where scores of hoses snaking to the hands of crewmen still poured water and foam into the wound. But they were cheering and waving. Aft, there was a great hole in the stern that still smoked but there was no fire. Fujita leaned close to the talker. "Tell the chief engineer that I want to get under way."

The talker spoke into the headpiece, listened and said to his commanding officer, "Chief Warrant Officer Tanesaki is the senior surviving engineering officer, and he suggests fourteen knots, sir. He can give you eighteen knots even without fire rooms nine, eleven, thirteen, and even if we lose engine room three. But many bulkheads are weakened and leaking."

"Very well. Come right to three-zero-seven, speed fourteen."

As the wounded leviathan swung slowly to her new course, stern a foot deeper in the water, shattered hangar deck still streaming wisps of brown and white smoke, the electrifying news came in. "Admiral," the talker shouted. "Commander Gakki reports one enemy carrier sunk, two carriers burning and sinking!"

"Banzai!" Cheers. The officers pounded each other on the back. Shook hands. Fujita grabbed a microphone from the windscreen. "This is Admiral Fujita. Our avenging eagles have destroyed all three enemy carriers." There were shouts of "banzai," a rolling thunder of pounding boots. The admiral's amplified voice silenced the bedlam. "*Yonaga* is wounded but still underway and ready to fight. Many of our comrades have journeyed to the Yasakuni Shrine, but we have shown Kadafi how 'little monkeys' can fight." More cheers. "There are still two enemy cruisers at

369

sea. We may engage them. Be alert. Damage control, heal our wounds." He glanced at the sky and then returned to the microphone. "Remember the *Naval Lament* — 'If I go to sea, I shall return a corpse awash. Thus for the sake of the emperor, I shall not die peacefully at home.' "

More cheers.

After replacing the microphone, the old admiral pointed grimly at the flight deck. "We cannot handle aircraft." He turned to the talker. "Radio room; bombers and fighter frequencies. Airgroups are to land at designated fields or alongside escorts." He looked upward. "CAP continue patrol until out of fuel then land near an escort."

"Good decision, admiral," Mark Allen said.

Fujita spoke to Naoyuki. "Command Center, any more red lights?"

"Commander Atsumi reports no new flooding, admiral."

"Good. Good. Get me a report from the chief engineer."

Naoyuki complied and listened. "Chief Warrant Officer Tanesaki reports engine room three bulkheads holding. His men and damage control four are shoring and caulking. They are rigging transverse and longitudinal reinforcing beams, and the pumps have dropped the water level below the floor plates."

"Fine crew, fine crew," Mark Allen said, awed.

"The best," Fujita agreed. Then grimly he said, "Those warheads were unbelievably powerful for aerial torpedoes."

"Those were big fish — much larger than ours," Allen agreed.

"Ours weigh seventeen hundred forty-two of your pounds, Admiral Allen."

"I would guess we were hit by one ton weapons with warheads yielding in the range of four to five tons of TNT."

"New Russian-shaped charges," Bernstein said. "The Arabs began using them against our shipping in the Med last year. One can blow a merchant ship out of the water."

Every head turned as engines roared to the southwest, and the first of *Yonaga*'s aircraft began to return from the battle to the south. In forty minutes, Brent counted only seven Zeros, eleven Aichis and no Nakajimas. Silently, the officers stared as plane after plane skimmed the sea and then splashed to bobbing halts next to the escorts. Then the engines of the CAP began to sputter and backfire, and within a half hour, the sky was empty.

However, there was good news from damage control. All fires were out and the bulkheads were holding. In fact, Tanesaki promised Fujita 24 knots in an emergency.

The roll call of death was sobering. The hit aft killed twenty-three men, wounded fourteen, destroyed one five inch gun and two twenty-five millimeter mounts. The bomb amidships killed thirty-seven men, wounded fifty-one and rendered the flight deck useless. The torpedoes had killed at least seventy-seven men, and sixty-three more were missing and presumed dead. But *Yonaga* was still underway, still bristled with 39 5 inch guns and 180 25 millimeter machine guns.

Naoyuki looked at the admiral. "Sir, the radio room

reports our aircraft have been landing on Palawan and airfields on Borneo and Sumatra, and over and over they are broadcasting reports of the sinking of three enemy carriers."

Rubbing his hands together, the old sailor said, "Thank the gods."

Brent's mind dwelled on Yoshi Matsuhara. Had the proud warrior found his destiny? Would he be forced to tell Kimio? "Please, Jesus, spare me that," he whispered to himself.

"Admiral," the talker said. "Radio room reports the two cruisers are retiring from Balikpapan into the Makassar Straits on course one-nine-zero."

Cheering, Bernstein and Allen shook hands and pounded each other. Brent laughed and joined in.

Fujita pointed at the ruins of the chart table and spoke to a lookout. "Get the top of the table and hold the chart up."

Obeying, the man ripped the top from the splintered legs smeared with Dempster's blood and gore and held up the chart. Fujita pointed. "They are here." He looked up at the dimming sky where the sun was slowly dying on the western horizon. "It will be dark soon. They can reverse course, and then at their high speed clear the straits, cross the Sulu Sea on a northwesterly headway." He stabbed his finger to the left. "And then west through the Balabac Straits into the South China Sea and interdict our course here at about longitude one-one-zero, latitude ten in about forty-eight hours from now."

"You suggested this before, admiral," Mark Allen noted. "Highly unlikely."

"With no air cover?" Bernstein asked, the tone of

his voice indicating what he thought.

But Brent wondered about World War Two and what the encyclopedic brain had in mind. The old Japanese did not disappoint him.

Eyes fixed on Mark Allen like twin gunsights, Fujita moved back to 1944. "Remember the Battle of the Philippine Sea, Admiral Allen?"

"Why, yes," Mark Allen responded uneasily. "You're thinking of Bull's Run."

"Precisely." The black eyes moved over Brent and then to Irving Bernstein. "Bull's Run, Adm. William F. 'Bull' Halsey's stupid blunder in thinking that a powerful force of our battleships and cruisers under Admiral Kurita, which, incidentally, included *Yonaga*'s sisters *Yamato* and *Musashi*, could not or would not change course when it appeared they were retiring after *Musashi* was lost in the San Bernardino Straits. Stupidly, Halsey took his fast carriers and battleships north at a high speed to intercept a decoy force of four carriers and two battleships, but with only one hundred thirty planes. He neglected to even post a picket destroyer at the mouth of the straits. Needless to say, Admiral Kurita reversed course and steamed unopposed into Leyte Gulf the next morning where he destroyed two small carriers and their escorts. With more fuel and aerial support he could have destroyed your whole transport force."

"Then you intend to post pickets here?" Allen indicated the Balabac Straits.

"If we had airgroups, yes—of course. But if we engage them, it will be a surface battle, anyway." He moved his eyes to Brent Ross. "A good commander anticipates even the most remote threats." He turned

373

back to the seaman holding the chart. "You may put it down." Then to Naoyuki, he said, "Radio room, bridge to bridge, all escorts to prepare for a possible surface engagement, which might develop with two cruisers and escorts in about forty-eight hours."

The man talked into his headpiece. Fujita continued. "Tell the carpentry shop I want the chart table on the flag bridge repaired immediately."

Fujita's estimate was off by two hours. It was forty-six hours later at 1600 hours that the enemy force was sighted. It had been a long, despairing afternoon for Brent Ross as lists of surviving aviators were compiled from the escorts and incomplete static-filled receptions on *Yonaga*'s own radios working from jury-rigged antennas. Some aviators had already been flown back to Japan from Indonesia, and the free world was rejoicing over the destruction of the enemy task force. Margaret Thatcher had personally broadcast her thanks to *Yonaga*. But Commander Yoshi Matsuhara's name was not listed amongst the survivors.

"Lord, Brent," Mark Allen had said as the two Americans sipped coffee in his cabin. "There are dozens of islands where our men could have landed. There must be many survivors."

"We lost most of them," Brent said, staring at the desk.

"I know. I know."

It was then the klaxons honked, and there was the usual pounding of boots, shriek of boatswains' pipes, shouted commands, and the rush to battle stations.

374

"AP! AP!" Fujita was shouting at the talker as Brent Ross, Mark Allen, Irving Bernstein, and Masao Kawamoto rushed onto the bridge, shrugging into life jackets and adjusting chin straps.

"AP, AP, all five inch guns load armor-piercing shells." Fujita turned to the newcomers. "The right hand lead vessel of the screen just picked up six vessels moving at a high speed, bearing zero-seven-zero, range three hundred kilometers. They are on a collision course with us."

"That's a hundred and eighty miles," Mark Allen said. "We should sight them in about two hours."

Naoyuki spoke. "ESM reports strong incoming S-band signals, sir. They are ranging us, admiral."

Looking down at the smashed flight deck, Fujita cursed. Then he said to the talker, "All stations prepare for surface engagement. Bridge to bridge, escorts prepare for torpedo actions and to make smoke. I will commit the divisions to torpedo runs myself." The talker repeated the commands. "Engineering, I will call for flank speed regardless of the conditions of the bulkheads."

"Chief Warrant Officer Tanesaki says he can give you twenty-six knots, but we may lose engine room three."

"Very well."

The next two hours were the longest in Brent Ross's life. Two cruisers: the *Dido* with eight 5.25 inch guns and the *Fiji* with nine 6 inch guns were bearing down on them. All the guns were mounted in turrets and outranged *Yonaga*'s 5 inch guns. Eyes rimmed with fatigue, he stared at solid banks of scudding low clouds and the gray lifeless sea. He felt frightened and restless, unbearably so, like some form of illness. And like all men before battle, he felt the helplessness of a victim of the fates; a convergence of uncontrollable circumstances forcing him to face a storm of steel and explosives and probable death with no choice whatsoever. However, he straightened, shamed by his fear and armed with the determination to stand up like a warrior to whatever came over the horizon. Meet it like Yoshi Matsuhara must have met it, he told himself.

For the next two hours, steady tracking by radar placed the enemy force north of *Yonaga* and off her starboard bow.

Fujita spoke calmly to the talker. "Destroyer divisions One and Two prepare for torpedo engagements and to lay smoke. Form up six kilometer and on a relative bearing of zero-four-five from the flag ship. Divisions Three and Four remain on standard screening stations."

The first calls came from the foretops. "Masts, smoke, off the starboard bow; range twenty kilometers."

"Twenty-one, twenty-two thousand yards," Mark Allen muttered. "The six inch will outrange us by a couple thousand yards."

"But we have the battleship hull, the armor belt, the eight inch steel box around our vitals."

"And two holes in our side, five thousand tons of seawater in our compartments and bilges, Admiral Fujita."

"What would you suggest, Admiral Allen?" Fujita said coldly.

"Sorry, Admiral Fujita. We have no choice." Allen

376

paused thoughtfully. "Close with them and blow them out of the water."

"Banzai," Hironaka croaked.

Fujita smiled. "Said like a samurai."

Brent saw a great flash on the horizon. "They've opened up, sir." Fujita nodded without lowering his glasses. Then he turned to the talker. "Destroyer divisions One and Two torpedo attack and make smoke."

There was a rumble and the terrible sound of canvas ripping the sky, and nine yellow towers of water erupted from the sea between the inner screen and *Yonaga*—flashes masked instantly by leaping waterspouts.

"Well, I'll be damned," Mark Allen observed. "Dye markers for visual control."

"Good idea," Fujita said. "The smaller cruiser will use a different color."

Seconds later, the howl of shells and orange-colored columns of water shot skyward a hundred yards short of the leading destroyer of Division One, which at flank speed and boiling great rolling clouds of black smoke from her two stacks slashed toward the enemy force.

"Whose division?"

"Gilliland's, admiral."

Fujita hunched over the voice tube. "Right to zero-seven-zero, all ahead flank."

Heeling and throbbing with new power, *Yonaga* charged toward the smoke on the horizon. Glasses pressed hard against his eyes until they watered with pain, Brent could see gunfire glowing and lighting up patches of smoke as again and again guns tore into the black shroud.

Fujita shouted at the other officers. "We will close the range while our destroyers keep them occupied. They only have four escorts. They must defend themselves against torpedoes—even the threat of torpedoes." He spoke to Naoyuki. "To gunnery, we want the six inch cruiser first. Open fire as soon as she is in range."

There was an orange glow on the far horizon. The great canvas sheets ripped again, and nine more yellow waterspouts erupted from the sea midway between Captain Fite's leading *Fletcher* and *Yonaga*.

"And he wants us first, admiral," Mark Allen observed.

"Good tactician," Fujita acknowledged. "He will engage our escorts with his four *Gearings* and his *Dido*."

"He probably has radar fire control," Mark Allen said.

"I would not trade radar for our optical range finder." Fujita gestured upward. "Especially on a clear day like this."

"Assistant Gunnery Officer Yanenaka has the *Fiji* in the range finder—fourteen thousand meters. Gunnery Officer Atsumi requests centralized control and that we come to a heading that will bring all of the port or starboard batteries to bear."

"Left to three-five-zero," Fujita shouted. Then to the talker: "Tell Commander Atsumi I will give him the starboard battery and to fire when ready."

As the great carrier's decks canted in the turn to port, Brent saw the lead *Fletcher* struck by a broadside that blew her number two gun mount and most

378

of the bridge completely off the hull. Turning wildly to port, a rain of shells raked her main deck, blowing men, guns, and shattered plating over the side. Slowly, she came to a stop and began to settle. But the next pair of *Fletchers* turned and launched their torpedoes. Then the trailing *Fletcher* lost her stern as the fast 5.25 inch guns of the *Dido* scored again. Brent watched in horror as the middle *Fletcher* exploded, struck by a full spread of torpedoes from a *Gearing* on her starboard side.

"Steady on the three-five-zero, admiral."

"Commence firing!"

Fired electrically by Atsumi from the CIC, the nineteen 5 inch guns of the starboard battery exploded simultaneously like a thunderclap. Groaning, Brent grabbed his ears, but his pulses pounded as cordite filled his lungs, and the clang of ejected brass casings on the deck and the excited shouts of gun layers hit his senses like a double shot of Chivas Regal. Firing over twenty rounds per minute per gun, the starboard battery set up a rolling, thunderous barrage. Then eight huge waterspouts leaped from the sea only 50 meters off the carrier's starboard side.

At that moment, Division Two with Fortino leading turned as one and launched eighteen torpedoes. Fortino was struck by a storm of shells that set off a forward magazine, blowing off the entire bow in a hundred foot searing orange flash.

"Sacred Buddha," Fujita muttered. "Bridge to bridge. Divisions Three and Four make your torpedo attacks."

While Fite led the remaining six *Fletchers* in a wide sweeping turn toward the smoke and flame on the horizon, Brent saw a *Gearing* explode, then the *Dido* staggered as two torpedoes struck her amidships and broke her keel. She began to drift aimlessly in a sea of flaming fuel, burning and exploding destroyers. The young ensign felt strength drain from his limbs, and he had the impulse to run from this nightmare of hell and destruction, which smeared across the whole northern horizon in a panorama of red flames and spark-dappled smoke. It was sheer madness, something which none of them could control.

Cheers as the *Dido*'s stern rose as she prepared for her final plunge. But the shouts were silenced by the roar of a full 6 inch salvo passing overhead. Tragically, one gun was short — perhaps with a defective barrel liner — and a 6 inch shell struck the forward gun director and blew it over the side with an orange flash, an ear-splitting blast that demolished the entire foretop, killing and wounding every man at the foretop range finder and the AA machine guns. Shrapnel raked the 25 millimeter tub just forward of the bridge, killing and wounding the entire nine man crew. Two men blown from the foretop tumbled past the flag bridge, screaming and spraying blood until they crashed into the flight deck and lay inert like bloody rag dolls.

"Good Lord," Allen muttered.

"Local control! Local control," Fujita shouted. A blanched Naoyuki relayed the order to the gunnery department and then said, "All radar and radios are out, sir." Fujita nodded.

Steadying his hands with a conscious effort, Brent glassed the enemy. He could see the *Fiji* clearly now only about 10,000 yards away. She was burning

380

amidships and 5 inch shells churned the water around her. Then she fired another salvo. Brent knew this one would not miss.

A tight salvo of nine 6 inch shells exploded along *Yonaga*'s starboard side. Four were near misses, but perhaps five projectiles hit the carrier at the waterline, sending tons of water to soak her gun crews and spray as high as the bridge.

"That is my three hundred millimeter armor belt. You can only scratch it," Fujita chortled, waving a wet fist.

Brent saw Fite's Division Three and Philbin's Division Four vanish into the flaming, smoking holocaust. He whispered a prayer.

Another roaring, ripping sound and every man on the bridge dropped as a full salvo struck *Yonaga*'s forward starboard galleries, blasting three 5 inch and a half-dozen 25 millimeter triple mounts from their mounts with a shock that jarred the carrier all the way to her keel. Torn chunks of metal plating whirled through the air like scraps of paper in the wind, while gun barrels were flung like sticks. Men and parts of men twisted in the wreckage, raining into the sea and onto the flight deck. Ready ammunition began to explode in the gallery on the starboard bow and choking brown smoke billowed from burning powder.

"Flood number one five inch magazine," Fujita ordered. "Damage control one to the starboard bow." Immediately, men pulled hoses across the flight deck to the gallery that looked like a burning junkyard peopled by green-clad dead and dying men.

Brent had his glasses on the *Fiji* when at least three torpedoes hit her squarely amidships. She seemed to rise straight up like an inverted V, and then settled back into the water and slowly began to roll onto her beam ends.

"Banzai! Banzai!" echoed through the carrier. Allen grabbed Brent's hand and Fujita pounded Bernstein's back while the Israeli jumped up and down shouting. Hironaka stared at the sky and gave thanks.

Recovering quickly, the admiral moved to the voice tube. "Right to zero-three-seven, speed sixteen." And the requests for damage reports and the inevitable casualty count. "Bridge to bridge — does Captain Fite answer?"

"Yes, sir."

"Order Captain Fite to take no prisoners."

"See here, sir," Mark Allen said sharply. "That's not human—"

"They are nothing but terrorists to me, and there is only one way to handle terrorism," Fujita lashed back.

"Kill them," Bernstein said matter-of-factly. "We've learned."

Because the thick oily smoke had been dissipated by the wind, Brent could see the hull of the *Fiji* clearly. Not one *Gearing* was afloat, and only seven *Fletchers* were visible. Two were stationary, one with a fire amidships and the other listing to port. The *Dido* was gone. Burning patches of oil and floating wreckage covered miles of ocean.

"Dust on the sea, they call it, Brent."

"After something like this?"

"Yes, Brent. When the killing ends."

"But it hasn't, yet." There were bursts of machine

382

gun fire, and Brent saw men swept from the red-leaded hull of the *Fiji* while others were shot in the water. Feeling sick, he turned away. Then the thought that comes to all men who survive battle: It's over and I'm alive. But he felt no joy, just numbness and a great fatigue.

"Flashing light to Captain Fite; radio silence. By visual signals, detail two destroyers to take damaged ships under tow, the remaining three destroyers form a standard screen ahead of the flagship and off my bows. Course zero-three-seven, speed sixteen." Fujita paused. "And well done!"

"Banzai! Banzai!"

Chapter Twenty-four

When *Yonaga* limped into Tokyo Bay seven days later, she was greeted by flotillas of gaily decorated boats and crowds lining the bluffs of Igu Hantō and Bōso Hantō. At first there was cheering, but then silence as the revelers studied the blackened and ripped bow, the two jagged holes in the flight deck, and the smashed foretop. As he stood next to Admiral Fujita on the flag bridge while the carrier made its way toward berth H-2, which was next to the graving dock at Yokasuka, Brent's feeling of horror and revulsion had faded despite the terrible punishment the carrier had taken: The dead crewmen numbered 264, 327 wounded, and the total count of dead aviators and aircrewmen still unknown. However, the realization that he had been terrified under fire gnawed at him like acid.

"You are a valued aide and a brave man, ensign," Fujita said staring through his glasses as *Yonaga* entered the Uraga Suida.

"Brave?" Brent said, lowering his glasses. "I've

never been so frightened, sir."

Dropping his glasses to his waist, the old man stared up at the ensign. "The shell fire was the worst."

"Yes, sir. At least you can see the planes. But the shells—the noise, and you can hear them coming in."

The old black eyes were clear and bright. "I was very frightened, ensign."

"You, sir?" Brent blurted incredulously.

"All men have fears, the brave man manages his. Only a fool or a madman would not have been frightened out there."

"You were calm—your fears didn't show, admiral."

"Nor did yours, Mr. Ross." Raising his glasses, he moved from the unsettling topic. "Kadafi and the rest of his thugs are not finished."

Brent welcomed the change in topic. "But, sir, we destroyed the whole force."

"Yes, ensign, but they have unlimited wealthy and Russian support. There will be work for *Yonaga*."

Brent sighed. "I hope not, admiral."

"We have taken heavy casualities; you are a valued aide—know the ship well and have adapted to, ah, our way of thinking with alacrity. *Yonaga* needs you, Brent-san."

"Thank you, admiral. But my career lies with NIS."

"Rot behind some desk in the Pentagon Brent-san when there may be samurai's work to be done?"

Brent felt like a trapped fly watching a hungry spider spinning a web around him. The man was a sorcerer. "Sir, I am an officer and will obey my orders."

"I intend to request that orders be cut assigning you permanently to my staff. But only if you agree."

"I'm flattered, admiral. Would you give me time to think it over—discuss it with Admiral Allen?"

"Of course. But I must put a new staff together so let me know within twenty-four hours."

"Aye, aye, sir."

"And Brent-san, remember. You have earned your sword, the distinguished sword of the Konoye family."

Brent felt steely pride stir deep within him. "Thank you, sir."

When *Yonaga* docked, row after row of ambulances were waiting behind a solid cordon of troops who manned machine guns in sandbagged positions. Enormous throngs of spectators stood outside the perimeter, staring in silence and pointing at the wounded giant.

As soon as the lines were over and the ladder secured, Capt. Takahashi Aogi, the liaison officer from the Maritime Self-Defense Force, the dock master, Lieutenant Commander Kamakura, and their staffs came aboard, brushing past an endless procession of stretchers on the accommodation ladder in their haste.

Meeting with the staff, the two officers listened grim-faced as first Admiral Fujita and then Commander Fukioka and Chief Warrant Officer Tanesaki described *Yonaga's* needs and peeled off sheet after sheet of requisitions.

"Eight months' work, sir," Kamakura said. "Besides the damage to your hull, the hangar and flight decks must be rebuilt."

"We have the time," Fujita responded. "When can you take us?"

"We will be ready in forty-eight hours, admiral."

"Very well." The admiral turned to Kawamoto. "Port and starboard liberty but maintain eight five inch ready guns and a dozen ready twenty-five millimeter mounts."

"Aye, aye, sir."

Aogi and Kamakura eyed each other but remained mute. Finally, Aogi spoke. "All of Japan—all of the free world is indebted to *Yonaga*. The Philippine and Indonesian governments wish to decorate you, sir."

Fujita smiled. "You know the Imperial Navy decorates no living men. Let them wait for my ashes. They can drop their baubles on my box." Brent restrained his laughter with a hand over his mouth.

Although there was no Imperial Navy, not one man objected. The admiral gestured to the end of the table at a very fatigued escort commander. "It was Captain Fite and his brave captains who defeated the cruisers. Without them . . ." He turned his palms up and shrugged.

"Thank you, sir," rumbled from the big man.

After nodding at Captain Fite, Aogi stood and handed Admiral Fujita a long white envelope. "From the emperor, sir."

Hastily, Fujita put on his steel-rimmed glasses and read. "He is pleased—has declared a holiday in honor

388

of *Yonaga* and will personally attend services at the Yasakumi Shrine to honor our dead."

"Banzai! Banzai!"

Brent found himself shouting and fell silent self-consciously under the curious stares of Adm. Mark Allen and Col. Irving Bernstein.

An hour later Brent was alone, stretched on his bunk, hands behind his head, staring at the overhead and wondering about Sarah Aranson. Certainly, she knew *Yonaga* was back, but of course, could not come aboard. And Bernstein had rushed ashore. The colonel would have told her he was well by now. He glanced at his watch. Liberty at 1500 hours; two more hours. He sighed. He would rush to a phone. None had been rigged on *Yonaga* as yet because of the battle damage, especially to the communications department.

He reflected on the conversation he had just finished with Admiral Allen. "I'm returning to Washington, Brent," the admiral had said. "You're my aide. You're due for a promotion."

"I know, sir."

"You don't show much enthusiasm," the older man noted "Fujita?"

There had been a long, hard silence. "He says he needs me on his staff. Claims he can request my permanent assignment."

"There's no doubt about that. At this moment he is one of the most powerful men in the free world. But

389

your future is in Washington, Brent."

"I know, sir."

"Admiral Winter will be at the embassy tomorrow at thirteen hundred. He has our new orders. You must make your decision by then, Brent."

Shaking his head, Brent put the conversation out of his mind. Then reaching up, he ran a hand over the curved, jeweled scabbard of the Konoye sword. "I earned it. I really earned it," he murmured.

A knock interrupted his thoughts. When he opened the door, Commander Yoshi Matsuhara was grinning at him.

"A ghost! A ghost!"

Laughing, Yoshi grabbed Brent's shoulders. "Does that feel like a ghost?"

Brent grasped both of the flyer's hands and pulled him into the cabin. "Our big receivers were out — we didn't know, Yoshi-san. How did you do it? Where have you been?"

"One thing at a time, Brent-san," the commander said, seating himself, laughing. Brent stared back from his bunk, shaking his head, unable to believe Yoshi was really there, alive, laughing.

"I was hit over the straits, lost part of my right wing at a very low altitude." He sighed. "I prepared to enter the Yasakuni Shrine but Amaterasu rode with me, guided me to a landing on a field at Kotadaik on Singkep Lingga. The Indonesians flew me back with thirty-two other survivors. I have been waiting for you for three days." He moved his eyes around the cabin. "*Yonaga* has been hit hard; very, very hard."

"Yes, Yoshi-san." Slowly, Brent described the horrors of the air attacks and the frightful slaughter of the surface engagement. "We're lucky *Yonaga* has battleship construction and a great crew," Brent concluded. And then he added, "Our escorts took a terrible beating, but now, maybe we can all rest."

Matsuhara knockled his forehead. "And perhaps not."

"What do you mean?"

"The Russians have developed a new Ilyushin fighter powered by a new three-thousand horsepower engine."

"But Grumman and Pratt and Whitney are developing a new fighter, too. And carriers are being converted. Let the Russians and Americans kill each other."

"You are an American!"

Brent felt his cheeks redden. "Why, of course."

Yoshi drummed his fingers on his knee. "I have seen Kimio," he announced suddenly.

"I'm glad."

"She loves me, Brent-san." He surprised the American again with his frankness.

"You're very lucky, Yoshi-san."

"I love her," the commander said with complete candor. "I never felt I would ever feel that emotion for a woman again. My only love for decades was the love of a samurai for his emperor."

"Will you marry?"

"Yes. Soon."

Brent grasped the flyer's hand. "Congratulations,

Yoshi-san. I'm happy for you." He smiled. "You have found what you've been looking for?"

Yoshi grinned back. "You mean like Captain Ahab?" Solemnly, he answered his own question. "No, I think not, Brent-san. You were right. His quest led to death, mine to life." He riveted the American with piercing black eyes. "If a man looks long enough, searches every corner of this earth, every byway and remote inlet, what he seeks will find him."

Brent sat back. "Yes, Yoshi-san. There's truth in that."

The pilot continued with a broad grin. "Sarah Aranson wishes to see you."

Brent came erect. "You've seen her?"

"Of course."

"I was going to phone her as soon as I got on the beach."

"Not necessary, Brent-san. She is waiting for you outside the gate in a cab."

It had been fierce and consuming and sometimes savage. Sarah lay back, her nude body limp and dampened by perspiration. Beside her, Brent stared at the ceiling until his breathing slowed and the weakening effects of their lovemaking faded. Turning and sitting up, he reached to the nightstand, found his scotch and soda and took a long drink. Then he sagged back.

Rolling to her lover, Sarah pressed her breasts

392

against his arm, lips to his cheek, and ran a finger through the hair on his chest until she found the long scar. She spoke into his ear. "Thank God, no new scars — at least none that show."

She had asked him about *Yonaga* and the battles while riding in the cab. "I saw you stand in," she said. "I was on the bluff at Uraga. The flight deck, the bow, stern, and she's low in the water. There were fires . . ."

"Please, please, Sarah," he had admonished, gently placing a big palm over lips. "Not now — not now. I want to hold you; must hold you." Then he kissed her with the hunger of a newly rescued starving man. And she kissed him back, mouth open, wet and demanding. When they entered her apartment, they began disrobing as they hurried to her bedroom.

"None that show," she repeated, moving her hand to his arm and testing the big bicep.

Perhaps the lovemaking had loosened his tongue. Certainly, he no longer felt the terrible edge of anxiety that slashed away composure and had invaded his fitful sleep with nightmares. Releasing air from his lungs audibly, he said, "We did take terrible losses. Hundred of crewmen and most of our pilots and aircrews. And, yes, *Yonaga* is badly damaged."

"Yoshi survived."

"Oh, yes, Sarah." Brent felt his spirits rise. "I know."

She nibbled at his ear. "Brent," she said softly. "You've never been like that."

"Like what?"

"When we made love, it was ferocious. More than just a hunger."

"I love you."

"And I love you, too, Brent. But it was more than that. You were wild, almost frightening."

"I didn't hurt you."

"Oh, no, no, darling." Propping herself up on an elbow, she kissed his forehead, eyes, nose, and then brushed her velvet lips across his mouth. "You're everything a girl dreams about."

He looked up at her with trouble-clouded eyes. "Maybe it was what happened out there." She looked puzzled. Stumbling, he tried to answer the question on her face. "It was killing — wholesale, savage, pitiless killing."

"Please, darling. Don't . . ."

"I must, Sarah." He pondered for a moment. "I was frightened; very frightened."

"That's normal."

He rushed on. "Of course I was hungry for you. You're everything war can never be." He stopped awkwardly. "I'm awfully corny."

She kissed the cord in his neck. "No, darling. I understand. What you were doing out there was a rite of death." He wondered at the serious timbre of her voice. She continued. "And this beautiful thing between us, I look on it — I guess all women do — as a celebration of life." She kissed his ear and ran fingers through his sweat-dampened hair. "Brent, remember, I don't care why you need me. Just keep on wanting me." Finding his lips, she kissed him hard, tongue darting, hand trailing down his flat stomach until she found the stiff hair and then she took him in her hand. Groaning, he rolled to her and covered her body with his.

Dawn was painting the eastern horizon with orange and golds when he left. Dressed in a sheer silk robe, she kissed him at the door. "The day after tomorrow. You promise?"

"Yes, Sarah. "I'll have port section liberty."

She lowered her eyes. "We've been so busy in there." She gestured at the bedroom. "I forgot to tell you I've been assigned to the Israeli Embassy in Washington."

"Great!"

"We can see each other." He turned away. "We will, won't we, Brent? NIS is headquartered there. You'll be sent—"

"I don't know."

Her voice rose. "Don't know? I saw Admiral Allen at the gate. He said both of you . . ."

He stepped back. "Admiral Fujita claims he needs me."

"Good, Lord, you've done enough." And then softly. "We could be together." She put her arms around his neck and kissed him.

For a long moment he held her. Then, pulling away, he said, "I'd better leave. I'm due back aboard at oh-eight hundred."

"You didn't answer!"

"I know. I know," he said, stepping through the

door.

"You have reached your decision, Ensign Ross?"

Standing at attention in front of the admiral's desk, Brent still felt the tranquility and peace the night of lovemaking with Sarah had brought him. Maybe the old sorcerer wanted this—delayed the decision until he had been sated by a woman. How could he know? But he seemed to know everything.

"Regardless of your decision, Brent-san, you have shown the finest qualities of the warrior—the samurai."

"Thank you, sir. But samurai?"

"Yes. I think there is some of the samurai in all men who wear the mantle of command. Each finds his own duty, and then with the help of his gods, or god, honors it." He leaned back. "Give more thought to your decision. Admiral Allen asked me to tell you to be at the American Embassy today at thirteen hundred hours."

"Yes, sir. I know."

The old Japanese placed gnarled fingers on the desk. "However, at the same hour a priest from the Yasakuni Shrine will conduct services in the Shrine of Infinite Salvation for our honored dead. My staff will attend in dress blues, white gloves, and swords." The black eyes gleamed like polished black stones. "You have been honored with the Konoye sword. Make your decision, Brent-san."

396

At 1200 hours Brent Ross shaved. Then, slowly, he began to dress. After adjusting his tie, he shrugged into his blue coat and stared into the mirror, pleased. "Almost finished," he said to the reflection, eyeing the broad expanse of cloth covering his shoulders, the gleaming buttons, and the single gold lace ring on each cuff. Carefully, he placed the peaked cap squarely on his head and turned for the door. Before leaving, he pulled on his white gloves and buckled on the Konoye sword.

DEPTH FORCE
by Irving Greenfield

Built in secrecy, launched in silence, and manned by a phantom crew *The Shark* is America's unique submarine whose mission is to stop the Russians from dominating the seas. There's no room for anything other than victory or death, and the only way to stay alive is to dive deep and strike hard.

ACTION ADVENTURE

SILENT WARRIORS   (1675, $3.95)
by Richard P. Henrick
The Red Star, Russia's newest, most technologically advanced submarine, outclasses anything in the U.S. fleet. But when the captain opens his sealed orders 24 hours early, he's staggered to read that he's to spearhead a massive nuclear first strike against the Americans!

THE PHOENIX ODYSSEY   (1789, $3.95)
by Richard P. Henrick
All communications to the USS *Phoenix* suddenly and mysteriously vanish. Even the urgent message from the president cancelling the War Alert is not received. In six short hours the *Phoenix* will unleash its nuclear arsenal against the Russian mainland.

COUNTERFORCE   (2013, $3.95)
Richard P. Henrick
In the silent deep, the chase is on to save a world from destruction. A single Russian Sub moves on a silent and sinister course for American shores. The men aboard the U.S.S. *Triton* must search for and destroy the Soviet killer Sub as an unsuspecting world races for the apocalypse.

EAGLE DOWN   (1644, $3.75)
by William Mason
To western eyes, the Russian Bear appears to be in hibernation — but half a world away, a plot is unfolding that will unleash it awesome, deadly power. When the Russian Bear rises up, God help the Eagle.

THE OASIS PROJECT   (1296, $3.50)
by William Mason
The President had a plan — a plan that by all rights should not exist. And it would be carried out by the ASP, a second generation space shuttle that would transport the laser weapons into positions — before the Red Tide hit U.S. shores.

Available wherever paperbacks are sold, or order direct from the Publisher. Send cover price plus 50¢ per copy for mailing and handling to Zebra Books, Dept. 2093, 475 Park Avenue South, New York, N.Y. 10016. Residents of New York, New Jersey and Pennsylvania must include sales tax. DO NOT SEND CASH.